D1585822

HAREM

EPIC ADVENTURE SERIES

Colin Falconer

PART I

The Spider's Web

'The spider spins her web in the palace of the Caesars'
- a verse from the Sa'adi

CHAPTER 1

Stamboul, 1522
now Istanbul, Turkey

When a new slave girl was brought to the Harem, in the Old Palace, she immediately received instruction in the language of the Osmanli court, and in the teachings of the Koran. She was also assigned to one of the Harem functionaries for training in a specific duty.

Hürrem had been given to the *kiaya,* the Mistress, of the Silk Room; an embittered Circassian with skin the color of leather. The old woman still clung to the memory of one fruitless night with Sultan Bayezid, Suleiman's grandfather. She had spent almost every day since then as a dressmaker in the harem, lost among the bolts of brocade, damask, and satin. Her temper was short.

Hürrem had nimble fingers and a good eye, and her handkerchiefs had won approving murmurs from the Sultan Valide, the Sultan's mother.

She hummed as she worked, embroidering a square of green Diba satin. She used gold and silver thread, sewing an intricate pattern of leaves and flowers into the cloth.

The tune she hummed was one she had learned from her father; a Tatar song about the steppes and the north wind.

She did not hear the *kiaya* enter the room behind her, but she felt the stinging slap to her ear. She started with shock, dropped her needle to the floor, and raised her hand to strike back.

The *kiaya's* eyes gleamed. 'Go on, hit me! I'll have the Kapi Aga put you to the *bastinado*!'

Hürrem lowered her hand.

'You do not sing in here, I have told you before. This is the Harem, and there is always silence.'

'I like to sing.'

'What the Great Lord likes is all that matters here.'

'He isn't even here. We could discharge a cannon in the courtyard, and he would be none the wiser.'

'Insolent little minx!' The *kiaya* slapped her again, but this time Hürrem braced herself for the blow. The *kiaya's* open hand left a pink imprint on her cheek.

The *kiaya* picked up the handkerchief and looked for fault. Finding none, she dropped it back on the bench in disgust. 'Get on with your work.'

Hürrem shared the sewing room with a raven-haired Jewish girl, who had been bought from slave traders in Alexandria. 'Market meat,' the *kiaya* called her. Her name was Meylissa. Hürrem watched her out of the corner of her eye, bent over her needlework, trying to make herself invisible behind the chemises and veils piled on the table in front of her. But she was too tempting a target for the *kiaya* in her present mood.

'Let me see that,' the *kiaya* said and snatched the work from Meylissa's fingers. 'Look at this. The finest Bursa brocade and you have ruined it.' She slapped her around the head. 'What were you thinking?'

Meylissa bowed her head and said nothing. The *kiaya* threw the piece of material onto the floor. 'Undo all these stitches and start again.'

'Fat old hind breath of a camel,' Hürrem hissed when she was gone. She started humming again, louder than before.

She heard muffled sobbing behind her and turned around. Meylissa was crying, her head cradled on her arms.

'Don't let her upset you.'

Meylissa shook her head, and the sobs came harder.

'Meylissa?' Hürrem got to her feet and put an arm around her shoulder.

'It's not her.'

'What then?'

And then she saw it, plain in the girl's eyes. Terror; naked and raw. Whatever it was, it had nothing to do with the *kiaya*.

Meylissa searched her face, looking for reassurance. 'I have to tell someone,' she said.

'You can trust me,' Hürrem said. 'Whatever it is, I won't tell anyone.'

'They'll kill me,' Meylissa whispered. She clutched at the hem of her kaftan, bunching the material into a ball in her fist.

'I can't help you if you don't tell me.'

'I'm pregnant,' Meylissa said.

Hürrem thought she had misheard. 'That doesn't make any sense,' she said.

'It's true. I missed my bleed.'

Hürrem laughed. Pregnant, she thought. In this prison? 'Meylissa, it's all right, it happens. Sometimes they come late, sometimes they don't come at all. It doesn't mean you're pregnant.'

Meylissa shook her head.

'You need a man to make you pregnant.'

Meylissa looked over Hürrem's shoulder to make sure no one could overhear. Until that moment Hürrem had thought herself the more worldly one, but in that unguarded moment she saw a knowing and a cunning in Meylissa that she had missed until now.

'The Kapi Aga,' Meylissa whispered.

The Kapi Aga! The Captain of the Guards and the Chief White Eunuch. Hürrem's jaw fell open in astonishment. Although he was in charge of the Harem Guard, he was supposed never to be alone with any of the girls as he was not *rasé,* a complete eunuch, like the Negroes. She had heard that most of the white eunuchs had only been partly castrated, their testicles had been tied or crushed, like young lambs.

She was stunned. While she had been wrestling with the new language, thinking herself superior, this farmer's girl had found a way to get herself bedded.

'They say sometimes a man can, well, regenerate,' Meylissa said. 'Even the black ones. They check them every year to make sure they haven't grown back.'

'Nonsense! When you geld a horse, it stays gelded!'

'The white eunuchs, you know, they are not *rasé* - their things are not shaved off, like with the Nubians.'

'But where did you do it?'

'There's a courtyard at the northern end of the palace. It's surrounded by high walls and shaded with plane trees. There's a door in the wall, but it's always locked and there's never a guard.'

'What were you doing there?'

'I was learning my Koran, as we were instructed. He must have seen me, from the northern tower. I heard a key in the lock. I was going to run away but...'

Hürrem cocked her head, waiting for this 'but'. Meylissa only shrugged her shoulders. 'He said I was the most beautiful woman in the harem. He said he would help me catch the Sultan's eye.'

'How many times did this happen?'

'Just once. Perhaps twice.' A breath. 'Six times.'

'Six! Do you know what they would have done if they had caught you?'

'But they have caught me. Haven't they?'

Hürrem wondered what she would have done if it had been her sitting in the shaded garden reading the Koran. Even mortal danger could be tempting compared with the stifling boredom of the palace.

'They are going to kill me,' Meylissa whispered. 'They will tie me in a sack and throw me in the Bosporus.'

'I'll help you,' Hürrem said. 'Trust me.'

CHAPTER 2

The room was as he had remembered it. For the first time since he had entered Stamboul in triumph three days before, Suleiman felt that he had come home. He threw himself on the couch. He tossed aside his silk turban and ran a hand across his skull to the scalp lock at the crown.

Ever since he had inherited the throne from his father three years before, he had felt like an actor in a shadow play. He thought the feeling would pass as he grew accustomed to his new role, but instead it grew stronger. Even in his diaries he referred to himself in the third person.

They called the Grand Vizier the 'bearer of the burden.' But the Grand Vizier was only a juggler; a balancing act of flattery, mathematics and duplicity. It was the Sultan who truly carried the great weight of expectation, not only of the six million Turks that he ruled, but of Islam itself.

Only the silence of the Harem brought him respite. Scented wood burned in the copper hearths, firelight rippled on the tiled walls. There were no viziers, generals, or responsibilities.

And there was Gülbehar.

He heard the rustle of fabric as she entered through the damask curtain at the far end of the room. She wore a sheer chemise, and two diamond buttons danced against her flesh. Her waistcoat was of Bursa brocade, her pantaloons a white waterfall of silk. Her hair was tied in a single, long braid down her back.

She is like sunlight rippling on the water, he thought. Gülbehar, Rose of Spring. What a perfect name they gave you.

She fell on her knees and touched her forehead to the carpet. '*Salaam*, Lord of my Life. Sultan of Sultans, Lord of the World, King of Kings.'

He motioned to her, impatiently. How many times had he told her there was no need? He was a man come home; that was all he wanted to be tonight. But she always greeted him this same way, keeping to the ancient formula.

'Come here,' he said.

She ran the last few steps and buried her face in his neck. He felt the wetness of her tears on his cheek and the scent of dried jasmine from her hair.

'When there was snow on the minarets and you had not returned I thought you were never coming back,' she said. 'I was so frightened without you. There are many whispers.' She pulled away from him and stared into his face. 'You were not hurt?'

'No scars that will ever show. How is Mustapha?'

'He has missed you. He talks of you often.'

'Let me see him.'

Gülbehar took his hand and led him through the apartments to the prince's bedchamber. A candle burned in a golden candlestick at one corner of the bed, attended by a turbaned page. Another page stood waiting in the shadows. Whenever the boy turned in his sleep, the candle on that side would be extinguished and another lit on the other side.

Suleiman leaned over the mattress. Mustapha had fair hair like his mother, and the same serene features. He was nine years old, growing tall, and as skilled at throwing a javelin as he was at learning the Koran and reading mathematics.

The next Osmanli sultan, Suleiman thought. Enjoy your youth while you can. It is good you are growing broad shoulders.

Such irony that his son looked so little like him, even less like one of the Turks he would one day rule. But every Sultan's wife was an infidel, since the Koran decreed that no Muslim could be sold into slavery. So every Sultan was the son of a slave, yet divinely chosen as the Protector of the Great Faith. God's web was indeed a large one.

'He is well?' he said.

'Sturdy and strong. He wishes to be like his father.'

He stroked a lock of hair from his son's forehead. 'Bless you Mustapha,' he said. He turned to Gülbehar. Her silhouette was outlined against the candle flame. Desire was like a physical blow. He wanted to have her now. But that would not do.

Instead he said, 'We should eat.'

Gülbehar served the food herself; tiny squares of lamb cooked in aromatic herbs, pieces of chicken baked over a slow fire, eggplants stuffed with rice. Afterwards there were figs in sour cream. Silent pages refilled their cups and bowls.

'What is the talk in the Harem?' Suleiman asked her. It always amused him to hear the gossip.

'They say you are a hero,' Gülbehar said. 'When the news came that you had taken Rhodes, everyone said you would be remembered by history as a great conqueror, like your great-grandfather. Some say you are destined to be the greatest of all the Sultans.'

'The price of glory was very high. We lost many men.'

'You must not think about that,' Gülbehar said. 'Our army will soon be strong again.'

The remark irritated him. What did she know of armies? He dipped his fingers into a silver bowl of scented rosewater. A page appeared instantly to dry them.

'By day it is easy not to remember. But at night, in the dark, it is harder not to hear the screams.'

How can I talk to her about it? he thought. I am not like my father or my grandfather. They lived for war.

This is a burden I must shoulder alone.

CHAPTER 3

Bathing was frowned upon, even feared, among her own people. Everyone knew it led to chills, sickness and death.

But in here the girls were made to bathe twice a day and to shave every hair from their bodies. Hürrem hated it, all of it. It seemed to her that the Turks wanted to pile one humiliation upon another.

There were three rooms in the baths: a dressing chamber, a warming room, and the large, central steam room. She stripped off her clothes and one of the *gediçli*, the negress slaves, handed her a perfumed towel. She slipped a pair of rosewood sandals on her feet and went into the warming room. There was a large marble fountain in the center, with water that had been heated in the massive boiler below. Girls were sitting or standing around it, scooping up the water in copper bowls and pouring it over their heads. Hürrem joined them.

On the steppe, women all looked much the same. Until she had come to the harem, she had not known the world was such a vast place, and that human beings could be so different. As she looked around, she saw *gediçli* with mahogany skins; Greek girls with dark eyes, their hair teased in a thousand ringlets; golden-haired Circassians with blue eyes and pink nipples; Persians with hair the color of night and eyes deep and dark as wells.

She looked down at herself, slim and small like a boy, and wondered why they had chosen her.

The steam seared her lungs and clung to her skin in a scorching veil. Instantly, perspiration oozed from her in a thousand tiny droplets. Willowy shapes moved in and out of the mist like wraiths. The silence was broken only by the clank of a copper bowl or the splash as a girl got in or out of the bath.

Light filtered from high windows in the domed ceiling, the vapor and walls of grey marble bleeding into one another so that it seemed there were no walls at all.

Hürrem lowered herself into one of the warm pools and closed her eyes, the water lapping around her shoulders. She rested her head on the marble lip, scooped a handful of water over her face and pushed the damp hair from her eyes.

She felt movement in the water. A tall fair-haired woman was sitting on the edge of the bath, while two slave girls scooped water over her body and massaged the muscles of her shoulders. She was leaning back, looking up at the ceiling, her hair almost touching the marble floor behind her. Gülbehar.

Hürrem felt a rush of envy. With all these women here at his command, she thought, why does he choose only her? Is she so beguiling or is he so easy to bewitch?

Marble columns and arches led off the steam room into smaller side chambers, where the *gediçli* tended to the girls. They massaged their bodies, minutely inspecting their noses and ears, their legs and arms, their pubis, vagina and anus, ensuring no trace of body hair remained. Hürrem had long abandoned protest at such indignity.

Her *gediçli's* name was Muomi. She was a sullen girl with tight jet curls. The other concubines spoke about her in whispers. They said she was a witch, and avoided her if they could. She had large hands that knuckled deep into joints and sinews, and made the girls scream.

Muomi started to knead the muscles at her neck and shoulders. Hürrem gasped, took a deep breath and endured. Muomi shifted her position to start on her back muscles.

'They say you're a witch,' Hürrem said.

'Who says it?'

'The other girls.'

'They choose them for their beauty not their brains. They are all as stupid as camels.'

'Are you a witch?'

Muomi's hands moved along her spine. It felt like she was driving her knuckles between the bones. Hürrem felt the wellspring of tears in her eyes and buried her face in her arms to hide them.

'Well, are you?' she repeated.

'If I were a witch, I would have cast a spell and got myself out of here a long time ago.'

She pressed both her fists deep into Hürrem's buttocks. Hürrem clenched her teeth to keep from crying out. 'Your muscles are as hard as a boy's,' Muomi conceded.

'A bit harder,' Hürrem said. 'I can hardly feel it.'

Meylissa found Hürrem lying on her back while Muomi performed her depilatory. She applied a paste made with quicklime, and expertly scraped away small hairs with the sharp edge of a mussel shell. Hürrem's breasts rose and fell tremulously with her breathing. Her cheeks were wet.

'Are you all right?' Meylissa said.

'From now on, Muomi will be the Sultan's new head torturer.'

Muomi ignored her, shoving her legs apart and examining the perineum minutely for hairs.

13

'What's the point of all this?' Meylissa said. 'Muomi is the only one who will ever see if we shave or not. The Sultan never will.'

'We must be ready,' Hürrem said. 'We cannot let one golden opportunity be lost for one golden hair.'

Meylissa perched on the edge of the marble and lowered her voice to a whisper. She put a hand on her own slender, brown stomach. 'Soon I'll be starting to show.' Her eyes filled with tears.

Muomi's head jerked up. 'What's wrong with her?'

'She remembers the last time you rubbed her back,' Hürrem said. She clutched Melissa's arm. 'Don't talk about it here.'

'What am I going to do?'

'Don't worry. I have a plan.'

CHAPTER 4

For two months, the Kapi Aga had known, by turns, abject terror, tremulous anticipation and delirious pleasure. He knew what they would do to him if his secret was discovered. But he could not stop now. The sexual pleasure - and she was a beautiful woman, made doubly so by being forbidden - was only part of it.

He had his manhood again.

Each Thursday afternoon, an hour before dusk, she would come to the garden to read her Koran. His entire existence now revolved around the dreadful, exquisite moment when he would turn the key in that rusted lock and enter the garden. Each time he pushed open the door he could never be sure if he would find Meylissa and her kittenish smile or his own soldiers, their razor-edged *killiç* swords drawn. Even as Head of the Palace Guard and Keeper of the Girls, he could not pull off his own dogs if he were discovered.

The iron-barred door creaked open. It sounded like a cannon shot in the silence of the harem. He crept through, locking it behind him and glanced up at the north tower. The only way he might be seen was from the room at the very top - it was from there he had first seen Meylissa - but he had just locked the door to that room himself.

He still felt as if every member of the Divan were watching him, ordering the chief executioner to sharpen the steel hooks that would tear him apart.

The garden was shaded by high walls, the paths flanked by columns of white Paros marble and overhung with cypress and willow. It was always twilight here. The late afternoon sun caught the tiles on the minaret of the harem mosque, turning them rose pink.

He looked around for Meylissa, thought to find her as usual on the marble seat beneath the colonnades, but there was no sign of her. He felt a thrill of fear. He held his breath and listened; the only sound was a lone nightingale calling softly in the willow branches above his head.

'She cannot come today.'

The voice came from behind him. He jerked around, instinctively drawing his *killiç* from its leather scabbard.

The girl crossed her arms and laughed at him.

He did not recognize her, but then there were so many new ones. She was small and slim, with flaming red hair and green eyes. She wore a yellow cotton kaftan, with a gold brocade jacket and a little green cap on her head. There was a single pearl tied at the cap's tassel.

She was so tiny a breath of wind might blow her away. 'Where is Meylissa?' he said.

'In the Harem of course, safe from the attentions of men.'

'What are you laughing at?'

'You are as white as your turban. It's all right, as you can see, I'm not one of the Sultan's Janissaries. I'm just a sewing girl. Look, I'm unarmed. I don't even have my needle.'

'Who do you think you're talking to, girl? I'll have you put to the *bastinado*.' He grabbed her by the arm, put his sword point to her eyes to intimidate her. Hürrem smiled back and her fingers closed around his groin.

'Meylissa is going to have your baby.'

He took a step backward and his sword slipped from his fingers and clattered onto the marble.

'You are thinking it's not possible? That's what she thought, too. But I promise you, Kapi Aga, you have defied their efforts to unman you.'

'Who are you? What do you want?'

'I'm Meylissa's friend. It's alright, I want to help you.'

'Who else knows?' he said.

'It would be easy to toss us both into the Bosporus in the middle of the night, and be done with the whole thing. That's what you're thinking, isn't it? That's why we have told one other. Someone whose name you will never know.'

He sheathed his sword. 'How could you help me?'

'I want to help Meylissa, but it will help you too. Or perhaps you do not wish my help. You could marry her and raise a family together.'

'Do not mock me!' He took a step towards her, bold again.

'One night the Sultan will appear in your quarters with two sacks. One for my friend Meylissa when they throw her in the Bosporus. The other sack will be to collect the pieces of his former Kapi Aga after his chief executioner has finished cutting him into small pieces.'

'What can you do?'

'I can eliminate your problem for you.'

'How?'

'That's not your concern. But in return you will do something for me.'

He wanted to kill her, but that would not do him any good. 'All right,' he said, at last. 'What is it you want? A better position? Clothes? Money?'

'You value your life so cheap?'

The sun was low in the sky now, and the minaret had turned blood-red. 'So what is it you are after?'

'I want you to get me into the Sultan's bed.'

'I cannot do that. It's impossible!'

'Then you must make it possible. Or else it is very possible that the Sultan will discover your perfidy, have you hung on a hook and leave you to turn black in the sun. You know the punishment.'

'The Sultan never sleeps with any woman but Gülbehar. What you are asking is not in my power.'

She stopped smiling. 'Enjoy your death. I believe they will give you plenty of time to savor it.'

She walked away.

The shadows crept across the garden and the Kapi Aga watched them come, frozen with terror.

CHAPTER 5

The Harem dated back to the time when the Osmanli Turks were no more than nomadic traders living on the wild plains of Anatolia and Azerbaijan. The idea of the harem was borrowed from the Persians. When the Osmanlis gave up their nomadic lifestyle, creating a capital first at Bursa, then at Stamboul, the Sultan's Harem had become an institution in itself and a rigid hierarchy had evolved, with its own protocols and government.

This reclusive community of eunuchs and virgins was governed by the Sultan's mother, the Valide. She was assisted by the Kapi Aga, the Chief White Eunuch, who was both Captain of the Guard and intermediary between the Valide and the Sultan himself.

Any of the hundreds of concubines might rise through the ranks to a position of importance in the Harem administration through her own merits. But the only path to real power was by catching the eye of the Sultan.

If he invited her to his bed, she was given apartments and an allowance of her own. She might have one night with the Lord of Life or a hundred. But it all counted for nothing unless she bore him a son and became one of his wives or *kadins*. There were only ever four wives. After that, the abortionist was called in. These four wives remained just a breath from real power, for only one of them would one day become the mother of the next Osmanli Sultan.

But Suleiman had broken with tradition. Even though he was thirty years old, he had only one *kadin* and one son. It was a tenuous thread for an exalted bloodline such as the Osmanlis, and Suleiman's mother fretted over this reticence on her son's part to ensure he had enough heirs.

The Valide received the Kapi Aga in her audience chamber, an immense vault of gleaming onyx and veined marble.

A yellow bolt of sunlight angled in from the glass cupola high above.

She regarded him from a high-backed, ebony chair upholstered with purple brocade. 'You wanted to see me, Kapi Aga?' she said.

The Chief White Eunuch licked his lips. He had practiced his speech long into the night but now every word of it deserted him and he was overcome with a black panic. 'Crown of Veiled Heads,' he mumbled, addressing her by her formal title.

'What's the matter? Are you unwell?'

'A slight chill.'

'A visit to the apothecary perhaps?'

'I shall do as your Highness suggests.'

'Something is troubling you?'

'I have word of unrest among the girls.'

The Valide frowned. 'What kind of unrest?'

'Well, some of them, they are…'

'The point, Kapi Aga.'

'They are jealous.'

'Harem girls are always jealous of something.'

'This is not a passing envy. The discontent is growing. I think we should pay attention to it.'

The Valide gazed at him steadily. It was unnerving. 'Go on,' she said.

'It is Gülbehar. She is well loved by everyone, of course.'

'Except me.'

Well yes, except you, the Kapi Aga thought. I was counting on that. 'Some of the girls feel it is neither right nor just that the Lord of Life ignores them. They are becoming almost unmanageable.'

'Well that is your job, and that of the Kislar Aghasi. To manage them.'

'Of course, My Lady. But if only there was something I could tell them, to encourage them.'

The Valide put a jeweled index finger to her cheek. 'What might prove sufficient encouragement, do you think?'

'That perhaps the Lord of Life would have use for them one day soon?'

'Who is to say what he will or will not do?'

He had touched a nerve. If anyone was unhappy about Suleiman's exclusive attachment to Gülbehar, it was his mother. 'They all cherish the opportunity to serve their master as best they can,' he said.

'But are any of them a match for Gülbehar?'

'They all think they are,' he said with a tight smile.

The Valide looked through the window and across the gleaming cupolas of the Harem. She tapped the fingers of her left hand against her thumb as if she were silently calculating figures in her head. 'I shall talk to the Lord of Life,' she said. 'Thank you for bringing this subject to my attention.'

The Kapi Aga wanted to shout, 'Wait, there's more!' Too late. He had been dismissed. He bowed and backed towards the door.

'One other thing.'

'Yes, Highness?'

'Do you have any particular girl in mind?'

He tried to hide his relief. He had thought she might not ask him. 'There is one girl I think might turn our Lord's head. She has the sort of quick mind and lively nature he may find more than pleasing.'

'Her name?'

'Hürrem, Highness. Her name is Hürrem.'

CHAPTER 6

Whenever Suleiman came to his harem in the old palace, he was required to visit his mother first.

The Valide received him on the terrace. She was wearing a flowered brocade kaftan, and the spring sunshine sparkled on the dusting of baroque pearl and garnets in her hair. She enjoyed these useless baubles more than real gems.

'Mother.' Suleiman kissed her hand. He sat down on the divan beside her, while one of her maids hurried to fetch sherbets and rosewater.

'You are well?'

'I feel the chill more than I once did. At my age you look forward to spring.'

'You are not so old.'

'I am a grandmother,' she said. 'Well, I have one grandson. It is hardly overwhelming.'

Suleiman threw back his head and laughed. 'Not that again.'

'I am saddened at how lightly you treat an old woman's fears.' She pulled her hand away and chose a fig from the bowl of fruit in front of her. 'And what of the conqueror of Rhodes? Where does the Divan urge you to strike next?'

'You will hear no war drums this year. My generals are still licking their wounds. It will be some time before they are ready to stretch their claws again.'

'And what about you?'

He sighed. 'The thought of another campaign sickens me to my soul.'

'A Sultan who will not carry the banner of Muhammad into battle will not remain a Sultan for long. The Janissaries will see to that.'

Suleiman remembered his father's words to him before he sent him to Manisa as governor, on his first official post, 'If a Turk climbs down from the saddle to sit on a carpet, he becomes nothing.'

But then his father was a barbarian.

'You do not need to remind me of my duty, to them or to God. But for this season at least I have had enough of war.'

'A Sultan's duty lies not only on the battlefield.'

So, here was the real business; her first words to him that morning should have warned him. They were to talk of Gülbehar again. 'The Osmanlis have an heir,' he said.

'And what if he sickens? A Sultan should have many sons.'

'So they can murder each other when I am dead?' Suleiman thought about his father. Selim the Grim, as the people had called him, had deposed his own father with the support of the Janissaries and had him poisoned him on his way to exile. He had then murdered his two brothers and eight nephews, so his sultanate could not be challenged. He had even dispatched Suleiman's own brothers, so that Suleiman himself would not be burdened with this grisly business. Did he doubt that he would have had the stomach for it?

'You have a duty.'

'I have many duties.'

'And you should not neglect a single one of them.'

'But Gülbehar makes me happy.'

'We are not talking about happiness, we are talking about heirs to the line of Osman.'

Suleiman turned away, stared at the panorama of minarets and cupolas that punctuated the jumble of wooden houses above the Golden Horn.

'At this moment, the house of Osman has only two heartbeats,' the Valide said. 'It is not enough.'

'What would you have me do?'

'I do not ask you to give up your Gülbehar. It is only natural that you should have a favorite. But there are many girls in the Harem. Some of them must be pleasing to the eye.'

'So I must play the bull for the house of Osman?'

'Indelicately put, especially in front of an old woman, but yes, that is exactly what you should do. It would be different if Gülbehar had given you more sons. But she has been your *kadin* now for nine years.'

'She pleases me.'

'And another woman cannot?'

Suleiman jumped to his feet. He saw one of his mother's handmaids glance at him shyly from under her kohl-darkened eyelashes. He felt a surge of impatience, with her and with himself. What was wrong with him? Most men would not find it such an onerous duty. Perhaps it is the way I prove to everyone, and to myself, that I am not like the beasts who sat on the throne before me.

'I will do as you ask,' he said and kissed his mother's hand. I'll bull them all, one at a time, if that is what you want, he thought. I'll fill the palace with cradles.

And then I'll go back to Gülbehar.

The *kiaya* snatched the cushion slip from Meylissa's hands, flung it on the floor and stamped on it. 'What is this? Are you deliberately trying to provoke me?'

Meylissa shook her head miserably.

'Look at these stitches! I would not give this to a peasant in the field, never mind to the Valide!'

'I'm sorry.'

'What is the matter with you? These last few weeks you have been quite impossible.' The *kiaya* pinched Meylissa hard on the cheek. The girl's howls encouraged her, and she did it again.

Hürrem got up from her workbench and snatched up the silk cushion at the *kiaya*'s feet. 'It is not so bad. Leave her alone.'

'You cannot sit still when you see fur flying, can you my sweet?' the *kiaya* said

'She is not feeling well.'

'Well, let's send her to the infirmary then. And if your stitching is so fine, you can do her work as well as your own.'

Hürrem flung the piece of material at her.

The *kiaya* raised her hand, but this time Hürrem was quicker. She hit the *kiaya* on the side of the head, almost knocking her off her feet. The sound of the slap was followed by silence.

The *kiaya*'s face split into a slow, triumphant smile. 'For that you get the *bastinado*,' she whispered. 'The Kapi Aga will have them strip the flesh from the soles of your feet with whips. It is spring now. If you are lucky you might take your first steps again in the winter.'

Two guards appeared in the doorway. One stepped into the room and took Hürrem's arm. 'You are to come with me,' he said. 'Bring your sewing with you.'

Hürrem looked bewildered. How had the guards come for her so quickly, had they been waiting outside the door? She did as she was commanded. She snatched up her needles, her little bag of emery powder, and the green square of silk she had been embroidering.

'Where are you taking her?' the *kiaya* said.

'The Kapi Aga has given us our orders,' he said and pulled Hürrem to the door.

'She must be put to the *bastinado*!' the *kiaya* shouted.

25

Hürrem let the guards hurry her away down the corridor. If the Kapi Aga had sent for her, it could mean only one thing, and it was not the *bastinado*.

CHAPTER 7

The Valide's courtyard was paved with almond-shaped cobblestones and dominated by an ornate marble fountain. Windows looked down from all sides.

The guards hurried Hürrem to the center of the court and released her. 'The Kapi Aga says you are to wait. And be sure to sing.'

'Sing, why? What is happening?'

But the men wheeled away without another word. Hürrem stared after them.

Perhaps the Kapi Aga has arranged an interview with the Sultan's mother, she thought.

She found a cool spot in the shade of the fountain and sat down, crossing her legs beneath her, Osmanli style. She spread the handkerchief on her lap, took out her needle and embroidery. She started to hum a love song her mother had taught her, about a boy whose horse had fallen in the snow, trapping him. As he died by inches on the winter steppe, he told the wind how much he loved a certain girl and how he had never had the courage to tell her. He asked the wind to carry his words across the plain so that she would remember him. It was a stupid, sentimental song, Hürrem thought, but she had always liked the tune.

She did not notice the tall, slender figure in the white turban until his shadow fell across her lap.

'The first law of the Harem is silence.'

She looked up, startled. The man was standing with the sun behind his back and she had to shield her eyes against the glare. He did not speak like a eunuch and he was not black like a Nubian. There was only one other man who might walk freely here.

'Perhaps we should cut out the tongues of all the nightingales then. And the bees. We should do something about them also. All this incessant buzzing. Don't they know the rules?' It was out of her mouth before she could stop herself.

For a moment he stared at her. She remembered that her first action before speaking should have been to lower her forehead to the ground to make her obeisance. She put down her embroidery and went to her knees. She should beg his forgiveness for breaking the silence, she thought. But it was a little late now.

The old Kislar Aghasi - the Chief Black Eunuch - was standing behind Suleiman, his face beaded with perspiration, fanning himself with a silk handkerchief. He looked as if he were about to faint.

'Do you know who I am?' Suleiman asked her.

'You are the Lord of Life.'

'What were you singing?'

'It was a song I learned from my mother, my Lord. A love song. About a boy who let his horse fall on top of him.'

'He was singing to the horse?'

'I think not. I dare to say the horse had lost much of its charm by then.'

'What is your name?'

'They call me Hürrem, my lord.'

'Hürrem? Laughing one. Who gave you that name?'

'The men who brought me here. Because they said I was always smiling.'

'Why were you always smiling?'

'So they would not see me cry.'

He frowned. Her answer had taken him by surprise. 'Where are you from, Hürrem?'

She squinted up at him. This was the moment for which she had gambled so much, and all she could think about was the pain in her knees. How long would he leave her down here on these cobblestones? 'I am a Tatar,' she said. 'A Krim.'

'Do all Tatars have hair of such amazing color?'

'No, my Lord. I was the only one in my clan burdened this way.'

'Burdened? I think not. It is quite beautiful.' He stroked her hair and held a lock of it in his fingers, as if he were examining a piece of material in the bazaar for quality and strength. 'It is like burnished gold. Is it not, Ali?'

The Kislar Aghasi murmured his agreement. 'Beautiful, my Lord. '

'Stand up, Hürrem.'

At last. She got to her feet. She knew she should lower her eyes, as she had been trained to do, but curiosity got the better of her. So this was the Lord of Life, the Possessor of Men's Necks, the Lord of the Seven Worlds. He was handsome, she supposed, but not especially so. There was the shadow of a beard on his face, which lent a certain majesty to his beaked nose. He had grey eyes.

He examined her from head to toe, as the Sultan's soldiers had done the day her father had traded her. He did not seem especially displeased with what he saw, yet when he had done he gave a long sigh. 'What is that you are embroidering?' he asked her.

'A handkerchief, my lord.'

'Let me see it.' She handed it to him. 'A fine piece of work. You have great skill. May I have it?'

'It is not finished.'

'Have it ready for me tonight,' he said and placed it carefully over her left shoulder. She saw the Kislar Aghasi's eyes widened in shock. Placing a handkerchief on a girl's shoulder signified that she was now *gözde*, in the eye, and the Sultan wished to sleep with her. She had been told that no girl had been so favored since he had assumed the throne.

Suleiman walked away without another word. The Kislar Aghasi hurried after him.

Hürrem watched them go. In the eye, she thought. Now I just have to stay there.

Suleiman hurried along the cloister. He felt angry, but also a little relieved. After his mother's lecture to him that morning he had realized he had no choice in the matter. He had asked the Kapi Aga to arrange a suitable girl. This Hürrem that he had picked out for him was appealing in an elfin way, and she intrigued him, a little. She had spirit. Most Harem girls were insufferably empty and vain.

And if she got pregnant his mother would be satisfied, and he could return to Gülbehar and continue his life in peace.

CHAPTER 8

A crescent moon trembled in the night sky. Suleiman and Ibrahim had dined on sturgeon, lobster and swordfish, taken that same morning from the Bosporus, washed down with sherbets made with violets and honey. They had finished the meal with a bottle of Cyprus wine, even though it was forbidden by the Koran.

It was a small transgression, but one that gave Suleiman a measure of satisfaction, for in all other ways his life was proscribed by protocol.

At soon as he was awake, the Parer of the Nails and the Chief Barber arrived. Then the Master of the Wardrobe laid out his day's clothes, each piece scented with aloe wood. The Chief Turban Winder curled yards of linen around his fez.

Dawn saw him hurrying to attend the Divan, except on Fridays when he rode to prayers at the Aya Sofia with his court; his Grand Vizier, his Chief Huntsman, the Chief Keeper of the Nightingales, the Master of the Keys and four thousand of his Janissaries.

In the afternoon he would take a short nap, as required by custom, whether he was tired or not. He was attended at all times by five guards. Then back to the Divan and the endless affairs of state.

A glass of wine seemed like an act of rebellion.

Ibrahim was his greatest scandal. During the siege they had slept in the same pavilion and had worn each other's clothes. He knew he outraged the whole court by showing such favor to a slave. But then, to Suleiman, Ibrahim was not just a slave; he was both confessor and counsellor. If anyone helped him shoulder the burden, it was not Gülbehar or the Valide or even the Grand Vizier. It was Ibrahim.

After they had drunk the wine, Ibrahim sat cross-legged beneath the window and strummed his viol. Though they were the same age, Suleiman felt much older. Careworn might be a better word.

Ibrahim had been born in a village on the western coast of Greece. He was stolen by traders and taken to the slave markets in Stamboul, where he was bought by a widow from Manisa. She raised him a Muslim, and when she discovered his flair for music and languages, she had arranged for him to have a good education. He learned to play the viol and he could speak Persian, Turkish, Greek and Italian.

Later she sold him for a handsome profit into Suleiman's service when he went to Manisa as the new governor of Kaffa province.

When he became Sultan in 1520, Suleiman brought Ibrahim with him to the Porte and made him head of his household. He sought him out for counsel more often than Piri Pasha, his old Grand Vizier. After Rhodes he made him one of his counsellors, just below the Grand Vizier in rank.

This is why we Osmanlis have become supreme in the world, Suleiman thought. Even a Christian slave can rise by his own merits to become pre-eminent in the greatest Islamic empire the world has ever seen.

'So solemn, my lord?' Ibrahim said, setting the viol aside.

Suleiman sighed. 'Do you ever have regrets, Ibrahim?'

'Regrets? Look at all this. Good food. Good wine. A palace to live in. What is there to regret?'

'But do you not sometimes wish you were someone else? Do you ever wonder what might have happened if the pirates had not come to the village that day and snatched you away?'

'I know what would have happened. I would be eating fish for breakfast and supper, and mending nets on the beach all day. Instead I sleep in a palace, drink the best Cyprian wine and am held in favor by the greatest Emperor on the earth.'

'Your life would have been simpler.'

'My life would have been worthless.'

'You enjoy all this, don't you? You enjoy going to war and you relish the endless politicking in the Divan.'

'We are at the hub of the world, my Lord. We are writing history.'

'We are serving Islam.'

'Well yes, that too.' He picked up the viol again. 'We are Islam's greatest servants.'

No, you do all this for its own sake, Suleiman thought. That is why I love you and envy you so much. I wish I were more like you. 'I think sometimes you should have been Sultan and I the son of a Greek fisherman,' he said. 'We might have been happier that way.' He got to his feet.

'Shall we sleep now, my Lord?'

'You may sleep, Ibrahim. I have yet one more duty to perform.'

Hürrem had been escorted to the Keeper of the Baths to be bathed and massaged. Her nails were dyed, her hair perfumed with jasmine, her skin pomaded with henna to prevent sweating, her eyes blackened with kohl.

She was then taken to the Mistress of the Robes, who dressed her in a rose-colored chemise and purple velvet kaftan, with a robe of silver and apricot brocade. The Mistress of the Jewels brought a diamond necklace as heavy as an iron collar, a string of fat Arabian pearls to plait into her hair, and a pair of heavy ruby earrings that reached to her shoulders.

They must all be returned in the morning, she was told.

A *gediçli* held up a mirror so that she could inspect her reflection. She regarded the apparition that stared back at her with something close to disbelief. 'I look completely hideous.'

The Mistress of the Robes put her hands on her hips. 'It is the way.'

'It is the way to make a man fall on the floor laughing.'

'Do you not realize the great honor that has fallen on you? I know what it's like, I was in the eye once, when Bayezid was Sultan. Let me tell you what you should do to please him…'

'I know what I have to do,' Hürrem said. 'I have to get pregnant.'

CHAPTER 9

There were two guards, the same pair who had led her to the courtyard earlier in the day. They escorted her along a maze of gloomy, cold cloisters and down a narrow staircase. The hem of her gown and the trailing sleeves of her kaftan kept catching and tearing on the wood. She felt a chill draft of air on her cheek as she was propelled into the night through a heavy iron door. A boxlike carriage was waiting for her. She caught a whiff of horse and ancient leather and then a soft, fleshy hand pulled her inside.

The carriage jerked forward and the horse's hoofs clattered on the cobbles. As her eyes adjusted to the dark, she made out the bulky silhouette of the Kislar Aghasi opposite her.

'Where are we going?' she said.

'To the Sultan. He is waiting for you in the Topkapi palace.'

The curtains were drawn. Hürrem tried to shift them aside to peek out but he snatched her hand away. 'Is it far?' she said.

'No, not far.' She could feel him staring at her. 'The Kapi Aga arranged this for you,' he said.

'Why would he do that?'

'A question I have been asking myself all day.'

'And what answer did you arrive at?'

'I have none. He looks very pale these days, like a man awaiting execution. Or perhaps he is unwell.'

'Perhaps.'

'Do not misunderstand me. Should the Kapi Aga fall into disfavor I shall not weep for him. But I should like to know what ails him.' He gave her a hard look. He suspects something, Hürrem thought.

The coach clattered to a halt and the door was thrown open. Hürrem looked quickly around as she stepped down. So, this was the Topkapi! The great tower of the Divan loomed above her and torches dotted around the gardens flickered among the bushes. A thousand trees rustled in the night wind.

Two halberdiers, the heavy-tressed plumes on their helmets covering half their faces, ushered her through a massive iron-studded door, and into the heart of the seraglio. The Kislar Aghasi wheezed and puffed as he struggled along behind. She was struck by how orderly and spacious it all seemed after the drabness of the Old Palace. The walls here were stone, not wood, and the corridors wider and better lit.

They reached two wooden doors, inlaid with mother of pearl and tortoiseshell, which led to the Sultan's private chambers. Two soldiers from his personal bodyguard stood on guard on either side.

Hürrem took a deep breath. She had staked so much on this one night. You don't have to beguile him, she reminded herself. Just accept his seed and let it flower into freedom.

The Kislar Aghasi threw open the doors and led her inside.

Hürrem looked around in awe.

The walls were decorated with Iznik tiles, orange and peacock blue, in dazzling patterns of flowers and fruit. The ceiling rose to a high dome and, below it, censers on long golden chains glittered with rubies. There was a fireplace shaped like a copper pyramid, and oil lamps glimmered in niches on the walls.

The bed was on a raised platform in the corner, hung with a canopy of green and gold Bursa brocade, supported on columns of fluted silver. There were quilts and cushions of crimson velvet, every one of them laced with pearls. Tapers burned in platinum candlesticks at the four corners.

Suleiman reclined on a divan of shimmering gold velvet. He wore an apple-green robe, and a turban of pure white silk with a clasp of heron feathers. An emerald, the size of a baby's fist, glinted from the folds. He looked faintly bored.

The door shut gently behind her as the Kislar Aghasi crept from the room. They were alone.

He stared at her for a long time in silence. She could almost hear him thinking: What have they done to you?

She untied the robe and let it slip to the floor, then unfastened the diamond buttons of the kaftan and pulled it over her head. She ripped off the diamond necklace and tossed it on top of the robe with the earrings. Finally, she loosened the pearls from her hair and shook it free.

When she was done, she had on only her chemise and harem trousers. She pointed to the rich pile of garments at her feet. 'The Mistress of the Robes chose my wardrobe personally. Of course, these days she is half blind.'

He shrugged.

She must shake him from this torpor, she thought, and she knew only one way to do that. She fell to her knees, covered her face in her hands and started to weep.

'What is wrong?'

'Lord of my Life, why did you choose me? There are so many beautiful girls in the Harem. I am not good enough for you.'

He rose from the divan and put a hand on her shoulder. She let him lift her to her feet. 'I never wanted this,' she whispered. 'I am frightened.'

'Hush now. Come and sit down.' He led her to the divan and sat her down beside him. 'You are wrong,' he said. 'I think you are quite exceptional.' He stroked her cheek.

He brought her face towards him and kissed her gently. He tasted of wine.

She undid the pearl buttons of her chemise.

CHAPTER 10

Hürrem was given an allowance of two hundred aspers, her own apartment, and enough organza, silk, taffeta, brocade and satin for the Mistress of the Robes to outfit a complete wardrobe. She even had use of her own bath, carved from pink marble, with its own cascading fountain of scented rosewater. Nightingales twittered in cedar cages on her private terrace.

She was also allowed her own *gediçli*. Hürrem asked for Muomi.

The girl seemed neither pleased nor surprised to receive Hürrem's summons. When they brought her to her new quarters, she stood, shuffling her feet, her face a sullen mask of indifference.

Hürrem studied her, her legs drawn under her on the divan. 'Are you happy with your work in the baths?' she asked her.

Muomi shrugged her shoulders by way of answer.

'As one of his favorites, I am allowed to choose my own handmaid. The work will be much easier than you are accustomed to.' Hürrem got to her feet and put her lips to the other girl's ear. 'I want you to help me. Tell me what you want in return.'

'What do I want?' She lifted her eyes. 'When I was seven years old, the magic man in our tribe came to our family's hut with a stinging nettle. He parted my legs and rubbed the nettle into my cleft. That was to make it swell. The next day he came back and washed between my legs with butter and honey, then cut away everything that gives a woman pleasure and cauterized the wound with a red-hot ember. My mother pretended to cry with joy to cover my screams. When I married, my husband cut me open with a knife to take me. Then he had me sewn up again, until the next time. It was the same when the baby came. When the traders stole me, they took my baby away because he was a boy child. I do not know if he is dead or alive. If he is alive, they will castrate him, the same as they castrated me. As for me, I will spend the rest of my life in this place. So, tell me, what could you possibly offer me?'

Hürrem smiled and stroked her cheek. 'Revenge,' she said.

The *Okjmeydan*, the Place of Arrows, looked down through groves of rosebushes to the dark waters of the Golden Horn. It was nearly summer; time for the war drum to sound in the Court of the Janissaries, and for the Grande Turke to set out again for the Lands of War.

But this year there would be no war. Instead, Suleiman was to remove the court to Edirne for the hunting.

He and Ibrahim went out every day with their arrows and spears to practice. Ibrahim had set up the statues they had plundered from Belgrade along the length of the esplanade. The notion of using Greek Gods as targets amused him.

Afterwards they rested in the broad shade of a fig tree and pages brought them olives, cheese and sherbets.

'Your aim is excellent, Ibrahim. If I were a boar, I should start running towards Russia now.'

'Your eye is good also.'

'No, you flatter me. My mind is on other things today.'

Ibrahim drained his silver goblet and took an olive, chewing it slowly as he placed the chalice an arm's length away in the grass. Then, with great theatrics, he spat the stone into the empty cup. He repeated this several times, without missing once.

'What is troubling you, my Lord?'

'Let me ask you something first. When we came from Manisa, you were able to establish your own harem?'

'Of course, though it is not as extensive as yours, my Lord.'

'But you have a favorite?'

'Whenever I am with a woman, she is my favorite.'

It was not the answer he wanted. How could he explain his problem to a man like Ibrahim, he thought. The night after he bedded Hürrem he had chosen another of the Harem girls, fulfilling his duty to the Osmanli line, as the Valide had insisted. The girl was a Georgian, with the most startling black eyes. Her eyes must have taken up her whole head for when she opened her mouth, she had nothing to say. When he took her to bed she just lay there.

She did not wake him three times during the night, as Hürrem had done, begging for more.

Gülbehar had been his favorite for ten years. Until Hürrem she had satisfied all his needs. Now a door had opened on other possibilities.

He had promised himself that he would not lie with any but Gülbehar more than once. But he was tempted to summon Hürrem a second time.

Yet he hesitated. Surely, it was not good for a woman to find as much pleasure in the flesh as a man. This Hürrem's soul was tainted by the sins of Rachel. If he encouraged her in her vice, was he not tainted also? And what of Gülbehar? He would be breaking the promise he had made to her, and to himself. He experienced the first sour gnawing of an emotion he had never expected to feel with any woman other than his mother.

Guilt.

'Does a woman have a soul, Ibrahim?'

'Does it matter?' Ibrahim sensed the shift in his mood and leaned in. 'Is it Gülbehar who troubles you?'

'No, it is another.'

'May I enquire her name?'

'Her name is Hürrem,' Suleiman said.

Ibrahim raised an eyebrow.

He aimed another olive stone at the goblet but this time it landed softly in the grass, well wide of the mark.

CHAPTER 11

Meylissa lay in the bath. The milky mist of the steam room made it appear that her face was floating. Her eyes followed Hürrem all the way to the water's edge. Hürrem stopped beside the pool to allow Muomi to remove her gauze shift, then lowered herself into the water.

'You look ill,' Hürrem said to her.

'I am sick every morning. The *kiaya* wants to send me to the infirmary.'

'Don't let her.'

'Do you think I'm stupid?' Meylissa moved closer. 'Every day my waist gets thicker. I cannot pretend forever that it is the sweetbreads. You said you would help me!'

'I am going to help you, just as I promised.'

'How? Will you plead for me with the Lord of Life while he shares your pillow?'

Hürrem nodded her head in the direction of her maidservant. 'Muomi.'

'What can she do?'

'She is a witch. She is going to make you a potion, an abortive.'

Meylissa's bottom lip quivered.

'Be brave,' Hürrem whispered.

'It is too late.'

Hürrem grabbed her arm. 'Of course it's not too late. Do you think this is any easier for me? If the Kislar Aghasi finds out, they'll kill me too.'

Meylissa bit her lip. 'When?'

'I will send Muomi to you tomorrow. Everything will be all right, you'll see.'

Meylissa nodded and climbed out of the pool. Hürrem studied her silhouette through the steam. She had hardly any waist at all. They didn't have much time.

Suleiman lay among the pillows and silks, Gülbehar naked beside him. He put a hand to her breast, and with his finger he tracked the blue vein from her nipple to the hollow of her shoulder. He felt a stirring of doubt. It was not the same. Something had changed.

She moved her legs apart, in readiness for him. He eased himself on top of her, watched her face intently for evidence of what she was feeling. She is so eager to please me, he thought. She has never wanted anything more but to sate my hunger. Why should I want any more than that?

When he was inside her he closed his eyes and thought about Hürrem, her head thrown back, her mouth open in a silent scream, the mane of gold-red hair splayed across the pillow, her body arched beneath him as if she were in the grip of some great torment. His sublime moment came swiftly.

He groaned and his strength left him. Gülbehar's arms pulled him down on top of her in warm embrace. She was still smiling.

'It was good, my Lord?' she whispered.

'Yes. Yes, it was good.'

But it wasn't good, he wanted more, he wanted her. He wanted Hürrem.

Hürrem sat on the terrace, watching the dawn break over the city. A silver sliver of moon faded into the deepening blue of the morning as the calls of the muezzin broke the crystal silence. Another night passed without him, another night he had spent instead with Gülbehar.

It had been a week since he had asked for her. She could not remain a mere favorite forever. If she did not become pregnant, and the Sultan continued to ignore her, she would have to return to the sewing room, without prospect of more.

She would not allow that to happen.

CHAPTER 12

The Kapi Aga had died a thousand deaths in the week since his encounter with Hürrem. He lived in unholy terror and every time he heard footsteps in the corridor, he thought it was the Sultan's torturers come to fetch him. He slept fitfully and dreamed about escape. But where could he hide where the Sultan could not find him? The empire spanned three continents.

One warm-scented evening he ventured back down to the garden. Nightingales sang in the plane trees. Such a pretty hell. Every stone of this accursed place was dangerous, he thought, no matter how many birds fluttered in the trees.

He turned the ancient key in the lock and inched it open.

Hürrem knelt on the grass beside the fountain, a Koran, illuminated in green and gold, lying open on the wooden stool in front of her. She wore a chemise of emerald damask and white silk pantaloons.

'I did as you asked,' he said.

Hürrem glanced up at him, then returned her attention to her Koran.

'I said, I did as you asked.'

'Good.'

'And now?'

'Now?'

'You must fulfil your part of the bargain.'

She turned a page of her Koran. The Kapi Aga tried to control his temper. How thoroughly satisfying it would be, he thought, to slice off her head. Be done with this upstart right now. Watch her life's blood spurt over the word of Mohammed and up the grey stone wall. If only that would solve the problem.

'When does the Sultan return?' she said.

'He goes north to Edirne tomorrow for the hunting. He will not be back until the leaves fall.'

'There is one more condition.'

'I have done as you asked. You may make no more demands of me.'

'While I keep your secret for you, I may do as I please.'

She is right, he thought. Once more, someone has me by the balls. I will see her suffer for this one day. 'You said you would help me.'

Hürrem closed the book. She got to her feet and came up to him. To his amazement she ran a fingernail down the length of his arm and took his hand.

'I will help you. After tonight, you will no longer have a problem. You will live in fear no more.'

Meylissa was embroidering a kaftan the color of burnished gold for the young *shahzade*, Mustapha. She took her handiwork to the window to examine it in the fading light of the afternoon. She heard someone enter the room behind her.

'Did I frighten you?' Muomi said.

'No,' Meylissa said and shook her head, but it was a lie.

'I have what you needed.' Muomi put a small blue and white jar on her workbench.

Meylissa removed the rounded cork stopper and sniffed. 'It's foul.'

'Of course it is. It's a kind of poison. Swallow it all, it will make you sick and kill the baby.'

Meylissa replaced the stopper. Her hands shook. 'Thank you.'

'It has nothing to do with me,' Muomi said.

CHAPTER 13

The Kislar Aghasi woke to the sound of a woman screaming. At first, he thought it might be just one of the girls crying in her sleep - the new ones did that. But as he came awake, he realized this was no milksop's nightmare. He had heard screams like that before, coming from the torture chamber. He swung his legs off the cot and reached for his wooden pattens.

The candle had not burned down far, so he guessed he could not have been asleep more than an hour. He took the candle and hurried out into the corridor in his nightshirt.

The screams came from the dormitory on the floor above. He summoned two of his guards and ran up the stairs.

Meylissa rolled naked on the floor, tearing at the bare, wooden boards with her fingernails. Another spasm shook her, and she curled her knees into her chest and retched. There was blood everywhere, soaked into her bedding and smeared across her face. There was a pink froth around her lips.

The other girls had gathered round her, pale and terrified. When Meylissa writhed again, they screamed and jumped back as if she might infect them all. Meylissa tried to say something, but her mouth just gaped open like a fish and the sounds she made were barely human. She clutched her belly and screamed again.

The guards tried to pick her up and she kicked out at them. She stared up at the Kislar Aghasi and her lips drew back from her teeth in a snarl, like a rabid dog. Someone came to stand at his shoulder. He turned around; it was Hürrem.

Meylissa pointed at her and tried to say something but then her mouth filled with blood and she choked on the words.

The hunting dogs flushed the partridge from its lair in the sagebrush. It exploded out of its hiding place, its short wings beating frantically at the air. Ibrahim laughed and raised the heavy leather gauntlet on his left wrist. The peregrine falcon quivered with excitement.

Ibrahim removed the hood. The golden eyes blinked once, then the bird launched itself upwards.

Ibrahim and Suleiman spurred their horses and went after it.

The falcon dipped its wings. One moment it was riding the currents, as weightless as the air itself; the next it fell from the sky like a rock. The partridge flapped in panic, but it had no chance of escape; the peregrine hit it from above in an explosion of feathers and its talons took purchase on its back with a blow so violent that its victim died mid-flight.

The falcon released its death grip at the last moment. It wheeled away and the dead partridge fell into the swamp.

Ibrahim whooped and galloped to the edge of the black water. The dogs splashed in directly under his horse's hoofs, vying with each other to be first to retrieve the prize.

Ibrahim looked up and stretched out a gloved arm for his falcon, now wheeling above him.

The boar watched the intruder from its sanctuary in a grove of wild rose, its yellow eyes bright with terror. It backed further into the gorse and thorns. From one side came the yapping of the hunting dogs, from the other the thunder of horses and the shouts of the archers.

It was trapped. It had no choice.

Snorting with rage, it charged from the brambles.

Suleiman saw it and shouted a warning. The beast struck Ibrahim's Arab mare high on its flank, one yellow tusk piercing its belly and tearing a bloodied hole. She bellowed in agony and reared back. The boar charged again, and Ibrahim was thrown to the ground.

Suleiman was fifty paces away. He pulled his bow from the leather scabbard on his saddle and took aim. His first arrow buried itself in the boar's flank, throwing it on its side. It staggered to its feet, squealing, and turned to face this new tormentor.

Suleiman reined in, took another arrow from the jeweled quiver. This time he hit the beast behind the shoulder, the steel tip angling in towards the heart, burying itself to the flight.

The boar's hind legs gave way.

In moments arrow after arrow thudded into its grey body and it died. The archers cheered and ran forward. Immediately Suleiman's horse was surrounded by cavalry from his personal bodyguard. He ignored the captain's shouted apologies and jumped from the saddle.

'Ibrahim?'

The Arab mare was still on her feet, wheeling and bellowing, as the hunting dogs ran around her legs, jumping at the purple viscera trailing from her flank. The Janissaries milled amongst them. One tried to catch her reins, another swore and slashed at the dogs with his *killiç* .

The wounded horse, eyes bulging, galloped towards him. Suleiman staggered back, but then the dogs were at her again and she turned away once more and took off through the quince trees.

Suleiman looked around, dazed.

Suddenly he saw Ibrahim, knee deep in the swamp, his white kaftan covered with mud. His turban was askew, lending an air of madness. In his right hand he held the partridge by its bloodied neck.

'We have our prize!' he shouted to Suleiman.

'I thought you were dead!'

'While I have my Sultan to protect me, how could I die?'

He laughed as if it had all been a game. He looked so pleased with himself that Suleiman threw back his head and laughed, too.

They were in Suleiman's pavilion; the music of Ibrahim's viol had to compete with the croaking of frogs from the swamp. The light from the candles rippled on the billowing folds of the tent.

Suleiman was elated from the hunt and could not sleep. He sat cross-legged on the divan listening to Ibrahim play, but his mind was not on the music. He had finally resolved a matter that had troubled him for some weeks. He had weighed his choice against the demands of court protocol and had now justified his decision to his own conscience.

'I am replacing Piri Pasha as Grand Vizier,' he said suddenly.

Ibrahim stopped playing. 'Has he been derelict in his duty?'

'No, he has not been remiss. I just do not believe that he is still capable.'

'But he has served in the Divan these many years.'

'Yes, yes. Once he may have been adequate for the position. But he has lost those powers he once possessed. I intend for him to be my governor in Egypt. I shall not humiliate him.'

'Who will be his replacement?'

Suleiman felt like a father passing on a treasured heirloom to his son. 'You, Ibrahim.'

'Me?'

'Yes, you will be my new Grand Vizier!'

Suleiman waited for a show of gratitude, but it did not come. Ibrahim cradled his viol in his arms and stared at his hands.

'What's the matter?'

'The Divan will wonder why you have elevated me at the expense of such an experienced man.'

'It is not for them to question my judgment on anything.'

'But what they will say privately concerns me.'

'What they say privately cannot harm you.'

'It will seem that I have been appointed in his place only because of our friendship.'

Suleiman stared at him in astonishment. This was not what he had expected at all.

'I am afraid,' Ibrahim murmured.

'You are not scared of being gored by a wild boar or trampled by your own horse but you are worried about the Divan?'

'No, my Lord. I am afraid of you.'

'Me?

'The Grand Vizier's neck is always under the sword.'

Suleiman was shocked that he should think this of him. It was true that Suleiman's own father had disposed of eight of his viziers in as many years. But he was nothing like his father.

'You have nothing to fear from me, Ibrahim.'

'You do me great honor. I always thought that I wanted this, until now. But you should not raise me so high that when I fall, I will die.'

Suleiman placed a hand on Ibrahim's shoulder. 'I give you my word. While I live, I shall see that you never come to harm. May God be my judge!'

Ibrahim took Suleiman's hand and kissed the ruby ring. 'Very well,' he whispered. 'You have brought me fame beyond my wildest dreams. I pledge myself to serve you until the day I die.'

CHAPTER 14

The Valide sat on the terrace overlooking the shaded, eastern court of the Palace and regarded her son's new favorite with a practiced eye. She could tell at once that this one was a different proposition to Gülbehar, you could see it in the way she walked, the way she held herself.

They said she was more clever than beautiful. But that was not such a bad thing. She, herself, had not survived so many years in the harem of Selim the Grim without a certain quickness of mind.

'Hürrem,' she said warmly, extending her hand. 'I am delighted with your news. Come and sit here beside me.'

It was a warm afternoon and finches twittered in the ornate cedar cages hanging from the eaves. Sherbets, melon and *rahat lokum* - the sweet pistachio-flavored 'rest for the throat' - were laid out on the low table in front of them. Behind them the city shimmered in the afternoon haze, the cupolas of the mosques shining like diamonds through the dust.

'Suleiman is hunting at Adrianople, as I am sure you have heard. I have sent a courier today with a message for him. He will be overjoyed with this news.'

Hürrem put a hand to her stomach. 'We must wait many months to discover the extent of his pleasure.'

A good answer, the Valide thought. If it's a girl, we are all back where we started. 'If God wills it.' She reached out a hand to take a lock of the girl's hair, held a few strands towards the light. 'You have beautiful hair. Not red, not gold. Where are you from?'

'My father was a khan of the Krim Tatars, Crown of Veiled Heads.'

'And how did you come to us?'

'My father saw an opportunity.'

The Valide smiled. 'For you, or for himself?'

'The Spahis tied him to the ground so they could force the money into his pockets. He struggled and screamed. I had to avert my eyes.'

'You smile when you say this. Does his betrayal amuse you?'

'He still lives in a tent, I am in a palace. In the end I got more from the trade.'

'So you are happy here?'

'I will be happier when my lord returns.'

'I was married to the Sultan Selim for many years. I can count the number of weeks we spent together on my fingers. It is a lonely life, Hürrem.'

'I will go back to my father, then. Can you arrange a horse for me?'

The Valide laughed, in spite of herself. She had a point. Why be miserable over things you do not have the power to change? 'Now you have the Sultan's child, this harem will be your home for the rest of your life.'

'Then I shall have to arrange larger rooms.'

'Like mine, perhaps?'

'If God wills it.'

'I should not be at all surprised if that is His design.' The Valide took a piece of *lokum* and bit into it. 'If there is anything that you need, you must tell me. Everything will be done to ensure your comfort.'

'There is one thing, Highness.'

'Yes?'

'I want a bodyguard.'

'A bodyguard. Why?'

'I am frightened.'

'Of what?'

'I have heard rumors that I will not live to see my baby born.'

'Who dares threaten you - threaten the Sultan's child?'

Hürrem averted her eyes. 'I don't know. It could just be harem gossip.'

She is lying, the Valide thought. She knows who it is but dares not say. There is only one person who would wish her dead. Gülbehar. But surely Gülbehar was not capable of such an act?

'If you think such rumors might have any base, you should have your servant girl taste all your food, even try on your clothes before you wear them, in case the fabric has been impregnated with poison. As a precaution I will have the Kislar Aghasi assign you one of his eunuchs.'

'Thank you, Crown of Veiled Heads.'

'Nothing - nothing - must endanger the Sultan's son.'

The Kapi Aga watched from the North Tower as Hürrem appeared from the shadows and sat down on the marble bench beside the fountain. She opened her Koran. She had come to the garden three days in a row. Why would she take such a risk, he thought. Soon she might be one of Suleiman's *kadins*. Wasn't that enough for her?

He had to find out what she wanted.

He hurried from the room, locking the door behind him, and went down the wooden steps to the courtyard.

He hesitated for a moment when he reached the iron gate, then slipped inside.

Hürrem looked up at him and her eyes widened in surprise. She dropped the Koran, stood up and screamed. The Kapi Aga froze. Too late, he realized what she had done. He turned to run, and dropped his keys on the marble flags.

She screamed twice more as he fumbled for them on the ground. When he finally threw open the gate, he found himself staring into the startled face of one of his own guards.

He ran back into the garden. 'You little whore,' he shouted, drew the jeweled dagger from his pelisse and slashed at her. Hürrem shouted for help and fell backwards, over the bench, the blade missing her by inches.

The guard rushed at him. His sword scythed through the air and then his dagger was gone, and with it his right hand. There was no pain, just the horror and the spurting of bright blood.

He fell to his knees and tried to prize the dagger from the fingers of his own severed hand. If he could kill her, it would be all right. They could do what they wanted with him as long as he knew she was dead. But then the guards were dragging him away, leaving a long trail of blood across the cobblestones. He screamed a string of curses at the witch with the red hair, but then another guard appeared and struck him with the hilt of his sword. He groaned and his head fell back.

The hawk soared on the updraught from the baked cobblestones of the city, then wheeled towards the Bosporus, hovering again over the walls of the Topkapi. Its golden eye picked out the twin towers of the Gate of Felicity, where the head of the Kapi Aga was turning black as an olive, high in its niche in the wall. His decapitated body still hung from the steel hook where it had been tormented for three days. A rope had been lashed from the scaffold to hold it upright. It would be there till the carrion crows had finished their work, and the meat and sinew rotted from the bones.

The hawk wheeled again, now towards the Golden Horn and the wooden palace high on the hill beside the great mosque of Bayezit II. On a balcony among the brass domes stood a woman with hair the color of fire.

The months would pass quickly, she thought. She stroked her belly.

Let it be a son.

There was snow on the roofs of the Harem.

A birthing chair and swaddling bandages were brought to Hürrem's apartment. Incense was burned and rose petals strewn over the marble floors. Amulets and blue beads were hung around the room to ward off the evil eye.

Hürrem had never experienced such pain. When the baby would not come, the midwife sat on her stomach to force the child from her womb.

Hürrem screamed. The midwife jammed a stick of ivory between her teeth to silence her.

Crouched over the chair, supported on each side by the midwives, she delivered up the child. The midwife received the infant in a cloth of linen while she recited the declaration of the Faith.

The Kislar Aghasi watched, as Osmanli law demanded, to ensure that no substitution was made. He took the child to the white marble fountain and washed the baby three times, according to custom. Sugared oil was placed in its mouth to ensure a sweet and amiable tongue; kohl was smeared around its eyes to ensure a profound gaze and a diamond-encrusted Koran was touched to its forehead.

Hürrem clutched the midwife's shoulders. 'What is it?'

It was the Kislar Aghasi who answered her. 'You are delivered of a son, my Lady.'

PART 2

Dark Angel

CHAPTER 15

Venice, 1528

She was a vision in velvet, a dark angel, with hair as black and lustrous as coal. She had skin like ivory. The bodice of her vesture was fashionably low-cut and the small gold cross at her throat - he could imagine the soft pulse just below it – was further provocation.

White and Christian; twice forbidden.

The street was crowded, and rang to the cries of the hawkers and the cursing of the sailors gambling in the arcades. An Albanian pushed past in baggy trousers, chewing a nub of garlic like a sweet. Several people saluted the passage of a senator in purple robes, who replied with a casual wave of the hand.

Abbas elbowed his way through the mob, following her to the portal of a church. She looked up just once, and their eyes met.

The old woman who escorted her gave him a contemptuous glance as they walked through the doors of the *Santa Maria dei Miracoli*.

'Did you see her?' he whispered to his friend, Ludovici.

'Of course I saw her. That's Julia Gonzaga.'

'You know her?'

'My step-sister, Lucia, knows her. She's her cousin.'

Abbas grabbed Ludovici and pulled him towards the steps. 'I want to get closer.'

'You're mad!' Ludovici pulled him back. 'Do you know who her father is? Antonio Gonzaga - he's a *Consigliatore*!'

'I don't care.'

Ludovici was alarmed, but not altogether surprised. Abbas was the most headstrong man he'd ever known. Reckless, his father called him. It was in his blood; a Moor is a Moor. This time Ludovici would not let him make a fool of himself. Besides, there was real danger here.

He pushed his friend against a wall and held him there. 'Abbas, no!'

'I just want to look at her.'

'You are not meant to look. She's a Gonzaga.'

Abbas jerked free and sprinted up the steps.

To hell with him! Ludovici thought. He started to walk away, then changed his mind and went into the church after him.

The saints watched, disapproving, from the gilt ceiling. A bust of the *Vergine della Santa Clara* frowned from her balustrade on a wall of pink coral marble.

It was cool after the heat of the piazza. Two figures dressed in black knelt at the altar. Saint Francis and the Archangel Gabriel stood guard on either side.

Abbas heard Ludovici's footsteps echo on the marble behind him. 'She is the loveliest thing I have ever seen,' Abbas whispered.

'She is not for you, my friend.'

Her *duenna* heard them and raised her head from her prayers. Abbas and Ludovici ducked behind one of the pillars. Ludovici put a finger to his lips.

When they peered out again, the two women were gone. The old woman was hurrying her charge out through a side door. Julia Gonzaga looked back once before she was pulled away.

'There, you've had your look,' Ludovici said. 'Now forget about it.'

The Captain General of the Republic watched the sun set behind the snow-capped peaks of the Cadore, setting aflame the backdrop of mushrooming clouds. The gondolas and galleys faded into dark relief against the pearl of the lagoon. Such a harbor, such a city; sometimes it was easy to feel a part of it. But they did not belong here. His son sometimes forgot that.

'It is quite impossible,' he said. 'You do not seem to understand the first thing about these people.'

'We can protect their lives but not marry their daughters. Is that it?'

'Marry? Is that what is on your mind?' He rounded on his son, who fell back a step. Mahmud was a bear of a man and his thick, grizzled beard added to his size and his ferocity. 'No Venetian wants a black Muslim son any more than I want a white infidel daughter.'

They would not be in Venice at all, of course, if the Doge could trust his army to the command of one of his own noblemen. The Captain-General of Venice was rarely even Italian and sometimes, as now, not even a Christian.

'They treat us like dirt,' Abbas said.

'They treat everyone like dirt. They mean nothing by it.'

'But we have royal blood.'

'What do you think the royal blood of a Muslim means to them? We are mercenaries, that's all. You may live in a fine palazzo and dress like the son of a senator but you are still a foreigner. Even if you may sometimes forget that, I assure you that they do not.'

'Then what am I to do?'

'Do as the other young bloods do and find what you need on the *Ponte delle Tette*.' Abbas knew the place; women stood stripped to the waist in its doorways, calling out to the young men who passed. 'It is nothing you can't get for a few coins. You are too young to think about a wife.'

'I want to meet Julia Gonzaga.'

Mahmud sighed. Gonzaga would never entertain the thought of his daughter even breathing the same air as a blackamoor. A *magnifico* of the

Council of Ten, like Gonzaga, could not speak to a foreigner in private, even the Captain General of the Army.

'It is just youth, Abbas. Believe me, it will pass. Tomorrow you will have forgotten all about her.'

'If that's what you think, then you don't know me at all,' Abbas said.

Julia Gonzaga watched the theatre of the Venetian evening from behind the latticed screen of her loggia. The lanterns hanging from the sterns of the gondolas left rippling tracks on the surface of the canal, and she heard voices and laughter echo along an alleyway as a young couple vanished arm in arm into the shadows.

She felt a stab of envy.

She thought again about what had happened that afternoon in the church of *Santa Maria dei Miracoli*. Why had that boy stared at her like that? A blackamoor. He looked like a gondolier, though he did not dress like one. He had a jeweled cap on his head, and his linen shirt had been open at the front in the manner of a fashionable young nobleman.

According to her *duenna,* Signora Cavalcanti, young men were the Devil's work, and would put her soul in jeopardy. Sometimes Julia wondered if even damnation might be better than this.

She was already buried alive.

CHAPTER 16

The girl reeked of wine and sweat. She collapsed, laughing, onto Ludovici's lap. He put his hand inside her dress and popped out her breast, weighing it in his hand as if it were on sale at the market. The nipple, Abbas noticed, had been rouged.

'Now look, Abbas!' Ludovici said. 'What are you getting so lathered about? They're all the same underneath!'

The girl cuffed Ludovici playfully around the head. She pulled up her bodice in a feigned attempt at modesty and flounced away. Ludovici picked up his goblet and drained the thick rosso, some of it spilling on his white shirt, where it spread like a bloodstain across his chest.

The tavern was crowded with the sons of the well-to-do and their tarts. The girls were a riot of color beside their young suitors. Under the strict laws of *La Serenissima* – as the Venetians liked to call their city - only the working class and prostitutes could wear what they liked; the wives and daughters of patricians always wore black.

'You take life too seriously,' Ludovici said.

'I'm tired of all this,' Abbas said. He pulled Ludovici to his feet. 'Let's go.' His goblet clattered onto the wooden floor.

Ludovici protested but he was too drunk to resist. Abbas dragged him outside and stood him against the wall of the tavern, holding him up by his shirt. It was sodden with wine. 'Listen' he said, 'you have to help me.'

'Help you do what?'

'Julia. Can you get a letter to her?'

Ludovici started to laugh.

'I'm serious. Will you do it?'

'Gonzaga will kill you.'

'You said she is Lucia's cousin.'

'It makes no difference.'

'She can take the letter for me.'

Ludovici sagged in his arms. 'It will come to no good.'

'Please, do this for me. I beg you.'

Ludovici groaned. 'All right, I'll ask her. Now let me go.' He shook his head. 'It's dangerous.'

'Danger gives meaning to life.'

'More often it ends it. If you do meet with her - and that is impossible for she goes nowhere unescorted - even your father will not be able to help you. You cannot toy with the honor of a man like Gonzaga.'

'What of my honor, Ludovici?' Abbas said. 'My father may be content to be the Doge's lapdog, but I am my own man. I will write the letter tonight.' He put a hand around his friend's shoulder and led him down the street toward the Piazza San Marco.

Julia draped her lacework across her knees, the warmth of the yellow sun on her skin as she worked. Lucia sat beside her, whispering the petty gossips she had heard from her brother. She visited her often during the summer - escorted by her *duenna* of course - to chatter and to sew.

'I hear you are to be married,' Lucia said.

'Yes. In the autumn.'

'Is he handsome?'

'I have only heard my father speak of him.' Julia pretended to examine her stitches. 'He is his closest ally on the Doge's inner council, the *Consiglio di Dieci*. His wife died three summers ago.'

'How old is he?'

'He is in his sixtieth year. But he may yet be handsome.' She fought to keep the tremor from her voice.

Signora Cavalcanti looked up sharply and frowned at her. Julia lowered her eyes.

'I have seen him,' Lucia said. 'He is very important.'

They lapsed into silence. Signora Cavalcanti put down her embroidery. 'I think I shall rest,' she said and went inside. Julia heard her draw the drapes at her bedroom window on the terrazzo above.

Sunlight bounced from the canal and threw dappled shadows onto the walls. A line tagged with clothes danced in the breeze. On the other side of the canal a woman leaned out of her window to haul up a basket of provisions from a gondola moored below.

Lucia's *duenna* excused herself for a moment, and the two girls were left alone. Lucia reached into the folds of her robe and produced a letter, sealed with red wax. She almost threw it into Julia's lap, as if it were alight.

Julia stared at it, astonished. 'What is this?'

Lucia glanced over her shoulder. 'Quickly, open it!'

Julia broke the seal. She read: *I have seen you in the church. I must meet you. You are perfection itself. A.*

'Who is this from?'

'I don't know. A friend of my brother.'

'What is his name?'

'He would not say. He just asked me to give it to you. Show it to me.'

Lucia tried to snatch it from her, but Julia folded it and slipped it down the front of her robe. She tore the envelope into small pieces and dropped them over the balcony into the canal.

'Why does this friend of your brother's send me letters? Does he want to disgrace me?'

'Ludovici said it was the only way.'

'The only way for what?'

'The only way you might ever meet, I suppose.'

Julia tried to compose herself. Her cheeks felt hot. She fanned herself with her embroidery. She would burn the letter as soon as she was alone. If its author were a suitable companion he would have arranged a meeting through her father. That he had persuaded a friend to smuggle his message only proved that he could not be a member of any family of note, or even a gentleman.

'What are you going to do?' Lucia whispered.

'I am going to find out who he is,' Julia said. 'Signora Cavalcanti sleeps every afternoon between noon and Vespers, while I study my Bible. Tell your brother that his friend should have a gondola waiting by the canal. If he is any earlier, or later, I will not come down, and he is not to bother me again.'

CHAPTER 17

Julia wrapped the long cape around her shoulders and pulled the hood low over her face. Not too late to turn back, she thought.

She heard Signora Cavalcanti's snores coming from her bedroom window and smiled. There was a certain satisfaction in outwitting her.

She opened the heavy wooden door and peered down the stone steps that led to the water stairs.

His gondolier had slung a line carelessly over the striped mooring pole. He was a tall Moor in a satin shirt with slashed sleeves, and his broad-brimmed hat was trimmed with scarlet ribbon. He leaned on the bargepole, with arrogant ease.

She inched the door shut behind her and took a deep breath.

She ran down the steps. When she reached the gondola, she pulled the curtains aside and jumped in. She stifled a gasp.

She recognized him immediately.

'They tell me I have all the makings of a fine gondolier,' he said. 'But my father would not permit it. He thinks the son of the Defender of the Republic should aspire to greater things.'

'Your father is the Captain General of the Army?'

'Yes. My name is Abbas. Should you find my appearance too shocking, my Lady, you may leave now, and I promise you will never hear from me again.'

He was young, almost as young as her. His skin was the color of mahogany and his hair tightly curled. A ruby glinted in his left ear.

She sat down. 'I may only be away for a few minutes.'

There were blue velvet curtains on all sides, so they were safe from prying eyes. The only thing she could see outside the tiny cabin was the gaily colored hose of their gondolier as he stood at his position at the stern. The boat smelled of mildew and walnut.

He leaned through the curtain and said something to the gondolier. The boatman unhitched the rope, and she heard the gentle splash of the pole as he steered them towards the center of the canal.

She reached inside her cape. 'Here is your letter.'

'I do not want it back.'

'It is too dangerous for me to keep. If you like, I will burn it.'

'No, I don't want you to do that.' He took it from her. 'I meant everything I said. Since I saw you, I have not been able to think about anything else.'

She felt her cheeks grow hot. 'You know Ludovici Gambetto?'

'His father is a general and an adviser to my father. We are both renegades, I suppose. Outsiders.'

'But the Gambettos are one of the noble families of Venice.'

Abbas looked embarrassed. 'Ludovici came from outside the marriage. Signor Gambetto had a mistress. She died when Ludovici was still a baby. Signor Gambetto is a good man and he raised him as one of his own but Ludovici will never be accepted here, among the people who matter. I assumed that you knew.'

Why would she know? No one ever told her anything.

'I am sorry for all this.' He spread his hands to take in the little velvet canopy. 'I wanted my father to speak to your father for me. He said it was impossible. But I am a man who believes nothing is impossible.' He reached out a hand and pulled back her hood.

She caught her breath. Suddenly the risks of the afternoon were all worthwhile.

She had no idea what she was meant to do or say. She pulled her hood back over her face, overwhelmed. 'I should be getting back.'

'Not yet.'

'If my *duenna* discovers I am gone, I will be in terrible trouble.'

A shadow passed over the canopy as the gondola slipped under a bridge. She heard the shouts of children playing on the cobbles.

'I have to see you again,' he said.

'I cannot. I am to be married in the autumn. My husband will return from Cyprus for the wedding at the end of summer.'

He took her hand. 'Could you love a Moor like I love an infidel?'

She didn't answer. He sighed, leaned through the curtain and gave the orders to the gondolier. Moments later she felt the boat scrape along the steps outside her palazzo.

'You can never see me again,' she said, scrambled out of the gondola and ran inside. She did not stop running until she reached her bedroom, where she threw herself on her knees before the wooden crucifix on the wall and prayed for forgiveness.

A little while later she was overcome with another emotion - regret. She should have stayed with him a little longer.

She wondered if she might be afforded a second chance.

CHAPTER 18

Antonio Gonzaga had noticed a subtle and worrying change in his daughter. He fretted over the flush in her cheeks and the nervousness in her manner. Such signs, small as they were, were not commensurate with a young lady whose time should have been fully occupied with religious instruction and lacework.

The maid set two plates in front of them. Gonzaga watched his daughter take up her spoon.

'Put your shoulders back.'

Julia did as she was told.

He frowned, irritated. The sooner she was married and off his hands, the better he would like it. 'Soon you will be the wife of a member of the *Consiglio di Dieci*. He will expect proper manners.'

He had seen such cow eyes on a woman before; his wife, on their wedding night, and his mistress whenever she was pregnant with another bastard, something that happened with too frequent regularity.

He drank his wine, ignoring his food. Surely the thought of marriage had not raised such a blush in her cheeks.

The realization came to him and he gave a long sigh. 'I feel unwell,' he said to her. 'I need to rest. You must excuse me.' He left, leaving her to finish her supper alone.

Ludovici and Abbas reeled out of the tavern, arm in arm and stinking of wine. Ludovici bent over, his hands on his knees, and retched on the cobbles. Abbas leaned against the balustrade of a stone bridge and stared at the moonlight at the canal. 'I have never felt so alive,' he said. 'I love her.'

Ludovici wiped his mouth. 'You don't know anything about her. If you enamored of anything, it is with your own daring.'

'You live in such a bitter world.'

'I am not bitter. I see the world as it is and no more. What is plain to me is that if you could marry this girl tomorrow with the blessing of her father, and yours, she would hold no more allure for you than a whore in a doorway.'

'One day it will happen to you.'

'Only if I lose my wits. Abbas, you are my greatest friend in the world. But I wish you would listen to me. A woman is just a woman, and the world is full of them. She is something soft to lie on, and a warm place to spill your seed. I allow that a woman might be a good companion, and one day I shall have a wife to keep my home and children. But when I marry, I will let my head do the choosing and not my heart. A man who does otherwise is a fool.'

'Then I am a fool because I promise you, I will love her forever.'

'If you love her until next week I will give you two gold ducats.'

'I feel sorry for you, Ludovici. You feel nothing inside. But one day life will seek you out and make you feel again.'

'You're just in love with loving.'

'You'll see. You should give me the two ducats now.'

Ludovici shook his head. He dropped the wine flask he was holding and it shattered on the cobblestones. Somewhere above them a man in a nightshirt ran up the shutters and called for the night watch. Ludovici and Abbas ran away down the street, laughing.

Gonzaga sat in his study, staring into the candle. A painting of the *Death of the Virgin* by Carpaccio dominated the room; two smaller offerings, a *Virgin and Child* by Bellini and a portrait of himself, for which he had commissioned Palma Vecchio five years before, hung on either side of it. Two bronzes by Il Riccio stood above the fireplace.

There was a knock at the door.

'Yes?'

'Signora Cavalcanti, Excellency.'

'Enter.'

The *duenna* crept into the room and bent to kiss the sleeve of his velvet gown. 'You sent for me, Excellency?'

'I did. I am deeply troubled, Signora Cavalcanti.'

'No failing on my part, I hope?'

Gonzaga picked at a piece of lint on his sleeve. He removed it with elaborate care. 'I do not know, Signora.'

She wrung her hands. 'I assure Your Excellency I have been most diligent in my duties.'

'Have you?'

The old lady looked terrified.

'I believe Mistress Julia is concealing something from you.'

'I do not think so, Excellency.'

'Really? Has she spoken much to you about the joyous occasion of her wedding?'

'Very little, Excellency.'

'The anticipation of it brings her no pleasure?'

Gonzaga gave her time to think, or at least invent something. He busied himself with the stole that hung around his shoulders. 'She is never left unattended?'

Ah, there it was. The slightest lowering of the eyes, the merest hint of a blush in her cheeks. He watched her prepare the lie. 'No, Excellency.'

He sighed and pretended to relent. 'Keep an eye on her. A very close eye. Do you understand?'

72

'Yes, Your Excellency. I understand very well indeed.' She turned with uncommon haste towards the door.

Well, that should do it, he thought. He had frightened her badly, as he had intended, and put her on notice.

If there was something he should know, she would find out about it now.

CHAPTER 19

She had not meant there to be a second time. But one afternoon, a week after their first meeting, the gondola had appeared again by the water gate and the temptation had been too great to resist.

Meeting him a second time made it easier to meet a third time. They had now met perhaps a dozen times. She could not believe her own daring.

'I can only stay a few moments,' she said.

She put out her hand and Abbas took it, cradled it in his palm.

'I love you,' he murmured.

'You cannot love me. I told you, it is impossible. This has to be the last time.'

'I cannot stop now. Perhaps I will stop when they put me in the earth.'

'Abbas, I am to be married soon.' She wondered how she would live without this now. How could she ever go back to watching the world through her window?

'Come away with me.'

'What?'

'I can arrange passage on a ship.'

'Leave Venice?' She could not believe he could contemplate such a thing.

'We can go to Spain. We will be safe from your father there. My father will give us money.'

'Stop it, please.'

'You don't have to marry an old man, spend the rest of your life shut up in a rich man's palace.'

Julia was horrified. It had been easy, until now, to pretend to herself that this was just a game without consequence.

'What should I do in Spain?' she heard herself say.

'You will be my wife. I can find employment as a soldier there.'

'Lucia has told me stories of men who have dishonored their women and abandoned them. This is madness!'

'You would rather spend the rest of your life trapped with an old man?'

'At least I should be safe. And what of sin, Abbas? If we should do this, God would punish us, if not in this life, then the next.'

He took her by the shoulders and pulled her towards him. She felt his lips brush against hers, as gentle as his grip was fierce. She closed her eyes and kept perfectly still, hardly daring to breathe, aware only of the soft scent of his clothes and the sweet cloves on his breath. Finally he pulled away from her.

'Come with me,' he repeated.

'You know nothing about me,' she said. 'I must go back.'

She jumped out of the gondola onto the water steps and climbed the stairs back to the palazzo in a daze. She looked back once, he had thrown aside the curtains and was watching her.

She inched open the door at the top of the stairs. It creaked slowly open. The *duenna* stood waiting, her arms crossed across her chest. 'So, you have deceived me,' she said.

Julia turned around, slamming the heavy door behind her. She ran back down to the canal, but the gondola was already gliding away from the steps. She would have shouted to him to come back, but then she heard her *duenna*'s footsteps on the stone flags behind her and knew that to call out his name would be to betray him.

The old lady grabbed her by the arm and wrestled her back inside. She was surprisingly strong. Julia looked around and thought she saw a movement of the curtains on the gondola as it rounded a bend in the canal, but she could not be sure.

Antonio Gonzaga stood at the window, hands clenched into fists at his sides, staring over the roofs to the campanile of San Marco and the Ducal Palace.

Julia stood in the middle of the room, her arms folded across her chest. She would not meet his eyes.

'Who is this boy?' he growled.

She did not answer.

'I said, who is this boy?'

Signora Cavalcanti waited in the shadows, her eyes glittering with satisfaction. He would deal with her later. This situation would never have come about if she had done her job properly. Besides, if she had leave to wag her tongue, the story would be all over Venice tomorrow.

He crossed the room and hit his daughter so hard across the cheek that the blow sent her crashing to the floor. He stood over her, daring her to stand up again and defy him. 'I will beat you like a dog until you give me his name.'

'Never,' she said.

The unexpected steel in her infuriated him further. He grabbed her hair and shook her, then dragged her across the room to the window. He kicked her in a rage. Julia put her hands over head to save herself from further abuse, and curled into a ball on the floor, sobbing.

'Excellency,' Signora Cavalcanti said. She seemed shocked. Did she think a man of affairs did not know the way of the street, he thought. A look from him sent her scurrying back into the corner.

'You will tell me his name.'

He hooked his fingers around the puffed sleeves of her jacket and pulled her to her feet. He cuffed her twice more around the head with his open hand while she twisted and writhed to try to escape the blows. Finally, he released her and she crumpled to the floor a second time.

It seemed he would get no sense out of her tonight. Well, no matter, there was plenty of time to change her mind.

He had torn the sleeve and bodice of her dress. 'Cover yourself up, whore,' he growled. She fumbled to reclaim her modesty, but her hands were shaking so violently she could not do it.

'Take her to her room,' Gonzaga said to the *duenna*. 'Lock it from the outside. Then come back here. I want to talk to you.'

Signora Cavalcanti had never been so frightened in all her life. She had always revered His Excellency as a stern man; grave and menacing, a little like God, she supposed. But the scene she had just witnessed had shaken her to her core.

When she returned to the study Gonzaga had composed himself. He sat at his desk, hands folded in his lap. His hair, still awry beneath his *bareta*, was the only sign of the violence that had taken place in the room just a short time before. 'My daughter is shamefully stubborn,' he said.

Signora Cavalcanti did not know what to say to that. She looked into the sorrowful face of Carpaccio's *Virgin* and felt ashamed.

'She seems not to realize the extent of the damage she has caused.'

'I have instructed her faithfully in her filial duties, as well as her duty to the Republic and to God, Excellency.'

'Perhaps.' He pursed his lips and tapped a forefinger against his temple, as if deliberating a change to the tax on wool. 'But if what you say is true, why does she defy me this way?'

The *duenna* realized that it was she who was now on trial. She should have kept her discovery to herself, dealt with it her own way. Well, it was too late now.

'Many questions arise from this,' Gonzaga said. 'For instance, how were these meetings arranged?'

Signora Cavalcanti swallowed the urge to say: 'I don't know.' It would be tantamount to admitting incompetence. 'I will find out,' she said.

'I hope so, Signora Cavalcanti,' he said and smiled. 'In fact, I rely on it.'

CHAPTER 20

Abbas followed the coach on foot from the palazzo. He lost it along the narrow alleyways but caught up with it again in the bustle of the market around the *Campo Santa Maria Nuova*. He pushed his way through the fruit sellers and peddlers, and vaulted a handcart loaded down with bolts of silk.

The church of *Santa Maria dei Miracoli* was one of the city's most beautiful churches, its façade built from antique marble. The coach stopped below the steps, and Abbas watched two figures step out; one was short and stocky, the other tall, lean and graceful. Her face was covered with a veil, but he knew it was her, just from the way that she moved.

'Please, Abbas. Don't do this,' Ludovici said. He was out of breath after pursuing him through the streets.

'Have you really never been in love, Ludovici?'

'This is not love, this is an escapade!'

'I cannot live without her now.'

'You breathe, you eat, you drink. That's all there is to living. It's simple. Anyone can manage it.'

'That's not life. That's just taking up space.' He started toward the church.

The church was empty. Saint Francis pointed a marble finger in his direction, as if singling him out for the Doge's soldiers.

One moment they were there, and then they were gone, shadows among shadows. They were already behind him, scuttling out of the doors.

'Julia!'

When he got back outside, there was no sign of them. He sat down on the steps. Ludovici looked up at him, shaking his head in frustration. A coach rattled away down the *Via delle Botteghe*, the horse's hoofs ringing on the cobbles.

It had been a trap and he had fallen straight into it.

'Abbas Mahsouf? The Moor's son?'

Signora Cavalcanti nodded eagerly, reveling in her own mendacity. She had lured him out so easily. She was sure His Excellency would be delighted with her.

Gonzaga jumped to his feet, his oak chair crashing onto the tiles behind him. 'A Moor?'

'He followed us inside, just like he did the first time. I saw him with my own eyes. He called her name as we left the church.'

'The first time? What was the first time? You said nothing of this to me.'

The *duenna* realized her mistake and her breath caught in her throat. 'It seemed like a trifle.'

'How did this trifle occur?'

'I thought nothing of it. Men stare all the time.'

'That is why she has a veil.'

'In summer she says it is too hot. Sometimes she pulls it back.'

'And you let her?'

'She is headstrong.'

'Do I pay you to be compliant to her?'

Signora Cavalcanti knew she must deflect his line of questioning, shift the focus elsewhere. 'I saw someone else there.'

'Who?'

'Ludovici Gambetto.'

80

He stared at her, appalled. 'You think she has had commerce with both of them?'

'No, of course not, Your Excellency. He was just looking on. I saw him watching as we left the church. I believe the Moor is friendly with him.'

Gonzaga went to the window. He watched the gondolas and barges moving up and down the Great Canal. He had to think about this intriguing revelation. 'So, my brother-in-law's bastard! You think this is how messages were passed?'

'His sister Lucia visits here often.'

Gonzaga nodded. 'Of course. I congratulate you on your discoveries. You shall have your reward Signora Cavalcanti. You may leave me now.'

The door closed softly behind her. Gonzaga considered his options. If he brought the matter before the courts, he would be the laughing stock of all Venice. He would lose his seat on the *Consiglio di Dieci*.

He could bring the matter to the attention of Ludovici's father, but that was just as perilous. Old Gambetto's wife - his sister - had been a long time dead, and now he was maneuvering to be elected the next Doge, a rival to Gonzaga himself, and might welcome the opportunity to create a scandal.

The matter called for subtlety and patience, he decided. Ludovici could be punished in due course. The Moor must be dealt with now.

When Lucia arrived that afternoon her *duenna* was dismissed and, instead of being escorted to Julia's loggia, Signora Cavalcanti ushered her into Gonzaga's private study.

'Ah Lucia,' he said. 'How pleasant to see you again.'

'Excellency,' Lucia said, alarmed. She bent to one knee and kissed the hem of his sleeve.

'Come and sit here beside me,' he said. He dismissed Signora Cavalcanti with a glance.

They sat together on the divan by the window and he watched her, his face frozen in a smile. Lucia squirmed in the silence. She wondered if he knew about the letter.

'I believe you have something to tell me,' he said finally.

'I did nothing wrong.'

'I know you didn't. It's all right. Julia has told me everything.'

'You are not angry?'

'With her, yes. With you? Yes, I am angry with you, too, my dear.' He fixed his executioner's eyes on her, still smiling. 'But you may yet find pardon in my eyes. You were, after all, only a messenger.'

'I did not know what was in it. My brother asked me to give it to her. That's all I know.'

'You think this excuses your conduct in deceiving me and Signora Cavalcanti?'

She stared at her hands. 'I don't know.'

'Perhaps you are right. I think it does excuse you.'

'You do, Your Excellency?'

'You were asked to convey a message from a friend. Where is the sin in that?'

'There is none.'

'Of course. So you will not mind, then, extending me the same favor?'

Lucia stared at him, bewildered.

'Tell me, did you ever deliver letters to your brother from Julia herself?'

'Oh no, Excellency. Only that once through my brother to her. She never gave me anything to take back.'

'Good. Because that is about to change.' He unlocked the drawer of his desk and produced an envelope with a heavy wax seal. He passed it to her. 'This is for Abbas.'

'For Abbas? From whom, Excellency?'

'From Julia, of course.'

She hesitated.

Gonzaga leaned across the desk and his smile vanished. 'Understand me well. You will give this to your brother and tell him to hand it to Abbas, and you will say that you took this from Julia's own hand. You will tell no one of our conversation. If you fail me in this, I shall inform your father of the role you and your brother have played, and bring down such calumny on both your heads that neither of you will be able to share polite society in *La Serenissima* ever again. The scandal may cost your father his place on the Council of Ten, and he will blame you. Am I making myself clear?'

Lucia nodded. The envelope trembled in her fingers.

'May I see Julia now?'

'I am afraid not. She is unwell and unable to receive visitors.' He stood up and opened the door. 'Signora Cavalcanti will show you the way out.' He put a hand on her shoulder as she passed him. 'Be sure that Abbas gets this message. I shall know if he does not.'

Lucia nodded, unable to find her voice. As the door closed behind her she clutched at a table for support. She felt dizzy with fear. She wished that she had never let her brother talk her into this. All she wanted to do now was give Ludovici the Signor's missive and be done with this business forever.

CHAPTER 21

My Dearest Abbas,

I am to be sent to the convent at Brescia until my marriage. Time is short. I put my trust in you. I can get away but once more. The door that leads to the canal is now forever locked, but there may be another way. If you will wait for me at midnight tomorrow on the Ponte Antico, I will come to you there. I will go wherever you choose to take me. My life is now in your hands.

May the hours pass swiftly until tomorrow night!
Julia

He read the letter twice more. Ludovici watched him, impatient. 'What does she say?'

Abbas tore the vellum in half and held the pieces over the candle. Soon it was no more than a few wispy black leaves on the table. 'Nothing,' he said.

'Nothing?'

'You are a good friend,' he said. 'I can't put you in danger anymore.'

Abbas was ushered into his father's council chamber at the Ministry of War. Mahmud glanced up from the charts on the table in front of him; maps of the Peninsula and the surrounding Ottoman possessions.

'What is so urgent that you disturb me here?'

'I am sorry, Father. But I need money.'

'Is your commission as an officer in my army not enough?'

Abbas drew a deep breath. 'I have to go away.'

Mahmud straightened up and tucked his thumbs into his broad silver belt. He reminded Abbas of a huge brown bear he had once seen in the forests near Belluno. On that occasion there had been ten archers at his back. He wished they were there now.

'Go where?'

'Spain.'

'Why do you wish to go to Spain?'

'I have been meeting a woman secretly. We plan to leave Venice together as soon as possible.'

Mahmud shook his head. 'You fool,' he said.

'I love her.'

'How you feel is meaningless to me. You have put both our necks on the block.'

'When it is done, Gonzaga will have to accept it. A year, perhaps two, and I will be back in Venice.'

Mahmud shook his head. 'Your resourcefulness far outweighs your intelligence. How you have managed to deceive Gonzaga for so long I do not know, but do not think he will ever forgive you when he finds out what you have done. Or me. He was weaned on venom.'

'Once we are married, what can he do?'

'There are many things he can do. Does anyone else know of this?'

Abbas shook his head.

'Good.'

The blow was so sudden and so unexpected that it lifted Abbas off his feet. He found himself suddenly on his back, staring at the vaulted ceiling. There was a buzzing in his ears and he tasted his own blood in his mouth.

Mahmud lifted him easily from the floor with one hand and pushed him against the wall. 'Now listen to me. I love you and I will not let you ruin your life - and mine - by one rush of youthful lust. Buy yourself a mistress and leave Julia Gonzaga alone. Do you understand me?'

Abbas rested his head on his father's shoulder until his senses cleared. He felt his father's grip relax. When it did, he pushed himself away, swaying slightly on his feet. 'Goodbye Father,' he said and stumbled out of the door.

No *Magnifico* was allowed, by law, to speak with the Captain General of the Army alone. The *Consiglio di Dieci* was wary of any nobleman trying to use their own army against them. So Mahmud was accompanied everywhere he went by two senators. They were with Mahmud early that morning when he burst into the private chambers of Antonio Gonzaga.

Gonzaga sat at the far end of the room, the lead-paned windows at his back. Behind him the domes of the San Marco loomed against a mauve sky.

'Most reverend Signore,' Mahmud murmured and bent to kiss the sleeve of Gonzaga's robe.

'I am told you wish to see me on a matter of urgency,' Gonzaga said, with a glance at the two senators. 'A matter of private and not state importance, I presume?'

Mahmud fidgeted with embarrassment. Better to have discussed this with Gonzaga alone, but the law made that impossible.

'A matter of the utmost delicacy, Signore.'

'Is it to do with matters of the heart?'

Mahmud was relieved that Gonzaga already knew. It would make it easier to discuss this with the two senators present. The senators were licking their lips in anticipation of a scandal. They would have to be prudent before these two gentlemen. 'You already have some knowledge of the matter?'

'All I know is that a certain lady has been impudent enough to pass letters between her friend and a young man who should have known better. I put it down to the tempestuousness of youth.'

'I needed to be sure that you were apprised of the situation.'

'Such indiscretions will never be allowed, of course. But I appreciate that you came here to warn me. I assure you all precautions have been taken to stop this foolishness from getting out of hand.'

'I am most relieved to find you so informed.'

'You have my thanks, General. But may I ask how you came by this information?'

Mahmud hesitated. Now that there was a way to contain this scandal it was not necessary to reveal to Gonzaga that he had not seen his son since the last evening. 'From the young gentleman in question. His duty is to Venice. As is mine.'

'Do not upset yourself. All matters are in hand.'

Mahmud bowed and made his leave. As he left the palazzo he persuaded himself that everything would end well.

CHAPTER 22

Abbas kept to the shadows. With the little money he had, he had paid for passage to Pescati on a merchant galley that would sail with the morning tide. He did not know how they might reach Naples from there, but Abbas was sure he would think of something. All that mattered to him was to get Julia out of Gonzaga's palazzo, and escape Venice.

Abbas had hidden all that day in the apartment that Ludovici kept for his mistress at Giudecca. When Ludovici came to see him that evening, he told him Mahmud's soldiers had been searching for him, turning out the inns and taverns.

'What will you do?'

'Don't worry about me,' Abbas said. 'I have already involved you too much in this.'

'This game is deadly serious now. I warned you.'

'It's not a game and I have always been deadly serious.' Abbas nodded at the somber, dark-haired girl watching them from a corner of the room. 'She thought you intended to share her with me. Reassure her that I shall leave tonight, with your house and your mistress intact.'

'Where will you go?'

'I cannot even tell you that.' Abbas embraced him. 'Thank you. You are the greatest friend a man could ever have.'

Ludovici pressed a purse into his palm. Abbas did not protest. Without it, he would have had scarce enough to buy a loaf of bread when they reached Pescati.

He heard the clock in the *Piazza San Marco* chime the twelfth hour and pulled his cape tighter around his shoulders. The gondola was moored by the steps below the bridge, waiting.

Ludovici was right, he knew nothing about her, he thought. But that was not what love was; knowing everything about someone was marriage. Love was excitement, it was mystery.

A shadow darted from the alley on the other side of the bridge. 'Julia!'

He ran across the bridge after her. She saw him and turned back. But just before he reached her, he heard footsteps on the cobblestones behind him. He looked over his shoulder. The night police.

'Julia!'

Her hood fell back. In the light of the half-moon he made out the crooked, bearded grin of a stranger.

'Am I not the beauty you were expecting?' the man said. Abbas saw the flash of a blade and felt the point of it jabbed hard between his ribs. 'I may not be your Julia, but I know the way to a man's heart.'

Abbas brought up his knee. The man doubled over, collapsing at his feet. Abbas gasped. As he fell, the man had sliced into his side with the dagger.

He turned around, drawing his sword, knowing the man's accomplices were behind him in the shadows.

He tried to run but the man in the hood grabbed his ankle. Abbas stabbed down with his sword and felt the blade crunch against bone. The man shrieked in pain and released his grip.

They had surrounded him. Abbas backed away until the cold stone of the bridge was against his back. He heard his gondolier poling away from the steps. Now the shadows came alive; two men rushed him from either side, neither as cocky nor as amateur as the wretch still sobbing in his death agony at his feet. Abbas slashed with his sword, and they backed off again.

He did not see their accomplice. There was suddenly a shadow on the moon and a net fell over his head and shoulders. He tried to throw it off, but tripped over the dying man and fell, enveloping them both in the mesh. His struggles only succeeded in working the net tighter. Abbas remembered the dying man might still have his dagger.

He felt a searing pain in his face and yelled out. But then they were on him. Something clubbed him hard on the back of the head and he blacked out.

When he opened his eyes, it was pitch black. He could smell bilge water and hear the slow slap of waves against the hull of a ship.

And there was something else he knew, something he remembered from the battlefield. The smell of corpses.

Whoever his assailants were, they were not cutthroats after his money. They had cudgeled him when he was tangled in the net, when they could as easily have killed him. He tried to move but they had bound his wrists and feet. His face burned like fire.

He tried to reason out his predicament.

These must be Gonzaga's men. If Julia had written the letter, then she had deliberately led him into this trap; the other possibility was that it had come from her father's hand. He hoped so. But why hadn't they killed him and dumped his body in the canal?

There were footsteps on the companionway, and men's voices. A hatch was thrown open and torchlight flooded the hold.

He turned away and found himself staring at the hooded stranger from the bridge. He was dead. Beside him lay another corpse, an old woman dressed in black. Her throat had been cut.

He heard a man laughing. His tormentors were bearded, shoeless sailors, the kind who could be bought at the Marghero wharf any day for a few denari. One of them - Abbas smelled cheap wine and body stench - bent down and held the flaming torch next to his face.

'Well, my boy, look at you. You don't look so pretty now. Bartolomeo here split your cheek in two with his knife before he died. Not that you'll care about that, soon enough.'

The two men behind him laughed again.

He leaned closer. 'See that other one next to Bartolomeo? She was Gonzaga's *duenna*. Put up a real fight she did. Not that it did her much good. Ever slaughtered a pig, have you? It was a bit like that.' He grinned. 'But she was luckier than you, that's a fact. You'll wish you were her before the night's out.'

One of the men tugged down his breeches while the other sliced the ropes at his ankles. They gripped his knees and forced his legs apart. He shrieked in panic and tried to kick out, but they were too strong.

The first man drew his knife. Abbas twisted and bucked. Now he knew why they had not killed him on the Ponte Antico.

'You wanted Signore Gonzaga's daughter to play with these little toys, did you? Well, how about we give them to the *Consigliore* and he can give them to her himself.'

He let go of his bladder in his terror and the men laughed.

'Say goodbye to them, Moor,' the man sneered. The blade flashed in the light of the torch and the world sheered into a hot and infernal place.

A milky dawn. A funeral procession of gondolas, draped with black velvet, emerged from beneath the *Ponte Molino*. They slipped silently along the *Sacca della Misericordia* and across the lagoon toward the cemetery island of San Michele. Julia watched until they disappeared into the mist.

Her father was sending her to the convent at Brescia, to await what he referred to as 'the joyous occasion of her wedding.'

She thought about that last afternoon in the gondola.

I should have said yes, she thought. It was my one chance, and I threw it away. Now I am to be buried alive.

PART 3

Rose of Spring

CHAPTER 23

Stamboul, 1528

Fields of sunflowers dazzled the eye. On the other side of the Horn, the city rippled in dusty amber behind its gray land walls. It was a view of the city some of the girls had never seen. Today the entire Harem had been transported in canopied skiffs - *caïques* - along the Bosporus; a welcome respite from the oppressive monotony of the Old Palace.

The girls gossiped on the blue and crimson Persian carpets thrown in the shade of the cypress trees, while the *gediçli* fed them peaches and grapes from silver salvers. Musicians entertained them with flutes and viols; piles of silk cushions kept their pampered bottoms from the hard ground; dancing bears performed for them on the grass.

Gülbehar kept herself apart. One of her *gediçli* produced a mirror and held it up for her inspection. The handle was encrusted with sapphires, a gift from Suleiman after the birth of Mustapha. She studied her reflection and brushed an errant lock of hair back into place.

The other girls watched. 'Where is Hürrem?' one of them said.

'The Kislar Aghasi says she is with Suleiman,' another girl said. 'Now he spends all his days with her, as well as his nights.'

Sirhane, a raven-haired Persian, popped a grape into her mouth. 'In the bazaars they say she is a witch, that she has cast a spell over the Lord of the Earth.'

'Look at her,' another whispered, watching Gülbehar's *gediçli* combing out her hair. 'She is so beautiful. If the Lord of Life will not look at her anymore, what chance is there for the rest of us?'

'They say even the Grand Vizier fears Hürrem,' Sirhane said. 'The Kislar Aghasi told me that the Sultan now goes to her to discuss politics, and that she advises him on military campaigns.'

'The Kislar Aghasi has a fertile imagination.'

'He swears it is true.'

'The Grand Vizier would have her drowned in the Bosporus.'

'Perhaps he cannot,' Sirhane said and they all fell silent. Was that really the truth of it? Surely no one was more powerful than the Grand Vizier? 'Anyway, I feel sorry for Gülbehar,' Sirhane added. 'The Lord of Life has disgraced her.'

'Gülbehar is still first *kadin*,' another girl said. 'And one day she will be the Sultan Valide. Her day will come.'

'They say God is punishing the Lord of Life for making a witch his *kadin*. That is why his last son died in the cradle.'

'But Hürrem has three sons still living.'

'None of them will ever rival Mustapha,' another girl said and there the conversation ended. The girls' attention returned to the dancing bear.

Sirhane kept to herself the other whisper she had heard from the Kislar Aghasi; Hürrem was plotting to get rid of Mustapha.

It was quiet among the kiosks and the ornamental ponds. Only the sigh of the wind through the chestnut trees, and the gentle murmur of water in the ornamental fountains disturbed the gazelles grazing on the lawns.

Suleiman had always liked to walk here to compose his thoughts and find respite from the endless demands and entreaties that came every day from the Divan and the Harem. Once he would come alone. Lately he brought a companion with him.

The last five years had been many times blessed, he thought. When he returned from hunting at Edirne, shortly after their first union, he had found Hürrem already plump with new life. Early the following year she gave birth to a boy.

He had not shared his mother's excitement. While she celebrated the consolidation of the Osmanli line, he brooded over future conflicts. He knew what his father had done to secure his throne. He supposed his sons would have to do the same.

Hürrem was his second *kadin*, but she had replaced the first in his affections. Gülbehar had been his sanctuary for so long, but he had never been able to share the burdens of his sultanate with her. That had been Ibrahim's role.

But when Achmed Pasha rose in revolt in Egypt, he had been forced to send Ibrahim to crush him. While he was gone, he had brought the problems of state to Hürrem instead. To his surprise he found her shrewd beyond her years, and with an innate grasp of the intricacies of court politics. He continued to confide in her, even after Ibrahim's return. Her caution was a counterfoil to Ibrahim's aggression.

She had opened a new world to him. While Gülbehar was pliant and predictable, Hürrem continually surprised him. On one visit she might be sullen but passionate; on another effusive and playful. She could soothe him with her singing and her viol or excite him with her dancing. She could dress like a boy in a soldier's tunic, or like a dancing girl in gossamer. He never knew what to expect from her, though she had an uncanny ability to anticipate his own moods.

True, her love of making love was unholy and he knew he must one day send her to the mufti for education. But for now her infidel soul afforded him endless pleasures. One cry of ecstasy gave him more pleasure than all the groveling of foreign ambassadors in the Divan.

Hürrem was now his joy; everything else was duty.

She had carefully cultivated her friendship with the Valide, and Nature had helped her cement the alliance by providing her with another two sons. She had failed in the labor chamber only once when she had produced a girl twin. The boy, Abdullah, had died, but his sister Mihrmah was now three years old.

She was not the devoted mother that Gülbehar had been, but that did not trouble him overmuch; he wanted her all for himself.

'I want to talk to you,' he said to her as they walked in the garden.

'Yes, my Lord?'

'It is the Hungarian question again. Frederick is sending an envoy to treat with us. He does not know that the local governor, Zapolya, has sent his man also who has already met in secret with Ibrahim.'

He did not need to explain the problem to her; she had already learned so much about foreign policy just from listening to him.

Suleiman's army, marshaled by Ibrahim, had annihilated the Hungarians on the plain of Mohacs just two years before. Their king had drowned in the swamp when his horse fell on him during the retreat. Since Hungary was too far away for permanent occupation, Suleiman had withdrawn his troops after the battle. It had become a wasteland of warring bandits, coveted by noblemen such as Zapolya and the great Hapsburg family, under Frederick. But they could not have it without coming to terms with him first.

'What are your thoughts, my Lord?'

'Why should I treat with either of them? I am the King of Hungary now.'

'But every summer you have to send your army to regain what it conquered the year before. One day you will grow tired of it.'

'The dogs are always at the door when there are scraps to be had.'

'Then you need a dog of your own, to keep them out.'

'Zapolya is an upstart. He is no king.'

'What is a king? It is not the crown that makes a king, it is the sword. Make Zapolya your gatekeeper and let him have a piece of iron for his head. In return demand his tribute and free passage for your army. While there is no border, you remain his master.'

'He is not strong enough to hold back Frederick's armies.'

'He can keep the borders until a real army is assembled against him, one that is worthy of your attention. You may even use Zapolya to lure Frederick into the contest and drown him in the swamp also.'

'Very well. Zapolya, then.'

'If my Lord considers my counsel proper. In all things I defer to your greater wisdom.'

Suleiman nodded, pleased with Hürrem's diplomacy. She was a rare treasure indeed.

Suleiman and Gülbehar ate kebabs of lamb on silver skewers and drank perfumed rosewater from goblets of Iznik glass. After the *gediçli* had removed the bowls they sat in silence.

'Have I offended you in some way, my Lord?' Gülbehar said at last.

'No. Why?'

'You have not asked for me these many months. When you do come, it is only to see Mustapha.'

'Do not question me.'

Gülbehar hung her head. Suleiman felt sorry for her; she had been a good wife. All she had ever asked of him until now was some Venetian satin, or Baghdad silk, or a tortoiseshell comb. And she had given him Mustapha.

He had not wanted to hurt her, but each moment he spent with her he compared her to Hürrem and his impatience grew.

He got to his feet. Gülbehar looked up at him, startled. 'You are leaving, my Lord?'

'I have matters of state to deal with.'

'Hürrem.'

It was an unpardonable breach of protocol, but Suleiman decided to ignore it. 'My Lady,' he said and took his leave.

It was always dusk in the Old Palace. Even in summer, the sun could not chase the shadows from the warren of dark paneled rooms and endless corridors. It was a world of dusty lanterns and baroque mirrors coated with ancient grime. Sloe-eyed women with rubies in their hair appeared on the gloomy staircases like ghosts, ungratified and forgotten.

It infected Hürrem's mood. One day, that could be me, she thought.

She had come so far. She had given him sons and somehow kept him from this neglected storehouse of pleasures. None of these things had been easy. The strain of childbearing had sapped her energies and after each confinement she had surrendered herself to Muomi's ministrations and to vials of her foul potions in order to restore her figure. She had wet nurses for the children so her infants would not suckle her breasts dry.

Yet it could all be snatched away from her in an instant.

Suleiman's great grandfather, the one they called the Conqueror, had set the precedent for every generation to follow when he had made his bloody *kanun*:

The ulema have declared it allowable that whoever among my illustrious children and grandchildren may come to the throne should, for securing the peace of the world, order his brothers to be executed. Let them hereafter act accordingly.

She knew that if Suleiman should die, Mustapha would become the new sultan. She would find herself in exile, or worse, and all her children dead.

'Muomi!'

Her *gediçli* appeared instantly. She had been hovering at her post outside the door. 'My Lady?'

'There is something I want you to do.'

CHAPTER 24

The stone kitchens below the Old Palace were cramped and hot, and smelled of spice, sweat and steam. Heat rose in waves from the open furnaces, and there was a constant clatter of pots and kettles. Cooks shouted at underlings and at each other, while veiled *gediçli* scurried through the fug of heat and noise with dishes and teas.

In this hubbub the harried pages, servants and cooks paid no particular attention to the tall, black girl carrying the tray of oranges. Even if they had, the most observant of them would not have realized that the platter she had with her as she left was not the one she had brought in with her.

At fourteen years, Mustapha was everything Suleiman had hoped for in a son. Like every prince he was trained at the Palace School, with the elite of the boys recruited in the *devshirme*, a system unique to the Osmanlis. He had proved an outstanding rider and swordsman, as well as being an outgoing and popular boy. He had become a favorite among the Janissaries who came to cheer him at the *çerit* - a horseback game using wooden javelins - in the Hippodrome. He was also a talented scholar; he had learned his Koran, Persian and mathematics.

But today he sported a plum-colored bruise above his right eye, which was almost swollen shut. Suleiman shook his head in feigned horror as his son knelt to kiss the ruby ring on his right hand.

'What happened to you?'

'He was hit by a javelin in the *çerit*,' Gülbehar said. 'Tell him to take more care. Nothing I say to him seems to make any difference.'

'Should I be more careful, father?' Mustapha asked him and grinned.

'You should take care not to get hit so often.'

'He would spend all day on his horse if he could,' Gülbehar said.

'There is nothing wrong with that. There was a time when the Osmanlis did not have fine palaces to sit in, or laws to make. It is good the next Sultan knows how it feels to have a horse under him.'

Look how tall the boy has grown, Suleiman thought. He was as tall as Suleiman himself, and he had the first sprouting of a beard on his chin. His eyes were bright with the eagerness of youth. When I was his age I was consumed with terror, wondering when Selim's shadow would fall across my face. Thank God Mustapha will never know such a father.

Gülbehar sat on the divan and folded her hands on her lap. 'Leave us now, Mustapha, I wish to talk to the Lord of Life alone.'

Mustapha *salaamed* to Suleiman, kissed his mother on the cheek and left the room.

'You are too severe with him,' Suleiman said, after he had gone.

'I have to be. He is all I have.'

'A young man should enjoy his youthful pleasures while he can. He will have responsibilities soon enough.'

'Every day he brings back from the Hippodrome some fresh injury. Last week he was thrown from his horse three times. What if he gets killed in that stupid game?'

'As God wills,' he said.

'Do you not worry what may happen to him?'

'A Sultan must be a soldier as well as a statesman. A few scars from the Hippodrome will only make him stronger. And how are you?'

'What does it matter to you? You only ever come here to see Mustapha.'

'That is my right.'

'Do I no longer have rights?'

She did not have to remind him. He knew he had ignored the night turn that was the prerogative of every *kadin*. He should, by custom, sleep with her at least once a week.

But it was not her place to rebuke him. He leaped to his feet. 'You may be first *kadin*, but you are also still my slave. You will do as I say, and you will not presume to question me.'

'Once you would never have spoken to me so,' she murmured and hung her head. 'She has bedeviled you. She wants dominion over the entire Harem - even over you.'

'Isn't that what you want also?'

She looked up. 'I just want to serve you.'

'Then serve me by keeping your silence,' he said.

That night, after the final prayer, silent pages brought Mustapha his meal on a gold tray. There were tiny cubes of meat broiled in herbs, squash stuffed with rice, figs in sour cream and fresh oranges.

The food was served in blue and white porcelain bowls, each hand-painted with intricate scrollwork. A servant tasted each dish for poison, as he did at every meal, then bowed and left the room. Mustapha sat cross-legged on the carpet and ate in silence. Occasionally he raised the index finger of his right hand and a page would step forward to refill his golden goblet with sherbet.

When he had finished, he looked at the oranges. He chose one, peeled the skin from one side of it, and tasted it. It was dry and slightly sour. He dropped it on the tray and pushed it away.

Instantly another of the pages stepped forward with a bowl of perfumed water. Mustapha dipped his fingers in the bowl and allowed him to dry them. Then he got up and went to his bedchamber. It was customary for the pages to eat whatever he left and as he left the room, he saw them fall on his leftover dishes like starving street dogs.

Other servants unrolled his sleeping mattress for him, but he did not feel tired. He sat at the Koran stand and read two more suras by the light of the candle, before the first spasm gripped his stomach.

By the time Gülbehar arrived, the pages who had served the prince's meal were already dead. Mustapha was pale and shaken but still alive. The Palace physician had administered an emetic and Mustapha groaned as his empty stomach rebelled once more.

Gülbehar cradled her son in her arms. He must be really ill, she thought, for he lets me do it. 'How could you let this happen?' she shouted at the terrified guards. 'Who did this to my son?'

'We will find them,' the Kapi Aga promised. By the prophet's Holy Beard, he thought, if Mustapha had died my own head would already be moldering on the Gate of Felicity.

Gülbehar rocked Mustapha in her arms, sobbing with rage and fear.

Mustapha's food taster was delivered to the chief executioner in the torture chamber. He insisted on his innocence between his screams. However he was able to show them which food had contained the poison, by the simple expedient of force-feeding him each morsel that remained from the supper.

'It was the oranges,' his physician reported. 'Somehow they poisoned the oranges.'

Suleiman ordered that everyone involved in the preparation of the prince's food be examined also. The two cooks died, begging for mercy.

It never came.

CHAPTER 25

Gold spigots dripped warm water into the marble bath. Naked bodies glided through the steam under a cavernous dome. Black *gediçli* in gauzy bath chemises scooped water into bowls, and poured it over the heads of the concubines.

Hürrem perched on the edge of the navel-stone, a huge hexagonal slab heated from beneath by an underground furnace. Muomi worked the muscles in her back. Later she would have her work on her stomach and thighs. She would not allow herself to grow old and fat in here.

She tried not to brood over her recent failure. The oranges had been her idea. She knew they would not suspect a whole fruit. She had pierced the oranges with needles and Muomi had poured the hemlock in through the tiny pinpricks in the rind. Fate and a fussy nature had saved Mustapha.

Gülbehar walked past. The bath chemise clung to her heavy breasts and Hürrem noted that her waistline was growing thicker. 'I know it was you,' she said. 'You tried to murder my son.'

'You are getting old, your mind is playing tricks.'

'It was you!'

'Why don't you run to Suleiman and tell him your suspicions then.'

Gülbehar was on the edge of tears. 'If you hurt my son, I will kill you.'

'I do not think so,' Hürrem said. 'Mustapha is all you have. I have three and I may yet have many more, since the Sultan no longer comes to your bed.'

'Leave my son alone.'

Hürrem lowered her voice so that only Gülbehar heard her murmur, 'Say goodbye to your little bud, Rose of Spring.'

Gülbehar lashed out. The slap stung Hürrem's cheek. She struck back but at the last moment she pulled back so that she caught Gülbehar a glancing blow on the side of the head. Gülbehar raked her face with her nails. Hürrem grabbed her and wrestled her onto the floor. The *gediçli* jumped back, screaming for the guards.

Muomi helped Hürrem back to her apartments. Her hair hung in wet tangles and there were streaks of thin, watery blood on her cheek.

She slumped onto a divan.

'Shall I send for the physician?' Muomi said.

Hürrem shook her head but then a spasm of pain in her belly made her gasp and she doubled over. She had landed heavily when she had tussled Gülbehar to the floor.

'You are badly hurt.'

'Fetch me a mirror.'

Muomi brought her a jeweled looking glass. Hürrem held it up and examined her reflection. There were small scratches on her cheek, two deeper ones on her forehead. 'Scratch me,' Hürrem said.

'My lady?'

'Scratch me!' Hürrem grabbed Muomi's wrist and drew her nails down her neck.

With elaborate care Muomi brought her fingernails to Hürrem's neck and raked deep scratches to the collarbone. Then she made others, not as deep - she did not want to leave scars - on her cheek. She held up the mirror again.

'Are you satisfied?' Muomi said.

CHAPTER 26

The Eski Saraya trembled.

Suleiman strode through the cloisters. The Kislar Aghasi shuffled behind, his face beaded with perspiration.

He stopped in front of the doors to Hürrem's apartment. The two eunuchs who guarded the entrance blanched when they saw him, but continued to stare resolutely ahead.

The Kislar Aghasi caught up, his breath sawing in his chest.

'Tell her I am here.'

The old eunuch nodded and went inside but it was Muomi, not Hürrem, who was waiting to greet him. She *salaamed* and remained on her knees.

'The Lord of Life wishes to see your mistress.'

'She cannot see him at present.'

The eunuch stared at her as if she had answered in a foreign language. 'What did you say?'

'My mistress is distressed beyond words that she cannot accept the honor he does her by visiting her here. But she cannot receive him. She could not allow the Lord of Life to gaze upon her in her present condition.'

The Kislar Aghasi felt the pain in his chest growing worse. There was no precedent for this in the protocols.

'But she must see him,' he said.

Muomi stared back and said nothing.

He hurried past her, into the private dining room. Hürrem was sitting on a divan of green brocade, a heavy veil covering her face.

'My Lady,' he said.

She said nothing. This is intolerable, he thought dabbing at the perspiration on his face with a silk handkerchief.

Hürrem lifted the veil and the old eunuch gasped. There were ugly red scabs over her nose and cheeks, and her neck looked as if she had been clawed by a mountain lion. This was not the way he had heard it. He had been told that although the altercation had been unseemly, neither girl had been badly hurt.

He stared at her in disbelief.

'Too disfigured to see me?' Suleiman said. He stared at his Chief Black Eunuch. The old man looked as if he were about to faint.

'It is as she says, my Lord.'

'I do not believe it,' he said. 'I am here to see my *kadin*. I will see her.' He swept past the guards into the apartments.

Hürrem looked up from the divan. When she saw him, she slowly raised her veil a second time. Suleiman took one look at the ruin of her face, turned on his heel and walked out again.

Gülbehar could hardly contain her excitement. The Kislar Aghasi's messenger had informed her that the Lord of Life was in the old palace. He had no doubt been told of the outrage that minx had inflicted on her. The snake had bared its fangs at last, she thought. Suleiman must see her now for what she was. She would tell him how she had tried to murder his beloved Mustapha. He would send her and her black sorceress to the *bastinado* and the truth would come out.

Then Suleiman would come back to her and everything would be as it was before.

She prepared the table herself, setting out sweetmeats, *rahat lokum* and sherbet, and then settled down to wait on the divan. Her hair was braided and brushed, and she was freshly bathed and perfumed.

The door crashed open.

There was no sweating old eunuch to usher the Lord of Life into her chamber. Suleiman stood in the doorway, his face ugly with rage. He slammed the door shut behind him, shattering the silence of the Harem, and stamped into the center of the room.

Gülbehar dropped to her knees. '*Salaam*, Lord of my Life, Sultan of Sult…'

He grabbed her arm and forced her to her feet. 'Take off your veil.'

Gülbehar felt weak. She pulled back her veil and his face twisted in contempt. 'Not one scratch.'

'I do not understand.'

His voice was so soft, she could scarce hear him. 'If you ever again take from me the pleasure of looking on her face, I swear I shall kill you.'

'Please, my Lord, I…'

'Your jealousy poisons the whole harem!'

'What have I done?'

'One day you will be Valide. Can you not be content with that?'

'What did she say to you?'

'Silence! You will never try to keep me from her again, do you understand?'

She nodded.

Now that his anger was spent, he felt sorry for her. 'You must leave here,' he said, 'it is best for you. I shall make the arrangements.'

CHAPTER 27

The sun setting on the stone of Ibrahim's palace had turned it rose pink. The high walls and wooden shuttered windows echoed the splendor of the great Topkapi, which stood less than half a mile away. It was a reminder to everyone, from the horsemen playing *çerit* on the Hippodrome below, to the faithful filing into the Aya Sofia mosque, that this was the greatest, wealthiest and most trusted Vizier the Osmanlis had ever known. They said the Sultan himself had built the palace out of the public purse. He had even given him his sister in marriage.

Güzül stared at the ivory and tortoiseshell throne, the silver candle holders and the copper-and-turquoise censers. They were all fit for a Sultan. With the thick band of gold around his sugar loaf turban and white satin robes, Ibrahim looked every inch as Güzül imagined the Lord of Life himself must look. The ruby on his finger was the size of a bird's egg.

His clerk and money man, Rüstem, sat cross-legged at the foot of the marble steps, facing away from her. She had heard a lot about him, a Bulgar who had risen rapidly through the ranks, as Ibrahim had done.

Güzül had come here directly from the Harem, where she was allowed to sell gems and trinkets. But that was not her true function; in the closed world of the Harem, she was that most precious of creatures - a go-between. Over the course of the years she had become Gülbehar's voice in the outside world.

To compensate for her fading youth she dyed her hair with henna and tied it with bright ribbons. The silver bracelets on her ankles and wrists made her look like a brigand queen.

'Well Güzül,' Ibrahim said. 'Tell me what brings you to my humble seraglio.'

'My mistress, Rose of Spring, sends her felicitations. May your house always increase in wealth and prosperity.'

'I thank her for her good wishes. May God always protect her and may her beauty never fade.'

'Insha'Allah.'

'I have heard whispers, Güzül.'

'What whispers, my Lord?'

'That your mistress quarrels with the Lady Hürrem in the Eski Saraya. One may only pray the conflict will be resolved to the satisfaction of all.'

'She is to be exiled, my Lord.'

Ibrahim did not seem surprised by this news.

'That is why I am here, my Lord. My mistress begs for your intercession.'

'I do not have such power, Güzül.'

That's not what they say in the bazaars, she thought. There they say you are Sultan in all but name. 'My mistress asks only that you speak for her with the Lord of Life.'

'This is the business of the Harem, and no affair of mine. I would like to help your mistress, but this is beyond any small power I may have. She should take her case to the Kislar Aghasi.'

'My mistress only suggests that you could examine more closely the consequences of her departure.'

Ibrahim leaned forward, one arm resting on the arm of his throne. 'Go on.'

'You have always been a friend to Mustapha. One day he will be the next Sultan. His mother hopes she will always remember you kindly.'

'Is that a threat?'

'My mistress has never sought to challenge the power of the Grand Vizier.'

'Of course not.'

'But Hürrem might.'

Ibrahim stared at her, his fist clenched on the arm of the throne. 'You think so?'

'In the bazaars they say she has bewitched him.'

'The Empire is not ruled by carpet salesmen.'

'He spends long days and nights with her, my Lord. Not all of their time together concerns the pleasures of the bedchamber. He talks to her of politics.'

'Thank you. You have made your point.'

'My Lord.' Güzül crept forward, kissed the carpet at the foot of the throne and crept out again.

He watched her leave, his face creased into a frown of uncertainty.

He looked at Rüstem kneeling patiently at the foot of the throne. 'Well, what do you think?'

'It is always wise not to make more enemies than is absolutely necessary,' Rüstem said.

'I agree. But it is true that he indulges this harem girl of his. Would she really dare to challenge me?'

It occurred to him that the real problem was that the harem was the only part of the Empire over which he had little influence.

'Perhaps a gentle word to the Sultan to gauge his thinking in this matter,' Rüstem said. 'How he responds to your advice should allow you to measure the extent of this Hürrem's influence.'

Ibrahim had not considered that. Suleiman had never over-ruled him before. If he suggested to him that he should keep Gülbehar in Stamboul, then that is what Suleiman would do.

Rüstem was right. He must test him out on it.

CHAPTER 28

Suleiman stared into his hands while the servants removed the last of the dishes. Ibrahim finished the ballad he was playing on the viol and laid the instrument on the carpet beside him. 'Something is troubling you, my Lord?'

Suleiman nodded.

'Is it Haberdansky?'

Suleiman scowled. Frederick had had the temerity to dispatch an ambassador to Suleiman's court with no tribute and no terms, other than to claim Hungary was part of Frederick's empire by birth and demand its return.

It had given Suleiman great pleasure to show him the rougher edge of Osman hospitality in the dungeons at Yedikule.

'No, it is not politics that wearies me, old friend.'

'Yet the Hapsburg question must be resolved.'

Suleiman sighed. 'What do you think of this Zapolya now you have met him?'

'He will make a poor king and a fine vassal.'

That was what Hürrem had said, Suleiman thought. 'Very well. We can make him our gatekeeper,' he said. 'He may wear the crown, but as long as he gives us tribute, in gold and slaves, the kingdom remains ours.'

'It is settled then?'

'Yes. Give his envoy our decision.'

Ibrahim picked up the viol again and gently plucked at the strings.

Suleiman felt a prickle of irritation. He could not rest, even here. All he could think about was the war of nerves taking place in his own Harem. He would not rest until Gülbehar was safely removed. 'There is something I must discuss with you. It is about Mustapha.'

'A fine boy,' Ibrahim said.

'Indeed, he shows great promise as a leader and as a warrior. He is fourteen years old now and it is time he is given a governorship, to test his mettle for the great burden he must one day accept.'

'He is still young.'

'Only a year younger than I was when my father sent me to Manisa.'

'A year is not a long time when one is forty, but a lifetime when one is fourteen.'

'Still I think it is time. But I accept what you say about his youth. We should have his mother accompany him, to guide him. They are very close. Do you agree?'

'I would counsel against it, my Lord.'

'No, I have made up my mind.'

Ibrahim blinked in surprise. 'There is danger in blooding him too soon. We should weigh this carefully over time.'

'I cannot see anything further that we should trouble ourselves with.'

'I would counsel forbearance. Can we not wait at least one year?'

'He is my son. I know him best.'

'But to give him a governorship so soon…'

'Will you give me peace, Ibrahim! I have told you that I have made up my mind. You are a fine Vizier, but sometimes it seems you think yourself the Sultan.'

'As you say, my Lord. I defer to your greater wisdom.'

There was a tense silence.

Finally Suleiman got to his feet. 'I shall go to bed now,' he said. 'I am tired.'

Ibrahim stayed where he was, strumming a melancholy tune on the viol.

As he played he closed his eyes. He saw the music drift beyond the walls of the seraglio, over the seven hills of Stamboul, across the Black Sea and the Aegean and the Mediterranean. A phrase drifted on the hot desert winds of Africa. One sad note echoed along the valleys of Persia and Greece, and then along the wide slow rivers of the Danube and the Euphrates. A refrain was carried with the wind over the wide plains of Hungary, and the steppes of the Ukraine, and even found its way along the winding streets of Jerusalem.

Princes and pashas, shahs and sheiks danced to the music, for this was the empire the Osmanlis had built, and it was here within the walls of the Topkapi that they plucked the strings.

But tonight, he heard a discordant note competing with the harmony he and the Divan had created. It came from the old palace where the Sultan kept his harem, and the hands that played it were soft and white, and the nails were painted scarlet.

For the first time in his life Ibrahim was afraid.

Suleiman sat astride a white horse in the cobbled courtyard. His face was drawn in a stern mask. It would have been impossible to decipher his expression, even if the pages and guards who stood nearby had dared look up at him. On pain of death, none of them would.

Mustapha jumped into his saddle, nudged his stallion forward with the slightest pressure of his knees, and reined in alongside his father. Suleiman put a hand on the boy's arm. 'May God bless your journey and keep you safe.'

'Thank you, Father.'

'Do well.'

'I shall do all I can to serve you.'

'Remember it is not me you serve but Islam. Even Sultans and their princes are only servants of Allah. Go in peace.'

Suleiman turned around and saw three veiled figures hurry across the courtyard and climb inside a waiting coach; Gülbehar and her two handmaidens.

He waited until the tiny procession had left the court and the great doors of the Old Palace were shut behind them. He felt both sorrow and elation. Had he lost her or was he free of her?

He felt a great weight on his chest. All the women in the world and he still did not feel complete.

PART 4

The Custodian of Felicity

CHAPTER 29

The Ionian Sea

The galley resembled a giant water beetle, twenty-seven sets of oars on each side like spindly legs pushing it across the surface of a pond. The Golden Lion of Venice hung limp, asleep in the sun. The elaborately carved poop was shaded with an awning of purple silk, under which the officers and more gentle cargo reclined at their ease on rugs and low divans. They held perfumed handkerchiefs to their noses to block out the appalling smells wafting from below.

The sails were braided along the two yards above the fore and main masts while in the bowels rows of naked slaves pushed her across the ocean. They were chained to wooden benches, their own feces swirling in the bilge around their ankles. They had been rowing for eighteen hours without a break. An under-officer moved down the rows with bread soaked in wine, cramming it into the gasping mouths of those wretches who seemed closest to exhaustion. Several men had already passed out in their chains. They were flogged back to consciousness with rope dipped in brine. Two who did not recover quickly enough were unshackled and tossed over the side.

Julia Gonzaga saw nothing of this from her chair under the purple tabernacle above. Brocade curtains spared the passengers such unpleasantness, though they had all caught glimpses of those unfortunates at the oars several times during the journey. Julia had never seen such despair, or such filth. It had haunted her all the ten days they had been at sea.

The captain explained to her and her *duenna,* that she should not trouble herself as they were only heathen, captured Turkish sailors and

Arab pirates, and no better than animals. But she felt ashamed anyway. Whenever she caught a whiff from below, she closed her eyes against the glare of the ocean and fingered her rosary.

She looked down at the beads and remembered how they had trembled between her fingers the night of her wedding. She had sat in the marriage bed staring at the walnut paneled door, hardly able to breathe, waiting for her new husband.

Finally there had been a knock, and when it opened her husband stood framed in the doorway, still in his wedding clothes. They had stared at each other in embarrassed silence.

'I am accustomed to sleeping in my own bedchamber,' he had said. 'I wish you a goodnight.'

Soon afterwards he had left to visit his estates in Cyprus. He had been gone no more than a few days when her father succumbed to a chill and could not leave his bed. He was running a fever and the physician was called and bled him. He sent for her and required that she sit beside him and read to him from Plato.

Her husband had written to tell her his business might keep him in Cyprus for some time, and he had arranged passage for her to join him. She supposed he did not trust to leave her alone in Venice, since her father was no longer well enough to supervise her.

She had anticipated this adventure with great excitement. She reveled in the salt air and the wide expanses of ocean. One morning she glimpsed bright spring flowers blooming on the islands off the coast of Greece. After the cloistered palazzo, with its smell of must, the monotony of lacework and daily prayers, she felt as if she had been released from prison. Only two things spoiled it for her; one was the stench coming from below; the other was the knowledge of what awaited her at the end of her journey.

She went to stand at the rail. Her *duenna* was below decks, seasick again.

She could still hear Abbas' voice.

She smiled at the memory.

'Pleasant thoughts, my lady?'

She looked around, startled. It was the captain, Bellini, a plump young man with florid cheeks and furtive eyes.

'I beg your pardon?' Had he seen her smiling through the black lace?

'One has so much time for reflection on these long voyages.'

'I was thinking of my husband.'

'Ah.' Bellini pointed to the sails. 'Still no wind. But another few days and I am sure you will be reunited. The voyage has taken longer than usual, because of the calm. The oars are a poor substitute for sail.' He held his handkerchief to his nose for a moment and breathed deeply. 'How long since you have seen him?'

'Nearly six months.'

'A long time. You must miss him.'

'Not especially,' she said and saw the blood rise to his cheeks. It was not the answer he had expected, and she had embarrassed him.

'For a lady such as yourself…' She never found out what he was about to say. The sentence caught in his throat. '*Corpo di Dio!*' he shouted and ran across the deck to fetch his eyeglass. Another cry from the sailor in the yards confirmed his fears.

The triangular lateen sails of the galleot appeared suddenly from behind the cliffs of an island on their port side. The blades of its oars hovered and dipped.

'Turks!' Bellini shouted, panicked. He ran down the companionway from the poop to the slave deck. 'Row!' he screamed. 'Make these scum row!'

The galley captains gave a blast on their whistles. Julia heard the slap of their whips as they ran up and down the rows of benches, kicking, lashing and swearing at the exhausted slaves. The ship lurched as the helmsman leaned on the long tiller, swinging them hard to starboard, away from the Turkish pirates.

Suddenly the deck swarmed with sailors, clambering from the yards to their positions in the prow and poop. Soldiers fumbled for their harquebuses and crossbows, cursing God and their luck in their terror.

The long beaked prow of the galleot came on.

'Where's our escort?' Bellini searched the horizon for the warship he had allowed to slip away across the horizon.

Julia gripped his arm. 'Can't we outrun them?'

'They're lighter and faster, and their oarsmen are all freemen and rested.' He shook her off. 'They must have been waiting for us,' he said. He pushed her aside and ran to the poop deck. The screams from below got louder as their galley masters worked the slaves with their whips.

She looked back to the stern and gasped. The galleot was almost on top of them.

A primitive wail came from the slave deck, over the beat of the war drum. The galley slaves were defying the officers, their voices raised in a guttural chant.

'*La illah ilallah Muhammadu rasul allah... la illah ilallah Muhammadu rasul allah...*'

God is great and Mohammed is his prophet.

The green flag of Islam fluttered at the mast of the galleot. So this was the heathen they had been fighting all her life, this was the Devil Islam.

Their captain - the *rais* - stood at the poop, urging even greater effort from his oarsmen, while a huge Arab, bald and bare-chested, gave the stroke on the tambour. The blades rose and fell in perfect unison. A white puff of smoke drifted from the prow as the Turks opened fire with their harquebuses.

One of the soldiers on the bridge screamed, clutching at his face, and disappeared over the side. The galley slaves cheered.

The galleot swept towards them from the starboard aft, safe from their bow-chasers. There was a roar as the Turks fired their cannon. The water churned to foam and part of the rigging in the main mast collapsed in a scream of cracking timber.

Julia was so frightened she could not think. Her legs shook and then gave way under her. She tried to cover her ears with her hands but could not block out the sound of the chant sent up by the Turkish rowers to frighten their enemy. *'Allahu Akbar! Allaaaah!'*

One of Bellini's officers pulled her to her feet and pushed her towards the hold. 'For the love of God!' he shouted. 'Get below!'

She ran blindly.

But when she reached the companionway she stopped. She saw the Turk's iron-tipped fighting prow scything through the waves towards them.

Within moments it crashed through the oars as if they were twigs, the looms snapping back into the chests and faces of the oarsmen. The bilges turned red, the screams deafened her. She saw one man trying to push his own viscera back into his stomach.

Then the prow crashed through the starboard bulwark and the galleon lurched. Julia toppled forward into the hold.

When she came round, she found herself lying on her back at the foot of the companionway. A filmy mist of white smoke drifted across the deck above her. She could hear men shouting orders, others crying in pain or begging quarter.

The clash of steel and the boom of the harquebuses stopped abruptly. It was replaced by a terrible rattling and howling. She realized it was the galley slaves, begging for their freedom.

She was too terrified to move. She crawled into a corner, hugged her knees to her chest and waited. She closed her fingers around her rosary and started to whisper a prayer to the Madonna.

There were footsteps on the companionway. Three men were silhouetted against the hatchway. They wore turbans and carried curved swords.

They stopped halfway down and stared at her. Then one of the men said something in a language she did not understand, and the others laughed. They pulled her to her feet and dragged her back up to the deck.

CHAPTER 30

The coast of Africa rose from the horizon, the villages stark and white against the scorched red earth. As the galleot sailed past the headland, the lateens filled with the sort of brisk wind that might have saved the miserable huddle of humanity now chained together in its hold. They were dragged on deck, one by one, at sword point, blinking in the harsh sunlight.

The fortress of Algiers loomed from the sea. Below it, whitewashed buildings piled up the hillside, safe beneath the Osmanli cannon and the green crescent banner of Mohammed.

As they slipped into the harbor several of the prisoners gave an audible sigh, knowing their lives as free men were over.

Julia, being a woman, was kept separate from the others. She dared a glance at them from behind her veil. They had been stripped naked, except for thin strips of material around their loins, and their hands and feet were chained. None of them raised their eyes from the deck.

She barely recognized Bellini. He looked smaller and fatter without his uniform.

The galleot moored at the quay in front of the harbor mosque. The men were led away first, the pirates shoving back the crowd that had rushed from the souk to gawk at them. They wore burnooses and *djellabas*, and they spat at the Venetians as they passed, screaming curses.

One of the Turks grabbed her by the arm and led her away, dragging her along behind him.

Julia had not given up hope. Her husband was an esteemed member of the *Consiglio di Dieci*. Venice had brokered a peace with the Osmanlis, and her husband traded with them. He had once even entertained members of Suleiman's court at his own table. The worst that might happen, she told herself, is that she would be shut up in a castle somewhere until they organize the ransom.

The crowd jostled and a man hawked phlegm at her. The *rais* ignored the curses and hurried her along.

The mob followed them along narrow alleys piled with filth. The men were herded along in front of her. Julia kept her eyes down, ashamed to witness their humiliation.

The palace loomed ahead of them. They were led through a gate, past the black slave corrals where caravans from the Sahara brought the Nubians and Sudanese for market. Some of the women had babies at their breasts and the men were naked.

They entered an esplanade of white sand enclosed on all four sides by arched colonnades. There was a din of voices shouting in languages she did not understand, some barking orders, others babbling in fear. She stopped, overwhelmed. The *rais* cursed her and slapped her across the shoulders with the handle of his whip.

He dragged her into yet another court. This one was smaller, but almost empty, though there were countless footprints in the bleached sand.

A man sat in the shade on a pile of cushions, staring at her. He had dark skin, almost mahogany. His white kaftan was trimmed with gold thread, and there was a large turquoise in his muslin turban. A young Nubian boy stood behind him, cooling him with a fan of ostrich feathers.

The *rais* and the fat man started shouting at each other. Julia heard one word repeated over and over: *Gaiour*.

The man lifted an arm to signal that he was about to rise. The Nubian boy dropped the fan and helped him to his feet. '*Como se chiame?*' the man said.

'You speak Italian?'

He smiled. 'Of course. And many other languages beside. What do you think I am, a barbarian?' He came closer. 'Do you speak Turkish?'

'A little.'

'Good.' He lifted her veil. Despite her situation Julia felt outraged. No Venetian gentleman would dare such a thing. She lowered her eyes. He glanced at the *rais*. 'He is right. You are very beautiful. Again, what is your name?'

'Julia Gonzaga. My husband is a *Consigliatore* in Venice. He will reward you richly for my safe return.'

'The Sultan might pay me more.' The Nubian boy shooed a fly from the fat man's face with his ostrich fan. 'Allow me to introduce myself. My name is Ali-Osman. I am Bey of Algiers, in the service of Sultan Suleiman, King of Kings, Lord of Lords, Emperor of the Seven Worlds.' He effected a mock bow. 'I am his lifelong servant. You may soon have the honor of being his servant, also.'

'I am no one's servant.'

'Ah, so proud. Pride and beauty often accompany each other. But that is no matter.' He walked around her, inspecting her for flaws. She endured this new humiliation in silence. He faced her again and then gently squeezed her breast. Julia screamed and jumped back.

The *rais* growled at her but Ali-Osman roared with laughter. 'Your modesty will not be worth much to you where you are going, *bellissima!*'

He turned to the *rais* and the two men fell into a heated argument. Julia could understand none of it, but from the expression on the pirate's face, and the angry tone of his voice, she dared to hope that he was about to draw his sword and pin this Ali-Osman to the wall.

They both laughed and slapped each other on the shoulders. The Bey reached into the folds of his robe and produced a leather pouch. He loosened the drawstrings and tipped a number of gold coins into the other man's palm.

The pirate walked away without another word, leaving her with Ali-Osman.

'Julia Gonzaga, my *bellissima*, you belong to Sultan Suleiman now!'

'But my husband…'

'Your husband no longer exists. The Kislar Aghasi has a deeper purse than any Venetian, I assure you. I shall make a tenfold profit on our transaction today.' He clapped his hands and two turbaned soldiers appeared from the shadows. 'Take her inside and keep her under guard. Make sure she is given food and water. Treat her well, who knows, one day she may be the mother of the next Sultan.'

Ali-Osman settled himself back on his cushions, and shouted at his Nubian to fan him faster, he was getting hot.

First, there was an endless bright ocean that hurt the eyes. Then they were overtaken by a violent summer storm that left her weak with nausea, with no escape from the vile stench of bile and vomit. For two weeks they sailed across the Osmanli empire, now and then glimpsing the inverted mirages of islands or a distant coast. Occasionally they would call in at this port or that dirty village to load a giraffe, or a slave, or a bale of silk.

Julia prayed to die. She even contemplated throwing herself over the side. But she convinced herself that when they arrived in Stamboul, there would be a legation from the Venetian ambassador waiting for her on the dock.

The Turks watched her, their eyes bright, hungry and hard, but none dared offend or touch her. They brought her food. It was not fit for a dog, though it was the same mess of rice and dried meat they ate themselves.

They gave her a cabin below deck, guarded day and night by two of the crew. She could scream or she could cry. They ignored her.

One morning when she came up on deck, one of the sailors pointed over the bow and she saw the great city of Stamboul rise from the mist. A little while later they sailed through the Bosporus strait. The sea was as flat and as silver as the blade of a sword. The morning sun caught the golden domes of the mosques, burning off the fog that clung to the sea walls and the jutting arm of Seraglio Point. The water teemed with fishing boats and fast *caïques*. She saw the golden lion of Venice hoist on one of the galleys and she felt a physical pain.

Then they were round the point and inside the sweeping arms of the Golden Horn. There was no delegation from *La Serenissima* waiting for her at the quay. She closed her eyes, knowing that everything she had ever known was gone forever.

CHAPTER 31

Manisa

Gülbehar watched the riders from behind the latticed windows of the palace. The iron on the horses' hoofs rang on the smooth stones of the Roman road and echoed along the valley walls. It reminded her of the bells that rang every hour in the Old Palace. That was another world away now. She did not miss the dusty stairwells or the draughty rooms; she missed Suleiman. Now, for all the freedom of her new life, her bed was always cold.

The evening sun dipped below the wheat fields. The breeze carried with it the smell of wood smoke.

The riders drew closer. There were a dozen of them, one riding ahead of the rest. She could hear his voice booming up the valley even from up here. He was dark, with a sparse beard, and wore a loose-fitting robe. A stag, its throat pierced by an arrow, lay across his saddle. Blood from the wound had stained the horse's flank.

Mustapha.

'So tonight we shall be dining on venison,' she murmured. Her son looked pleased with himself.

He rides like a true *shahzade*, she thought. He shouted something to his escort. It was lost to her on the wind, but she heard the men shout with laughter.

My son will be the finest of all the Osmanli sultans, she thought. One day he may even surpass his father. So many talents, so few flaws. He hunts, he speaks half a dozen languages, he excels in mathematics. Everyone loves him.

The riders dismounted in the courtyard below. Mustapha looked up at the window and waved. He could not see her, but he knew she would be there, watching.

They ate in silence. Three times Mustapha described how he had killed a stag before he ran out of conversation. Elated with his success, he resented his mother's dark mood.

'What is it, Mother?'

'We must think about your future,' she said.

'Not that again.' He laughed. 'I have the simplest future of any man living. For now I am governor of Manisa. And one day I will be Sultan of the Osmanlis. What is there to think about?'

'But will you really? Be the Sultan?'

His smile vanished. 'Mother, please.'

'How often does your father come to visit you? Meanwhile the witch insinuates herself further and further into his court.'

'How he conducts his Harem is no business of mine.'

'You are blind.'

'You see conspiracy everywhere.'

'She tried to have you poisoned!'

'No one thinks that but you.'

'Who else would want you dead?'

'The Osmanlis have many enemies.'

Gülbehar slammed her hand on the table, startling him. 'Of course it was her. You are all that stands in her way.'

'My father would never betray me.'

'I thought that once, too. '

Mustapha pushed his plate away. 'What would you have me do?'

'You have many friends at the Sublime Porte. Perhaps it is time you thought to use them.'

'For what purpose?'

'Your grandfather knew the answer to that.'

Mustapha turned pale. 'I will not raise my hand against my father. It would be a sin before God.'

'There are greater sins and they are being committed as we speak in the palace at Stamboul.'

Mustapha raised a finger and a deaf-mute hurried forward with a scented bowl. He washed his fingers and held them out to be dried. 'The throne will come to us as God wills. I will not turn against him.' He reached across the low table and took Gülbehar's hands in his own. 'I love you, Mother. But you see phantoms everywhere. If Hürrem is my enemy then she will answer for it one day. But I will not harm him.'

After he had left, Gülbehar brooded in silence. Then she clapped her hands for the servants to remove the dishes and had a maid send a summons to Güzül.

The Kislar Aghasi was not much older than Julia herself. He wore a kaftan of flowered silk, over which was an emerald-green pelisse, lined with ermine. Its long sleeves swept the ground. There were thick rubies on his plump fingers. A white cat dozed in his lap.

He was disfigured by an ancient scar that ran from one side of his face to the other.

He pointed at her. 'Take off her veil.'

Julia had learned enough Turkish on the way from Algiers to understand what he meant. She had also learned that she could avoid humiliation by submitting. So as soon as he spoke, she reached up and pulled back the black lace.

The Kislar Aghasi jerked in his seat, as if he had been stabbed in the back. His mouth fell open. Then he leaped up, spilling the sleeping cat onto the floor. 'Get her out of here.'

The guards hesitated.

'Now!'

Before they could drag her away, he had already turned for the door. It crashed shut behind him.

CHAPTER 32

The Kubbealti, the Hall of the Divan, was the hub of the Empire. For eighty years, in this small chamber under the watch tower of the Second Court, Osmanli Sultans had held court for four days in every week, receiving petitions, resolving legal matters, meeting foreign envoys, and deciding foreign and state policy. Every decision, from the humblest legal dispute between merchants to the declaration of war, had been made in this room.

On the morning of the Divan, a long line extended across the garden outside as petitioners waited their turn to bring their case before the Sultan. Suleiman would sit on a cushioned dais opposite the door with the Grand Vizier on his right, and the governors of Rumelia and Anatolia behind him. Agas, pashas and mufti would sit in their proper order of rank to either side. Notaries would record the imperial decrees and judgments.

Only the Sultan had the right to speak. Others could offer their opinion as requested, or when sought out on a particular point of secular or religious law that was their specialty. The Sultan's decree in all matters was final.

Suleiman had grown tired of it all. Lately he had abrogated the duties of the Divan to Ibrahim, and allowed him to preside in his place. He reported to the Lord of Life on his decisions twice a week, and the Sultan would ratify them. A small, latticed window had been cut in the wall high above Ibrahim's divan so that Suleiman might watch the proceedings whenever he chose, without being seen. It was a measure to safeguard Ibrahim's conduct, even though Suleiman rarely used it.

Ibrahim was increasingly troubled by the changes he had witnessed in Suleiman. Perhaps, he thought, he has come too far too quickly. He has conquered Rhodes and Belgrade, then crushed the Hungarians and their king at Mohacs. He had already achieved what his father or even the legendary Mehmet the Conqueror had been unable to do, and so his greatness was assured.

He delegates too much to me, Ibrahim thought. It does not bode well for him, or for me.

On this morning, the petitioners were made to wait as the Grand Vizier debated with his generals the matter of that summer's campaign in the Lands of War. Ibrahim allowed the mufti to speak first.

'Sooner or later the Lord of Life must deal with the Persian Shah, Tahmasp, who dares shelter the Shi'a heretics and raids our border constantly. He offends not only the Osmanlis but Islam itself. It is the Sultan's duty to bring him to heel!'

Ibrahim bowed his head in deference to the Islamic judge. If he had his way, he would have the charlatan's head on a spike at the front gate.

He turned to address the other generals, 'I agree with the mufti, the shah is indeed an offense against God. But should we use cannon to squash a mosquito? Though Shah Tahmasp is a heretic, the greatest prize we might present before God is the capture of the Green Apple.'

The Green Apple was a reference to Rome. Every Sultan, before he ascended the throne of the Osmanlis, was traditionally asked at the ceremony, 'Can you bite from the Green Apple?' Suleiman's achievements might already rank alongside those of his father and grandfather, but in Ibrahim's opinion he had the opportunity to stand in heaven next to Mohammed himself if he could take away the infidel's greatest prize.

Can you capture Rome?

Ibrahim paused to let his words take effect. 'Surely our greatest threat must be the man who calls himself the Holy Roman Emperor. At this moment he is troubled on his southern flank by Francis. The Christian heretic Luther is inciting rebellion against the Pope, and his own nobles are warring among themselves. The time to strike is when your enemy is weakest and there is no doubt he is deeply divided at this moment. Vienna's walls are ready to fall and, when they do, the whole of Christendom will tremble at our approach.'

He turned to the Aga of the Janissaries. 'What say you, Achmed?'

'As long as our kettle is full, my Lord, we will eat. My men are restless for another chance to blood their swords.'

Ibrahim turned to his other generals. They all spoke for Vienna.

'We can deal with the heretic Tahmasp at our leisure,' one of them said. 'But Frederick is ripe for the plucking right now. Let us lay Vienna at the feet of our Sultan!'

Ibrahim smiled. It had been six years since their last great victory. No empire could stand still. The ghazis of old knew that as soon as a man climbed down from the saddle his muscles started to get soft. Perhaps on the long road to Vienna Suleiman would find himself again, and forget this harem girl.

'It is decided then,' Ibrahim said. 'This summer the Sultan goes to Vienna.'

CHAPTER 33

Julia removed her bath chemise and slipped into the water. Two other girls - one an Egyptian with a skin the color of hazelnuts, the other alabaster-white with startling blue-black hair - sat on the edge of the bath and examined each other for hair.

The girls saw her watching them and the Egyptian gave her a mocking smile.

Julia got as far away from them as she could. She heard someone move towards her through the water and found herself staring into the blackest eyes she had ever seen.

'You are the *Gaiour*,' the woman said.

She nodded. *Gaiour*, she had learned, meant Christian.

'Don't be frightened. It must all be strange to you now, but you'll get used to it.'

It was the first kindness she had found since she had come here.

'What is your name?' the girl asked her.

'Julia.'

'I am Sirhane. I am from Syria. My father gave me to the devshirme.'

'Devshirme?' So far she had understood most of what Sirhane had said, but this was a new word.

'It is like a tax, only instead of money you pay it with young men or women. The Sultan's men travel the empire taking the best boys and girls for royal service.'

'So you are a prisoner, too?'

'A woman is always a prisoner, isn't she? I'm glad my father gave me up, I prefer my life here. Do you know what I would be doing if I was not lying here in this bath? Picking cotton in a field.'

'Do all of these women belong to the Sultan? Are they all his wives?'

'He has only two *kadins,* and one of them is far away in Manisa. Only Hürrem is here, but she is not young anymore, so that leaves hope for the rest of us.'

'I do not understand. Speak slower, please.'

Sirhane smiled and edged closer. To Julia's horror she put her arm around her. 'You will need someone to take care of you in here. You don't know anything, do you *Gaiour*?'

The Kislar Aghasi leaned against the lattice window that overlooked the steam room, closed his eyes and groaned aloud. What devil in all the hells could have devised a torture more exquisite, he thought, than to take from a man all means of loving a woman but leave him still the desire, as fierce as it was when he was complete? If he were not so weak, he would have ended his life long ago.

Light poured in brilliant tendrils from the small, rounded windows high in the cupola and one picked out Julia's milky silhouette. His fingers curled around the iron lattice as if he would wrench it from the wall.

Suleiman held the flickering candle above the crib. The infant looked so scrawny and so pale. He reached out a tentative finger, stroked the suckling's back and recoiled from the unnatural lump on his spine.

Hürrem watched him. She was surprised; he had never paid any attention to their other children when they were in the cradle. Yet every day he came to stare at the grotesque and deformed son she had delivered him.

'He eats?' he asked her.

'His wet nurse says he has little appetite. She does not think he will survive.'

'You must pick him up every day and croon to him. It will help.'

'Yes, my Lord.'

Suleiman handed the wet nurse a gold coin. 'Look after him well,' he said and led Hürrem from the chamber.

When they were alone, she helped him remove his turban and brought his head to her breast. He was unusually quiet.

'My Lord is troubled?'

'Matters of the Divan, *russelana*.'

'You wish to talk?'

Suleiman sighed. ' Every spring my Agas press me for another campaign. This year they wish to go north again, against Vienna.'

'And what does Ibrahim say?'

'Ibrahim clamors louder than any of them.'

'He longs for glory. For Islam, of course. Yet I wonder if it wise.'

'Tell me your thoughts.'

'It is a long road to Vienna. Too far to take an army, even the army of the Osmanlis.'

'The real prize is not Vienna, it is Frederick.'

'He will not come out to fight you. Why should he risk everything in a battle against the greatest army in the world? He will quit Vienna when you approach, and when you withdraw for the winter he will take the city back again, and everything will be as it was before. You will have nothing to show for it but a long trek through the mud.'

'I cannot hold the leash on the Janissaries for another year.'

'The Persians have been raiding the eastern borders and murdering our mufti. Send them to Asia if they want a fight so badly. We could serve God by preserving his judges from the heretics.'

'The Persians are just flies nipping at the rump of a lion. We only have to swat our tail to remove them.'

'Perhaps God wishes us to be his swatter of flies even though there is little glory in it.'

Suleiman laughed. 'What I would not give to put you into a debate with Ibrahim!'

Hürrem stroked his forehead, felt the tiny pulse of blood at his temple. This is all I have, she thought. When this pulsing stops, life will stop for me as well, unless I can find a way to rid myself of the curse of Mustapha.

'Do not go, my Lord. Let Ibrahim shoulder the burden and chase Frederick through the Austrian mud if that is what he wants.'

'Impossible. If the army goes into battle I must be at their head. It is the way, the Janissaries expect it.'

'Do you love war so much?'

'You know I do not.'

'Then why?'

'It is my duty, Hürrem.'

'Duty has made the king of kings a slave.'

Suleiman sat up, his face flushed. 'Enough.'

Hürrem bit her lip, contrite. She cursed her own impetuosity. A wasp was trapped with honey, not vinegar. 'My Lord, I did not mean to offend you.'

'The place of the Sultan of the Osmanlis is with his army. They cannot go to war without him. It is our way.'

She cradled his face in both her hands. 'Forgive me. It is just that I love you so much, my Lord. The summers are endless without you. And I am so afraid that one winter you will not return.'

Suleiman stroked her face; then his fingers traced the line of her throat to her breast. 'Enough of politics,' he whispered. 'We will talk of this another time.'

She put her arms around his neck and smiled.

CHAPTER 34

The Venetian community of Stamboul lived in a quarter of the city known as Pera. It overlooked the Horn, looking directly south towards the city and the Topkapi palace.

Ludovici had built his own palazzo there. It had a marble terrace that faced onto the water. From there he could watch his ships sail past Seraglio Point into the Marmara Sea, loaded down with Turkish grain, Nubian slaves, Arab horses and Oriental spices.

He had done well for himself coming here. As a *bastardo*, the Venetian court was closed to him, so while his peers had donned senators' black robes, he had come to Pera and established himself as a merchant. Feeling no special allegiance to either his hosts or his former countrymen, he had quickly learned to manipulate both to his advantage.

His father had helped him. Senator Gambetto appreciated Ludovici's decision not to remain in Venice where his presence among the merchant community might have caused embarrassment. It was Gambetto's money that founded the business. But it was Ludovici's acumen that expanded it.

At first it was difficult. The great merchant families of Venice and Genoa dominated the spice and pepper trades. He could not compete. He soon realized that greater profits were to be made from smuggling wheat.

Suleiman had placed restrictions on the export of Turkish grain, with a rigorous price-fixing policy. But a resourceful man could find a way around such regulations, if he had daring and a little imagination.

Ludovici chartered a fleet of Greek merchantmen to pick up wheat from Black Sea ports, and ferry it to the Venetian colonies at Crete and Corfu. Avoiding the Turkish harbor patrols in the Bosporus was simply a matter of knowing which palm to grease in the Topkapi.

The Venetian community in Pera regarded his success with a benign contempt. He did not really care much for them either. He could do business without their patronage. He had gradually become more Turkish than Italian and had even acquired a small harem.

Tonight he sipped his Cyprian wine, well satisfied with the course his life had taken. He had money, he had a fine residence on the water, and he had women. He was content.

One of his servants, Hyacinth, appeared on the terrace. Many eunuchs took the names of flowers. 'There is someone to see you, Excellency. '

'Who is this fellow? Did he give a name?'

Hyacinth shook his head.

Someone newly arrived from Venice, Ludovici supposed. 'Show him in,' he sighed.

He was expecting a nobleman's son fresh off the boat from *La Serenissima*, or an old acquaintance from university, not the fearsome apparition that presented itself on the terrace. The man was wearing a vast silk *ferijde* – a long-sleeved cloak with a hood that made the wearer all but invisible - and soft leather boots.

Ludovici stood up, alarmed. 'Who are you?'

The man pulled back his hood. It was difficult to tell if he was Moor or Nubian as his face had been so disfigured by the scar that slanted across his nose and right eye. He wore a great sugarloaf turban, in the courtly style.

'Hello Ludovici,' he said.

'Do we know each other?' Ludovici wondered how this man might presume to address him by his Christian name when he was clearly a slave.

'I am the Kislar Aghasi of the Sultan Suleiman.'

The Kislar Aghasi! The Custodian of Felicity, Captain of the Sultan's Girls, and one of the most powerful figures in the Harem. Ludovici was too surprised to speak.

'Don't you recognize me?'

'We have never met.'

'I know I have changed greatly since we last saw each other but think about the warning you gave to a young friend of yours outside the *Chiesa Santa Maria dei Miracoli*. Looking back on it now, it was very good advice.'

Ludovici slumped down onto the divan, speechless.

'*Corpo di Dio*,' he murmured. 'Abbas!'

Suleiman reined in his Arab and watched the goshawk floating on the air currents, waiting for its prey. Ibrahim walked his stallion through the long grass to flush out their quarry. The hawk twitched its wings and hovered.

Then its golden eye found its target. Seeing it scamper from Ibrahim's approach far below, it tucked in its wings and swooped, its razor-sharp claws crushing the hare's back. The hare kicked and then was still. The bird settled on its kill. There was a scarlet blossoming on the fur clutched between its talons.

The pages ran forward to collect their game.

When it was done Ibrahim returned, the hawk held aloft on his gloved left arm. It was hooded in its leather rufter. Behind him the pages carried their day's trophies; a dozen hares and rabbits, strung from poles, and a brace of pheasant.

She was an efficient killer this bird. It had always struck Suleiman as curious that the female hawks were better at this deadly game than the males. All the falconers preferred them for hunting.

'A fine day's sport, my Lord.'

'The sun is low, Ibrahim. We should return to the *caïque*.'

'It has been a long time since we hunted together like this.'

'There should be many days like today this summer.'

Ibrahim's smile fell away. 'I should like that also, but the Divan has recommended another campaign against Frederick's brother, Charles.'

'You did not agree to this? Two years ago, on your advice, we besieged Vienna. Frederick did not come then, and nor did his brother. What good is it to go after them again? They will not fight us.'

'We were stopped then by the unseasonal rains. If we had been able to bring our cannons to the walls, we could have taken the city.'

'If we take Vienna, how do we keep it? If one goes through a door one must be sure one can get out again.'

'But we must go back to the Lands of War. It is our duty to Islam.'

'Ah yes. I forgot what a good Muslim you are, Ibrahim.'

Ibrahim bridled at this jibe. 'We cannot leave the Janissaries inside the city for another summer. They grow impatient for battle.'

Suleiman shrugged. 'Perhaps we should look in another direction.'

'Shah Tahmasp?'

'He is trying to infect our eastern borders with his Shi'a heresy, and he is still killing our muftis. He should be taught a lesson.'

'He is nothing. We could crush him at our leisure.'

'Then let us do so.'

'Charles is the Holy Roman Emperor, the avowed enemy of our faith. It is our duty to Islam to confront him.'

'What is Vienna?' Suleiman said. 'A distant outpost that Frederick will recapture as soon as we withdraw. The destruction of Tahmasp should be our first aim.'

The goshawk on Ibrahim's wrist grew restless. She batted her wings and Ibrahim cooed softly to gentle her. 'If we take Vienna, Rome is at our mercy. If we threaten the Green Apple, we will flush out the Emperor.'

Suleiman fell silent. The scent of the pines lay heavy on the dusk. 'Then I shall let you decide, Ibrahim, for you will be leading them.'

'As your *seraskier*, of course. But you will be with me.'

'No, not this time. There is too much to do in Stamboul. I have decided to remain here.'

Ibrahim was too stunned to speak.

'You cannot do this,' he said, finally.

'Cannot?' Suleiman stopped and Ibrahim reined in beside him. 'Who says to me 'cannot'? Am I not the Sultan? Am I not King of Kings? The King of Kings shall do as he pleases.'

'Your place is at the head of your armies.'

'My place is wherever I choose to be.'

'The soldiers take their inspiration from you.'

'They are my soldiers, and they will do as I command.'

'No Sultan has ever…'

'A Sultan makes tradition, he is not slave to it.'

'You will lose their faith!'

Suleiman leaned across the saddle so that his face was inches from his Vizier's. 'Ibrahim, you are my friend and my counselor. Please. I have had enough of war, take this burden from me. They just want blood, so let them wallow in it. It does not matter whose blood it is, not to them. But I do not wish for another campaign.'

'You must reconsider!'

'No, I have made up my mind.' He put his hand on his friend's shoulder. 'I trust you like I would trust no other. You are my brother. Do this for me.'

Even his voice has changed, Ludovici thought. The color of his skin, too. It was paler, and sickly looking. He was obese, and the light had gone out of his eyes. It was Abbas and yet it was not.

'I should have listened to you, Ludovici. You tried to warn me.'

'I never knew what had happened to you. No one did. I assumed you were dead.'

'What happened to my father?'

'Gonzaga brought false charges of drunkenness against him after you disappeared. The *Consiglio* dismissed him as Captain-General. He is soldiering in Naples now.' Ludovici felt sick to his stomach. Better you had died, old friend. 'I always hoped that perhaps you had just run away.'

'As a wiser man would have done.'

'I should have tried harder to dissuade you.'

'There is nothing you could have done.'

'It was Gonzaga, wasn't it?'

Abbas took a long time to answer. 'Do you remember giving me a letter? Lucia handed it to you, she told you it was from Julia. But it wasn't, it was from Gonzaga. It was how he baited the trap. The letter said I should meet her on the Ponte Antico. Instead I made my rendezvous with four gentlemen he had hired on the waterfront. I fought them but there were too many of them.

'They razored me Ludovici, right there in the bilge in the galleot. They thought I would die, I think. But somehow, I survived and every day since I have wished I had not. I was sold in the slave market here in Stamboul and taken into the royal Harem to be trained as a page. The old Kislar Aghasi took a liking to me. He could see I had more learning than the rest of the poor wretches they sold on the blocks. I could speak

Turkish and Arabi, as well as Italian. He groomed me for better things, if you can call it that.

'So I learned my tasks well and when the old Kislar Aghasi died, the Sultan's mother appointed me in his place.' He stopped and hung his head. 'They have made a ghost of me, Ludovici. A ghost who walks, talks, and breathes, but a ghost just the same.'

Ludovici did not know what to say. 'Why did you not come here before?' he managed finally.

'We both know the answer to that.'

'Then why did you come today?'

'Because I need your help.'

'Name it. Anything.'

'Do not be so quick to offer favors to a stranger.'

'You are no stranger to me. Abbas, I will never deny you.'

'You don't understand,' Abbas said. 'How could you?' His fingers strayed to his cheek where the dagger had sliced his face.

'Tell me what you want me to do.'

'She is here, in Stamboul.'

'Who?' Ludovici shook his head in astonishment. 'Not her? Not Julia Gonzaga?' Impossible, he thought. If she had come to Pera, he would have heard of it.

'She is a slave in the Harem,' Abbas said. 'She was captured by corsairs. I have seen her, Ludovici, I have seen her with my own eyes. She is as lovely as ever.'

'Does she know?'

'No, she does not recognize me. I do not want her to know. I just want to get her out of there.'

'But Abbas, how? No woman ever escapes from the Topkapi.'

'There must be a way. I only know I cannot do it alone.'

'It is an enormous risk. Why would you do it? You have sacrificed too much for her already.'

'Look at me, Ludovici. What do I have to lose? You told me once that women were just women, that I was a fool to moon over just one. Perhaps you were right. But if I was a fool then, I am a bigger fool now, do you not think so?'

'I don't know what to think any more.'

'You owe me nothing. This could be dangerous for you. If we do this and we are found out, you won't be able to hide from the Sultan's wrath here in Pera.'

'You were my friend, Abbas. I count you as one still. Just tell me what you want me to do.'

Abbas seemed overcome. 'Thank you. As yet I don't know how this might be done. I will think of something. When I have a plan, I shall get a message to you.'

'I would rather you come here yourself. I have missed you old friend.'

'I cannot come again. If I am seen here, and something goes wrong, it will put you in danger. And it is painful for me, this. I am sure you understand.'

He left. Ludovici stayed where he was, staring at the black water.

CHAPTER 35

Ibrahim stood on the balcony in the gathering darkness, staring at the rose-pink walls of the Aya Sofia and the cupolas of the Palace beyond. The distinctive tower rose above the Divan. Güzül thought he looked tired. His shoulders were hunched.

'I trust Rose of Spring is well,' he said.

'She is well in her body, my Lord. But she is sick at heart.'

'I am her servant, as always.'

Güzül hesitated. 'She has heard whispers, my Lord. About the lady Hürrem.'

'Go on.'

'She believes that she conspires against her son.'

A cool wind accompanied the dusk, guttering the candles. 'She has proof?'

'Not yet, my Lord.'

'Then there is nothing to be done.'

'My Lord, she thinks that even you may be in danger.'

'Suleiman loves me with his life. He is the only one who might threaten me.'

'But Hürrem has his ear.'

Ibrahim shook his head. 'Tell Rose of Spring I will do all in my power to help her, for I am as troubled by what is happening in the Old Palace as she is. But I will never do anything to harm the Lord of Life. Even if it costs me my life.'

'I shall convey your words exactly.'

'One other thing,' Ibrahim said. 'I am curious. Have you ever seen this Hürrem?'

'I have seen her many times.'

'Describe her to me.'

'She is pretty, or pretty enough. But no beauty. Yet she has a certain way with her. She is brighter and more spirited than most of the girls in there.'

'What color is her hair?'

'Gold and red. Like wheat and rust.'

'And her face?'

'Her eyes are her best feature. Green and bright. Piercing, one might say, my Lord.'

She could see Ibrahim trying to form a picture of his adversary in his mind. But it would be like trying to imagine the dome on the mosque by describing each tile separately. Hürrem was much more than the sum of her parts. You only had to be in the same room as her to know that.

He turned away and leaned on the balustrade, his forehead creased into deep furrows. 'Thank you, Güzül, you may go.'

Güzül touched her forehead to the carpets and hurried away.

After she had gone, Ibrahim watched the night come. He had risen so far; his own barge, eight guards of honor, and a salary twice that of the previous Vizier. He had more power than any slave could dream of; he ruled the Divan, now he even commanded the army. And yet he had been more content when he had been in Suleiman's shadow.

Was he really in danger, he wondered. Suleiman was his friend, surely, as well as his Sultan. He would never betray him for a woman. He might give up the Divan and give up the Army, but he would never give up his best friend.

CHAPTER 36

Suleiman and Ibrahim dined off green and blue Chinese porcelain, a gift from a long-forgotten ambassador. There was honey from Wallachia; butter brought in ox hides across the Black Sea from Moldavia; sherbets iced with snow and carried in felt sacks from Mount Olympus; and dates and plums from Egypt.

'I think we have eaten our way around the Empire,' Ibrahim said.

The dishes were collected by the servants, and Suleiman asked Ibrahim to play for him on the viol.

'My Lord, I hope you will pardon me, but tonight I am too troubled to play.'

'What ails you, old friend? Do you still wish for me to charge the walls of Vienna with you and help fill the moats with our soldiers?'

'It is a matter of greater import, my Lord.'

Suleiman sighed. Ibrahim had changed, always needing to talk about matters of state. He seldom laughed any more. 'Well, tell me, then. Is it to do with the Divan?'

Ibrahim shook his head. 'It is a matter I should normally tremble to mention in your presence.'

'You have mated with your horse?' Suleiman had spent the day with Hürrem and was in high spirits.

Ibrahim did not even smile. 'There is talk among the Janissaries and in the bazaars.'

'You want to fill my head with rumors?'

'Rumors are like the pestilence. A few hundred cases a year are to be expected. When there is an epidemic, one should take notice.'

'An epidemic?'

'The talk fills the bazaars and even spreads along the cloisters of the Palace itself.'

'What are these rumors?'

'They concern the lady Hürrem.'

Suleiman stiffened. 'What happens in the Harem is of no concern to anyone but me.'

'I only repeat what I hear.'

'What is it that you hear?'

'They say she is a witch. They say she has enchanted you and clouded your reason, and that is why you will not take the army to Vienna or attend the Divan.'

Suleiman leaped to his feet, stamping the room in search of someone to strike down. 'A witch? Find me who says it. Bring these wretches to me and I will have every one of their heads hung on the gate!'

Ibrahim remained resolutely cross-legged while Suleiman paced the floor behind him. 'The reports are brought to me by my spies. They do not bring me names.'

Suleiman snatched up the nearest object within reach - Ibrahim's viol - and smashed it against the wall. Ibrahim stared at the mess of splinters and strings lying about the carpet.

'Leave me,' Suleiman said.

'My Lord?'

'Leave. And never presume to mention her to me again.'

Ibrahim turned pale and fled.

CHAPTER 37

They had given her to the Mistress of the Robes. She had proven her skill with fine needlework and the *kiaya* had professed herself pleased with her.

Abbas found her hunched over a satin robe that was intended for young Bayezid, working a pattern into the cloth with gold thread. When she saw him, she dropped to her knees to make the proper *salaam*, but he stopped her.

'Just sit down,' he said.

Julia did as she was told.

'Look at me,' he said.

She raised her eyes and he saw her wince. The scar was not pretty, close up. It would have been better if the dagger had taken his eye out completely than leave just the white of it staring at the world. He waited for some dawning of recognition but there was none. He knew his body had bloated, even his voice had changed. The scar on his face had obliterated all trace of how he used to look.

'Do you know who I am?'

'You are the Kislar Aghasi.'

'Yes, the Kislar Aghasi. Your well-being is my responsibility from this moment on. Do you understand?'

Julia nodded.

'Do they look after you in here?'

'The *kiaya* is very kind to me.'

Abbas nodded; better than the last one by all accounts, and more fortunate, too. Hürrem had ordered that the foot that had once been raised against her be lopped off, and then had the *kiaya* exiled to Diyarbakir.

'You have learned much of the language already. That is very good,' he said.

'I have an ear for it.'

You are clever then, as well as beautiful. But I always knew that, he thought. What would you do, I wonder, if I spoke to you in Italian, told you that you are still the most beautiful woman in the world, even though I spend all my days surrounded by beauty? 'You are a *Gaiour*?' he said.

'I am.'

'It will not help you here. No one will force you to give up your religion, but you will rise faster if you learn your Koran. They have given you a holy book?'

'I cannot read it. It is in Arabic.'

'Then you must learn to read Arabic.' He lowered his voice and said more gently. 'You must forget about Venice. That world is gone now. You can never go back there.'

'I know.'

He searched for something else to say. He understood how it must feel to be a ghost, to see the physical world and be unable to join it. 'If you need for anything, let me know,' he said.

She bowed her head. He hesitated. Once I waited a week just for the moment when you drew back the veil that covered your face, he thought. Now I see you naked every day. I watch you from my lattice window high above the baths and I still burn for you.

'My Lord?'

He realized he had groaned aloud.

'Is something wrong?'

'It is nothing.' He turned and left the room. He made his way slowly through the darkened cloisters of the Harem to the tiny cell that was now his home. He sat down on his cot, hung his head, and wept.

The Marmara Sea looked like rose-tinted glass, the gray humps of islands breaking the surface like spouting whales. Below the Valide's window, new fruit had bowed the branches of a cherry tree. She still loved the view from here, though she had seen it every day for most of her life.

Behind her three small boys in skullcaps and baggy trousers scuffed the marble floor with their soft slipper boots, impatient for the audience to be over.

'So have you all been working hard at your studies?'

Bayezid looked at his older brothers and waited for them to speak, but Mehmet looked surly, and Selim just sniffed and stared at the floor. So Bayezid took up the responsibility. 'Yes, Grandmother,' he said. 'I can recite the Surah Fatiha and the Surah Al Kahf by heart.'

'That is good.' She studied them in turn; Bayezid and Mehmet were both fine looking boys, she thought. They had their father's long limbs and lean good looks. But she was not sure about Selim.

'Do you learn your Koran, Selim?'

'Our tutor beats us,' he mumbled.

'Why does he beat you? Are you lazy?'

'I don't know.'

The Valide picked up a silver salver from the table in front of her, arranged with *rahat lokum*. Her pastry cooks prepared it fresh for her every day using the pulp from white grapes mixed with semolina, flour, rosewater, apricot kernels and wild honey. She took a piece and popped it into her mouth.

'Would you like a piece, children?'

The boys came forward eagerly. Bayezid and Mehmet, she noticed, took one piece each. Selim took three.

She wondered what the future held in store for them. None of them would ever grow to be as fine a prince as Mustapha, but if anything should happen to him, one of them might one day be the next Sultan.

'Tell me what you have learned at the Enderun.'

'I can throw a javelin from the back of a horse!' Mehmet shouted.

'But you are only seven years old.'

'And hit a target with an arrow.'

'What about your Koran?'

Mehmet lowered his eyes. He nudged Bayezid, who dutifully recited ten verses from the first sura of the holy book. The Valide clapped her hands in appreciation.

'And what about you, Selim? What have you learned?'

He shrugged and said nothing.

'Come now, Selim. Recite a verse from the first sura for me. You must be able to do that by now.'

Selim mumbled a few words and then stopped.

'Well, go on.'

'I can't remember any more, grandmother.'

She frowned. 'No wonder your tutor beats you,' she said, 'at your age Mustapha could recite the first chapter without taking breath.' She sighed. 'I am tired. I need to rest for a while. Come and kiss your grandmother, boys, then be off with you.'

Bayezid and Mehmet dutifully kissed her. Selim was the last. His lips barely brushed her cheek, and as he left she saw him scoop up three more pieces of *rahat lokum* and hide them in his robe. She almost called him back to reprimand him. What was the point, she thought. He was greedy and stupid and God had seen fit to make him that way.

She went back to the window and watched them playing in the courtyard below. Selim showed his two little brothers the sweetmeats he had stolen and when they threw out their hands for a share he laughed and stuffed all the pieces in his own mouth at once.

Praise God there was Mustapha.

There is a currency in the Hall of Kings, Rüstem thought, and it is not jewels or gold. Money of itself has no value; the only thing that can be traded for power and for life is information.

Which was why the Kislar Aghasi was worth more to him than his own substantial weight in gold.

Abbas visited the Treasury once a week and was always ushered into Rüstem's office without being made to wait, as most others were. While he drank his chai and ate his halwa, he gave him all the news from the Harem.

'How is the Valide?' Rüstem asked him.

'She sickens. The physician sends her potions, but they do little good.'

'May God protect her,' Rüstem said.

'She is in all our prayers,' the Kislar Aghasi said with little enthusiasm.

Rüstem tapped a finger on the arm of his chair. 'I have a crumb for you to peck at.'

'What is it you wish to know?'

'It is not something I wish to know this time. It is something I wish to tell. You have heard the war drum beating?'

'The blacksmiths in Galata keep their foundries burning day and night. Do we make war on Frederick again?'

'We shall. But this time the campaign will go a little differently.'

'How so?'

'This time the Grand Vizier will lead the army.'

'Of course. He is the *seraskier*.'

'Indeed, no one could replace him in that role, thanks be to God. But this time the Sultan will remain behind, here in the palace.'

Abbas cocked his head. 'This is true?'

'Another crumb for you. It was the Lady Hürrem who persuaded him to abandon his duties in the Lands of War. She means to sing and dance for him, while his Janissaries bleed and die for Islam at the Gates of Vienna.'

'He must be mad!'

'Something very like it.' Rüstem yawned. 'Soon the whole palace will know of it, Kislar Aghasi. But the Sultan Valide will remember you kindly if you tell her of it first.'

CHAPTER 38

There was a kiosk at the end of the long peninsula of Seraglio Point. Its silver-plated dome was decorated in arabesque, with flower motifs in blue and white. The woodwork was inlaid with ivory, and it had windows of stained glass in patterns of claret and pavonine. There were fretted gold sofas, and even a conical bronze fireplace against one wall.

It was Suleiman's refuge from the furnace heat of the palace on these warm nights. The evening breeze from the Marmara Sea whispered among the plane trees.

Hürrem lay with him on the long divan, listening to his musicians playing unseen somewhere in the garden.

She made a shadow play on the wall of the kiosk with her fingers. 'Look,' she whispered.

'A camel!' Suleiman laughed.

'Now this.'

'A sheep?'

'It's a horse!'

'It looks like a sheep.'

'Did you ever see a sheep with such a long nose?'

'I have never seen such a long nose anywhere. Perhaps Ibrahim,' he laughed.

Hürrem frowned in concentration as she manipulated her fingers. Suleiman watched her, smiling indulgently.

'What about this?'

'A cat?'

'The Kislar Aghasi's cat. See? It has nothing between its legs!'

This time he did not laugh. 'You should not make such jokes.'

'Why not?'

'You offend against Islam.'

'Oh, you're such a hypocrite.'

Suleiman was lost for reply. How dare she say such a thing to him? Did she have no sense of her place? But it was what he loved most about her. He would let no one else speak so freely in front of him.

In the garden, tortoises with lighted candles on their backs ambled through the roses and carnations. A full moon threw long shadows through the trees. He closed his eyes to the music. It is so peaceful here, I could stay here forever.

But then the breeze died away, and in the stillness he heard the ringing of hammers as the smithies at the Galata arsenal set to forging new cannon for the coming campaign in Austria. He was overcome with guilt.

God forgive me, he thought. I should be going with them.

The Valide was growing old. Her once black hair was dyed with henna to disguise the gray, and all her kohl and powders could not hide the pouches under her eyes and her chin. Her limbs trembled even when she was sitting down.

Abbas placed his forehead to the silk carpet in reverence before addressing her. 'Crown of Veiled Heads.'

'Kislar Aghasi.' The Valide sounded breathless even though she had been resting. 'You wished to speak with me?'

'Indeed, on a matter which, I hope, will be of no import.'

'Come now, I know you better than that.'

'It is just a rumor that has come to me through my various sources.'

The Valide sat forward, suddenly young and viperous again. 'Concerning who?'

'Concerning the Lady Hürrem.'

'That one!'

'It is, as I say, only a rumor.'

'I have more faith in your rumors than the official pronouncements from the Divan. Tell me what you have heard.'

'Soon the army will march against Frederick in Vienna.'

'The whole world knows that.'

'What they do not know is that the Lord of Life will not lead his army to the Lands of War this year.'

'What?'

'I am told the Lady Hürrem has persuaded the Sultan to remain behind with her.'

For a moment Abbas thought she was going to choke.

'This cannot be true.'

'I only repeat what I hear. I felt it was my duty to report it.'

The Valide slapped the palm of her right hand against the divan. 'She presumes too much! I warned him about her. First Gülbehar and now this little Russian. My son has not the faintest idea about women.'

'I hope I have not caused you offence,' Abbas said.

'On the contrary, you have done me a great service.' She picked up a cushion from beside her and threw it across the room with surprising force. The effort exhausted her. Her two maidservants rushed forward but she waved them away. She took some time to get her breath back. Then she said in a quiet voice, 'What happened to your face?'

'Madam?'

'Your face. I have known you these few years now and I have never asked you before. I shall be gone soon, and I should like to know before I die.'

Abbas contained himself with difficulty. Until now the Valide had treated him respectfully. Why would she shame him now, just to serve curiosity? 'I received the injury in a street fight.'

'What were you fighting over?'

'My manhood.'

She was silent, and he realized that she had seen him for the first time as a man and not as a slave.

'I wish my son would fight as hard for his own manhood,' she said. 'Thank you for your service. I will remember it. Leave us. I have business to attend to.'

CHAPTER 39

Suleiman was dismayed when he saw his mother. She seemed to grow a little older, a little frailer, each time he came. He had always thought her indestructible.

But age had not dulled her mind - or her tongue. 'Have you seen your sons?' she said the moment he had settled beside her on the divan.

'I have seen them. Çehangir is still sickly, but the others prosper. Their tutor seems pleased.'

'What do you think of Selim?'

Suleiman shrugged his shoulders.

'I do not like him,' she said. 'He is a sullen child. I do not trust him. He eats too many sweetmeats for a boy, and he carps like a woman.'

'You have nothing better to say about him?'

'In all other ways he is a model prince.'

'Well his tutors have said nothing to me.'

'Of course not. They do not dare. It is his mother's fault; she spends no time with him. It is a wonder that Bayezid and Mehmet are as pleasant as they are.'

'Ah! Do I detect some kind words?'

'You may laugh, Suleiman, but it is fortunate for you that you have a son like Mustapha.' She tapped her finger on the back of the divan. 'You will leave soon?'

'The army rides within the week,' he said, avoiding her eyes.

'To look for Frederick?'

'Frederick is just a small man of Vienna. His brother Charles is the great prize, but we do not expect to flush him out. He will skulk in his castle in Germany.'

'The preparations go well?'

'Ibrahim plans for thirty cannon to pummel the walls, provided the mud does not lay claim to them again on the journey north.'

She placed her hand on top of his. 'You will truly be the greatest of all the Sultans, my son. The gypsies prophesied as much when you were born.'

'I have done my best,' Suleiman said. He answered the pressure of her hand and was shocked by how frail she was. He could feel every bone and every knuckle. There was no flesh on her at all.

'I have heard whispers,' she said.

'From where?'

'A little bird flies through my window every morning and sings to me. This morning he told me that the army is going to leave here without a general.'

Suleiman tried to pull his hand away, but the withered leaf of a hand was suddenly as strong and powerful as a man's. 'Of course they will have a general, the very best.'

'The best general in Stamboul is sitting here with me. So the whispers are not true? You are going to lead your army into the Lands of War, as every Osmanli Sultan before you has done?'

'They do not need me. Ibrahim is my *seraskier* and he will manage the campaign just as well as if I am there.'

The Valide fell silent.

It was Suleiman who broke. 'Who told you about this?'

She ignored his question in favor of her own. 'How long did you think you could keep this from me?'

'I decide matters of war, no one else.'

'There are some things that no Sultan, however great, may decide on his own. You are first of all a Muslim and you must surrender to the will of God.'

'I have had enough of these wars. It is pointless.'

'It is your duty to the Osmanlis and to God!'

'Which I have always, until now, put above all else.'

'Until now.' The Valide's eyes were suddenly hard. 'It's her, isn't it? She has done this to you.'

Suleiman turned away. Someone has put her up to this, he thought. Whoever it was knew she was the only woman or man in the world who might speak like this to him.

'In the bazaar they say she has bewitched you.'

'So I am told. If any man repeats this calumny, I will cut out his tongue and make him eat it.'

'Then half the city would be mute.'

'I make sure there is bread on their tables and meat enough for every one of them. They live under my protection, safe from the ravages of the armies that enslave half of Europe. I have given them Rhodes, Belgrade and Hungary. What more do they want from me?'

'They want their Sultan.'

'They have him.'

'They do not.' They have a Greek slave to listen to their complaints in the Divan, and a Greek slave to lead their armies against the infidel. The only one who has the Sultan's ear and the Sultan's love is a harem girl.'

'There are other things to life than the petty quarreling in the Divan and the endless, pointless spilling of blood. I will tell you how I shall become the greatest of all Osmanli sultans; by giving the people laws, mosques, and schools. I want to build, not to destroy endlessly and for no good reason.'

'You have abdicated your power to Ibrahim and your manhood to a woman.' She took his hand again and held it tight. 'Listen to me. I do not want you to be unhappy. Only you know what has passed between you and this woman. But you must remember also that you are a ghazi. Do not grow too fond of the ways of the Harem. Its purpose was to make us strong and to create sons; it was not intended for indolence and indulgence.'

'It is the law that makes us strong, the *kanun* and the *sheria*.'

'Suleiman, my whole life has been for you and for your Sultanate. I have been so proud of you. You are not cruel the way your father was cruel, and that has been your strength. But it has also been your weakness. I have seen it with Gülbehar and with Ibrahim, and now with Hürrem. You must learn to stand alone.'

'If I am alone, then what is left for me?'

'The world is what is left for you, the empire of the Osmanlis. Your grandfather's grandfather rode out of the desert so that you might live in a palace. Stamboul is not yours by right. It is a sacred trust, and you must earn it by your devotion to God and to your people.'

'But I have earned it, not only for my lifetime but every generation to follow. I did it by giving this city and this empire written laws. I send my armies against Christendom because that is what I am required to do, what does it matter if I ride with them or I do not, as long as they go? After all this, there must be something left for Suleiman.'

'Everything is left for you. The palaces, the finest harem in the world. Your ancestors lived in tents and ate from the saddle of a horse. You have grown soft.'

Suleiman gritted his teeth. 'They do not need me in Vienna.'

'Of course they do. Now take back your authority before it is taken from you.'

'You mean Ibrahim? He would never turn against me.'

'What about Hürrem?'

'She is a woman!'

Too late he realized what he had said. His mother smiled bitterly. 'Yes, a woman. Do you think I cannot read her better than you? You have allowed her to twist you to her own ends. I know this game.'

'What do you want from me?'

'I want you to be Sultan. You have hundreds of women to choose from here in this palace, why do you choose just one?'

'Because I can be myself when I am with her. Not the Sultan, not the Possessor of Men's Necks, just myself.'

'And what does she want? For you to be yourself or for her to be the next Valide?'

'Insha'Allah! Please, give me peace. I love her, let it be.'

'I cannot let it be, Suleiman. If you wanted peace, then you should have been born a fisherman or a goatherd. You are a Sultan. Your harem, your Cyprian wine and your pages do not come without a price. They are there to serve the Sultan, and in return the Sultan must serve the Osmanlis.'

'It is time I made my own decisions.'

'Then let them be yours and not Hürrem's. Do your duty, Suleiman. It is what you were born for.'

CHAPTER 40

The great bazaar had been built in the time of Mehmet the Conqueror, Suleiman's great-grandfather. The riches of the empire were crammed into its tiny shops along the warren of stone alleyways; gold and silver, brocades and silk, crimson rugs from Damascus and peacock blue silk carpets from Baghdad.

Outside the gates, hawkers grilled corn cobs on charcoal braziers, fanning the flames with turkey wings and brushing ineffectually at the small, persistent black flies. Other hawkers sold tripe flavored with garlic, or warm almond cream sprinkled with cinnamon.

Suleiman marveled at it all, lost in his own city.

But even among the tumult he recognized the order his ancestors had imposed. Everyone knew their place. The Turks wore white turbans, the Greeks' turbans were blue, though their boots were black. The Jews had yellow turbans, as did the Armenians, but their boots were a startling crimson.

A spice merchant had been nailed to the door of his shop by his ears. The sign that hung around his neck said that he had been convicted of giving false measures. One of the crowd spat in his face, and Suleiman did the same. He felt no pity for him. It was the law and it had been made to protect the people.

His mother was right, he thought, he had lived in palaces too long and he had grown soft. The smell of filth and offal made him gag and the gabble of voices hurt his ears. These were the people that came with their petitions to the Divan. He had seen them every day, begging his clemency, his judgment or his justice. But he had never seen for himself how they lived in their own world.

Night fell quickly. A crescent moon rose above the roofs of the bazaars.

It was the first time that he had not been surrounded by a bodyguard. Yet he felt safe. What enemy would recognize him in these rags? Besides the Janissaries patrolled the streets every night, and any act of violence was treated as an insult against Islam itself and punished accordingly.

He knew the Valide would have apoplexy if she knew what he had done. But what better way was there to discover if this so-called gossip was true?

He strolled through the vaulted bazaar, lit by a thousand lamps. He lingered at the stall of a spice merchant, staring at the sacks of sesame seeds, saffron and liquorice root as if deliberating over a purchase. The vendor was engaged in a heated debate with one of his customers. Suleiman heard the name Hürrem and stopped to listen.

'He does not even look at another woman,' the merchant said. He hawked abundantly onto the cobbles next to his stall, narrowly missing Suleiman's sleeve.

'That is not possible,' a customer said. By his white turban, Suleiman knew he was a Turk like himself. 'He has a harem with three hundred of the most beautiful women in the Empire.'

'Unless he is bewitched!' the Greek shouted and hawked again.

'You talk out of your ass so often your tongue should be at the other end.'

'They say she is not a woman; she is a foul spirit from the forests of Wallachia.'

'Well, there you are. Everyone knows she is not from Wallachia, she is Russian. And if she is an evil spirit, like you say, why is Suleiman the greatest Sultan we have ever had? Look at what he has conquered -

Belgrade, Rhodes, Buda-Pesth. Why two summers ago he was at the gates of Vienna itself.'

The merchant threw his hands in the air. 'Exactly! Why did we not take Vienna when it was there for the asking? The witch made it rain right through summer, so our cannons were bogged and useless.' He hawked and spat on the floor of his shop with such violence that even the Turk took a step back.

'They say he cannot even pass his water without receiving her permission first.'

'If anyone has him in their power it is Ibrahim!'

'Ibrahim is a great soldier. We need a strong Vizier, especially when our Sultan has moon eyes for one of his slave girls. When a Sultan ignores his concubines it means some other woman has him by the thick member and she will lead him around like a donkey with reins.' He turned to Suleiman. 'What is it you want?'

What I want is to take a sword and lop off your ugly head, Suleiman thought. Then I would hang it on the gates of the Sublime Porte and invite it to spit one more time. Instead he said. 'I want nothing here.'

But the insults echoed in his mind as he made his way through the bazaar. What Ibrahim and his mother had told him was true. His people were turning against him over her.

He would have to show them he was master of his own house, he thought. He would do his duty and then perhaps they would give him some peace.

CHAPTER 41

There was a protocol for choosing a girl.

As he rode in, the Kislar Aghasi was waiting to greet him, in a long-sleeved ceremonial pelisse and white sugarloaf turban. A hundred girls, pearls and jewels glittering in the sun, waited in the shaded area of the courtyard.

Any other man would tremble with anticipation, Suleiman thought.

The great iron door creaked shut behind him and he dismounted. The girls' eyes were hooded, none would dare look at him directly, yet he felt each one of them imploring him. A whole lifetime could turn on such moments, or so they believed.

The eunuch touched his forehead to the cobblestones. 'Great Lord.'

'You are to be complimented,' Suleiman told him, keeping to the protocols. 'They are all quite exquisite.'

'Thank you, my Lord.'

The Kislar Aghasi moved into step behind him. Suleiman breathed in the scent, jasmine and orange. Silks and satins shimmered, cheeks blushed pink. He bowed and greeted each one of the girls, and as he did so, the eunuch whispered their names.

They are all so beautiful that even beauty itself becomes meaningless, he thought.

'What is your name?' he said to one of the girls.

She murmured a response, but her voice was so soft he did not hear what she said. He turned to the Kislar Aghasi.

His Chief Eunuch hesitated. 'Julia,' he said at last.

Suleiman looked at the girl a second time. Perfection indeed. He took a green handkerchief from the sleeve of his robe and draped it over her shoulder. It was one Hürrem had embroidered for him herself. He knew she would be watching, unseen, and he hoped he had made his point.

Hürrem turned from the window. Her fingers closed around the nearest object, a silver candlestick that stood on a low table by the divan. She flung it across the room, splintering the blue Iznik tiles on the wall. Muomi ducked away, out of range.

Hürrem stood stock still, the muscles working in her jaw. 'I have to stop this,' she said.

'He is the Sultan,' Muomi said. 'How can you stop him?'

'Who is she?'

'I don't know her name, she's new. She came here from Algiers. She was taken from a Venetian galley that was captured by corsairs.'

'I want you to make me one of your potions.'

'If you kill her, he will only choose another,' Muomi said. 'If she dies like Mustapha's servants, it will make them suspicious.'

'What then? There has to be a way.'

Muomi looked at her, her eyes glittering. 'Can you sup with him tonight?'

'Suleiman will not come to me now. He will not know how to face me.'

'Then you have to find a way to persuade him.'

'What is your plan?'

'There is a mixture. It can take away a man's passion. If he does not have her, then he cannot fall in love with her.'

Hürrem allowed herself a smile. 'Can you get what you need?'

'There is an apothecary in the bazaar who has what is necessary.'

'Then I will send one of the pages to get it for you straight away.'

After it was arranged, Hürrem settled herself back on the divan. As Muomi was leaving she called her back. 'Fetch the Kislar Aghasi for me,' she said. 'Tell him I need to talk with him urgently.'

Hürrem had a handkerchief bunched in her fist, and she twisted it around and around her fingers. Her eyes were red and swollen. Abbas almost felt sorry for her.

He executed a *temennah*, his right hand touching his heart, his lips and forehead. 'My Lady, you wished to see me.'

'What am I to do, Abbas?'

'My lady?'

'The Lord of Life has chosen to spend the night with another of his concubines.'

'It is his right, my Lady. You should not upset yourself. You are still second *kadin*. Nothing can change that.'

Hürrem dabbed at her eyes. 'What is her name?'

Abbas hesitated, suddenly alarmed. 'As I said, my Lady, you should not upset yourself over trifles.'

'I did not ask your advice, Abbas, I asked you her name.'

He paused. But if he did not tell her, she could as easily find out from someone else. 'Her name is Julia. A very dull girl. Italian. She can barely speak a word of our language and though she has a pretty face she is spectacularly stupid. You can rest easy.'

Hürrem tossed the handkerchief onto the floor. When she spoke, her voice was icy. 'Do not presume to tell me when I may rest and when I may not. In fact, Kislar Aghasi, remember your place and do not advise me on anything. All you need to do is answer my questions.'

'Yes, My Lady.'

'I wish to see the Lord of Life. Could he perhaps sup with me tonight?'

'I do not think that is possible.'

'Again, I did not ask your opinion!' Her voice was like a whip crack 'You presume too much, Kislar Aghasi.'

'A thousand apologies.'

'I wish to see the Lord of Life. Tonight. I did not ask if it were possible. I only meant that you should arrange it for me. He is still in the palace, visiting with the Valide, is that not correct?'

'As you say, My Lady.'

'Then arrange for him to dine with me tonight. Tell him I am contrite for those things I have said to him most recently and I wish to make my peace.'

'But it may not be possible.'

She sighed. 'Do you remember what happened to the last Mistress of the Robes? Perhaps you were not part of our Harem family then.'

His mouth was suddenly very dry. 'I am not sure I follow you.'

She stood up and walked up to him. 'The woman had the temerity to cross me. She kicked me when I was one of her charges in the sewing room. Do you know what I did to her?'

Abbas nodded.

'They say you could hear her screams in Üsküdar. Yet she did not offend me nearly as much as you offend me now.'

'I meant no offence.'

'I do not want your contrition, or your excuses. I suggest you remember what happened to the *kiaya* and ensure the Lord of Life sups with me tonight.'

'She wants to dine with me, tonight?'

174

'She believes you are punishing her. She wishes to show her contrition.'

'No, Kislar Aghasi, it is impossible.'

'Perhaps if you explained this to her yourself. She has become accustomed to your exclusive use of her, I am afraid. To ignore her now would be only to accentuate her suffering.'

'You explain it to her. You seem to have a better understanding of her moods.'

Abbas could smell his own sweat. I cannot push him too hard or he will have the guards throw me out and put me to the *bastinado*. But if I do not leave here with his agreement to this excruciating arrangement, I shall forfeit a foot to Hürrem's temper.

'My Lord, a few kind words from you at supper would perhaps save you a lengthy speech at breakfast.'

Suleiman sighed. 'Do you really think so, Kislar Aghasi?'

'I am convinced of it.'

Suleiman drummed his fingers on the back of the divan. 'Very well. But tell her I cannot stay long.'

CHAPTER 42

Abbas did not recognize her.

They had dressed her in a rose-pink silk chemise, with blue harem pantaloons and a headdress glittering with emeralds, diamonds and opals. Her face was concealed beneath a bead-fringed yashmak. All that was visible was her eyes, and they had been completely ringed with kohl. Her wrists and ankles were dripping with gold.

As she rose to her feet, a *gediçli* held out a heavy cloak for her to put on. The broad hood and long sleeves hid her completely, so that not even a finger was visible.

Abbas escorted her down the winding passageways to a narrow door. A coach waited for her in the cobblestone courtyard. They climbed in and set off in silence. The last time you were alone with me like this, he thought, I pulled back your veil and asked you to run away to Spain with me.

'Are you frightened?' he said.

'Yes.'

'Don't be. The Sultan means you no harm.'

'What must I do?' she murmured, and he heard the panic in her voice.

'Have you ever lain with a man?'

'No.'

'But you were on your way to meet your husband when you were captured.'

'He never touched me the whole time we were married.'

Abbas closed his eyes. *Corpo di Dio!* A virgin and the eunuch who loves her. Surely, this must be one of the Devil's jokes. 'You must simply do everything he wants,' he said.

'Why did he choose me?'

'Because you are the most beautiful woman in the world,' he heard himself say. The carriage drove through the gates of the Sublime Porte.

Suleiman lay on the bed in a simple white robe. The room was fragrant with frankincense burning in the brass censers that hung from the ceiling.

Abbas touched his head to the carpet three times. 'Great Lord.'

'Kislar Aghasi,' Suleiman said, as was the protocol, 'I have mislaid my handkerchief. Do you know who has it?'

'Yes, my Lord. I will have her bring it to you.'

Suleiman sensed there was something amiss with his Chief Black Eunuch. He was sweating heavily though it was not a hot night, and his eyes had a vacant look. He had seen that look sometimes after a battle, in men who had endured too much. He hoped the Kislar Aghasi was not sickening. He would be a hard man to replace.

Abbas went to the door and ushered in a small, cloaked figure. He removed her *ferijde* and whispered something to her. He pushed her forward.

The door shut softly, and they were alone.

The girl took out the handkerchief he had placed across her shoulder that morning, fell to her knees and crawled on all fours to the bed. She lifted the coverlet, raised it to her forehead and to her lips, and crept up the bed, exactly as the Mistress of the Baths had told her to do.

Suleiman closed his eyes and wished with all his soul that he were with Hürrem.

CHAPTER 43

Suleiman rose naked from the bed, glared at the girl who lay curled on her side beside him. The candlelight cast long shadows over the hills and valleys of her body. She was perfect. Her skin was like satin to the touch, a paradise for the eyes, yet he had been unable to raise any passion for her.

He threw on a silk robe and went to the open window.

Fear, anger and confusion tumbled over inside him. This had never happened to him before, and it could never be allowed to happen again.

The girl watched him from the bed, doe-eyed. She had not uttered a word the whole time. He was sure she would find her voice later, in the Harem, when the other girls asked her what it was like to lie with the Sultan.

He could not let her gossip that the Lord of Life and the Possessor of Men's Necks had been unable to bull her.

He went to the door and threw it open. 'Kislar Aghasi!' The guards outside the door looked startled. 'Where is the Chief Black Eunuch?' he shouted at them. One of them ran off to find him.

Suleiman slammed the door and went back to the bed. He picked up the girl's clothes and flung them at her. 'Get dressed.'

A few moments later Abbas appeared in the doorway, his eyes wide with fright. Suleiman pointed to Julia. 'Get her out of here.'

'She does not please you, my Lord?'

'Get her out.' He grabbed Julia's arm, dragged her across the carpets and pushed her through the door. 'She is to speak to no one when she leaves here. If she is alive tomorrow morning your head will be feeding the crows on the Gate of Felicity.'

Abbas stumbled through the cloisters of the Topkapi, a sealed parchment clutched in his hand. He found the Aga of the Messengers, whispered his instructions and slipped something into his palm as added incentive to complete the task quickly.

It was midnight, which meant that by the time Ludovici received the missive he would have less than five hours to make his preparations.

Abbas was not sure that it would be enough time.

CHAPTER 44

Just before dawn, Abbas led Julia through the gate at the Bosporus wall, and down the stone steps to the water's edge. Something made him look up. He saw a flock of white birds, that the Stamboulis called the Damned Souls, wheeling in the sky above them. The strange thing about these birds was that they never made any sound; even the beat of their wings was silent. No one ever saw them roosting or feeding. They just seemed to drift over the black waters, night and day. It was said they were the souls of the harem girls who had been drowned in the waters below.

This was the traditional way for a Sultan to be rid of his brother's wives when he assumed the throne, or to punish a girl who had somehow found a way to get pregnant by one of the white eunuchs.

Julia had been crying all night, and the kohl had run down her cheeks. Her braids hung in a tangle round her face. She wore only her chemise and harem pants. She hugged her arms to her chest, shivering in the cold of the morning. He could see the gooseflesh on her.

'Where are we going?' she asked him.

He had two of the executioner's men with him. They were there to report that the job had been done correctly. He intended to give them no cause for doubts. 'You will not be returning to the Old Palace,' he said. He took her arm and pulled her down the bank to the waiting *caïque*.

'What's happening?'

'Just do as you are told.'

He slung her into the boat. She looked down then and saw the sack. He took a silver cord from the folds of his pelisse and tied her hands behind her.

'Please, no,' she whispered.

He put her feet in the sack and tugged it up around her hips. There was a pile of smooth stones in the stern and he placed them in the bottom of the sack. Then he lifted it over her head and knotted it with rope.

He threw her on her back. 'Don't struggle until you hit the water,' he whispered to her in Italian. 'It will be all right. Trust me.'

Then he stepped out of the *caïque* and joined the two men in the other boat.

They rowed past the promontory of Seraglio Point and the somber sea walls of the palace, towing the *caïque* to a spot midway between the peninsula and the Asian side. It was still dark, but he knew dawn could not be far off. They had to do this now. Mist swirled over the water.

The two men decked their oars and they drifted with the current. Abbas looked at the tiny boat drifting behind them, lit by the lantern at the stern. The shapeless bundle was still struggling in the sack so that the boat rocked gently in the water.

'Take the lines,' Abbas said. The two men picked up the ropes that trailed over the stern and twisted them, so that the *caïque* began to roll and then take water. Finally it listed to starboard and capsized. There was a splash as the sack tumbled into the water; a rash of bubbles floated on the surface and then was gone.

One of the men cut the ropes. Abbas sat in the bow and let them row him back to Seraglio Point. They heard a splash behind them and looked over their shoulders.

'A fishing boat,' Abbas said.

'They're out early in the fog.'

'You want to go back?' he said casually and held his breath.

Then they heard nets going into the water. It was too misty anyway, he could see them thinking, they risked a collision. And besides, what was the point? They shrugged and kept rowing.

The morning kept her secrets.

Julia gasped as she hit the water, the stones in the sack dragging her feet first to the bottom. She knew it was pointless to struggle. She had resolved to suck in the water straight away to get it over with quickly. But as soon as she felt the *caïque* capsize, she had instinctively breathed in a lungful of air and held it.

She had worked her hands free on the boat. She tore at the sack, and the ropes that the Kislar Aghasi had supposedly tied around it fell away. He had given her a chance.

She struck out blindly, that one last breath of air carrying her up, her chest pumping. As she broke the surface, she tried to take another breath, but her mouth and nose was full of water and she started to choke. She paddled furiously at the water, felt herself going under. She was too exhausted to keep herself afloat any longer and everything went black.

CHAPTER 45

Ludovici and his men glided silently through the water. In the letter he had received, Abbas had told him to look for his riding lights. There would be no other boats trying to navigate Seraglio Point at that time of night.

The mist that clung to the water had made their job both easier and harder; harder to find Abbas, but easier to remain unseen. He and his two crew dared not even breathe. Every small sound carried over the flat water as if they were in a church.

There was just the creak of timber and rope.

Then he saw it, a light blinking close by, and the helmsman pulled the tiller hard over. They could not come too close, not until they knew she was in the water.

He heard a splash, and for a moment the *caïque* was silhouetted against the mist. He heard Abbas' voice.

She came up, right beside them, gasping. His helmsman reacted straight away, lighting a lantern and shouting a command to his fellow, who hoisted the nets over the other side, making as much noise as he could to disguise Julia's groans. Ludovici reached out a hand and dragged her to the side. The other sailor let go of the nets and helped him pull her aboard.

She lay there, blue and still. He thought she was dead, but the sailor shook her roughly and she coughed and vomited water onto the deck.

A fresh breeze ruffled the Bosporus. The cries of the muezzin called the faithful to prayer. The tower of the Divan rose through the mist, sunlight glinting off the spire.

Did I do enough, Abbas wondered. What if the knot he had tied in the sack was too tight; what if she did not get out in time; what if Ludovici did not find her in the fog?

A messenger arrived and placed a scroll in his hands. He broke the seal and read it through quickly. The goods had arrived safely and were in good order. Ludovici would put them in the warehouse until he was ready to ship them on.

Abbas swayed on his feet. He put a hand out to steady himself against the sill.

'Is the Kislar Aghasi unwell?' one of the pages asked him.

Abbas shook his head. 'I am quite well,' he said. He took the letter to the fire and burned it.

CHAPTER 46

The Valide had been propped up on pillows, while her servants hovered. She appeared lost in the bedclothes. There was no artifice to support her now. Her *gediçli* had applied kohl to her eyes and put a little cap on her head, but it had only made her look older. The Kislar Aghasi looked terrified.

'Is she dying?' Hürrem asked him.

'She cannot move or speak. She sleeps most of the time. Who knows when Almighty God will call her home.'

'She cannot speak?'

He shook his head.

'She has no way of communicating with us?'

'We put a pen in her hand, but she is unable to use it. Her fingers twitch a little, that is all.'

'Can she understand what is said to her?'

'It appears so. But she slips in and out of this world.'

Hürrem smiled. 'You see how quickly the world turns, Kislar Aghasi. Just the other night you were ready to defy me.'

'I should never defy you.'

'No, you never should. It would be unwise. Your life is in my hands now. Where is the Sultan?'

'He has just left. He is greatly distressed.'

Hürrem went to the bed. 'You are sure she cannot speak?'

'She has had an apoplexy. It has taken away all her powers.'

Hürrem looked at the Valide. 'I want everyone out of the room,' she said.

'My lady?'

He thinks I am going to put a pillow over her head, she thought. Look at her. I don't need to.

'The law says that the Kislar Aghasi and her *gediçli* should stay with her at all times,' he said.

'Do as I say.'

He rapped out a short command to the maidservants and ushered them out of the door.

'You too, Kislar Aghasi.'

He hesitated for just a moment, then left.

Hürrem bent over the bed. Saliva had pooled on the Valide's cheek and against the pillow, but her eyes were bright.

'I envy you,' Hürrem said. 'You are about to do what I long to do. You are going to get out of this place.'

The old woman's breath was foul. Already, she smelled of the grave.

'One day I will be the Valide and I will rule here. Do you think that is what I truly want? What I want is to go home, to ride the steppe with my brothers and sisters, to feel the wind in my hair again. Instead I will be your son's prisoner for the rest of my life.'

She moved closer so that her lips were close to the old woman's ear.

'Hürrem. The Laughing One. That is what you all call me. But my laughter is a disguise. I don't want any of you to see how much I hate you, all of you. Most of all, your son.'

There was froth on the old woman's lips and she writhed as if she was trying to get off the bed.

'Kislar Aghasi!' Hürrem shouted.

The Chief Black Eunuch rushed in. He must have been standing with his ear to the door. Never mind, she thought, he could not have heard her and would not dare say a word even if he had.

'I think she is having another seizure,' she said.

He called for her *gediçli* and they tried to hold her down.

'You should send a message to the Lord of Life,' Hürrem said. 'I do not think she is long for this world.'

She gave the Valide's hand a last, reassuring squeeze and left the room.

CHAPTER 47

Julia stood at the water's edge staring at the lights flickering on in the palace. She was wrapped in a fur cloak, but she could not stop shivering.

'How could I not have recognized him?' she said.

'He is much changed by what happened to him.'

'Tell me.'

Ludovici nodded. 'Abbas got a letter. Lucia gave it to me and said it came from you. I had no cause to think otherwise. So in one respect I was the instrument of his downfall. He was lured to the Ponte Antico and taken to a ship in the harbor…' His voice trailed off.

'How did he not die after what they did to him?'

'He was lucky, or unlucky, depending on how you see it. I have been told by those who know about these things that most men die when they are razored. I cannot imagine what he has been through.'

'So my father did this to him?'

'It seems so.'

'And yet he still loves me?'

'It was hardly your fault.'

'How long have you known about this?'

'He came to visit me for the first time soon after you appeared in the Harem. He wanted me to help him get you out, but at the time he had no way of doing it. When I received his message I had only a few hours to act. Because of my business I was able to procure a small *caramusali* straight away. You are very fortunate.'

'I need to see him.'

'That will not be possible.'

'Is there nothing we can do? After all he has done, all he has been through on my account. I cannot bear what I have brought him to. I owe him at least one word of thanks.'

'It will be enough for him to know you are safe.'

She turned away from the window. 'So what now?'

'Now?'

'I was shut up first in my father's house, then the Sultan's house. I suppose now I shall be shut away in your house.'

'You are not my prisoner. But you cannot leave here. It is too dangerous. No one can know you're alive.'

'And I cannot go back to Venice. That would be to trade one prison for another. But I don't wish to sound ungrateful. It was very brave of you also, to do what you did.'

'I did it for him. I have to tell you, I tried many times in Venice to dissuade him from pursuing you.'

'And you were right. It would have saved him so much pain. What will they do to him when they find out he has tricked the Sultan?'

'Let's hope they never do,' Ludovici said.

Suleiman knelt distraught beside his mother's bed, and when she finally died, he threw back his head and howled.

Ibrahim thought he heard him, as he paced the terrace of his palace near the Hippodrome. Gülbehar thought she heard it, too.

Abbas stopped to listen, but there was only silence. Just an owl, he thought. He stood at the window of his tiny cell and looked across the Golden Horn to Galata. A shadow passed across the moon.

He took out the small velvet pouch that had arrived that afternoon from the Venetian quarter, sent by messenger. He opened the drawstring and emptied the contents into his palm.

Two gold ducats. For the first time since he arrived at the Harem he smiled.

PART 5

The Passage of Dust

CHAPTER 48

Stamboul, 1535

There are lines around Mother's eyes, Selim thought. I never noticed them before. He kissed her hand and Bayezid did the same. Then they stood back, their arms crossed on their breasts as they had been taught to do in the Enderun.

Hürrem turned to Bayezid. 'You've grown into a fine boy,' she said. 'Your tutors say you are a wonderful horseman and athlete. Almost as good as Mehmet.'

'Thank you, Mother.'

'But you must try harder at your studies. Even when you leave the Enderun, you should never stop learning. If you ever become Sultan, you will need more than your skill with a javelin and a horse.'

'I will do my best.'

'And you Selim.' Hürrem sighed. 'Your tutors say they have to pound every lesson into your head with their knuckles.'

'I do my best, Mother,' he said, testing the defense his brother had used.

'Your best is not good enough.'

Not good enough, Selim thought. I will never be good enough, no matter what I do. Your hopes reside elsewhere. And it is no secret that Mehmet is my father's favorite. He loves him even more than Mustapha, if such a thing were possible.

My only hope is that when one of them takes the throne, they dismiss me as a threat, as casually as my mother does. As for Bayezid, my one prayer is that the fool falls off his horse playing *çerit*.

Selim often wondered who it was he hated the most; himself for not being more like Mehmet and Bayezid; or his mother, for constantly reminding him of it.

'Leave me now, both of you' Hürrem said. 'I have urgent business to attend to. And Selim,' she added, as the boys turned for the door. She seemed to be struggling for the right words. 'Try to be more like your brothers.'

Güzül was ushered through the apartment by a *gediçli*. She was impressed, despite herself.

Hürrem had her own garden with a marble fountain. There was an aviary with nightingales and canaries. It was whispered in the bazaar that Suleiman had even presented her with a bed brought from far away in China. Made from ivory, and inlaid with sandalwood and large pieces of pink coral, it was supposed to have cost more than ninety thousand *scudi*, a fortune.

Hürrem lay on a slab of marble, warmed from below by the palace boilers, while Muomi massaged her neck and shoulders. Her private steam room, Güzül noted, was as large as the Grand Vizier's audience chamber.

She executed a ceremonial *salaam* on the floor and waited on her knees for Hürrem to acknowledge her presence.

Hürrem blinked open one eye.

'Would my lady honor me so as to examine my poor wares?' Güzül said.

Hürrem assented with a slight movement of her head. Güzül bent down, unknotted a green silk handkerchief and spread an assortment of ribbons and lace trinkets on the floor, repositioning each one so that it might catch the morning sun to better advantage.

She looks like a cat, Güzül thought, sleek and self-satisfied. You would not think she has had five babies. By all accounts she had a wet nurse for all of them and lost all attachment to them after the cord was cut.

'How is your mistress?' Hürrem said.

Güzül felt the blood drain from her face. 'Mistress, my Lady?'

'Rose of Spring.'

Güzül rearranged the baubles on the carpet in front of her. 'My Lady is mistaken.'

'My Lady is never mistaken,' Hürrem said, and yawned. 'You are Gülbehar's creature. You come to Stamboul to bring messages for her and spy on the Harem. These trinkets you sell are a ruse, are they not?'

Güzül said nothing.

'Don't be afraid. All I want is a little information from you. It is the only merchandise that you have that I am interested in.'

Hürrem scratched the calf of one leg with the big toe of the other. She stretched, and Güzül watched the muscles of her buttocks tense. While Gülbehar grows fat and lazy on sweetmeats in Manisa, she thought, Hürrem starves herself and drinks from some secret fountain of eternal youth.

'For instance, can you tell me who is Lady Gülbehar's friend in the court?' Hürrem said.

Güzül bit her lip and tried to think how best to answer.

'Tonight I shall be whispering to the Sultan in the quiet moments,' Hürrem said, 'and if I choose, I could tell him that a certain gypsy peddler came to the Harem and called his favorite *kadin* a witch, to her face, and insulted her beyond all imagining. You will deny it, of course. But who will he believe?'

Güzül put out a hand to steady herself.

'The choice is yours. Think about it for a moment.'

Hürrem closed her eyes and surrendered to Muomi's attentions. Güzül felt faint.

'Ibrahim,' she said.

'Ah, the Chief Vizier,' Hürrem said. 'He has never liked me, has he?'

Güzül felt the room spin.

'You have a choice to make. You cannot serve two mistresses while you have only one life.'

'My Lady, I will do anything you ask.'

'Don't make the bargain before you know what it is. Come now, you have been a hawker all your life, you should know better than that.'

'What would you have me do?'

'Over there, on the table, is a small bottle. I want you to put it in your robe and take it with you to Manisa. Then you must find a way to pour the contents into Mustapha's drink. Do you think you could do that, Güzül?'

Güzül stared at her.

'A difficult choice, I understand. But before you rise from your knees, you will have made it. You or Mustapha. If it is you, I shall make sure your death is not swift. Three days hanging by a steel hook in the executioner's yard should not be overlong. What is it to be?'

'It is impossible, my Lady, the food tasters sample everything.'

'Ah, I see. You are stalling now, thinking that the Chief Vizier will save you. It is true that he also has the Sultan's ear. But there are other parts of the Sultan that are more desirable to possess, and whoever holds them leaves him open to the greater persuasion. Who would you gamble on, in your situation?'

'My Lady, please, anything else.'

'There is nothing else. What do you decide?'

She means it, Güzül thought. A string of saliva spilled from her lips onto the carpet. She gathered up her jewels with trembling fingers, then she went to the marble table and picked up the pretty blue and white Iznik bottle.

Hürrem closed her eyes and groaned softly as Muomi worked her strong hands into her neck muscles. I will have to settle with the Grand Vizier very soon, she thought. He wants Suleiman for his own.

But I will share him with no one.

CHAPTER 49

Topkapi Palace

Ibrahim did not look forward to the Sultan's company as he had done in the past. Suleiman had become a tiresome companion, talking endlessly about the plans he had made with his architect for a new mosque or school. He seemed to have forgotten that the lifeblood of the Empire was conquest. When a warrior no longer saddled his horse and sharpened his sword every day, he became the prey and not the hunter.

After the servants had removed the plates, Ibrahim filled two crystal goblets with Cyprian wine and began to read aloud from the history of Alexander. He recited his march into Persia, the defeat of the Persian king Darius at Gaugamela, and the capture of Babylon.

He paused in his reading and looked at Suleiman. 'We must go to Persia too, my Lord.'

Suleiman nodded. They had received news in the Divan that the Persian heretic, Shah Tahmasp, had recaptured Baghdad and killed its entire garrison. As Defender of the Faith, Suleiman could not ignore such a challenge to his authority.

'Why so solemn, my Lord?'

Suleiman sighed. 'We subdue one attack, there is the sound of trumpets from another wall.'

'It is the way of it for emperors and kings.'

'There is more to Empire than fighting wars. I want to leave behind something that will endure after the dust of armies has vanished over the horizon.'

'There will always be armies, my Lord.'

'I am tired of it Ibrahim.'

'A man cannot be Sultan and live his life without conflict. He must subdue others or be subdued himself. It can never be otherwise.'

'Then we are no better than dogs in the street.'

'It was Mohammed who urged us to jihad, my Lord. When we go to the Lands of War, we take the green banner of Islam with us.'

'What do you care for Islam?'

'It is my religion, my Lord.'

'Religion is a convenience for you. You use it to justify doing what you love, which is going to war.'

'I am a faithful soldier of Islam.'

'You are a loyal Vizier. The rest is between you and God.'

'You mock me, my Lord.'

'You mock all of us.'

'In a few days we will ride together under the green banner once more. Once we ride out, you will forget all your misgivings.'

'No, Ibrahim, I did not wish to go to Vienna and I was persuaded. For five months I watched our cannon sinking deeper into the mud under the walls of a fortress whose name even now I cannot remember. The Roman Emperor did not come to fight us. I warned you that would happen. This time I will not be swayed. You will take my army to Persia alone.'

Ibrahim stared at the floor in stony silence.

'Is this such a terrible burden? Other men would weep at such an honor.'

'A Sultan's place is with his army.'

'Do not lecture me on my duty. Can you crush this Shah Tahmasp and rid me of this meddlesome mosquito?'

'Of course.'

'Then do it, Ibrahim. From now on, you will be my guardian at the gate.'

'I wish that you would not do this.'

'I have decided.'

Ibrahim hesitated. It was time he was told; he had delayed the news long enough. 'My Lord there is a matter you should know of. A messenger came to me today from Manisa. There has been an attempt on the life of your son, Mustapha.'

'Who brought you this news?'

'It was one of Gülbehar's couriers, my Lord. There is no mistake.'

'What happened?'

'He sat down to dine with the captain of his personal bodyguard. The man drank some wine and fell ill abruptly. He died in agony an hour later.'

'And Mustapha?'

'He had not yet drunk from his cup, praise be to God.'

'Who did this?'

'There is no proof,' Ibrahim said. He would not meet his eyes.

'You are wrong,' Suleiman said.

'My Lord, who else could it be?'

'It is another of Gülbehar's fantasies. Bring me one shred of proof.'

'My Lord, you have given her too much power. How often do I see you now? We no longer hunt, we eat together like this but rarely. She occupies your every waking minute.'

'So you are jealous.'

'I am afraid of what is happening to you. The Suleiman I knew would never let his army go to battle without him.'

'The Suleiman you knew was a boy who simply did what his father did. I am my own man now.'

'She wants Mustapha dead so one of her sons will be Sultan.'

'You have been my friend a long time, Ibrahim. Do not make me hate you.'

'My Lord…'

'Go now. I must think.'

Ibrahim rose to his feet and left the room. Damn her, he thought. Perhaps he had already left it too late.

Mohammed Dürgün knew they called Rüstem 'The Man Who Never Smiled.' Yet there was nothing remarkable, or even fearsome, about him. He looked like any one of the hundred clerks in the palace.

He did not look up as Mohammed entered. He studied the document on the table in front of him.

'You are Muhammed Dürgün?'

'I am.'

'You are from Kirklareli?'

'Yes.'

'Your father served at Mohacs and the siege of Buda-Pesth?'

'He did.' Mohammed hesitated, unsure what to do or say next. He hoped that what he had heard about this man was true or he had come all this way for nothing. 'He died last year, from the pestilence.'

'If so, then by law the lands return to the Sultan.' Rüstem took a quill from the desk and made a notation on the parchment in front of him.

'Is there not some way?'

Rüstem paused. 'Your father's name was Hakim Dürgün?'

'Yes.'

'According to my records you are mistaken. He is not dead. It says here he still lives. He should return to the Treasury the equivalent of one asper per sheep per year. Do you have any questions?'

'No.'

'Then that is all.'

He left, stunned at the simplicity of what had just happened. The law forbade any fiefdom passing from father to son. Yet in the few moments he had been with the Treasurer, he had become the owner of his father's land - for a price. His father had been taxed at one asper per two head of sheep. Rüstem had doubled the tax in order to mislay the record of his father's death. Mohammed knew where that extra money would go.

But it was worth it.

CHAPTER 50

A path of colored pebbles wound through the dappled shadows under the black cypress trees, to a six-sided kiosk behind the Gate of Felicity. It dominated the selamlik gardens. The marble dazzled the eyes. Even the windows were fretted with gold. The floor had been so carefully crafted by Suleiman's artisans that it appeared to be made from a single piece of rock crystal.

A garland of honeysuckle dripped from the trellis. It was a paradise within a paradise.

Suleiman rested on a gold-embroidered mattress watching the sunlight dance from the damascened lantern hanging from the cupola above him. Hürrem lay beside him. She reached up and stroked his cheek. 'You are frowning again. What are you thinking about?'

'Someone tried to poison Mustapha.'

She stared at him. 'Is he all right?'

'Praise be to God, yes.'

'Who did this?'

'We don't know.' He watched her, looking for some clue. 'Ibrahim accuses you.'

'Of course he does. He thinks all the evil in the world comes through me.'

'He says you want one of your own sons to be Sultan.'

'That is obviously so. Do you think Gülbehar will be gentle with me if Mustapha takes the throne? She'll have me tied in a sack and thrown in the Horn and all my boys throttled. I pray every day that God will be merciful and spare us, though I don't see how. But Ibrahim flatters me if he thinks that I have the power, here in your Harem, to harm a great prince five days ride from Stamboul.'

Suleiman said nothing.

Hürrem snatched the ceremonial dagger from the scabbard at his waist. She held it against the soft flesh of her wrist. The rubies studded in the handle glittered in the afternoon sun.

'If you believe it of me, tell me to open my veins and I will do it. I would rather die than have you suspect me of such a crime.'

Suleiman wanted to believe her, with every fiber of his being.

Hürrem slashed downwards and blood spurted onto the pure white of her chemise and down her arm. He wrenched the dagger from her hand before she could cut herself again. 'Hürrem!'

He ripped the rich brocade from his own pelisse to bind the wound, and held her tight, shocked by what she had done. She would have bled to death if he had not stopped her. He wished Ibrahim had seen this.

By the flickering light of the candle, Muomi carefully unwound the brocade around Hürrem's wrist and examined the wound. Hürrem watched her, her face shining with sweat.

'Is it bad?'

'The blade missed the main vein, my lady. If you had cut there, it would have been much worse.' She redressed the wound with a poultice of herbs and put on a fresh linen bandage. 'You must have cut very carefully.'

CHAPTER 51

Hürrem smiled as the Kislar Aghasi was ushered into her presence. Abbas knew that could be a good thing or a bad thing. The fact that she was in a good mood might mean anything. He imagined she would be in excellent spirits the day she ordered his execution.

Since the death of Suleiman's mother, Hürrem had assumed the position of Valide. It meant that Abbas was now her chief servant, and subject to her caprices. It was an impossible position. She had the ear of the Sultan, while Abbas himself was captain of three hundred increasingly restive concubines, a harem in name only.

He executed three ceremonial *salaams* and allowed two pages to help him back to his feet.

Hürrem dismissed the pages with an almost imperceptible nod of the head. The fountains that bubbled from the golden spigots on the walls would disguise their conversation from eavesdroppers.

'You're trembling. Is something the matter?' she said. 'Are you wondering if the palace executioner is standing behind you with his cord.'

Abbas felt sweat erupt on his face. He did not dare turn around to look.

He stared at her.

'The information you gave me about Güzül was true. I compliment you.' She leaned forward, resting her chin on her hand. 'As the Lord of Life seems to have little use for his Harem, you are redundant, are you not?'

'As My Lady says.'

'Since the death of the Valide, may God bless her and keep her in Paradise, your main function has been to supervise my household. Our fortunes seem to be interwoven.'

'I am much blessed.'

'Yes, you are. But am I blessed with an obedient servant?'

'Veil of Crowned Heads, I live to serve you.'

'Perhaps.'

Abbas felt dread settle in his chest like cold lead.

'Do you remember Julia Gonzaga?'

Abbas swayed slightly on his feet. 'One of the harem girls?'

Hürrem smiled.

'I remember now. She did not please the Lord of Life. She sleeps in the Bosporus.'

'She sleeps in Pera, with the *Gaiour*s.'

He caught his breath. She knows, he thought. Dear God, I am at her mercy now.

'Why did you do it, Abbas?'

'She paid me,' he said.

'You defied the Sultan for money?'

'Wouldn't you?'

Hürrem clapped her hands, delighted at this answer. 'I like it so much better when you are honest with me and do not pretend to be servile. You are a snake pretending to be a sheep. I like it when you show your fangs.'

'Am I to die?'

'Do you want to die?'

'A part of me does.'

'I would not try to stop you. Do you know the punishment for disobeying the Sultan in this way? They hang you on a sharpened spike and leave you to turn black in the sun. I am still not sure where they insert the hook but they tell me the effect is not pleasant.'

'Please, my Lady.'

'I do not expect you to beg, Abbas. You know that is not my way.'

'What is it you want?'

'Your obedience. That is all. Your obedience until the day I die.'

Abbas stared at the rug at his feet. 'I am already a slave. It does not matter to me who the master is.'

'Then you will find me someone who can bring me Ibrahim's head?'

The very notion took his breath away. 'Ibrahim?'

'You think escaping the Sultan's hook is worth nothing? I will not trade your three days of mortal agony lightly.'

'I know someone,' he said.

CHAPTER 52

They lay on the divan, in the candlelight, the crescent moon framed by the open window.

'Stay here forever,' Hürrem whispered.

Suleiman smiled. 'And what would happen to the Osmanlis if I did?'

'The Empire would crumble into dust. I don't care.'

'Sometimes...' He left the sentence unfinished. 'There have never been enough hours.'

'Will there be another war drum and another campaign this year?'

'The Shah of Persia has become impudent. It is time to swat the mosquito.'

Hürrem frowned. 'Will you lead the army?'

'All the way to Persia for one troublesome insect? I shall leave that to Ibrahim.'

'What about the Roman Emperor, Charles?'

'The Pope has called for an alliance against us. He wants Naples and Venice to join with him to secure the Mediterranean. Ibrahim is delighted, of course. He would fight all year long if he could.'

'So we will fight two wars this summer?'

'No, it will be years before the Christians agree on who will lead their crusade and when, if at all. Ibrahim says the infidels cannot agree on which direction the sun comes up. They will have to wait for another time.'

'He is sure?'

'I trust his judgment.'

'My Lord, forgive my impudence but last night I had a dream. I dreamed you sued the King of Naples and the Doge of Venice for peace. You offered them a treaty and in return they would secure the ocean against Charles. You said that if they did not agree, it would give your admirals an excuse to raid their coasts all summer long. Do you think that a fine dream?'

Suleiman laughed. Such a calculating mind was wasted on a woman. 'One day I will make you my Grand Vizier,' he said.

'Perhaps you should. I will have Ibrahim as my scribe.'

'He would die first.' He grew serious. 'Do not mock him. Without Ibrahim we would not have this time together. He is the only one who can help me shoulder the burden.'

Hürrem stroked his beard, watched the play of thoughts on his face. She chewed on her bottom lip.

'What is it *russelana*?'

'It is nothing.'

'Tell me.'

She looked into his face. 'Do you not worry sometimes that he might abuse his power?'

'Ibrahim? Of course not.'

'There are such rumors in the Harem. Because I never know the truth, I worry for you.'

'What rumors?'

'I do not wish to speak against Ibrahim. I know he doesn't like me, but that is not the reason.'

'But what rumors?' he repeated.

'That he mocks Islam and consorts with *Gaiour*s. That when he meets with ambassadors, he calls himself Sultan.'

'Women's fantasies.'

'I'm sorry. I should not repeat the stories I hear. You're right it is almost always vicious nonsense.'

'Ibrahim is rash and boastful, but he would never betray me.'

She got to her feet. Her hair, hands and feet had been dyed with henna, and there were thick circles of kohl around her eyes.

Without warning she performed the three conventional *salaam*s expected from any concubine brought to his bed for the first time. Then she unfastened the pearl buttons of her silk *gömlek*. Her nipples had been painted with hashish. When he suckled her breasts, it would enhance the sublime moment later.

Bare to the waist she dropped to her knees and approached the divan like a common slave. His breath caught in his throat. Just when he thought he knew all her tricks she surprised him.

She kissed his feet in the traditional act of humility. He gasped as her fingers loosened his robes for her ministrations.

She is my harem, he thought. She is like a thousand women.

The city was a vast mosaic of color below the long fingers of the minarets and the gleaming cupolas of the mosques. Mehmet the Conqueror had long ago ordered that all houses should be painted for the religion of their inhabitants. There were clusters of grey houses where the Armenians lived, ghettoes of yellow for the Jews, while Turks themselves had red.

It made the house he was looking for easier to find. It was painted black, to signify a member of the Sultan's Court.

Abbas rarely ventured into the crowded alleys of Stamboul, and he assured his anonymity now with a black *ferijde*. Rüstem's house had a private courtyard at the back. A page ushered him inside. Rüstem was seated in a kiosk at the rear. A marble fountain murmured nearby.

Rüstem executed a brief *temennah* and indicated that Abbas should sit opposite him on the carpet. A page brought sherbets and laid a silver platter of pastries between them.

'I have come at the request of the lady Hürrem,' Abbas said. 'You have a common interest.'

'What might that be?' Rüstem said.

'Yourselves.'

'Explain yourself, Kislar Aghasi.'

'The Veil of Crowned heads has asked me to tell you about a man named Hakim Dürgün. It seems that last year he died of the pestilence. Yet he still farms his allotment at Edirne. A remarkably diligent ghost, do you not agree?'

'Remarkable. I will look into it.'

'You should also look into the case of another landlord in Rumelia, who died four years ago. About the time you became treasurer, in fact. Since then he has taxed the farmers on his land eight aspers per sheep. And yet you have done nothing about this avaricious spirit. Is it because you are afraid of the dead or because his ghost passes you two aspers per sheep for yourself?'

'How do you know so much about ghosts?'

'Wherever there is a black man, I have a pair of ears. And there is not a palace or a treasury in the entire kingdom that does not have a supposedly deaf mute who hears everything.'

Rüstem selected a pastry and chewed slowly. 'What is it you want? A cut of the business?'

Abbas admired his composure. 'Nothing so common. Please. I have not come here to line my own pockets. The Lady Hürrem sent me.'

'She does not need money.'

'Of course not.'

'A favor then?'

'More than a favor. We are talking about an alliance.'

Rüstem looked directly at Abbas. He had November eyes, Abbas thought. Not cold, just grey and empty.

'That would be an interesting arrangement,' Rüstem said. 'Does she realize that Ibrahim is my patron?'

'Of course. I understand you are to accompany the Vizier on campaign in the east.'

'What interest could the second *kadin* possibly have in a military expedition to Persia?'

'None. Her interest is Ibrahim. His boasting is already the scandal of the court and the bazaars.'

'Why should that concern her? I know she does not care for him overmuch, but his arrogance cannot reach as far as the Harem.'

'Her reasons are not your affair. But the Vizier is heading for a fall, and she would like it very much if you hurried it along. She would like evidence of his treachery.'

'He is hardly a traitor.'

'It does not matter to my mistress if he is or he isn't. She just wants you to collect evidence of it.'

Rüstem took another pastry while he thought this over. 'That might be difficult.'

'Not too difficult, I hope. Or one night, when the Sultan is wrapped in the embrace of his second *kadin*, she will whisper to him how you have embezzled taxes from the *timariots* and corrupted the fiefs.'

Rüstem did not look afraid. He merely frowned, as if he had been outmaneuvered at chess. 'And what reward should I hope for, should I prove a resourceful ally?'

Abbas was surprised by the question. 'Your life?'

'If we are bargaining, Kislar Aghasi, as you say we are, then I should like to make a counter-offer. Tell her that should I give her Ibrahim, I would like to enter into a more permanent arrangement with her. We might be very good for each other.'

'I will tell her,' he said.

The Man Who Never Smiled almost did. But he restrained himself.

CHAPTER 53

Galata was built on one of Stamboul's seven hills, just across the Horn from Seraglio Point. It was dominated by the Galata Kulesi, a round tower built by the Genoese as part of the city's fortifications. Tiny houses and shops clustered at its foot, next to the harbor, and this was where the Jewish and Genoese commission agents kept their homes. Berbers and Red Sea Arabs had warehouses here also, and filled them with spices, ivory, silks, glass and pearls. There were even small shops where wine and arak were served.

Ludovici kept a house in the quarter, although no one ever lived in it. Its purpose was a safe house where he might receive his spies and pay bribes to palace officials. Endless comings and goings at his palazzo in Pera by government pashas might excite too much comment.

The house was painted yellow, the color of the Jews. Most of the rooms were empty. The only room that was furnished was an upstairs audience chamber. There was a low cedar table and cushions were scattered about a rich Persian silk carpet. They belied the humble surroundings.

Abbas came once a month, disguised in his black *ferijde*. Ludovici had tried at first to speak to him as he did in the old days, but the Abbas he had once known was gone. Aside from discussing politics he seemed to gain no pleasure from his visits, though he provided invaluable insights into the workings of the Topkapi. He never wanted payment for his information. There was only one reason for his visits.

'How is Julia?' he said.

Ludovici remembered how he had pulled her from the water that morning three years ago. He had wrapped her in blankets and carried her up the steps of his palazzo from the *caramusali*. She had been as pale and

213

cold as marble. She had remained that way ever since; beautiful and remote, like a statue in the *Santa Maria dei Miracoli*. A ghost drifting through the gardens and the gilt rooms.

'She is well,' he said.

'You know she cannot stay in Stamboul much longer. It is not safe here.'

'What has happened?'

'I cannot tell you that.'

'But Abbas…'

'Please. Get her out of Stamboul. As soon as you can.'

'Where could she go?'

'It doesn't matter as long as it is not Stamboul. I have done all I can to protect her, but the situation is impossible now.'

'I will do what I can.'

'No, that is not good enough. You have to get her out.'

'Has someone found out about her?'

'Just promise me that you will do this.'

'I promise,' Ludovici said.

Suleiman sat on a pure white Cappadocian horse, watching his army march through the main square, the *Atmeydani*. Ferries were waiting to take them across to Üsküdar and Asia.

The Hippodrome shook to the rumble of supply wagons and siege engines. Choking clouds of dust swept across the square, whipped up by the horse's hoofs and the iron spiked shoes of his infantry.

Ibrahim appeared through the haze, resplendent in a white cloak. 'Your blessing on our endeavor, my Lord. Would that you were with us.'

'You must defend Baghdad against the devil.'

'I will crush the Shah as you have commanded me.' He reined in his horse to review the army at Suleiman's side.

First came the *azabs*. This was the irregular infantry; criminals, jailbirds and cutthroats come to fight for loot, or else die and go straight to Paradise. They had nothing to lose and were sent in first at every charge. 'Moat fillers', Ibrahim called them.

The regular cavalry thundered past, their horses caparisoned in gold and silver cloth, their conical helmets and burnished steel chain mail gleaming.

Next came the Janissaries, enormous Bird of Paradise plumes waving in the wind and blue-skirted cloaks swinging with every stride. The huge copper cauldrons that served as each regiment's standard went with them.

Behind them were the dervishes, naked except for green aprons, and towering hats of brown camelhair. They chanted verses from the Koran as they marched. Madcaps rode up and down the lines, long hair straggling from under their leopard skin caps.

At the rear came the mullahs in green turbans. They had with them a camel bearing a sacred fragment of the holy Ka'aba.

Finally there were the supply wagons, camel trains and bronze siege cannons. A white banner emblazoned with the flaming sword of Mohammed fluttered in the wind, embroidered with gold text from the Koran.

I should be with them, Suleiman thought.

'I will bring you back the Shah's head!' Ibrahim shouted.

Suleiman felt a stirring of unease. I have put all my faith in you, Ibrahim, he thought. God grant that I have not trusted you too much.

CHAPTER 54

Rüstem had calculated that, provided he did not commit himself too soon, he could profit from the Kislar Aghasi regardless of how the dice fell. It was plain that there would soon be a confrontation between the Harem and the Divan. It would be politic to have a foot in both camps.

He would encourage Ibrahim in his ambition. If he emerged triumphant, he would be there at his side. If he failed, he would seek his reward from the witch, Hürrem.

It was a long march through the lonely steppes of Anatolia. The army trailed a cloud of dust that spiraled a hundred feet into the air. The jackals fled in their wake.

The scouts roamed ahead, while the camel trains and heavy guns creaked over the rutted roads, the column stretching from horizon to flat horizon. A summer passed as they made their way east, to finally arrive at the foot of the great mountains of Asia and the cool still waters of Lake Van.

They glimpsed the blue-tiled domes of Tabriz glittering in the sun. Ibrahim hurried on, but Shah Tahmasp would not risk his cavalry against his artillery; instead he chose to slip away into the mountains of Sultania.

Ibrahim's standard of six horsetails - only the Sultan had more - was jammed into the hard earth. The tent whipped in the wind. Razor-backed mountains rose against a mottled sky.

When Rüstem entered the tent, copper braziers had already been lit against the chill. Ibrahim sat on a throne of ivory and ebony wood. Rüstem touched his forehead to the carpet in salute.

'Rüstem? Should you not be guarding the camel train and the silks?' Ibrahim said. He was in a dangerous mood. The frustrations of the past weeks had begun to tell, as the quick, decisive victory he had counted on had not come.

'I thought I might be of service to you, my Lord,' Rüstem said.

'To help count the money?'

'In the matter of the Shah, my Lord.'

'The Shah is no better than a jackal. He runs away from us then doubles back to sniff at our spoor and snap at our heels.'

'Our scouts have still not located his army?'

'These are his mountains. He knows every valley, every ridge.'

'Perhaps there is a way to flush him out.'

'How?'

'If you offer him a treaty...'

'Never! I have vowed to crush him.'

'You are not treating with a European nobleman, my Lord. The Shah is a jackal, as you have said. There would be no dishonor in using an offer to treat, simply as a means to draw him close enough to strike.'

Ibrahim brooded on this. 'What do you suggest?' he said.

'If we can get a message to him, perhaps?'

'How can we do that?'

'I am sure the Safavids are watching us, even as we speak. Any lone messenger travelling east will be intercepted. They will find us - we do not have to find them.'

'They will cut off his ears and nose and send them back in a leather pouch.'

'They might. But then again, perhaps the Shah does not wish to spend every summer skulking in the mountains. He cannot make war on us forever.'

Ibrahim got up and paced the tent. Outside, the sky had turned lead grey. Rain clouds swept towards them with the swiftness of charging cavalry.

Rüstem watched Ibrahim think it through. He held his breath. This was the moment; if Ibrahim took the bait, his fortune was assured. He would not be a clerk for ever.

'Let me take the message.'

'You, Rüstem?'

'I will coax the jackal from his lair.'

'When does a clerk become an ambassador?'

'When he has ambition.'

'What is your plan?'

'A sealed message from you, my Lord, offering him Tabriz and Azerbaijan in return for the holy city of Baghdad. We respect his borders to the east.'

'He will never believe we would make such a bargain.'

'I can persuade him if I have him face to face. And you have a duplicate of Suleiman's personal seal. If it is affixed to the offer, he must believe it is genuine.'

'Supposing he listens to you. What then?'

'We bring him and his escort to the plain under flag of truce and we massacre them like the dogs they are.' The rainstorm was overhead now and broke like a volley of cannon fire, thundering onto the hard ground and slapping violently on the roof of the tent.

'He will never believe it.'

'Let me try. He will know of the alliance the Pope wants to bring against us. I will convince him we are more concerned for our borders to the west and wish to be rid of him.'

Rüstem saw the play of emotion on Ibrahim's face. After Vienna he could not afford another failure, not with Hürrem whispering against him. He needed this victory.

'All right, Rüstem,' he said at last. 'If you can bring him to me, your reward will be beyond your wildest dreams.'

Rüstem bowed. Well, that was easy, he thought.

CHAPTER 55

Shah Tahmasp regarded the miserable creature in front of him. The man had been brought to the camp, chained and blindfolded, by two of his scouts. He lay face down in the dirt at the entrance to his pavilion, two scimitars pressed into the flesh of his neck, while the Shah read the contents of the missive he had brought with him.

The Shah showed the letter to his mullah, who passed it to one of his generals. They shook their heads. The Shah snatched it back and read the letter a third time. He was a young man, thin as a whip with cruel eyes. When he spoke his voice was high and sibilant. 'What is your name, messenger?'

The wretch raised his face from the ground. 'Rüstem, my Lord.' There was a trickle of blood on his lips.

'What is your rank in Suleiman's army?'

'I am his treasurer, my Lord.'

'A clerk. When do the Osmanlis send their money counters as couriers?'

'The Grand Vizier trusts me.'

The Shah frowned. 'So Ibrahim is persuaded to sue for peace. Is this what his Sultan wants, also?'

'Ibrahim has the confidence of the Lord of the Two Worlds. He has his personal seal.'

'Yes, I see that.'

'He has given him leave to make treaties in his name.'

'Can you tell me why your so-called Lord of the Two Worlds does not lead his army against us himself, as his father did?'

'He has tired of war, my Lord. He wishes for peace.'

Shah Tahmasp had heard these rumors. The offer was reasonable, he thought. If it were real, he could present his mullahs with a great political victory. They could not hold Baghdad for long in the face of the Osmanli armies.

'Such a treaty might be possible, messenger Rüstem. But we must meet at a place of my choosing, with only bodyguards in attendance.'

'You doubt Ibrahim's honor?'

'No. He's a Turk.'

'Greek,' Rüstem corrected him.

The shah nodded at the two guards, who dragged Rüstem to his feet. 'If he agrees to my conditions, tell him I accept his offer. Go in peace.'

The guards dragged him away. The Shah watched them put him on his horse, still chained and blindfolded. They led him through the rows of tents toward the south. He wondered again about Suleiman. An Osmanli who wanted peace? Was it the first sign of weakness? Well, as God wills.

'If you follow the spur, it will lead you to the valley where your friends are camped,' the Persian said and ripped the blindfold from Rüstem's face. The other rider unlocked his chains.

Rüstem blinked in the sunlight. One of his guards, a bearded ruffian in a battered conical helmet, tugged at his beard. 'Next time we meet, perhaps the Shah will let me wet my sword on your liver.'

Rüstem ignored the insults and took the reins of his horse. He had no time for Persians; his was a greater game.

Ibrahim was far too fond of the grand gesture to be a truly great Vizier, he thought. Greatness required calculation and planning. Someone with the ability to see opportunity in danger.

Someone like himself.

The two Persians galloped away, and he was left alone on the high steppe. He allowed himself a small smile. Then he rode back down the spur towards the camp. He rode like a clerk, but he had the heart of a bandit.

CHAPTER 56

Ibrahim's face betrayed both amusement and wonder. The silk tent flapped in the wind as it buffeted and sighed.

'So you found the Shah?'

'Yes, My Lord.'

'You astonish me, Rüstem. I thought never to see you alive again. They kept you blindfold, no doubt.'

'Indeed.'

'They treated you well?'

'Passably.'

His robe was torn and filthy. There was blood and matted dirt in his beard. The pale grey eyes betrayed nothing.

'Your lip is cut.'

'It is nothing.'

Ibrahim roared with laughter. 'What a loss you would have been to the world of poetry and good conversation!'

'I think not, my Lord,' Rüstem said.

Ibrahim shook his head. He sometimes entertained a fantasy in which he scooped off the top of Rüstem's skull with his sword, like an egg. When he peered inside there was no brain, just an abacus. 'So what does the Shah say to our offer of treaty?'

'He has refused it, my Lord.'

Ibrahim's face darkened, but the smile stayed doggedly in place. 'He does not trust us?'

'It was the authority of the letter he mistrusted.'

'The authority?'

'He said he could not treat with you.'

The smile vanished. 'Why not?'

'He said you were only a soldier, and that he could only accept such an offer as genuine if it were signed by the Sultan, not the Sultan's clerk.'

Ibrahim stood up. He clenched his fists to stop the trembling in his hands. Then he grabbed Rüstem and threw him across the tent. Rüstem lay on his side, looking neither frightened nor really all that surprised.

Ibrahim drew the *killiç* from the jeweled sheath at his waist. He raised it, double-handed, above his head, and brought it down on the back of the throne. Splinters of ivory and wood went spinning across the tent. 'The Sultan's clerk? Is it the Sultan's clerk who sits every day in the Divan and administers the Empire? Is it the Sultan's clerk who leads his armies into battle for him while he pleasures himself in his harem?'

'He spoke in ignorance, my Lord.'

'Does he think the Sultans sends clerks into battle? Does he, Rüstem?'

'I only repeat his words. He said he could not treat with any but the Sultan of the Osmanlis.'

'How long must I endure this? The Sultan has entrusted to me his kingdoms, his armies, his power. The making of war or the granting of peace are in my hand. Does the Shah know who it was called for the army to come here? It was I - not the Sultan. I take the burden and yet he calls me the Sultan's clerk?'

Ibrahim held the *killiç* in front of Rüstem's eyes, turning it slowly so that the light pooled and shivered on the blade. 'When we take him, we take him alive.'

'First we must lure him out. If we convey to the Lord of Life a message…'

'No. I swore I would bring him back his head. Should I now rush to him with entreaties for his aid?'

'Then perhaps there is another way?'

'What other way?'

'All the Empire knows how greatly the Sultan has honored and trusted you. You should impress this upon the Shah. You must show him that you have the authority to make such a treaty.'

'How?'

'You must extend the offer again. Only this time you must sign it as the Sultan.'

Ibrahim stared at him. Did this lunatic realize what he was saying? 'That is impossible.'

'What else may we do, my Lord? Except chase him around the mountains until winter comes.'

'I may do many things, Rüstem, but I cannot assume the title of Sultan.'

'Who will know once it is done? You may bury the document with the Shah.'

Ibrahim stared at him. It was unthinkable.

And yet why not, he thought. I am Sultan in everything but name. He has trusted me with his Divan and his armies; if he did not wish me to invoke his power, why would he give me so much?

'I cannot do it,' he said.

'In that case let us hurry and take back Baghdad but the Shah will take it back again as soon as we are gone.

Ibrahim closed his eyes. Rüstem was right. How could he return to Suleiman without securing their Asian border? Their destiny lay in the Green Apple, not here in this wilderness. It was the defeat of Rome that would carve his name alongside Alexander's in history. If he must take a hammer to swat this mosquito, then so be it.

He told Rüstem to fetch a quill and parchment.

To the Shah Tahmasp of Persia, greetings and health, may prosperity and glory signal your days. From sundry verbal communications we have cognizance of your desire for peace, and by the grace of the Most High, whose power be forever exalted! we ourselves have no desire to make war on our brothers in Islam. We therefore make it known that should you give up the holy city of Baghdad and all territories you have conquered by force of arms, we shall cede to you Tabriz, and the lands known as Azerbaijan, should you pay tribute each year of one thousand gold ducats. Night and day our horse is saddled to ride and meet with you to conclude our peace.

Written in the year of the Hejira, 941.

Ibrahim. Seraskier Sultan.

CHAPTER 57

Rüstem reined in his horse on the ridge overlooking the Osmanli camp. The smoke from the morning campfires drifted upwards, throwing gauze over the distant panorama of the mountains. From here he could see the scarlet tent of the Grand Vizier, his standard with the six horsetails limp in the still of the morning.

He turned and rode away towards the north. He spurred his horse beyond the first ridge, then wheeled around and galloped west. When he did not return Ibrahim would assume the Shah's men had murdered him. By the time he gave him up for lost, he would be in Stamboul.

Suleiman crumpled the letter in his fist, his face twisted with grief.

The pashas, muftis, and generals who surrounded him all fell silent. He knew what they were thinking: The vain boastful Greek had finally written his own death warrant.

Rüstem Pasha stood in the center of the Divan, waiting his turn to speak. There was no scent of perfume on him now. He stank of horse. He claimed to have ridden for three weeks from the borderlands of Azerbaijan to bring his news.

I would rather your horse had fallen and broken your neck, Suleiman thought.

'You wrote this at his command?' he said finally.

'Yes, great lord. He bid me take it to the Shah Tahmasp. He affixed your seal.'

Suleiman knew he was trapped. He could have forgiven Ibrahim anything but this. If Rüstem had come to him privately, he could have found a way to excuse it. But now it had been made public, there was nothing he could do. 'Why did you not do as he commanded and take this to the Shah?' he said.

'My Lord, I know my duty. I could not allow such treachery. I am your loyal servant.'

'The Sultan owes you a great debt,' he forced himself to say. He stared at the crumpled parchment in his fist. 'How does the campaign progress?'

'All we have seen of the Shah has been the dung of his horses. The Agas urge Ibrahim to Baghdad but he ignores their counsel. He says he is the only one capable of achieving victory. He says it has always been so.'

A sigh passed around the chamber. How dare Rüstem say such things, Suleiman wondered. He repeats these calumnies in front of everyone as if they were figures from a balance sheet.

'What of the morale of my army?'

'They clamor for you to lead them. Without you they believe they cannot achieve victory. The Janissaries believe Ibrahim will only lead them further into the mountains, to disaster.'

Suleiman watched the dust filtering through the shafts of yellow sunlight. Behind him, high on the wall, was the dangerous window where he often sat to spy on the Divan. He wished he were up there now, watching someone else make the terrible decision that he knew must finally be made.

CHAPTER 58

Hürrem entered silently through a velvet curtain and knelt at his feet. For once she had no smile to greet him. She kissed his hand and rested it against his cheek.

'You knew?'

'Yes, my Lord.'

'How?'

'Whispers in the Harem.'

'How is it the Harem know everything that happens even before I do?'

'When I came through the curtain and saw your face I knew the whispers must be true.'

He stroked her hair and his face softened. 'What am I to do?'

'May I see the letter, my Lord?'

He still held it crumpled in his fist. She took it from his fingers and unfolded it. It was barely legible, badly creased and the sweat from his hand had smudged the ink. But she could still read the signature.

Seraskier Sultan.

Oh Rüstem, she thought. Abbas chose well. You have a rare genius for intrigue.

'He sues for peace with the Shah under your name,' she said.

'It is madness. What could have possessed him to do such a thing?'

'Is this fellow Rüstem to be trusted?'

'He is just a clerk. In his misguided way he thinks he does well by me. The treason is there written beneath my own seal. There is no circumstance, no provocation, under which any man might call himself Sultan other than me. To do so is treason.'

'But he is your friend.'

'Much more than a friend. It only makes this even more unforgiveable.'

'Do not act too rashly, my Lord.'

He shook his head. 'You may be the only one today who speaks for him. Suddenly he has enemies I did not even dream of. They have swarmed from every rat's nest in the Palace walls to denounce him.'

Yes, I will speak for him, she thought, and when his head is rotting on the palace walls, you will remember that I did. 'You must go to him.'

He nodded. 'I cannot bring myself to harm him, *russelana*. It would be like cutting out my own heart.'

'There must be some way you can excuse him.'

He snatched the letter from her hand. 'What excuse can there be?' He jumped to his feet and went to the candle. He held it to the flame, watched it burn.

'He will tell me about this letter with his own lips when I arrive. If he is truly my friend, he will not try to hide anything from me.' He crushed the ashes with his boot.

Hürrem stood up and wrapped her arms around him. She pulled his head to her breast.

'Hürrem,' he said, 'what would I do without you?'

'Shh,' she murmured and stroked his head, despising his weakness more than ever.

CHAPTER 59

Suleiman crossed the Bosporus with three hundred cavalry, to Üsküdar and then east across the baked plains towards Asia. There would be a full cycle of the moon before he reached his destination, a month of choking dust and aching muscles.

He followed the trail of Alexander through orchards of figs and olives, fields of cotton and wheat. From Konia they roasted under the desert sun. The only signs of life they saw were the black tents of nomads and the baked walls of the caravanserais.

They passed through Edessa, the birthplace of Abraham, where old men sat in the shadow of the fortress and tossed chickpeas into a pool of sacred carp. From there they rode up into the mountains, and the air turned suddenly cool. The brown steppe gave way to bare rock and tumbling ravines. The wind savaged men and horses like a whip. Wild storms appeared from nowhere. It was a place only goats, sheep and the Kurds could survive.

And the Shah.

They rode twelve hours a day, stopping only when their horses were too exhausted to continue. Finally, they reached Azerbaijan.

The scouts rode ahead to find the camp. One afternoon they rode to the crest of a ridge and saw the army spread out on the plateau in front of them. Although he was exhausted beyond all measure, he drew himself taller in the saddle and rode down the slope to take command of God's regiments once more.

The tents had been erected in crisp lines, according to division and regiment. Holes had been dug at regular intervals as latrines. Horses had been corralled, siege engines, supply wagons and cannon drawn up in strict order.

The camp was silent, for no fighting, gambling or drinking was tolerated. But when the men recognized the Sultan's standard of seven horsetails and saw the bearded figure with his green robes and snow-white turban the hush erupted into wild cheering.

Word spread quickly. Suleiman had returned to lead them. He would guide them through these mountains and to victory.

He reined in his horse before the scarlet silk tent with the six-horsetail standard. Ibrahim emerged and quickly executed a ceremonial *salaam* on the ground in front of him.

'My lord,' he said.

Where is the boyish grin now? Suleiman wondered. Where is the young man who would rush to embrace me whenever we had been too long apart?

'Do you have the head of the Shah for me?' Suleiman said.

'Not yet, my Lord,' Ibrahim said.

'Then we will remove to Baghdad. Give the order.'

CHAPTER 60

'It is good you are here, my Lord. But the reason for your arrival distresses me. Do you no longer trust me as your Vizier?'

They were sitting on the thick carpets in Suleiman's pavilion. The coals in the copper brazier glowed, fanned by a sudden draught. Suleiman was so tired he could barely think. And he was cold. He pulled his ermine lined robe tighter around his shoulders.

'A Sultan's place is at the head of his army, as you never cease to remind me.'

'Is that the only reason, my Lord?'

'As protector of the Faith I am obliged to defend Baghdad, not have my army chase phantoms through the wilderness.'

'Once we defeat the Shah, Baghdad is ours anyway.'

Suleiman searched Ibrahim's face for the truth. Any moment, he thought, he will confess to me what he has done and why. There can be no secrets between us.

'Perhaps we should treat with the Shah,' Suleiman said, testing him.

'And what should we offer him?' Ibrahim said.

'What do you think?'

'Nothing. Except perhaps a rope for his neck.'

Suleiman shook his head. 'He is as elusive as our Holy Roman Emperor. We will never bring either of them to battle. It is more important that we do our duty and be patient. We defend the Faith.'

'The Faith!' It was clear Ibrahim regretted this blasphemy the moment it was spoken.

'It is the reason for my army, Ibrahim, there can be no other. The jihad is only for God.' The horses were growing restless outside, Suleiman could hear them stamping their hoofs, unsettled by the wind. 'Tomorrow we march on Baghdad. We will retake the city and, if necessary, we will winter there. The mountains are no place for an army.'

'As you command.' Ibrahim stared at the coals in the fire, his lips compressed in a thin line. 'Why did you do this to me?'

Suleiman wondered at his audacity. After your treachery, Suleiman thought, you dare question me? 'I am tired. I must sleep. Leave me now.'

'But My Lord...'

'Leave.'

It had been their tradition to sleep in the same pavilion when they were on campaign. But Ibrahim did not protest. He rose to his feet, made his *salaam* and left.

During the night, a blizzard swept down from the mountains. Suleiman woke to the sound of horses and camels screaming in the storm. A gust of wind shook his pavilion so violently he thought it must rip in two. He threw on his fur robe and went outside.

Curtains of driving sleet obliterated everything, and he had to shield his face with his hands to protect himself from the stinging slap of the ice. Torches flared for a moment and were instantly extinguished by the wind.

His pages trembled with terror. Even one of his bodyguard fell on his knees. 'May God protect us!' he screamed. 'It is the Persian magicians!'

'It's just a storm!' Suleiman roared. 'Get up, man!'

Damn Ibrahim, he thought. Damn him for his treachery and his stupidity.

Dawn, and the entire valley was blanketed in white. Soldiers staggered, dazed, through a landscape none could recognize from the night before.

Some clawed at the snow to release a comrade, or hauled on the rope of a camel half-buried under a drift.

Whole regiments had been lost, and their tents torn away by the wind. Pieces of canvas flapped on broken poles.

A terrible hush had fallen across the valley.

Ibrahim turned his eyes toward the jaws of the pass, dreading the arrival of Persian horsemen.

'Ibrahim!' Suleiman stood above him on the slope, his face contorted with rage. 'What have you done?'

Ibrahim spread his hands helplessly. Who knew there could be snow in summer?

'If the Persians come now,' Suleiman shouted, 'we will all die here!'

Ibrahim turned away and plunged through the thigh-deep snow towards the wreckage of the camp. They must reorganize quickly and make their retreat.

He was a stranger to failure. Even now, he could not believe this had happened to him.

CHAPTER 61

After they had concluded their business, Abbas said, 'These are dangerous days. You have made sure she is safe? She is out of Stamboul?' His face shone in the light of the candle.

'Yes,' Ludovici said. 'She is far away.'

Abbas grunted, satisfied.

'Do you ever think about the old days, Abbas, about Venice?'

'No, I don't. It is too painful. The past is done. Nothing can change it.'

'Do you ever wish you had done things differently?'

'A man's fate is written on his forehead by God at the time of his birth, and this was mine. I could not have done differently, as a cloud cannot decide which way it will travel through the sky.'

'I believe that on the day of Judgment it is God who should ask pardon of you for what He did.'

'That is blasphemy, Ludovici, and I shall not listen to it.' Abbas clapped his hands to signal to his deaf-mute slaves that he was ready to leave. It was the movement of his hands that was the signal, not the sound. They hurried to assist him to his feet. 'One last question. Did you ever take Julia into your harem?'

The question took Ludovici off guard. 'She is not a concubine. She is a Christian woman of high birth.'

'Yes, but did you do it?'

'No. I did not.'

'Good,' Abbas said. 'I am glad.'

He got to his feet and prepared to leave. 'And if I had?' Ludovici asked him.

'But you didn't,' Abbas said. 'So why ask?'

When Ludovici returned to Pera, he went to his study and stood at the window, looking over the Horn. He shouted instructions to Hyacinth to fetch Julia. The eunuch shuffled away along the corridor. Ludovici sat down at his desk and waited.

She entered silently, heralded by the rustling of her long skirts on the marble. 'You wanted to see me?'

Ludovici stood up and offered her a chair. 'Please, sit down.'

She did so, and he pulled up a chair next to her.

'Is something wrong?' she said.

'I have just met with Abbas. He wants you to leave here. He says it is dangerous for you.'

'Do you think someone at the Harem has found out I am alive?'

'Maybe. I don't see how. He just said it was dangerous for you to remain.'

'But where should I go?'

'I don't know. I can send you back to Italy, to a convent perhaps.'

She shook her head. 'Why would you think I would prefer that to being a concubine? Though the evening entertainments would be different.'

He turned away and stared at the twilight gathering over the Horn.

'Do I have a choice?'

'I'm not your jailer.'

'Do you have another plan?'

'No. But you can't stay here forever.'

'You want me gone?'

He took a deep breath. He might as well say it 'What do you think of me, Julia?'

'What do you mean?'

'You have lived with me in this house for three years. You must have formed an opinion.'

'You are a kind and decent man. I am very grateful to you. You saved my life and gave me sanctuary here.'

Ludovici felt his heart sink. It wasn't the answer he had hoped for. 'I made enquiries. Your husband is dead.'

She took a deep breath. 'When?'

'Three weeks ago in Cyprus. I learned the news today.'

'So I am a widow?'

He nodded.

'Well. It changes nothing though, does it?'

'Perhaps it does.' He turned away from the window. 'Marry me.'

She stared at him, astonished. 'But you have many women in your harem,' she said. 'Why would you want to marry me? How could it possibly serve you?' She got to her feet, then sat down again. It was the first time he had seen her agitated.

'I could tell Hyacinth to get rid of my concubines. I can marry them off to wealthy Turkish husbands. It is the custom here. If that is what you want.'

'Ludovici, stop. What is it you want from me?'

'I am afraid I am enchanted. Just as Abbas was.'

'And look what happened to him.' She touched his hand. 'You must understand. I don't feel anything anymore. It might be better to have me as your mistress for a short time. I don't mind, it is a way I can repay you for all your kindness. Afterwards you might more easily discard me, for I am sure you will be very disappointed.'

'I should never discard you.'

'Ludovici, you are Sultan here, in this house. Put your handkerchief on my shoulder, and I will come. Just let me stay here in your house a little longer. Please.'

'As Abbas said, it's dangerous for you here. I will look into things, see if there is somewhere else you can go.'

She stood up to go, then hesitated. 'Why have you never asked me this before? I know you wanted to.'

'Because of Abbas.'

'I see.' She kissed him on the cheek and left. Her perfume lingered in the room after she had gone. She was still as unattainable as she ever was, for him, for Abbas, and for even the Sultan himself.

Baghdad had been built from the same stones as the ancient city of Babylon. It straddled the Tigris and the Euphrates, palm trees framing the domes and minarets. Suleiman stared at the walls as the siege engines and cannon rumbled into position. He breathed a prayer of thanks. The crisis was past.

The Persians had not attacked the morning after the storm, through grace of God. His presence had galvanized the army, and by that evening they had reorganized and begun the long slow retreat from the mountains.

The Empire of Mohammad, the army of Islam, would have been destroyed, he thought, thanks to my *Seraskier* Sultan.

Ibrahim rode towards him, the rubies and emeralds embroidered on his saddle glittering in the sun. 'Why so solemn my Lord?'

'Why? Because you should have stood at these gates two months ago. Because a week ago you almost led my army to ruin.'

'Your generals were eager for a long campaign, and we have given them one. That old bear at the head of the Janissaries is still melting the snow out of his boots.'

'You may laugh, Ibrahim, but this was our objective. Baghdad! We did not come here to placate the Aga or find the Shah. We were here to chase away dogs from a holy place.'

Ibrahim grew sullen. 'You said you wanted the dog's head.'

'No, I did not say that. You did.' He squeezed the flanks of his horse with his knees and trotted ahead, leaving Ibrahim alone on the plain.

CHAPTER 62

Early Spring, but snow still clung to the roofs of the kiosks in the Topkapi, fell in minor avalanches from the dome of the Aya Sofia and froze the fountains in the courtyards of the Old Palace. All the shutters and doors were tightly closed against the cold, and the stale aroma of incense, charcoal and hashish mingled to create a suffocating fug. Hürrem had her servants spray her apartments with orange blossom and rosewater to relieve it.

The fall of Baghdad and the passing of the long winter months had not stilled the gossip about Suleiman and his *Seraskier* Sultan; if anything the anticipation of the army's return had intensified it.

It was the scandal of the whole city, how Ibrahim had defied the sultan even to the point of assuming his title. Rüstem had made sure everyone knew of it within days.

Merchants spat and cursed the Greek's name in the bazaars. The statues in front of his palace in the *Atmeydani* were defaced. All Stamboul had hated him for years, resenting the way he flaunted his wealth. No one was surprised or dismayed that he had finally gone too far.

Hürrem had assumed that Ibrahim was already dead, strangled in his tent by the Sultan's deaf-mute assassins – his *bostanji* - or hung on a gibbet in a Baghdad square. He should have been moldering in his grave for weeks, she thought, by the time Suleiman's messenger arrived with news. But the long winter was almost over, and the couriers said that Ibrahim still lived.

Abbas settled himself on his knees to deliver the latest news. 'A courtier has arrived at the palace my lady. Suleiman will be back in Stamboul in the next few days.'

'With Ibrahim?'

'Yes, My Lady.'

I do not believe this, Hürrem thought. It seems as if the Vizier could put a dagger through Suleiman's heart and he would just look up and kiss him on the lips.

'There is other news,' Abbas said,

'Tell me.'

'The Shah attacked the rearguard of the army on its return through Azerbaijan. Four generals were lost, eight hundred Janissaries surrendered.'

'Who was the commander?'

'Ibrahim. The Sultan had ridden ahead with his bodyguard.'

'It seems the Greek's golden touch has deserted him.'

'Yes, my Lady.'

'It is not the outcome we all prayed for, yet that is no fault of yours, Kislar Aghasi. You have done well.'

'Thank you.'

'Rüstem, too. He shows a great talent. I am sure we will find a use for him again in the near future. You should convey him my thanks and assure him he will be amply rewarded.'

'I will tell him.'

'Have you seen your Venetian friend?' Hürrem said, as he reached the door.

'No, my Lady.'

'Did you know that she is mistress now to Ludovici Gambetto, one of the Venetian merchants on Pera?'

He returned to his cell, fire burning in his heart.

Mistress? Ludovici had told him he had sent her out of Stamboul. Instead he had her in his bed.

The room started to spin.

CHAPTER 63

Suleiman looked suddenly old, as if all the juice had been squeezed out of him.

He sat at a low table, his hands clenched into fists in his lap. His homecoming had been muted. Hürrem had welcomed him in her apartments in the Old Palace and they had shared a meal together, though Suleiman had eaten hardly anything. Instead of ravishing her, as she had expected, he had fallen asleep on the divan. Now awake again, he seemed scarcely more refreshed than before.

'What is wrong, my Lord?'

'You know what is wrong. All Stamboul knows what is wrong.'

'You confronted him about the letter?'

'I waited for his confession, but it did not come. He acts as if nothing has happened. What should I do now? Bring Rüstem before him?'

'What good will it do?'

Suleiman shook his head. 'I wanted only his free admission. I could not bear to debate it with him and have to listen to his lies. But he didn't say a word about it.'

'And yet?'

'And yet I love him, Hürrem.'

You must get rid of him, Hürrem thought. Otherwise we are all in danger. If you give him time, he will make a move against you, he has no choice now. 'You might exile him, as you did Achmed Pasha,' she said.

'Achmed Pasha used his place of exile as a base for revolt. Do I dare take the same risk with Ibrahim, who is a far better general than Achmed ever was?'

'He has been your friend for so long, my Lord. I know you love him like a brother.'

'His ambition and his greed have clouded his judgment. As commander he should have been watchful for an attack at our rear. He was more concerned with guarding the bales of Persian silk he had looted. He allowed the Shah's cavalry to inflict the greatest defeat my army has ever suffered. Instead of celebrating our victory at Baghdad we are mourning the loss of a thousand good men.'

Hürrem held his hands in hers. 'He is guilty of negligence in his command, through his own self-interest. He has done the unthinkable and assumed the name of Sultan. My Lord, I feel your pain, but what else can you do?'

The sun set behind the roofs of the old palace. 'He comes to dine with me tonight alone at the Topkapi,' Suleiman said.

Hürrem put her head on his shoulder. 'What will you tell him, my Lord?'

'I do not know. I cannot end his life, Hürrem. I have given my word.'

'My Lord?'

'I made a vow when I made him Vizier - I swore to it before God - that while I lived, he should never fear for his own safety. He has my oath on that.'

They sat in silence. Long shadows crept across the carpet. Pages came into the room to light candles and oil lamps.

'Must he die?' Hürrem whispered.

'The law says he must.'

'Then there is a way, though I hesitate even to whisper it.'

'Tell me.'

'You have sworn not to put him to death while you are living. Then let the order be carried out while you are asleep. The muftis say that when a man sleeps, he enters another realm; that he is not really alive. It is like a small death. So you can fulfil the law, your duty to the throne and to Islam, and still not violate your oath.'

Suleiman said nothing for a long time.

'So be it,' he said at last.

CHAPTER 64

Ibrahim ran a finger around the rim of his cup, and stared into his wine. 'We have given a lashing to the Persian dogs,' he said. 'They will be licking their wounds for as very long time.'

'The campaign was not well advised,' Suleiman said. 'We were drawn into a trap. As it was, the final battle went to the Shah. He will be celebrating now, despite our victories at Baghdad and Tabriz.'

'There will be other summers.'

'To what purpose?'

'We have an empire that rivals that of Alexander the Great. Why should we engage in this moping? We have Baghdad, the Shah has the snow and the rocks.'

'We lost many good men for no reason. Rüstem, for example.'

Ibrahim felt the blood drain from his face. Why would Suleiman bring up Rüstem? Was he dead? His spies had whispered to him that he was still alive, and had been seen in Manisa.

'What do you know about my clerk?' Ibrahim said, unable to meet his eyes.

'That he was murdered by the Shah engaging in some secret diplomacy of yours. Did he volunteer for his mission or did you order him to go?'

'He volunteered. He seemed very eager.'

'And what was the purpose?'

'I wanted to lure the Shah out of the mountains through a minor deception.'

'It seems you failed.'

'I tried everything to find the Shah.'

'Well, it is done now,' Suleiman said.

'There will be other victories, my Lord. Like Rhodes and Mohacs. Do you remember how close we came to giving up then?'

'It was your counsel that prevailed at Rhodes, Ibrahim.'

'I only ever wish to serve you.'

'And you have served me well, many times. But our only true loyalty must be to God, and the Prophet.'

'I was not born in your faith,' Ibrahim said carefully. 'I still have much to learn.'

'It is too late for that. I do not think anyone can teach you anything now.' If he had smiled as he said that Ibrahim might have smiled along with him. But Suleiman looked away.

'Shall we go hunting in Edirne again this summer?' Ibrahim said.

'Only God sees the future.'

'We used to hunt all the time together. Do you remember when that boar rushed my horse from the thicket on the Marantza River? You saved my life.'

'I cannot always be there to save you. We must all face death alone eventually.'

'Yet you swore to me once that you would never abandon me.'

'I remember my oath. But let's not talk about this anymore. I need my bed.'

Suleiman rose to his feet. His head felt like lead. The drugged wine had affected him more than it had affected Ibrahim. He just wanted to sleep, longed only for this ordeal to be over. 'The pages will prepare your bed. Sleep well, my friend.'

Ibrahim rose to his feet and embraced him. 'Sleep well, my Lord.'

Suleiman went into his private chamber, locking the door behind him.

Hürrem rose from the bed and hurried over to him. He was gray. I must not let him change his mind, she thought.

She was naked except for rose damask trousers and a single pearl fastened around her waist. He did not even seem to notice.

'He all but begged me for his life.'

'Drink this,' she whispered, and offered him a goblet of wine.

He sank to his haunches, put his head in his hands. Hürrem refilled the goblet with more of the wine. She held the cup to his lips, and he gulped it with the desperation of a man dying of thirst. 'Do not let it happen while I am awake. I must not break my oath.

She cradled his head between her breasts. After a while she felt his head grow heavy. She lay on the floor beside him and held him while he twitched and muttered in his sleep. She prayed that the *bostanji* would hurry and do their work.

CHAPTER 65

Ibrahim paced the room, ignoring the bed the pages had made up for him, fighting the heaviness in his limbs and the numbing tiredness that had all but overwhelmed him.

I must stay awake, he thought. He would not let them find him sleeping. He was Ibrahim, Vizier to the Magnificent. He could not die at the Sultan's hand. He had his prince's word, his oath before God.

So why had the pages locked the door behind them?

He heard footsteps in the corridor outside and a noise that sounded like the yelp of a dog. A key creaked in the lock and the handle began to turn.

The door swung open.

There were five of them, all Nubians. Ibrahim staggered to the door that separated his room from Suleiman's. He hammered on it with his fists. 'My Lord!'

The *bostanji* edged towards him.

Each of the five *bostanji* held a silken bowstring, the ritual instrument of execution for those of high position or with royal blood. It was such a bowstring that had dispatched Suleiman's own uncles, cousins and nephews.

Ibrahim took out his dagger and turned to face them.

The first of them moved in. As he lunged, Ibrahim sidestepped him and the knife flashed in the candlelight.

The *bostanji* stared at him in dull surprise. Blood spurted rhythmically from his neck and up the wall. He put his hands to his throat in a vain attempt to staunch the flow and fell to his knees.

Ibrahim backed against the wall, as the other *bostanji* fanned out across the room, more wary now. Their comrade died, noisily.

They signaled to each other with deft, almost imperceptible hand signals. He tensed, ready.

When they moved again it was quickly and in unison. Ibrahim's knife flashed again, and then he leaped back, out of range. One of the assassins howled and dropped his bowstring. Blood poured from a gash in his arm.

'My Lord, call off your monsters!' Ibrahim shouted, but his cry for mercy was cut off as a bowstring closed around his throat. The other two *bostanji* tried to grab him. He slashed again, and another of them reeled back, clutching at his face.

But then his fellow had hold of his arm and tried to twist it behind him to break his grip on the dagger. The bowstring tightened around his throat.

Most men clawed at the bowstring; it was instinct. Instead Ibrahim used his free hand to plunge two splayed fingers into the eyes of the second attacker. The man screamed and loosened his grip just enough for Ibrahim to twist his dagger arm free, the blade slicing through the man's hands.

He reversed his grip and stabbed behind him. He felt a rush of hot blood on his back and the noose around his throat loosened. He stabbed twice more, but the second time the dagger was torn from his grip. It had jammed between the *bostanji* 's ribs as he fell, and he couldn't pull it free.

Another bowstring closed around his throat. His attacker was one he had already wounded; he could feel the blood dripping from the man's arm and down his neck. He tried to twist around but the assassin jerked backwards with the noose, pulling him off balance.

He put his hands to his throat, and in the moment his reflexes took over from his warrior's training he knew he was lost. He tried to slide his fingers under the bowstring, but it was drawn taut, biting deep into the flesh of his throat. His chest spasmed and he kicked out in panic, all reason gone. Flashes of light exploded in front of his eyes.

He tried to scream Suleiman's name, but no sound came. He could no longer control his limbs. The shadows closed in from all sides.

Güzül hurried along the *Atmeydani* under the imposing red walls of Ibrahim's palace. A messenger had brought an urgent summons to her house in the Jewish quarter a few minutes before. Ibrahim wanted to see her immediately.

She was ushered through the gates by the guards. She crossed the courtyard to the stairs that led to the pasha's hall of audience. She kept her head down, lifting the skirts of her *ferijde* as she ran, taking care not to slip on the thin film of ice on the cobblestones.

She was halfway up the stair when she was aware of the figure watching her from the shadows. He wore a fur-lined green pelisse and white sugarloaf turban. She stared at him in confusion.

'Ibrahim is dead,' Abbas said. His voice was flat.

Güzül turned and looked behind her. Two *bostanji* stood at the foot of the stairs, their *killiç* drawn.

'It is at the order of the Lady Hürrem,' Abbas said. 'Go with God.' He turned away, his duty done.

Suleiman watched from a window high above the Third Court as the Chief Executioner threw Ibrahim's body over a horse. A blanket of black velvet had been laid on the horse's back, and a special ointment had been put in its eyes to make it weep. He led the horse away. Ibrahim was to be taken to Galata and buried in an unmarked grave.

Two dead *bostanji* had been dragged from the room. None of them had escaped injury. One had lost an eye, another his nose. There were splashes of blood up each of the four walls. It looked as if two small armies had gone to war in there.

'He fought well,' Suleiman said. His face was ashen.

'Your orders were just,' Hürrem said. 'You could not do other than what you did.'

'I know,' Suleiman said. 'But I have broken my oath. I have murdered my friend.'

PART 6

This Woman Hürrem

CHAPTER 66

Çamlica 1541

Suleiman watched Mustapha spur his Arab to the crest of the hill. He has grown into a fine prince, he thought, with four sons of his own. He is already the same age that I was when I took the throne.

The awkward, bowed figure of Çehangir followed, a hooded gyrfalcon on his outstretched arm.

Suleiman spurred his horse to the rise to join them. He watched the archers and their dogs sweeping through the marsh below, flushing out prey.

Çehangir rode down the slope and released his gyrfalcon, as Mustapha had shown him. It swept into the air with a piercing cry.

'Look at him,' Mustapha said proudly. 'He tries hard to overcome what God has willed.'

'Promise me you will never harm him,' Suleiman said.

'Why would I harm him?'

'When the throne is yours. You know the law.'

'I am not my grandfather.'

'Yet it is your right if you wish it.'

'Then I give you my word - I shall not harm him, or any of my brothers.'

I wish I could believe you, Suleiman thought, but will you feel the same when your life and your throne are threatened? 'What you do after I am gone is with you and with God. But spare Çehangir.'

'None of them need fear me, my Lord. That bloody custom ended with my grandfather.'

'You may feel differently in time.'

'If they do not raise their hands against me, I shall not harm them. I don't want their blood on my hands.'

How can you be sure what you will do when the whispers start? Suleiman thought. How can any of us be sure?

I once told myself I could never harm Ibrahim.

The gyrfalcon swooped on its quarry and the dogs bayed and sprang forward. The archers let out a whoop of triumph.

Another life ended on a beautiful spring morning.

The shadows retreated across Asia toward the cold dark of Europe. Sunlight inched through the cloisters and dark gardens, dissolving the mist that curled around the roofs. An owl tolled the watch song of the dawn.

The muezzin called the city to prayer.

Hürrem stood at the lattice window, shrouded in a fur pelisse. Her hair hung loose about her shoulders, unkempt and unbraided. She shivered in the cold, staring at the minarets of the Aya Sofia flashing like the tips of lances as they broke through the morning mist.

She called for Muomi to perform her toilet, then sat in front of the mirror and watched her comb out her hair.

'Stop,' she said. She leaned closer to the glass.

You cannot deny me any longer, the mirror said. The tiny lines at the corner of your eyes will grow deeper until you can no longer disguise them with kohl, and the first gray hair will soon be followed by others.

What will happen when he sees me growing old, she thought. Will he still overlook the paradise of willing concubines eager to use their transient charms to replace me in his bed?

She took the ivory handled brush from Muomi.

'Get Abbas,' she said. 'There is something I need him to do.'

CHAPTER 67

The Sirocco originates in the Sahara, its hot breath scalding Tripoli, Algiers and the ruins of Carthage, before heading across the Mediterranean towards Europe. By the time it reaches the distant shores on the other side of the sea, the thunderheads are banked to the stars behind it. Everything wilts in the baking wind.

On the night Abbas had chosen to execute Hürrem's latest caprice, it rushed through the narrow streets of Stamboul like a gale. It bent the branches of the cypress trees in the palace gardens, whipped the red and green flags of the palace into a frenzy, and piled froth on the distant shores of the Bosporus.

Perfect weather, Abbas thought.

The Palace was in darkness when he set off with two *bostanji* through a little-used gate in the southern wall. They were gone for less than an hour and when they returned an orange stain was already creeping up the sky and over the roofs of the cramped wooden houses below.

As soon as they were back inside the palace, Abbas found the Chief Executioner and slipped an emerald ring into his palm. He used sign language to indicate that the two men who had accompanied him on his errand that night should not live to see the morning.

Then he returned to his cell and waited, wondering what other crimes he might yet commit in the name of love.

The booming of the tambours echoed through the dark streets. The Palace woke to the cries of, '*Yanghinvar!* Fire!'

Abbas ran from his cell. He could hear women screaming from one of the upstairs dormitories. In the courtyard below two guards had drawn their swords in confusion. Idiots, he thought impatiently. Couldn't they smell the smoke?

He did not hesitate. He had had days to rehearse each move and Hürrem had made it quite clear what his first duty should be. He rousted two of his pages from their beds and rattled off the list of instructions he had memorized: prepare the coaches; get all the women downstairs into the courtyard; send six other pages to the dressmaker and bring all of Lady Hürrem's possessions down to safety.

Naturally, she could not leave anything behind of hers, even if the whole city roasted.

Then he heaved himself up the stairs to her apartments.

He was astonished at her appearance. She must have been grooming herself all night, he decided. She had on a stunning emerald-green kaftan, over a white chemise emblazoned with *rumi* scrollwork in gold thread. Her hair was plaited with tiny emeralds and pearls, and her yashmak was in place. Muomi stood beside her, holding a *ferijde* of violet silk.

So this is what one wears to a fire, he thought. She was perfumed, of course, for she would not present herself to the Sultan after an inferno reeking of smoke.

'What took you so long?' she hissed. 'Did you want me to cook in my bed?'

'They have just sounded the alarm, My Lady,' he said.

'Why did you need to wait for the alarm? You already knew the city was alight.'

Abbas went to the window and groaned aloud. The wind had fanned the flames into a firestorm and the wooden buildings on the hill below were being gobbled up in moments. The fire was rolling towards them like a wave.

He watched a house catch light, flare, and then cave in, sending a shower of sparks into the night sky. Men and women rushed up the alley, carrying all they could on their backs, tripping over each other in panic. The mass of people looked like a river flooding through a chasm; a torrent of torches and wide-eyed oxen, blindfolded rearing horses and unveiled women.

God forgive me, Abbas thought.

A red-hot cinder hurtled towards him on the wind and caught his cheek. He jumped back. 'We must hurry!' he shouted.

'I have been waiting to hurry for hours,' Hürrem said, as if she were late for a formal entertainment at the Hippodrome.

Muomi helped her into her cloak, drawing the full veil of her *yashmak* over her face to preserve her anonymity and her dignity. Then she put on her own hooded cloak and Abbas led them out of the apartment and down the stairs.

He had thought they would have more time. The coaches were waiting on the cobblestones. 'Get inside!' he shouted. 'Quickly!'

The two shrouded figures pushed past him and climbed into the first coach. He shut the door behind them. A hand snaked from behind the taffeta curtain and grasped his own. Hürrem leaned out and for a moment he thought she was about to whisper her thanks.

'Leave behind anything of mine,' she said, 'and it will be your head.'

Abbas slumped to his knees to execute his *salaam* at the feet of the Lord of Life. He rested his forehead on the carpet a little longer than was necessary. His pelisse reeked of wood smoke, and his face and turban were smeared with grime.

Suleiman watched him, his face creased with anguish.

'A thousand pardons my Lord,' Abbas gasped.

'Does my servant need the physician?'

'I am merely fatigued.' Two pages helped him back to his feet.

'There has been a fire at the Old Palace?' Suleiman was impatient for the Kislar Aghasi to tell his story.

'The entire palace was in flames when I left. However all the women are safe.'

'And Hürrem?'

'She waits outside the door. I guarded her life as I might that of your most precious treasure.'

'We are in your debt,' Suleiman said. 'There were no injuries?'

'I fear a number of my pages and guards were burned in the fire as they were attempting to recover my Lady's jewels and clothes from her apartment.'

'The palace is destroyed?'

'My last vision of it, it was totally engulfed in flame.'

'I commend you Abbas, for your efforts. Send in the Lady Hürrem and then go and rest. We shall speak again in the morning.'

Moments later a figure swathed in violet silk appeared and almost immediately fell to the ground. Suleiman rushed to help her. 'Hürrem, are you all right?' He threw back her veil. Her face was pale and her eyes red from crying. 'Are you hurt?'

He felt her tremble in his arms. 'When the messenger told me about the fire, and I saw the glow above the palace... I do not know what I would have done if anything happened to you.'

'It was the smell of smoke that woke me. I thought I was going to die.'

'Until the coaches came, I thought you were gone,' he said.

'It was fate,' she said.

'You must accommodate Hürrem and the other women in the Palace here until other arrangements can be made,' Suleiman said to Abbas.

'It poses a problem, my Lord,' Abbas said.

'I do not wish to hear of problems.'

Suleiman does not look quite as well disposed to the mercies of the Great God this morning, Abbas thought. He looks a little sour. 'I would not burden you with such trivialities,' he said, 'but it requires your special permission.'

'How difficult can it be to find rooms for a few women and their servants?'

Abbas stared at him, appalled. Could it be that the Lord of Life was ignorant of the true size of his harem and, in particular, Hürrem's private arrangements? 'My Lord, my Lady Hürrem's retinue alone is a large one, as befitting the favored *kadin* of the Lord of Life.'

Suleiman shifted irritably on the divan. 'How large?'

'She has herself thirty pages and slaves, one hundred and three ladies in waiting, and of course there is her purveyor and her dressmaker. It makes a total of one hundred and thirty-seven people, including myself.'

Suleiman stared at him in disbelief.

'Add to that number the one hundred and nine girls who still remain in my Lord's harem, plus perhaps an equal number of pages and hand maidens.'

Suleiman tugged at his beard. He looked alarmed. 'My private quarters will be totally over run.'

'Until other arrangements are made.'

Suleiman sighed. 'Very well.'

'My Lord?'

'There is nothing else to be done. The harem must be housed somewhere. Take whatever rooms you need, I will authorize it. I shall summon my architect. We shall set to work on a new palace for the harem immediately.'

CHAPTER 68

They sought refuge from the hot August night on the slick still waters of the Bosporus. Suleiman and Hürrem sat together in the stern of a black and gold *caïque* off Seraglio Point, accompanied only by three deaf-mute *bostanji* to man the tiller and oars. They drifted with the current a stone's throw from the shore. Torches burned at prow and stern.

Black velvet curtains assured their privacy. Hürrem peered out and saw the dark cedar-grown cemeteries of Çamlica slide past in the darkness.

Suleiman seemed once again preoccupied. He seldom laughed anymore. He had dismissed all the musicians from the seraglio and had their instruments burned. He never even asked her to play for him now; he said the music of the viol reminded him too much of Ibrahim.

He had learned to punish himself in small ways. He sent his favorite green and white Chinese porcelain back to the treasure house at Yedikule, and ate instead from earthenware. He had drunk not one drop of wine since Ibrahim's death.

'I have consulted with my architect,' he said. 'I have asked him to design a new palace on the ruins of the Old Palace. I would like you to look at his plans and give them your approval.'

'Is it so terrible for you, having me here in the palace?'

'You know that is not the case. There is no room for the harem at the Topkapi. It cannot be part of the royal palace. It has always been separate.'

'It is a large harem, my Lord. Do you still hunger for the other girls?'

'Of course not.'

'Then perhaps if you no longer require them, you could order the Kislar Aghasi to find them husbands. Then it would be only me and my household that you would need house here.'

'What you are asking is unthinkable!'

'I am sorry if I gave you offense, my Lord.'

'What more do you want from me? I have sent Gülbehar away. The only time I ever visited the old Harem was to see you. I love you more than I have loved any woman.'

'So will you make me your queen one day?'

'The Sultan may never marry.'

'It is part of the holy laws, the *Sheri'at*?'

'There is nothing written.'

'It is not even in the laws of the Osmanlis?'

He shook his head.

'Then why not?'

'No Sultan has married since Bayezid the First,' he said.

'You are greater than him. You are greater than any Sultan there has ever been.'

'There are good reasons.'

'You are the *Kanuni*, the Lawgiver. You make the laws, not ghosts from the past.'

He sighed. 'I will tell you a story about our history and the very first Bayezid of the Osmanlis. He was a Sultan long before we came here to Stamboul. He married a Serbian princess, Despina.

'At the time we were struggling with the Tatars for control of Anatolia. Bayezid met Tamerlane in battle at Angora and was defeated. It was a terrible defeat; Bayezid was captured and so was Despina. Tamerlane wanted to humiliate us, so he forced Despina to wait naked on him and his generals at table.

'It was the darkest moment in our history. Our weakness, you see, is our women. Since then no Sultan has ever married, so that we can never be weak that way again.'

'That was long ago. Your people were nomads then. Now you are lord of the world's greatest empire. Who will ever take me prisoner my Lord?'

'No, Hürrem,' Suleiman said. 'What you ask is quite impossible.'

CHAPTER 69

The Aya Sofia had been the greatest church in Christendom until Mehmet had conquered Constantinople and claimed it as his mosque. It was vast, its dome soaring far overhead, seemingly unsupported, like the cupped hand of God.

It was sunset, the hour of lamp lighting, and the Reader's only light came from the stained windows far above. He stood on the prayer stand, a sword in his hand, a Koran in the other, his voice echoing around the church.

Hürrem was concealed behind a latticed screen, kneeling on a prayer rug of age-worn silk. Below her, thousands of turbans bobbed in unison, the mumbling of prayers susurrating around the walls. This ritual meant nothing to her, but it always impressed her.

Here, she thought, was the real power behind the Osmanlis.

The droning of the mufti and the repetition of movement focused her mind.

It was unbearable. Slave girls who had come to the Harem at the same time as she, had since been married off to a pasha or a cavalry officer and had their own property and status as a wife. She, the favorite of the Lord of Life, remained a slave. She was Suleiman's constant companion, but it was another woman's son who would inherit the throne after his death.

She touched her forehead to the carpet, murmuring her prayers, as the gloom gathered inside the church. A thousand candles were lit, one by one, around the walls. Duty, tradition, religion; these people were consumed by fear of their own God.

The answer lay here, she decided, with Islam.

The gardens of Mustapha's harem blazed with hundreds of tulips. Gülbehar sat alone in a kiosk below the fortress wall, listening to the hum of the bees. She did not hear her son approach.

'Hello, Mother.'

'Mustapha!'

'I find you well?'

She smiled with pleasure and held out her hand. He raised it to his lips and sat down beside her. 'Better for knowing you are returned!' she said. She clutched his hand in both of hers. 'I have missed you. How was Stamboul?'

'Rife with gossip as always. Everyone from the lowliest hawker to the Mixer of the Sultan's Cordials fancies himself as the next Commander-in-Chief and plans the next campaign against the Holy Roman Empire.'

'I am sure they will leave a part of it for you to conquer when you are Sultan.'

'As God wills.'

She searched his eyes. 'You saw your father?'

'I saw him.'

'Did he ask after me?'

'He sends his felicitations for your continued good health.'

She forced herself to smile. 'And what other news from the city?'

'All everyone talks about is the fire at the Old Palace. It was burned to ashes and most of the surrounding quarter.'

'Hürrem?'

'She was not harmed. She sleeps now in the seraglio.'

'She actually sleeps in the palace?'

Mustapha shrugged. 'For now.'

'She spins her web. Be careful.'

'You credit her with too much.' He raised Gülbehar's hand to his lips once more. 'He loves her more than you. I wish it were not so. But it is no more than that. Try to forget.'

He talked then about his family, asked about his sons and hoped she had not had trouble from his *kadin*s. Gülbehar ruled his harem; she knew all that happened, spoiled her grandsons, and barely tolerated his wives. So she told him what he needed to know and took care not to mention Suleiman again. But the pleasure of seeing her son once more was soured by old ghosts.

After he left, her hands bunched into fists in her lap. He would not listen.

He did not see the danger.

There were two codes of law. There were the *kanuni* - the laws formulated by the Sultan himself - and there was the *Sheri'at*, the sacred and immutable law of Islam. While the Sultan ruled with absolute power, even he was subject to the written word of God.

The *Sheri'at* was interpreted by a council of religious judges, who alone were able to issue fetwas, or opinions, on any question in accordance with Islamic jurisprudence. However, they could not issue a fetwa unless invited and could not speak unless their opinion was sought.

Each governor had their own mufti to guide them in matters of religious law. The foremost judge, the *Sheyhülislam*, was assigned for the spiritual guidance of the Sultan himself.

Suleiman's *Sheyhülislam*, Abu Sa'ad, was one of the most powerful men in the Ottoman empire.

His room was a simple chamber overlooking the gardens of the second court, and there was little furniture as befitting a man of ascetic tastes.

The room was dominated by a stand of ivory and tortoiseshell. A Koran lay open upon it, the pages illuminated in gold and blue script.

The Lady Hürrem was preceded into the room by the Kislar Aghasi. Hürrem was completely hidden by a chador of violet silk. Abu Sa'ad clapped his hands and pages fetched sherbets for his guests, although he knew Hürrem would leave her cup untouched; to drink from it would expose her hand and face, and disgrace them both.

'I am honored by your presence, My Lady,' Abu Sa'ad said. 'God rejoices in the great zeal with which you have forsaken the pagan gods of your youth and embraced the one true faith.'

'I still have much to learn,' Hürrem said.

'We all have much to learn.'

He glanced at Abbas, looking for a clue as to the purpose of this meeting. But the Kislar Aghasi stared stonily out of the window. The pages brought their iced sherbets and retired. Abu Sa'ad waited for Hürrem to speak.

'As you know, I have been much honored by the Lord of Life,' she said.

He bowed his head in recognition of the Sultan's generosity towards her.

'It has given me great pleasure to pass on some of my bounty to the glory of Islam. I have paid for both a hospital and a mosque to be built.'

'Your generosity has been most welcome.'

'But there is a question that has been troubling me. It is a matter of religion that a poor woman such as me does not understand. Have these donations increased the piety of my soul in the eyes of God?'

Abu Sa'ad blinked. 'Well, it is indeed a pious act.'

'And so they have been recorded in the great book in Paradise and count towards my salvation?'

He paused. The answer of course was plain, but he took care in how he phrased his reply. 'It is a gracious act, my Lady, yes. But as a bondswoman it may not be recorded against your own name in Paradise. Rather it increases the sanctity of the Sultan, may God keep him and grant him increase.'

'Then my good works are to no avail?'

'On the contrary. They are to the glory of God and the Sultan.'

'But there will be no place for me in Paradise?'

He thought he heard a sob catch in her throat. 'That I cannot say.'

'Thank you for seeing me,' Hürrem said.

Abu Sa'ad was convinced that she was weeping behind the chador. He felt sorry for her. But he supposed she would soon get over it, whatever it was. A woman did not feel the pain of the spirit as acutely as a man.

CHAPTER 70

The Çinili Kiosk offered an uninterrupted view of the Horn. There were verses from the Koran emblazoned on the walls in Arabic script, yellow on midnight blue. They might as well have been sitting in purgatory for all the pleasure it seemed to give his second *kadin*. She looked pale and had hardly said a word all afternoon.

'What is wrong, *russelana*?'

'My Lord, it is nothing. It will pass.'

'The last time I saw you, you told me it was your time of the moon. Before that you said it was a passing melancholy. I cannot remember the last time I saw you smile.'

'Forgive me. Perhaps you should send me away.'

'Perhaps I should,' he said. He jumped to his feet. The sudden movement startled the two black guards. Hürrem curled her knees up to her chest, avoiding his eyes.

'Tell me why you mope like this. I cannot tolerate such miserable spirits a moment longer!'

She covered her face with her hands. When he saw how wounded she looked, it softened him. 'Please tell me,' he said, this time more gently.

'My Lord, I fear for my soul.'

This abrupt confession caught him off balance. He almost laughed with relief. 'We all fear for our souls.'

'But you may find pardon in good works.'

'I do not understand.'

'You fear for your soul, why do you think I do not fear for mine?'

Suleiman realized she was quite serious. He had never thought about this before. Women did not have souls quite like a man. Although

Hürrem had accepted Islam from necessity, he had never considered that she might take it seriously.

'What is it you are afraid of?'

'I begged an audience with the *Sheyhülislam*. He told me that despite my many bequests for mosques and hospitals I receive no credit for it in God's eyes. I shall be ignored, even in Paradise.'

'What exactly did he tell you?'

'He told me that no bondswoman can earn credit in Paradise, and that as long as I remain a slave, I am just dust in the afterlife.' She took his face in her hands. 'I want so much to have a soul and be saved!'

The intense look on her face shocked him. 'If that is what you want, then I shall make you free. From today you will be a bondswoman no more. And God and all his prophets shall rejoice in another soul who has found the true path.'

'You mean it?'

'It is a simple thing. You need only to have asked me.'

She threw her arms around his neck. Suleiman felt pleased with himself. If only all his problems were as easily resolved.

The next day Abu Sa'ad again granted audience to Lady Hürrem, to counsel her on affairs of the spirit. What she asked him stunned him to silence. But he gave her his *fetwa*, and gave it honestly, as he was bound to do, according to the dictates of Islam and the teachings of the Koran.

CHAPTER 71

The Sultan's personal quarters were separated from the harem by a single door. It led from his bedroom onto a cloister, and then to a maze of courts and dormitories that had once belonged to the pages and eunuchs of his own retinue.

It had become known inside the palace as the Golden Road, for it led directly to Hürrem's apartments. It was along this cloister that Abbas hurried now, the sleeves and hem of his pelisse trailing the cobblestones, his cheeks puffing with exertion. He paused before going up the steps to the first-floor apartment, to catch his breath.

When Hürrem finally received him, he was still panting from his exertions. He dabbed at the slick of perspiration on his forehead with a silk handkerchief.

'Well?' Hürrem said.

'The Lord of Life commands your presence in his bedchamber, My Lady.'

'I see,' Hürrem said. 'I am sorry, Abbas, but you must inform him that I cannot come.'

This was the moment Abbas had dreaded. His fortune was inseparable from hers, and now she had quite plainly gone mad.

Suleiman lay sprawled on the divan, apparently calm. But his eyes were pinpoints. 'She refuses me?'

Abbas felt a bead of sweat trickle down his spine. 'She said, My Lord, that her life was at your command but that she might not come and lie with you without offending God and His sacred laws.'

'She lectures me on the *Sheri'at* now?'

'She says she wishes no offence. She says she heard it from the *Sheyhülislam*'s lips. He told her that as a bondswoman, she could be your mistress and give no offence to God. However, as a free woman, she would be acting in sin.'

'Abu Sa'ad told her this?'

'Yes, that was what he said.' Let him explain this mess, in the name of God.

'We must consult him then, since he knows God's mind better than I.'

Suleiman stormed out of the room. Abbas whispered a silent prayer and followed.

Any other man would have quaked at being roused from his bed to face the Lord of Life, the King of Kings, the Possessor of Men's Necks, and bear the brunt of his towering rage. But the *Sheyhülislam* feared only God and knew, with unwavering conviction, the heart and mind of the Infinite. He looked surprisingly calm.

There were only three men in the vast audience chamber; Suleiman, Abbas and Abu Sa'ad. The guards who had fetched the mufti from his bed now waited beyond the door.

Suleiman glowered at the cleric from his throne. 'I need a fetwa,' he said.

Abu Sa'ad bowed his head.

'It concerns Hürrem. I have released her from my slave family. She is now a free woman.'

'She has told me,' Abu Sa'ad said.

'As a free woman may she still lie with me in accordance with God's holy law?'

Abu Sa'ad had the answer to this question ready, as it was the same question Hürrem had sought his opinion on earlier that day. The answer remained immutable, no matter who was asking it. 'Even if you laid with her a thousand nights as a bondswoman, it would be a sin before God now that she is free. It would put her soul in mortal danger.'

'How might she resolve this problem?'

'She may only lie with you now without stain if she is your wife.'

'Get out,' Suleiman said. 'Both of you.'

Such a beautiful room, Suleiman thought. Such a vast room. How long had men labored over this faience on the walls? And these rich crimson and blue carpets! They still bore the impressions of his Kislar Aghasi's knees. He closed his eyes and listened to the murmuring of the fountains. There was frankincense in the censers. So perfect here. If only a man's surroundings were enough to make him happy.

It comes down to a simple choice, he thought - give her marriage or give her up.

His limbs felt frozen. He sat for hours, staring into the vaulted cupola above him, wondering what his life would be without her.

He was not alone through his despair; tradition, duty and fear sat beside him through his vigil, arguing back and forth like wives at the fish market. They all had an opinion and expressed it as forcefully as the *Sheyhülislam*. He wished he did not have to listen to their carping, but not one of them would go away and leave him be.

The Fourth Court of the Topkapi was a miniature forest of old pines and twisted cypress swarming up the slopes of Seraglio Point. On one side it overlooked the training fields of the *çerit* and the crumbling Byzantine monasteries that now served as stables; on the other was the sparkling blue of the Golden Horn. Suleiman liked to walk here sometimes, to admire the view, to watch the cavalry training.

Today he kept his head down, oblivious to everything but the tumbling confusion in his mind.

He climbed The Hill That Made The Camel Scream, to the very highest point of the court. From there he could look south to the islands of the Marmara; beyond lay the Mediterranean and his colonies in Egypt, Barbary and Algeria.

If he looked east across the wind-whipped Bosporus he could see Asia where the caravan roads led to Syria, Azerbaijan and Armenia.

Below him the harbor was fringed with the masts of galleys belonging to Dragut, his admiral, who had turned the Mediterranean into a Turkish lake. Just beyond lay Galata, and the warehouses and palaces of the Venetians, the Genoese and the Greeks, who all paid him tribute.

Look north and he could make out the *Gaiours*' palaces at Pera. Behind them were Rumelia, Bosnia, Wallachia and Transylvania; they were all fiefdoms of the Osmanlis.

'What king is there now who may conquer you and make me wait naked at his table?' he heard her saying. 'You are the most powerful man in the world and yet you dare not do what you most desire. You are ruled by your own fear.'

He imagined her eyes filled with tears. The fancy was so real that he even reached out to try to touch her. But there was no one, just the wind. If he gave her up no one would ever walk beside him again. He might sleep with the most beautiful women in the Empire, but without her he would be alone to shoulder the terrible burdens of rule. She was his conscience, his consolation, his counsel, his advocate and his ease.

She was the Vizier who could not betray him, as Ibrahim had done; she was his Harem, a thousand women in one.

She was his friend.

'I cannot give her up,' he said, and the decision was made. He would do the unthinkable because to do otherwise was unbearable.

When Abbas was summoned once more into the presence of the second *kadin*, he had prepared himself for every possibility except the one that presented itself. She was, he noted, in high spirits and wasted no time with pleasantries.

'How would you like to be rid of your girls, Abbas?' she asked him.

'My Lady?'

'The Sultan no longer has need of his harem. His concubines are to be married off. You are to start making the arrangements immediately.'

Abbas could not hide his astonishment. 'I shall proceed as you command.'

'Do you not wish to know why?'

'It is not for me to question the decisions of the Mighty.'

'Abbas, you are indeed a treasure. I shall tell you anyway since you will hear of it soon enough. The Lord of Life is to dispense with his harem because soon he is to take a queen.'

Abbas blinked at her.

'You are looking at the future wife of the Sultan of the Osmanlis.' She laughed. 'Are you not impressed?'

'As you say,' Abbas said.

Impossible, he thought.

On the occasion of the marriage of Suleiman to the Laughing One, Stamboul witnessed the greatest celebration it had ever seen. Bread and olives were distributed to the poor; cheese, fruit and rose-leaf jam to the middle classes. The streets were festooned with the scarlet flags of the Osmanlis and the green standards of Islam.

There was a public procession of wedding gifts; hundreds of camels laden with carpets, furniture, and gold and silver vases. Wrestlers, archers, jugglers and tumblers performed in the Hippodrome day and night.

In another procession a huge loaf of bread, the size of a small house, was dragged through the streets by ten oxen, while the city's master bakers threw hot loaves covered in sesame and fennel seeds to the crowd.

Lions, panthers and leopards were paraded in the *Atmeydani*. Thousands of people lined the arena, and those who could not get in climbed trees for a better view. The Sultan's slaves showered fruit, money or silk among the spectators. The arrival of giraffes elicited gasps of astonishment.

Meanwhile, in the seraglio, Hürrem became queen in a simple ceremony witnessed only by herself, Suleiman and Abu Sa'ad. Suleiman touched Hürrem's hand and whispered, 'This woman Hürrem I make my wife. All that belongs to her shall be her property.'

Finally, she was Hürrem Haseki, the Sultan's consort and Queen of the Osmanlis. It was her most perfect day.

PART 7

Paradise on Earth

CHAPTER 72

Pera, 1541

The carriage clattered to a halt in the courtyard below Julia's window. A eunuch jumped down to settle the horses while another opened the door. The windows were covered in black taffeta so she could not make out who it was. She was only mildly curious. Ludovici often entertained merchants and suppliers during the day.

A figure emerged from the coach, head and face invisible beneath the hood of a cloak and *yashmak*. Not a finger or toe was visible.

A few moments later Hyacinth tapped on her door to announce that she had a visitor. The woman entered behind him and threw back the hood of her cloak.

Sirhane hadn't changed. She was perhaps a little thinner, otherwise it was as if the last six years had not happened. Julia threw her arms around her. 'I never thought I would ever see you again,' she said. 'Tell me everything.'

She had servants bring them sherbets and sweetmeats, then sat her down on the divan beside her.

Sirhane told her she was now married. It had been arranged by the Kislar Aghasi, she said, when Suleiman disbanded his harem. Her husband was a captain in Suleiman's cavalry. His name was Abdul Sahine Pasha.

'He is a big brute of a man with a beard and his member is as thick as my wrist! He treats me well enough. I could even grow to love him if he were not a man.' She rested her head on Julia's shoulder. 'I have missed you.'

She looked glorious, as she always had. She wore a kaftan of green Bursa brocade, open in front and joined at the waist by three pearl buttons. Beneath it she was all snow-white silk, shimmering to her ankles. Rubies glinted on her fingers and in her hair.

Julia was dressed in somber black after the Venetian fashion. She felt drab beside her.

'How did you find out I was here,' she said.

'On the morning that I was to leave the Harem. The Kislar Aghasi came to me and told me you had not drowned after all. He said you were in Pera, married to a Venetian.'

'He told you?'

'For six years I mourned you. And now I find you married to a fine Venetian gentleman!'

'We are not married, and he is more pirate than Venetian gentleman. Still, look at us, whoever would have thought that we would have survived this long.'

The sun dipped below the seven hills, and the calls of the muezzin rose from the dusty city. Light pooled like liquid gold on the Horn, as the silhouettes of the cypress trees faded into the gloom below the walls of the seraglio. Julia and Sirhane sat on the terrazzo, talking in whispers.

'Is it really true?' Julia said. 'Suleiman has married off his entire harem?'

'Yes. There is no more honey in the honeypot. All that remains is Hürrem and her household. She has a hundred slaves in waiting now. She comes and goes whenever she likes, thirty eunuchs trailing along in her wake.'

'And yet, it is hard not to admire her.'

'How can you say that?'

'She has fire in her. She is not like the rest of us. The other women are either jealous of her or they are cowed by her reputation.'

'The Kislar Aghasi told me she was the reason the Sultan ordered you drowned.'

'Whatever she did or did not do, it cannot affect me now.'

'Then you are the only one in all the Empire who is not afraid of her. Foreign ambassadors include gifts for her as well as the Sultan now. They even send her letters to try to sway her opinion, hoping she will use her influence over him. The viziers, muftis and Agas pay her tribute through the Kislar Aghasi. Even my husband. He says she is more powerful than Ibrahim ever was.'

The lamps flickered to life in the old city and the echoes of the muezzin faded into the gathering violet dusk. A stillness settled over the city. 'I must go,' Sirhane said.

'So soon?'

'I should not be here at all. If Abdul ever found out, I might end up in a sack myself.'

CHAPTER 73

Fate had been kind to Ludovici Gambetto.

He had powerful and influential friends at the Sublime Porte and his business had prospered beyond his wildest dreams. Fortune had also delivered him a beautiful mistress from a noble Venetian family.

Yet his good fortune - the contacts Abbas had made for him inside the Sublime Porte - was founded on his best friend's anguish. Julia belonged to him only because she could not belong to anyone else.

He had built a new palazzo on the heights of Pera, dressed Julia in the finest velvets and put rubies and diamonds on her fingers. No one saw them, of course, for she was never allowed to be seen. The colony knew he kept an Italian mistress, and he had heard her identity was the source of gossip. It amused him to hear the names they came up with. One of them was a former mistress of the Pope himself.

He stood on the terrazzo and watched her. She was down in the garden, reading. The summer flowers were still in bloom, the air heavy with the scent of umbrella pines. He went down the marble steps to join her.

She looked up. 'You look pleased with yourself,' she said.

'No, I cannot take the credit.' He sat down beside her. On the harbor the *caïques* crisscrossed the bright water.

'What has happened?'

'I have heard a rumor from the Porte. They say Rüstem Pasha is to marry the Sultan's daughter.'

'Mihrmah?'

'That's what they are saying.'

'Then he will almost certainly be the next Vizier.'

'Yes.'

'That pleases you?'

'If I were on the side of the angels, it would not. But I am only a humble merchant and I cannot afford to be on God's side. I have not really been on the side of Heaven since I left Venice. That is why I have all this.'

'That is blasphemy, Ludovici. And I still do not understand.'

'Suleiman's present Vizier, Lütfi Pasha, is too difficult to do business with. He is too honest.'

'A fatal flaw in a Vizier.'

He smiled. 'Indeed. Rüstem on the other hand would sell his own mother for ten per cent commission. For fifteen, his grandmother and his canary.'

'He will be excellent for your purposes, then.'

'I am sure he will be a great success.'

'And you can send more *caramusalis* through the Dardanelles without fear of inspection. But what made Suleiman choose Rüstem for such a wonderful match?'

'His charm and good looks?'

Julia had already worked it out. 'Hürrem!'

'Yes that is what they are saying in the bazaars. Time will tell. Though what he has done to deserve her patronage I can only imagine.' He studied her. There was something different about her today; a bloom in her cheeks that had not been there before. 'You had a visitor yesterday,' he said.

'Is that wrong?'

'Who was it?'

'She was a concubine in the seraglio, as I was.'

'But how did she find you?'

'Abbas.'

'Abbas told her?' He sat up straighter. 'Abbas told her about you?'

'Yes. He wanted her to know that I was safe.'

So he knows I lied to him, Ludovici thought. He felt his cheeks burn with shame. How will I ever look him in the eye again?

'Are you alright?'

'I worry for you. Now that someone else knows about you, you are even less safe.'

'I am sorry,' she said. 'I am a burden. I put you in danger.'

He reached for her hand. 'I have been thinking about this lately. I have a vineyard in Cyprus. You could go there and live under another name. You would not have to live like a prisoner there.'

'You could give me another name but someone there would recognize me, eventually. Someone from Venice, someone from here. It would make no difference.' She drew herself up. 'I would rather stay in Stamboul.'

He shook his head. 'But why?'

'I have grown to like it here. I do not wish to go to Cyprus.'

I should just put her on a boat and make her go, he thought. If I were a better man. 'There is something else you should know,' he said. 'Remember I told you that Suleiman's navy defeated our Republic's fleet at Prevezzo.'

'Yes, I remember.'

'Venice is a city built on the sea and for the sea. It needs command of the ocean to survive. Suleiman has choked off all the sea routes, in and out. The only Venetians who have welcomed this state of affairs are men like me, here in Pera. We can charge a lot more for our contraband wheat.'

'How does this affect me?'

'There is a legation arriving soon from Venice. They have come to see the Sultan, to sue for peace.' He hesitated. 'Your father is to head the legation.'

She turned pale. 'I thought he must be dead by now,' she said. 'So even the Devil does not wish him in Hell. Will he come here?'

'I doubt it. The Venetians in Stamboul consider me little better than a pirate.'

'You surely do not imagine that I would wish to see him?'

'No, I did not think so. But I thought you should know.'

She closed her eyes. 'What about Abbas?'

'Yes, if he finds out, your father could be in danger.'

'You don't think I want to protect him after what he did? I think we should make sure Abbas knows about this. In fact, I should like to tell him myself.'

A meeting between Julia and Abbas? He didn't relish the thought, but he supposed it was about time. 'I will see if I can arrange it,' he said.

CHAPTER 74

The carriage was an oblong box on wheels, painted with flowers and fruit, no different from a hundred others in the city. It clattered through the filthy alley and stopped outside an anonymous two-story house, painted yellow like all the others in this Jewish quarter. A page opened the door and Julia stepped out.

She was also anonymous beneath her *ferijde*. It was black silk, the only clue to her station in life. She wore two veils; a gauzy yashmak that covered her face, nose and mouth, and a black *cazeta* that fell from her head to her waist, with just a square hole for her eyes.

She hurried into the house, leaving her pages to wait by the coach.

Abbas was sweating heavily, even though it was still early morning and not yet warm. He dabbed at his chin with a silk handkerchief.

He stopped when he saw her and stared in shock. 'Where is Ludovici?'

'He sent me in his place,' she said.

He tried to struggle to his feet, clapped his hands for his pages to come and assist him. After they had him back on his feet, he sent them all outside. 'Julia,' he breathed.

She lifted the *cazeta*, let it fall behind her, like a cape. Then she unpinned the yashmak. 'Hello Abbas.'

He covered his face with his hands and turned his back to her. 'What are you doing here?' he said. 'You should not be in Stamboul. I told Ludovici to send you away!'

'He tried to make me leave, but I wouldn't go. Anyway, where could he send me that would be safe? It's not his fault.'

'If you knew the pain you cause me, you would not have come here.' He slumped against the wall. 'Please, just go.'

'There is something I have to tell you. It is about my father. He is coming here to Stamboul.'

'How do you know this?'

'Ludovici was informed of this yesterday by the *bailo*. Venice is dispatching a peace legation to the Porte and my father will be the ambassador.'

Abbas slipped further down the wall until he sat on his haunches on the carpet. 'So the devil approaches Paradise,' he said.

There was nothing else to say. Julia desperately wanted to comfort him. She knelt down beside him and he did not protest as she leaned forward and gently kissed his cheek. 'I am sorry,' she whispered.

She got up, replaced the yashmak and the veil. She looked once over her shoulder, wanted to say something more, but could not find the words.

After she had gone Abbas stayed crouched against the wall, his kaftan bunched around his knees. He heard the clatter of the carriage wheels on the cobblestones as she left. Dust motes drifted through the chevrons of light from the window.

He drew his knees up to his chest and curled on his side on the floor. Just before evening his pages came, helped him to his feet and half-carried him downstairs to the carriage. Then they took him home; to Hürrem, and to hell.

Antonio Gonzaga stared at the Mohammedan skyline as they sailed past the battlement walls on Seraglio Point. The Kubbealti Tower at the Topkapi reminded him of the campanile in the Piazza San Marco.

'So that is the home of *Il Signore Turco*?' he said.

'We must treat warily with him,' the *bailo* said.

Gonzaga snorted with contempt. The *bailo* was more Turk than Venetian now himself, he thought. The man has gone native.

He despised the Venetian community in Pera, how they built Turkish palaces and dressed in Turkish gowns. What was more disturbing was how they spoke of the Sultan and the Divan, as if they were more important than the Doge.

'We should take care not to provoke him,' the *bailo* went on.

'Do not disturb yourself', he said. 'One day the Lion of Venice will consume all its enemies. Until then, I shall do as you suggest and play the lamb. But I shall not grovel to him. Our setbacks are only temporary. Do not forget that.'

CHAPTER 75

Gonzaga made the short trip across the Golden Horn in the royal *caïque*. When he reached Seraglio Point, two pashas and forty heralds escorted him and his delegation the rest of the way to the Gate of the Majestic One.

He tried to appear indifferent to the great arch of white marble and the contents of its mitered niches. The decapitated heads had ripened in the sun and there were more heads piled like cannonballs at the main gate. A group of urchins were playing with them.

He put a scented handkerchief to his nose.

The arch was a full fifteen paces long and when they emerged from it they entered the first court of the Topkapi, the Courtyard of the Janissaries. It was crowded shoulder to shoulder. There were servants carrying trays of hot rolls; a page being carried on a litter to the Infirmary; a troop of blue-coated Janissaries on the march, their Bird of Paradise plumes cascading almost to their knees. Yet he was struck by the hush, after the tumult of the street outside. In here no one spoke above a whisper.

The *Ortakapi*, the gateway to the second court, was flanked by two octagonal towers with conical tops, like candle snuffers. There was a huge iron door and Suleiman's *tugra*, his personal seal, hung above it on a brass shield. There were more heads blackening on spikes on the wall above.

Gonzaga was ordered to dismount.

'We must go on foot the rest of the way,' his interpreter told him.

Gonzaga reluctantly complied.

A waiting room led off from the gatehouse. While Gonzaga cooled his heels in a sparsely furnished cell, the interpreter passed the time by pointing out a cistern that was used for drowning prisoners. Next to it was the beheading block. The Chief High Executioner, he said with pride, could process up to fifty heads a day.

Gonzaga thanked him for this information and settled down to wait.

Three hours later he was escorted through the gate to the Second Court.

How dare they can make him wait like this, Gonzaga thought. He was so angry at the insult to his person and to *La Serenissima* that he did not spare a glance at the fountains or the box hedges or even the gazelles that grazed on the lawns. He stamped between the honor guard of Janissaries lining the pathway to the Divan, his retinue hurrying behind him.

The only thing to be heard was the sigh of the wind in the trees.

He was escorted into the Divan.

He was impressed, despite himself. He had never witnessed such a riot of color. Such a brilliance and variety of costumes; a Grand Vizier in bright green robes; the muftis of religion in dark blue; the *ulema*, Suleiman's religious judges, in violet; the court chamberlains in scarlet. Ostrich plumes waved like a forest, jewels flashed in turbans and from scimitars. There were silks, velvets and satins.

Hundreds of dishes were set out on the silver tables; guinea fowl, pigeon, goose, lamb, chicken. Gonzaga looked around for the chairs. Instead he was made to squat on the carpets with the rest of the company to eat his lunch.

'When may I see the Sultan?' he hissed at his interpreter, who was sweating profusely.

'Very soon,' the man whispered back. 'But we must be silent for the meal.'

Pages leaned over their shoulders and squirted rosewater into goblets, with unswerving accuracy, from goatskins slung over their backs. Attendants in red silk robes moved silently to and from the kitchen. A raised finger was enough to have a servant hurry over to fulfil any request. Figs, dates, watermelon and *rahat lokum* were served as dessert.

Not a word was spoken.

In fact the solemnity of the occasion was not broken until the meal was completed and the assembled dignitaries rose to their feet. At that point, the slaves descended on the plates and scrambled for the remains of the food like a pack of dogs. It only confirmed what Gonzaga had suspected all along. Underneath all the pomp and ceremony, they were just heathens.

The Gate of Felicity guarded the *selamlik*, the Sultan's inner sanctum. The double gate was surmounted by an ornamented canopy flanked by sixteen columns of porphyry and guarded, by Gonzaga's calculation, by at least thirty eunuchs. They wore vests of gold brocade and each had his curved sword drawn, the razor-sharp blades flashing in the sun.

Gonzaga was given a gold cloth to put over his clothes so that he would be fit to present to the Sultan. The Chief of Standard came to receive his gifts.

Four Parmesan cheeses.

The interpreter did not comment on this bounty. Gonzaga was made to wait while this treasure was presented to the Lord of Life.

Suddenly two chamberlains grabbed him by the neck and arms, pinioning him. They forced him to his knees to kiss the portal and then dragged him across a courtyard between another double line of guards, and into the Audience Hall. They ignored his protests. They could not understand his Italian anyway.

A throne, fashioned from beaten gold, stood in one corner of the hall like a four-poster bed, surrounded by a carpet of green satin. It was so vast that the Sultan's feet did not touch the ground. Pearls and rubies hung from silk tassels on the canopy.

Gonzaga's impression of the Lord of Life was fleeting; a white turban adorned with a huge egret feather, three diamond tiaras and a ruby the size of a hazelnut. His white satin gown was ablaze with even more rubies. He had a beard and a proud nose.

The Vizier, standing at Suleiman's right shoulder, turned to the interpreter. 'Has the dog been fed?'

'He has. The infidel now craves to lick the dust beneath His Majesty's throne.'

'Bring him here, then.'

Gonzaga was dragged into the middle of the chamber and they forced his head onto the carpets. Approaching the throne, they made him do it again.

'The dog has brought tribute?' the Vizier asked.

'Four cheeses, Great lord.'

'Store them in the Treasury with the other gifts.'

Gonzaga was dragged backwards to the door and propelled into the forecourt, where the chamberlains released him.

He was spluttering with rage. 'You humiliate me. I have not even addressed the Sultan!'

'You may not address the Lord of Life directly,' the interpreter said. 'Now we go to the Divan. You may put your entreaties to the Vizier and the Council.'

'What?'

'It is not possible to speak directly with the Sultan.'

'Then why did you bring me here?'

His interpreter looked terrified. 'Please, this way, My Lord,' he said. 'You will speak to the Vizier now and he will take your message personally to the Lord of Life. That is all.'

CHAPTER 76

It was two days since Gonzaga had been honored with an audience with the Sultan of the Osmanlis, and he was still shaken. 'We come here in peace and they spit on us,' Gonzaga said. 'How dare they treat us this way!'

Ludovici poured him wine from the crystal decanter to soothe his nerves. 'That is the protocol,' Ludovici said. 'All ambassadors are treated alike, ever since Murad the First was assassinated by a Serbian noble.'

'I was not even given the opportunity to speak to him. Who does he think he is?'

'He is the Lord of Life, the Emperor of the Two Worlds, Maker of Kings and Possessor of Men's Necks - that's who he thinks he is, your Excellency. Besides, all decisions on foreign policy are taken by the Vizier, for Suleiman to ratify. He never conducts negotiations directly. It would be too demeaning.'

They were in the drawing room of Ludovici's palazzo. He saw Gonzaga cast a critical gaze over the long table of polished chestnut, the carved chairs upholstered with crimson damask, the gilt Vicenzan mirrors on the walls.

Yes, Ludovici thought, not bad for a bastard, is it?

'You must understand,' he said, 'their whole system is built around a rigid hierarchy. To their mind the Sultan has no equal anywhere in the world. Not even the Pope - or the Doge.'

Gonzaga snorted with derision.

'The Sultan is the only one in this whole Empire who attains his position by virtue of his birth,' Ludovici continued. 'All others rise by their own abilities. They do not even have to be born a Muslim. The last Vizier, Ibrahim, was the son of a Greek fisherman. A Christian.

'They have a system called the devshirme. They take men and women from all over the Empire and train them to be part of the Sultan's slave family. Those with real ability can rise to pre-eminence. Those with more brawn than brain are conscripted into the Janissaries, which is their soldier elite. And they are elite; full time professionals and the reason they have conquered half of Europe. As for the women, the mother of the Sultan might start life as the daughter of a Circassian peasant farmer. The system is eminently fair and eternally surprising.'

'I understand the point you are making, but perhaps your admiration for them is tempered by your own bitterness for Venice,' Gonzaga said.

Ludovici bowed his head to concede the point. 'It is true, in the Republic men such as me must go abroad to find their own measure. However, even an impartial judge would see that their system is not only fair, but it also promotes peace inside the society. For instance, although the Turk fights us infidels with all the means at his disposal, nowhere else in the world can a man practice his religion as freely as he may inside the Osmanli empire. Even when they made war on Venice, we in Pera were allowed to practice our Catholic rites in peace. Down in Galata you will find Jews, Muslims, Christians all working side by side. In Rome, they are still putting Lutherans to the stake.'

'Is that why you asked me here Ludovici? To list the Sultan's virtues. Perhaps you will convert to Islam yourself?'

'I remain a loyal subject of *La Serenissima*. But I have lived here a long time, your Excellency, I understand their ways.'

'Thank you for the lecture. It has been most instructive. Now, you said you had a proposal for me.' Gonzaga finished his wine and helped himself to more.

'I understand your negotiations with the Vizier did not go well.'

'He wants us to pay tribute and cede the island of Cyprus. He will want the San Marco as his summer palace next.'

'Can we refuse his demands?'

'Ever since Preveza, Suleiman has had us by the throat, as you well know. Without uninterrupted trading routes our republic will sink into the Adriatic. Thanks to your enlightened Turk.'

'There might be another way to settle this, Excellency.'

'I'm listening.'

'As you know my activities do not always align with the strictest reading of the law.'

'You're a pirate.'

'Not quite.' Ludovici smiled. 'But I have made some unusual allegiances in the course of my business. They might be of use to *La Serenissima*.'

'How?'

'It is true that I admire the Turk, but I love my country more. Perhaps you should abandon your negotiations with the Sultan. I might instead be able to arrange a meeting for you with the Turkish admiral, Dragut.'

'Dragut?'

'Now *he* really is a pirate, for sale to the highest bidder. So, if Venice must pay tribute for use of the sea lanes, I am sure Dragut would not be quite as unreasonable in his demands as the Vizier.'

Gonzaga drained his glass. 'Continue'

'Dragut is a freebooter. Make him the right offer and he'll switch sides.'

Gonzaga smiled. 'Well my renegade merchant, perhaps you could be of service to the Republic after all.'

'I am so glad you think so,' Ludovici said.

Julia watched the conversation from the shadows at the top of the stairs. Her father! It was like looking at a total stranger. He looked grayer and smaller than she remembered. Twelve years since she had seen him, but his voice still put a chill through her. It brought back memories of silent meals, dusty Bibles and, of course, Abbas screaming in the hold of a privateer.

She searched in her soul for some ghost of filial affection but found nothing. She felt instead a deep kinship for Ludovici, as he handed yet another goblet of wine to the man who had destroyed his best friend and crushed the spirit of the woman he loved.

CHAPTER 77

A messenger arrived that afternoon at the *bailo's* residence with a sealed missive. It said that Dragut would be on the galleot Barbarossa, moored in the harbor at Galata. Gonzaga was to meet him there at midnight and he was to come alone.

Gonzaga informed no one but his host of his meeting with Dragut. Ludovici had impressed on him that the fewer who knew about it, the better. He omitted Ludovici's role in the arrangements. Gonzaga was prepared to protect him while he was still of possible future use.

That night he left Pera in a coach. The *bailo* wished him luck and waved him farewell. He disappeared down the hill towards the inky bowels of Galata.

A pink glow lit the sky from the nearby foundries. A carriage clattered out of one of the violently steep alleys that led onto the waterfront. Abbas watched from the shadows as a man stepped out. He was wearing the robes of a Venetian senator.

He passed close to the doorway where Abbas stood. So, this was him, this was Gonzaga.

A decade rolled back. He was in the hold of a stinking privateer and he felt the terror overwhelm him yet again.

There were three of them, a knifer and two assistants.

They tied a white bandage round his lower belly and thighs to slow the bleeding. He kicked and writhed but it did him no good. The knifer swore at him and they let him exhaust himself before they set to work.

He struggled with all the strength he possessed. But against three men, his hands tied behind his back, it was useless.

When it was done, they cauterized the wound with boiling pitch. He vomited and passed out.

When he came round, they were still binding the wound using paper saturated in cold water. They put a spigot in an opening in the bandages to restrict the flow of urine and blood.

Then the knifer's assistant dragged him to his feet and began to walk him around the hold. One circuit took in the blue lolling head of Julia's *duenna;* another a pool of blood-stained bilge, a coil of tarred rope and a broken winch cable.

They walked round and round for hours. What horrified him was the kindly way the two men talked to him, encouraging him, recalling other operations they had seen and telling him what a brave lad he was and that everything would be all right.

It was as if they were good friends come to rescue him, instead of his tormentors. What was worse, he sobbed and thanked them for helping him when they finally eased him back onto the floor, half crazed with pain and barely conscious.

He had no idea how long he lay there. A few hours later he started to burn up with fever. But they would not let him drink, and his tongue swelled in his mouth until it almost choked him. His lips cracked and he could not speak.

One day the men came back into the hold and bent down to examine the wound. They removed the bandages and nodded to each other, apparently satisfied. When they released the spigot a flow of urine spurted across the hold like a fountain.

'Well done,' one of them said and patted him on the shoulder. 'You're a tough one. You're going to be all right. Didn't I tell you?'

A few weeks later they sold him in the market square at Algiers.

In the years that followed, he had watched his body change, turning soft, then running to fat. He envied the eunuchs who had never really known what it was to be a man. He was one of the few who had survived such an operation when it was performed so late in life. Food had become his only solace.

And every day he cursed the name of Antonio Gonzaga.

He watched Gonzaga head towards the Barbarossa, lamp swinging. The galleot's outline was silhouetted by the glow from the arsenal at Top Hane. Abbas looked back up the hill. Two shadowy figures slipped into a doorway. He had not supposed that Gonzaga would be so foolish as to come alone. Well, that did not matter. His men would take care of them.

He moved out of the doorway and followed him.

Julia knelt in her private chapel, her gaze fixed on the wooden crucifix above the altar.

'Dear God, help me. I fear for my soul.' There was evil in her, she was sure of it. She knew something terrible was about to happen to her own father and yet she was going to do nothing to prevent it. What sort of woman would do that?

'Help me,' she repeated. But the words were hollow. She didn't want guidance, and she didn't want forgiveness. Instead she felt a reservoir of cold and visceral anger spill over inside her.

What kind of God would allow a boy like Abbas to suffer so terribly and a man like her father to prosper?

Her father's God. Not hers.

She rose from her knees. She would find her solace elsewhere.

CHAPTER 78

Gonzaga sensed that someone was behind him. He turned and peered into the shadows.

'Who is there?'

No answer.

But there was someone, he was sure of it. If it were one of Dragut's men, surely he would have shown himself. Perhaps it was one of his own men further along the wharf. He turned and hurried towards the gangway of the Barbarossa.

The galleot was deserted. The lamps that burned on the fore and main masts threw long shadows across the deck. There was no night watch and no sound from below.

He heard a noise somewhere along the dock and spun around. Four shapes melted out of the shadows, blocking the way back. He drew his sword.

No, wait. Perhaps they were Dragut's men.

'Which one of you is Dragut?' he said.

'Dragut is not here,' a falsetto voice replied in faultless Venetian dialect.

'Where is he then? I demand to see him.'

'He is getting drunk in Üsküdar. Now drop your sword or we will be forced to take it from you.'

Gonzaga heard the rasp of steel as swords were drawn from their scabbards.

'Who are you?'

'I said, drop your sword. You don't know how to use it anyway. I assure you these men here are expert.' Gonzaga uttered a sob of fear and did as he was told. The blade clattered onto the cobbles at his feet. He shouted for his bodyguards. No answer. He dropped the oil lamp and ran.

Two more shadows appeared from the darkness and grabbed him before he had gone even five paces. They wrestled him to the ground. 'Tie him up,' the falsetto said.

His hands were pinioned behind his back and tied with rough hemp. He screamed for help, so they stuffed a foul rag in his mouth. One of the men lashed out with his boot, kicking him in the ribs, then rolled him over onto his back.

The falsetto picked up the oil lamp that he had dropped and came over. Gonzaga found himself staring at a fat Moor with one eye, half his face mutilated by an ancient injury. In the lamp light he looked like a devil from hell.

'Antonio Gonzaga,' he said. 'Do you remember me?'

Remember him? His mind reeled. What was he talking about?

He squinted up at this apparition in panicked confusion. He was a Moor, yes, but not wharf side scum like the others. He wore a sable-lined pelisse, embroidered with pearls and silver and he had on soft yellow leather boots. There was a large round pearl in his ear. He crouched down and removed the sodden rag from Gonzaga's mouth. 'You really don't remember, do you?'

'Of course I don't remember you. I've never met you.'

'No, we have never met. But I knew your daughter.'

'My daughter's dead. She was murdered by pirates.'

'Perhaps.'

'Who are you? *Corpo di Dio,* I have money. Do you want money? Tell me what you want.'

'What do I want? I want you to remember, that's all. I want you to think about your daughter, the most beautiful woman I ever saw, that I ever will see. I want you to send your mind back twelve years, to the son of the Captain General of the Republic of Venice.'

Gonzaga remembered then and wet himself. The man holding the lamp shook his head. 'Yes, I did the same. It's terrible, knowing that you are utterly helpless, isn't it?' He stood up. 'Take him aboard!'

Gonzaga screamed but one of the men quickly shoved the rag back in his mouth. They lifted him easily, hands and feet, carried him onto the Barbarossa and down into the hold.

Perfect justice, Abbas thought.

CHAPTER 79

Abbas hung the lamp on a hook fixed to one of the beams and leaned against the bulwark as the men deposited their whimpering cargo in a lapping pool of tar and seawater. His eyes were starting from their sockets and he was trying to say something through the gag.

Abbas waited until they were alone, then he said, 'I will take the rag out of your mouth now. But if you scream, I shall replace it. Is that clear?'

Gonzaga nodded.

'There.'

The words came bubbling out in a torrent. 'I didn't know what was done to you, I swear, I only ordered them to beat you, to discourage you, that's all, if I have wronged you, I swear that I will make it up to you, I am a rich man, I have much I can offer you, I am a *Consig-*'

Abbas stuffed the gag back in his mouth. He's like a dog trying to vomit up its breakfast, he thought. It was like that for me once.

'What can you offer me, *Consigliatore*? Money? I have more than I shall ever need. The Sultan and his lady pay all my expenses. I have fine clothes and more diamonds than even you could fit in your long pockets. No, what I desire is only what every man is granted at his birth. And you took it away. You cannot give it back.'

Abbas drew a dagger from the sash at his waist. He held it close to Gonzaga's face, turning it in his hand so that the blade caught the reflection of the lamp. 'Look at this, Excellency. A simple instrument. You can cut bread with it or you can ruin a man's life. It depends on the intention. What is my intention, Excellency? Can you guess?'

He pulled up Gonzaga's robe, exposing his thighs and lower belly. He gripped Gonzaga's testicles in his fist, squeezing. Gonzaga's face suffused with blood as he tried to scream through the gag.

'Can you imagine what this is like? Did you imagine it when you ordered it done?'

Gonzaga shook his head violently. Abbas touched the knife to Gonzaga's flesh, drawing a thin line of blood. Gonzaga thrashed like a beached fish. Abbas put the knife back into the sash at his waist.

'No *Consigliatore*, I would not wish such a horror on even my worst enemy, and you are that, and more. I cannot do it, not even to you. I would never stain my own soul with such a sin.'

Gonzaga curled his knees into his chest and rolled onto his side. He started to weep.

'I will show you the mercy you never showed to me. I will give you your life, such as it is worth. Every second that remains of it is yours to savor. In the morning Dragut sails for Algiers. I have instructed him to sell you in the marketplace. When you are chained to a bench, awash in your own filth, toiling eighteen hours a day at the oars, you can think about what you did to me and to your daughter. You will have plenty of time for reflection. Some men survive five years before their strength gives out.' Abbas went to the companionway. 'If only you had shown me such consideration! Go with God, Excellency.'

He took the lamp from its hook and left Antonio Gonzaga to the terrible darkness.

The moon had fallen below the seven hills when Ludovici returned. Julia was still awake. She sat by the window staring into the candle.

He put a hand on her shoulder. 'It is done,' he whispered.

He felt the answering pressure from her fingers, but she did not reply. He left her there and went to bed, knowing he would not sleep.

Abbas selected his own key from the hundreds on the key ring in his sash. The former Kapi Aga was the last of the white eunuchs to have the keys to the Harem. Now the Sultan only entrusted a complete rasé with the responsibility.

He slumped on his cot. The cat jumped into his lap, purring, and he petted her absently. He removed his turban and put his head in his hands.

Revenge did not taste particularly sweet. What would he do with his pain now that he could no longer dream about retribution?

He had settled his score with Gonzaga, but nothing could ever change what had been done.

PART 8

The Dangerous Window

CHAPTER 80

Topkapi, 1553

Suleiman had lived fifty-nine years, and age gnawed at his bones. He spent more and more time closeted with the *Sheyhülislam* reading his Koran.

He had gout; his elbow and knees were sometimes so swollen and tender he could not bear the slightest touch. These attacks sometimes lasted as long as a week. He had taken to wearing rouge to hide the sickly pallor of his skin. He ate little.

Time was running out.

'I am so afraid,' Hürrem whispered to Suleiman one night as she lay in his arms.

'Of what *russelana*?'

She laid her head on his chest. 'My Lord, when you die - may that day never dawn - my life shall no longer be worth living, so I fear nothing on my own account. But when Mustapha attains the throne, he may execute all his brothers, even poor Çehangir.'

'We are beyond such barbarity,' Suleiman said. 'Mustapha has a good heart. He has vowed that as long as your sons do not take up arms against him, they will not be harmed.'

'But when he comes new to the throne, he will be surrounded by those not as well disposed. We know Mustapha shall be Sultan but who will be his Vizier? Would an old man like Lütfi Pasha feel the same compassion for my sons?'

Suleiman held her tighter. She was right, after his death she would be helpless, and so would Selim and Bayezit. He was relying on his son's nobility. The boy was no butcher; he was as loyal as he was brave. There was no malice in him. 'Mustapha is a good man,' he said.

'His mother still lives, and she hates me.'

'What would you have me do?'

'Never die.'

He smiled in the dark. 'We all die. It is God's path for us.'

'Then I shall pray I have a voice in the Divan to protect me. Rüstem perhaps?'

Yes, there was something in that, he thought. As his son-in-law, Rüstem would protect his wife and her brothers. He had proved his loyalty with Ibrahim. 'I will think about it,' he said.

Soon afterwards, when Lütfi Pasha died of the pestilence, Suleiman made Rüstem the new Grand Vizier, and the second most powerful man in the Osmanli empire.

Abbas was ushered into the presence of the Vizier, executed his *temennah*, and allowed his pages to lower him to the carpet.

'May I extend my congratulations on your great fortune,' Abbas greeted him. 'God indeed smiles on you. To be Vizier of the greatest of all Osmanli sultans is a blessing almost too great to comprehend.'

The Infinite had no hand in this, Rüstem thought. 'All thanks and praise to Him.'

'However my mistress has asked me to remind you that though God is great, there are times when his Bounty - as His vengeance - may need prompting by earthly angels.'

'Tell your mistress I shall not forget her words and that I am exceedingly grateful for them.'

'Well that is why I am here. To discuss the many ways you can prove your kind remembrance of her.'

Well, Rüstem thought, she wastes no time in calling in her favors. He clapped his hands and the pages scurried away to fetch sherbets and halwa while they settled to their discussion.

'You have heard the whispers in the bazaar?' Abbas said.

'People do more than whisper, Abbas. They shout to each other across the stalls how our Sultan has lost all appetite for war. He spends more time with his architects than with his generals.'

'My mistress worries that there are those who may seek to profit from his distractions.'

'Doubtless you have heard these other rumors from the barracks?' Rüstem said.

'Everyone in Stamboul has heard them.'

The trouble had started, as always, in Persia. Shah Tahmasp was once again raiding their eastern border, torturing and killing the muftis and flaunting his Safavid heresies, all the time growing bolder. Meanwhile Suleiman wrote poetry, dictated laws, and planned mosques in his summerhouses at Edirne and Çamlica.

His soldiers waited behind the palace walls, hungry for action.

Mustapha would not sit around drinking sherbet with his builders, they said. He would have taken us against the heretic Persian long ago. As soon as he takes the throne, we will be on the march again, there will be more victories and more plunder.

A new sultanate will be the end for Hürrem, Rüstem thought. And when she goes, I go as well. 'What would the Lady Hürrem have me do?' he said.

'Only remember where your loyalty lies.'

'I am loyal to my Sultan above all things.'

'Then you will be sure to root out any who might seek to bring him down?'

'Of course.'

'We shall rely on you to deal with this threat.'

There is no threat, Rüstem thought, just the jabber of soldiers and eggplant vendors. But this is our best opportunity to save our own necks.

'Assure your mistress that I remain her husband's faithful servant,' he said.

CHAPTER 81

Suleiman had his head in Hürrem's lap, his eyes closed. Insects murmured in the garden, but in the harem it was cool, almost chill. It was midday. The sun had not yet penetrated the plane trees and only a weak yellow light filtered through the windows.

'You look tired, my Lord,' Hürrem said.

'Yet there is so much to do before I sleep.'

'You should not work so hard.'

But working hard is my duty, he thought. I have abrogated the day to day running of the Empire to Rüstem and the Divan, so I can devote myself to the rebuilding of this city. Stamboul will be a worthier testimony to my reign than Rhodes, Mohacs or Buda-Pesth. When my grandfather conquered this city, much of it was abandoned and derelict. Before I die it will have surpassed its former glory.

The focus of the building work was the construction of imperial mosques. Each one included a *kulliye* - a cluster of charitable institutions such as a hospital, a religious school, baths, a cemetery, a library, sometimes even a hospice and a soup kitchen. New quarters with new populations soon built up around them.

He had commissioned work to start on the *Suleimaniye*, on the site of the old harem. It would be his masterpiece; the stone cupolas and minarets would dominate the Horn and the city of the Seven Hills for a thousand years.

He had also set himself the herculean task of drafting a complete legislature that would be the foundation of all future government. The thousands of laws that he was drafting would regulate the judgments of the Divans, and give the Osmanlis, for the first time, a complete code of law.

He prayed to God for enough time to finish the task he had set himself.

Hürrem stroked his cheek. 'So deep in thought, my Lord.'

'I was thinking how quickly time slips by.'

'Perhaps then you should not spend so much of it closeted with your scribes.'

'I cannot rest until the work is finished. I cannot leave it to Mustapha. He is a great soldier and an able governor, but he cannot apply himself to matters of law as I can. Besides, other matters press on me. I must go to Persia. I cannot ignore the Shah's provocations any longer.'

'Why send a professor of law to spank an errant child? Is Tahmasp so great a king that he should warrant your individual attention?'

'There is no choice.'

'Of course there is. Send Mustapha. The Janissaries adore him; they will follow him anywhere.'

A nerve in Suleiman's cheek twitched. 'Why do you say that?'

'Have I offended you my Lord?'

'What whispers have you heard concerning Mustapha?'

'I hear only good reports. They say he is a good man, as you have always said. A great horseman, a brilliant commander.'

'Too brilliant perhaps,' Suleiman murmured.

'Can a man be too brilliant?'

'I thought you were afraid of him.'

'You assured me I had nothing to fear. You know your son and I do not. I trust your word.'

'I do not fear him when I am dead. Yet in truth, I sometimes fear him while I still live. I fear the Janissaries.'

'They will never love him as they love you. You gave them Belgrade; you gave them Rhodes; you gave them Buda-Pesth.'

'That was a long time ago. Many of the young recruits in the army now were not even alive when we took Rhodes.'

It had been so long since he had seen Mustapha. He still thought of him as a lively, bright-eyed boy, but he was a man now with grey in his beard. He was capable and he was ambitious; how could he not be impatient for the throne?

And, as Hürrem said, the Janissaries adored him and that was what kept him awake at night. They had made the Osmanlis masters of Europe and Asia. The armies they fought against were mostly noblemen who had brought their peasants along with them as infantry.

The Janissaries were the difference. Whoever commanded them, commanded the world.

It was the Sultan who kept their bellies filled. A soup kettle was emblazoned on all their battle standards to symbolize this allegiance. Their general was even called the Head Soup Ladler, and had a brass spoon sewn on the front of his cap.

Their ranks were replenished from the devshirme. They lived harsh, celibate lives in Spartan barracks on poor pay. The only way they could enrich themselves was with the plunder they took in battle.

In theory they were his slaves. But with their constant demands for warring and loot, and the threat they posed to security, he wondered sometimes if he was not theirs.

They had once rebelled and forced his grandfather from his throne. If they had done it once, they might one day do it again.

'There have been times when I have gone to war just to satisfy the Janissaries,' he said, 'even though I deemed it unwise. If they can rule me, perhaps they can rule Mustapha also.'

'But years ago you sent him to Amasya to guard our eastern borders. It is twenty six days' ride from here. Surely, he is no threat to you there?'

'The threat lies in what my son intends. There are so many rumors. He is like a stranger to me now. How can I be sure of his loyalty? I fear what will happen if his ambition overtakes his patience.'

'Let us speak no more of it. You have always said that Mustapha is a good and just man. Forget about the whispers. The court is always full of them. Until you have hard evidence against him, then give none of it any thought.'

Suleiman took some consolation from what she said. She is right, he thought. I have no evidence against Mustapha.

And it was crucial that he could trust him. He had dreamed of an empire that would leave the Osmanli heritage of nomad tents and constant warring far behind. Stamboul now boasted the finest architecture in the Orient. Literature, painting and music were flourishing. Mustapha's peaceful accession to the throne after his death would make his dream real.

For Suleiman, his death was now as important to him as his life. Beyond all the conquests, beyond even the great city he would leave behind, that would be his true legacy to history and to the Osmanlis.

CHAPTER 82

Amasya

Clumps of cobalt forget-me-nots pushed through the patches of hard snow. Wild ducks rose from the grass, their wings whirring as they flapped away, panicked by their approach.

Mustapha turned his horse away from his escort and waited for Çehangir. Out here with only the wind for company he knew they would not be overheard.

'A fine day's hunting,' he said.

Çehangir looked flushed and tired. 'Yes, a wonderful day.' They rode together for a short while in silence while Mustapha decided how to best broach the subject on his mind. 'How is our father?' he said, finally.

'He suffers badly with the gout. It gives him a foul temper. I stay out of the way as best I can.'

'Does he seem troubled?'

'I see him only rarely. I don't know.'

'Does he speak to you of me?'

'Suleiman loves you,' Çehangir said. The sun retreated behind the mountains and there was ice in the air.

'Does he?' Mustapha said. 'Then why did he send me out here? Why have I not seen him in so long?' He could smell snow on the wind. 'We must hurry. The mountains are bitter here at night, even in spring.'

He patted Çehangir on the shoulder and together they rode back to join their escort. He wondered what his half-brother was not telling him. Or perhaps no one except Hürrem knew what Suleiman was thinking these days.

The fortress was perched high in the mountains overlooking the Green River. In the courtyard the guards stood motionless in their leather winter cloaks. Torches fixed in the walls set their shadows dancing over the cobbles.

In a room high above them, a page in a turban of apricot silk set a silver jug of steaming black coffee on the low table beside Gülbehar's divan. She warmed herself by the charcoal brazier as she waited for her son.

He burst in, his face bronzed by the cold wind. He has been hunting, she thought, and has ridden home in the dark, even though he knows the dangers of ice and swollen rivers this time of year.

He kissed her hand and settled on the divan beside her. Forty years old now, and he still had the energy of a raw youth. Which is just as well because he will be an old man by the time he is Sultan. If only Suleiman would spend more time on the battlefield, in harm's way.

'How are you, Mother?'

'I am well. Here, I have had the *kiaya* fetch us coffee.' She clapped her hands and one of her *gediçli* stepped forward and poured the coffee into two silver cups.

It was scalding and laced with honey. She disliked its bitter taste, but she had heard that it was the fashion in Stamboul to drink it. 'I hear Rüstem has reduced your allowance.'

'Do I have no secrets?'

'Not from your mother.'

'Do not upset yourself. It is nothing.'

'Nothing! It is an insult!'

'He is trying to provoke me into doing something that would benefit him far more than it would benefit me. He will regret it when I am Sultan.'

'If.'

'Mother…'

'You trust your father too much. Look what he did to me.' She put down her silver cup and the coffee spilled onto the tray. 'How many more of these insults will you bear? He marries the witch, makes her queen, then exiles you to the mountains and gives her devil's spawn the seat at Manisa. Now he turns his back while Rüstem makes you a pauper. If it is a goad, then accept it and let him deal with the consequences.'

'That would be foolish.'

'Would it, son?' Her eyes filled with tears. A fine boy; the finest prince the Osmanlis would ever see, and they were conspiring to ruin him. You deserve to be Sultan, she thought.

'He is my father, and he is my sultan. Any action against him would be a sin against Heaven.'

'I am sure no such noble thoughts have crossed the mind of his new queen.'

'In the matter of succession, Suleiman is the only judge.'

'How naïve you are!'

'I know you do not trust her. Neither do I. But I put my trust in my father.'

Do not trust her? Gülbehar thought. I hate her so much it makes my bones ache.

'In time we will balance all injustice,' he said. 'Perhaps if Mehmet were still alive, you would have cause for concern. But I do not fear Bayezid and I certainly have nothing to fear from his idiot brother. Suleiman could exile me to Cathay, and while I live the Janissaries will not accept either of them over me.'

'The Janissaries are not as patient as you. They want you to do something about this now.'

Mustapha shook his head. 'That would be wrong.'

'Suleiman's father did it.'

'And if I raise rebellion against him, what will happen when my own sons are of an age? We become no better than barbarians.'

'Mustapha, listen to me!'

'No, I will not do it. One day the throne will come to me by right. I will wait. I will not offend my father and I will not offend God!'

'He has to die,' Rüstem said.

Mihrmah blanched and lowered her eyes.

'Yes, Mihrmah and if he is ever Sultan what do you think will happen to us? I will tell you. The first thing he will do is put my head on a spike outside the Gate of Felicity and then send you into exile with only hyenas for company. And what do you think will happen to your brothers?'

She had never known anyone talk about death as dispassionately as her husband. He discussed it as if he were reciting the final moves of a chess game.

'Your father made me Vizier thinking I could protect you and your family,' he said. 'But Mustapha hates me almost as much as he hates your mother.'

Mihrmah turned her head away. It was spring and a warm breeze was blowing from the south. Dolphins were playing near the shore in the Sea of Marmara. Such a pretty day to be discussing murder. 'But if we are found out in this,' she said.

'There is more risk in doing nothing.'

'What shall I say to my father if he asks my opinion?'

'Tell him you live in mortal fear of Mustapha. That is what he will expect you to say anyway.'

She watched him eat, mechanically and without relish. Really, bread and water and an abacus and he would be in Paradise. 'Whose idea was this? Yours, or did it come from my mother?'

He smiled, and the effect was chilling. She knew what they called him, of course, and now she knew his secret; his two eye teeth were larger than the rest. When he smiled they made him look like a wolf.

'Does anything happen in Stamboul that your mother does not instigate?' he said.

'And if we fail?'

'If we fail, we have lost nothing, for Mustapha is already our enemy. If we succeed, we have power over this Sultan and the next.'

CHAPTER 83

The Sultan's apartments served two functions; to display the wealth of the Osmanlis, and to preserve their secrecy.

The wealth was quickly apparent. Verses from the Koran, in white and blue sülü script, circled the room. The stained-glass windows were masterpieces of emerald and crimson. Gilt Vicenzan mirrors hung on every wall, and the bed was raised on a canopied platform and strewn with coverlets of gold brocade and crimson velvet. Beside the bed was a golden ewer for washing the hands.

It was awe-inspiring, though no one ever saw it except his eunuch slaves and Hürrem.

The Osmanli's compulsion for secrecy inspired the fountains that had been cut into the walls; golden spigots murmured perfumed water into marble urns, preventing whispered conversations from being overheard. Gazebos jutted out from the walls so that the Sultan could sit and observe the gardens without being seen himself.

Soon after Hürrem became queen, a further refinement was introduced; a concealed doorway was carved into the wall behind one of the gilt mirrors. It opened onto a stairway that led directly to her apartments, so that she could come and go without being seen.

It was from this doorway that Hürrem emerged one afternoon to find Suleiman pacing the room like a caged beast, even though his right knee was still swollen from another episode of gout.

'My Lord,' she said and performed her *salaam*.

Suleiman was holding a piece of paper in his right hand and he waved it in her direction. 'What do you make of this?'

'I cannot tell from this distance. But if you were to ask me, I should say that it is a piece of parchment.'

'I am sorry, I forget myself.' He hobbled toward her and helped her to her feet. 'I can scarcely believe the evidence of my own eyes.' He handed her the document. 'Here, read this.'

Hürrem read it quickly. It was addressed to the Shah Tahmasp and signed under the seal of Mustapha. After a long soliloquy of greeting, Mustapha offered one of his daughters in marriage to the Shah's eldest son. It went on to outline the benefits to both parties from such an arrangement.

'Why would Mustapha do such a thing?' she said. 'The Shah is the sworn enemy of the Osmanlis.'

'It must be a forgery,' Suleiman said.

It is, she thought, and a very good one. Rüstem is to be commended.

'It could be Rüstem, trying to cause trouble' he went on. 'When Mustapha is Sultan, the first neck he will break will be the Vizier's.' Suleiman paused. 'But there are others who might gain from setting us against each other. The Holy Roman Emperor, for instance. It would certainly not be beyond the Shah himself to do this.'

'I hope you're right. Mustapha always appears so loyal.' She paused a moment, to let him wonder.

'There is a saying, Hürrem. 'The enemy of my enemy is my friend.' If Mustapha sees me as his enemy, then an allegiance with Tahmasp would make all the sense in the world.'

'I am so sorry, my lord. What can I do?'

'I live among snakes and vipers, *russelana*. Yours is the only voice of moderation.' He winced at the pain in his knee. His gout was bad today.

'Shall I send for the physician?'

'No stay here by my side. That is greater medicine than any potion that fool can give me.' After a while he closed his eyes and she thought he was asleep. But then he said: 'I must ride east again with the army.'

'My Lord, you are unwell.'

'We must finish with the Shah, there can be no peace while he is still conspiring against us in Asia. The Janissaries, my generals, the *ulema*, they are all are clamoring for me to do something about him. As Defender of the Faith I have no choice.'

'Send Rüstem in your place.'

'The Janissaries would riot. They expect me to lead them.'

'You are unwell and the mountains in Persia are cold, even in summer. You yourself have told me that a week in Azerbaijan is like an entire campaign in Hungary. I am being selfish, my Lord. I am terrified of losing you.'

'No, I must go.'

Hürrem had not expected this. The letter was meant to undermine Mustapha, not to spur Suleiman into another pointless campaign that could kill him.

'I know you do not fear hardship, but there is another way, a better way.'

'Tell me.'

'Send Rüstem to Amasya with orders for Mustapha. Tell Mustapha to accompany the vizier on a campaign against the Shah. Let him use his own troops.'

'To what purpose?'

'If Mustapha co-operates, you will know the document is a forgery and that Mustapha is loyal.'

'I might go myself and divine Mustapha's loyalties.'

'If Mustapha plans treason do you risk discovering his true ambitions so far form Stamboul? If he is seeking rebellion, you will have to rely on the Janissaries to support you against him. Remember how your grandfather lost his throne.'

'Do you think it will come to that?'

'I only counsel caution, my Lord.' She rested her head on his lap.

He stroked her hair. There was only one problem with power, he thought, and that was how to keep it.

He let the letter slip from his fingers to the floor.

CHAPTER 84

The black market trade in wheat was the worst kept secret in the Osmanli Empire. There was active complicity from every Turkish nobleman with arable land. Eighteen months previously even Rüstem had sailed his own roundships to Venice by way of Alexandria and had made a staggering profit on just one shipment.

Since the summer of 1548, Turkey had enjoyed five excellent wheat harvests, while Venice was starved for grain. The profits for the traders grew in proportion. Ludovici's *caramusalis* sailed regularly to Rodosto on the Black Sea, to load hides or wool. On the way they made clandestine calls to the port at Volos to take on wheat. On the return trip they were ignored by the Turkish warships that were supposed to enforce the embargo, but the privilege was expensive.

'Rüstem Pasha wants another thousand ducats a month,' Abbas said.

Ludovici threw up his hands. 'I can't afford that!'

'I'm sorry. But there is much *baksheesh* to pay.'

'Is there no limit to Rüstem's greed?'

'Apparently not.'

'Tell him I refuse.'

'Don't be rash, Ludovici. Even after the extra *baksheesh* you will still make a twofold profit on every kilo of grain unloaded in Venice. What do you pay here? Twelve aspers per kilo. Rüstem knows you are making thirty-five in Italy.'

'I have to make a profit.'

'Those were his words also.'

Ludovici sighed. There was nothing to be done. If you wanted to do business in the Empire you had to pay whatever the Vizier demanded. Everyone knew that.

They continued with their business; agreeing on routes for his ships and payments to minor officials in the provinces, and counting the ducats that Ludovici had brought with him in a leather pouch.

Abbas was Ludovici's prime source of information on the moods and internal politics of the Sublime Porte. After he had finished his tirade against Hürrem and the extent of the corruptions introduced by Rüstem pasha - of which he was now an integral part - he said, casually, 'It is said that Mustapha is planning a revolt.'

'Where did you hear that?'

Abbas shrugged. 'There is talk that he has arranged a marriage of his daughter to Shah Tahmasp's son. He solicits his support in a rebellion against Suleiman.'

'Suleiman knows about this?'

'You think you and I should know of something that was hidden from the Lord of Life?'

'This is disturbing news.'

'You and your friends should send a delegation to treat with Mustapha,' Abbas said. 'When he comes to the throne he may not be as well disposed to our business as Rüstem, and you will miss our Vizier's avarice then. It may be as well to make an accommodation with now. Have your money on both horses.'

'Could Mustapha actually do that?'

Abbas shrugged and the great dewlaps beneath his chin trembled. 'He has the support of the Janissaries.'

'Not if he allies with the Shah.'

'That may be just a ploy to make Suleiman move against him.'

If all this were true, Ludovici thought, and Abbas's information had always been accurate in the past, then he and his fellow traders should make their move now. When he came to the throne Mustapha might not be well disposed to those who had helped line his enemy Rüstem's pockets. Abbas was right, he should indeed place a bet on both cards, the knave and the king. 'What about you, Abbas, what will you do?' he said.

'I will accept the will of God.'

As Abbas was leaving, he hesitated at the door. 'If anything happens to me, take care of Julia.'

'It is done?' Hürrem asked.

Abbas bowed his head. 'I did as you asked me. The seed has been sown.'

'The whispers will find their way to Suleiman's ears?'

'How can they not?'

'Good.' She smiled. 'How is Julia?'

'Julia is well,' he said, refusing to take the bait.

'What a loyal friend you are. Thank you. You may go, Abbas.'

Çehangir's deformity made it impossible for him to stand upright. He always looks as if he has a sack on his shoulders, Suleiman thought, and is bent under the weight of it.

He could not ride a horse above a canter, could not aim a bow and arrow, could not even lift a sword. A fine son for a ghazi. Yet of all his sons, he was the one he loved best.

'You have seen Mustapha?'

Çehangir did not lift his eyes. He never does, Suleiman thought. He cowers in front of me like a stall keeper.

'He is well, my Lord. He sends his greetings.'

'His mother is well also?'

'Indeed, my Lord.'

Suleiman felt dispirited. The boy looks as if I am about to send him to the executioner. 'You look tired,' he said.

'It was a rigorous journey.'

'The hunting was good?'

'Yes, we hunted every day.'

'Mustapha has shown you great friendship,' Suleiman said. He wondered why. Did Mustapha love the boy so much, or was he using him as a spy?

'I think he feels sorry for me,' Çehangir said, as if he could read Suleiman's mind.

Suleiman was startled by this candid admission. Çehangir was more astute than he gave him credit for. 'I am sure that is not true,' Suleiman said, but he considered this possibility for a moment and then said, 'Did he speak of me?'

'He asked after your health.'

'Nothing else?'

Çehangir seemed to hesitate, then shook his head.

'I am happy to see you safely returned.'

Çehangir was eager to leave.

He is as terrified of me as I was of my own father, Suleiman thought. This is the real legacy of the Osmanlis. We destroy our children.

CHAPTER 85

Steam rose from the damp cobbles and the twitching flanks of the donkeys that trudged single file through the narrow, twisting streets around the fruit markets. It was melon season and the hawkers had piled their fruits in pyramids on their stalls and on the ground, flecked and striped, green and golden. The smells assaulted the senses; ripe fruit, sewage, wood smoke.

The wooden houses overhung the street, and the morning sun could not penetrate. It was cold.

Suleiman forced his aching joints up the hill. He followed one of the porters. The man was bent double, his hands at his ankles, boxes of figs roped in a huge tower on his back.

He had done this once before, leaving the palace anonymously to test the opinion in the street. He had decided it was time to do it again.

He stopped at one of the stalls and pretended to examine the peaches while he listened in on the hawker's conversation with his neighbor.

'They say the Sultan will ride east again, against the Shah,' the man said.

'He should have gone years ago. The Persians have tugged on our beards long enough. We have the greatest army in the world, and he leaves them sitting around in their barracks.'

'Mustapha would not have let the Shah humiliate us like this,' Suleiman said, goading them.

Both men looked at him warily. But the merchant could not help but take the bait. 'Mustapha is a great warrior. He would have had the Shah's head moldering on the gate long ago.'

'Perhaps it is time for Mustapha to be our new Sultan,' Suleiman said.

The men both looked at him as if he had gone mad. 'Keep your voice down. The Sultan has spies everywhere.'

'I am not afraid of the Sultan,' Suleiman said.

'He only says what everyone else is thinking,' another man chimed in. 'Suleiman is an old man. I was still drinking my mother's milk when he last won a great victory.'

'Still, he has done many great things,' the melon seller said. 'He has built us fine mosques to the glory of God, and his navies rule the Mediterranean.'

'What good is his navy when the Shah of Persia lives in the desert? I tell you, it is only a matter of time before Mustapha gets tired of talking to goats in Amasya and sweeps Suleiman from his throne. And everyone knows it!'

'Be still!' the merchant said to him and then turned to Suleiman. He looked angry. He obviously suspected Suleiman was a spy. 'If you want to buy some peaches let me see your money. If not, stop bruising the fruit and go away and talk someone else's head off their shoulders.'

Suleiman shrugged and walked away. He followed a donkey through the press, the wicker panniers on its flanks piled with cherries. The man's words still rang in his ears.

CHAPTER 86

A month later, Rüstem arrived below the cliffs on the Green River with a squadron of Spahis of the Porte and a regiment of Janissaries. He struck camp under the somber walls of Mustapha's citadel, planted his six-horsetail standard outside his tent, and waited.

He heard Mustapha's approach. Unlike the camps of Christian armies, the Turks maintained order and an iron silence. There was no drinking and no gambling and, except when in battle, prayers were observed five times a day. Not a single rider could approach the camp without Rüstem knowing of it.

What began as a few hoofbeats soon became an uproar, rolling like thunder through the lines. Rüstem went outside and waited.

There were no more than two dozen riders, all but one wearing the scarlet silk jackets of Spahi cavalry. Mustapha was the only one in white. There were heron's feathers in his turban, held by a diamond clasp that flashed in the morning sun so that Rüstem had to raise a hand to shield his eyes.

The Janissaries ran through the camp after him, blue coats flapping, letting loose a deafening ululation that echoed from the cliffs until the noise seemed to surround them on all sides. Now they milled around him and his escort, still whooping, happy to eat the dust of the Chosen. Mustapha did not acknowledge their acclaim. He kept his eyes fixed on the royal tent.

Rüstem had his bodyguards drawn up on either side. Dust drifted in an orange cloud over him and his generals. He spat grit from his mouth.

Mustapha dismounted and the cheers faded away. They waited, a savage, shuffling mass. He executed a swift *temennah*. 'Where is my father?'

'He is unwell,' Rüstem said. He has appointed me as Commander in Chief for the campaign.'

'How ill is he?'

'It is not mortal. But he could not bear the rigors of a long campaign.' Thousands of his men were listening to this exchange, some just a few paces away. 'I have never heard such loud cheers. Not even for the Sultan.'

'They cheer me because I am his son.'

'Let us withdraw inside. The dust has parched my throat.'

Rüstem led the way inside his pavilion. Pages brought halwa and rosewater and then Rüstem produced a letter from inside his robe. He handed it, without comment, to Mustapha.

It was the letter offering marriage to the Shah's son, under Mustapha's seal.

'This is monstrous,' Mustapha said.

'You deny it?'

'Deny that I would offer an alliance to an enemy of our Empire and of Islam? What do you think?'

'It bears your seal.'

'It is a forgery, of course. Has my father seen this?'

'He has.'

'And what does he say?'

'I am not privy to his deliberations. What is your reply?'

'I smell your stink on this!' Mustapha said and threw the letter in Rüstem's lap.

'I am not your enemy, Mustapha. Those soldiers outside are your enemy. They cheer too loudly for you.'

'I have never, and will never, say or do anything against my father. He knows that.'

'He awaits your reply.'

'He shall have it.'

'First I have orders from the Sultan himself. You are to assemble your troops and accompany me on the campaign against the Persian heretics. Under my command.'

'I shall do as he orders,' Mustapha said with disgust and got to his feet. He left without speaking another word.

After he had gone, Rüstem sent for the Aga of the Janissaries. He was a fair-haired wiry man, a Slav. The left side of his jaw gone where he had taken grapeshot during the siege of Rhodes. The Bird of Paradise plumes on his cap rustled as he performed his *salaam*. He stood to receive his orders.

'You should prepare a squadron of your best men,' Rüstem said. 'Mustapha is to be taken from the Palace tonight and returned to Stamboul in chains.'

The Aga hesitated. For a soldier trained from a child to unquestioning obedience, it was an alarming reaction. 'As you command,' he said.

'The men should be ready at dawn. That is all.'

The Golden Road led from the Harem mosque past the Sultan's apartments and through the Harem. Hürrem's silk kaftan rustled on the cobbles. She threw open a small door and followed a darkened staircase up to the Dangerous Window. She sat down close to the taffeta curtain and peered through a small chink. Through the latticework, she could glimpse the marble pillars of the Divan. She could not see much, but she could hear everything.

'You are sure of this?' she heard a man say. It was Suleiman. He had returned to his duties in the Divan in Rüstem's absence.

'My information is utterly reliable.' She did not recognize this other man; one of Rüstem's army of bureaucrats, no doubt.

'I have my information from several sources,' the man said. 'The Venetians in Pera are convinced that Mustapha is about to launch a rebellion. The *bailo* himself has sent a messenger in secret to Amasya with a letter. We do not know the contents, but we may surmise that they are making accommodations with him.'

How satisfying, Hürrem thought, to hear one's own rumor repeated in the Hall of the Divan as a hard truth! Abbas had done his work well. For years she had given him little titbits of the truth to feed the Italians. Now they had swallowed the big lie whole.

'I still do not believe this,' she heard Suleiman say.

'My Lord, my inform-'

'Enough! I do not want to hear any more about your spies!' Suleiman strode out of the hall.

Hürrem hurried away as well. Her Sultan would surely summon her to seek her advice about this latest blow. She must be there to comfort him.

CHAPTER 87

An angry murmur rose from the camp at Amasya. The two guards outside the pavilion shuffled nervously at their posts.

The discharge of the harquebus sounded like cannon fire, and the echo resounded from the cliffs after the guard had fallen, clutching at his chest. The second drew his sword in a futile effort to defend himself and his post. There was another bang and he screamed and fell, clutching his face.

Their attackers rushed from the shadows. They paused to deliver the finishing blows to the two men thrashing in pain on the ground, and ran into the tent. Rüstem recognized only one of the men, the Aga with the scar on his face, though it was plain from their uniforms that they were his Janissaries.

'It is fortunate I am not in my pavilion. I think those butchers are about to fire their harquebuses into my mattress,' he said.

On cue, there was a loud bang, followed by another.

Rüstem mounted his horse and turned to the captain of the Spahis, who waited alongside on the ridge above the camp. 'It seems we are faced with a rebellion.'

'So it appears.'

'We must ride hard back to Stamboul and report this to the Sultan. We should hurry in case Mustapha comes after us.' He spurred his horse and disappeared into the darkness with his escort.

Gülbehar had been woken from her sleep with the news of the rebellion in Rüstem's camp. She sat shivering in her ermine robe, huddled around the glowing coals of a brazier. Sirhane entered and performed her *salaam*.

She thinks she is a widow, Gülbehar thought, she believes that is why I have summoned her. Her husband has been captain of my son's bodyguard for ten years. She must have anticipated this moment every day since.

'Your husband is safe,' she said.

Sirhane's shoulders sagged with relief. 'Thanks be to God.'

'But we are all in great danger now.'

'We will leave Amasya?'

Gülbehar shook her head. 'There is nowhere to run.' She stared into the coals. 'There was a rebellion at the royal camp tonight. The Janissaries tried to murder Rüstem Pasha. It was not Mustapha's doing, but when Suleiman hears of this, he will certainly blame him for it. I need your help.'

'My help?'

'If Suleiman moves against my son, he will move against your household too. Your husband will be executed, his property confiscated, and you will be exiled. You will end your days as a beggar.'

Sirhane hung her head.

'Your fortunes are tied to ours now. So you must act quickly. You remember the Kislar Aghasi?'

'A good man, as I remember him.'

'I want you to go to Stamboul and find him.' She leaned forward. 'I want Hürrem dead. Offer him anything. Anything! If he can do this for me, my son will become Sultan and Abbas may have anything he desires. Persuade him, Sirhane. For my sake, and for your own.'

CHAPTER 88

Suleiman stared at Rüstem without speaking. The only movement was the flaring of his nostrils as he breathed.

'It grieves my heart to bring you this news,' Rüstem said.

'Did Mustapha order this?'

'I do not know, my Lord. The Janissaries came in the middle of the night and killed my guards hoping to find me defenseless in my tent. I was forewarned and was thus able to escape.'

'How many?'

'I do not know.'

Suleiman shook his head.

'What about Mustapha? You met with him?'

'When he rode into camp the Janissaries cheered him till they were hoarse. They shouted that he would lead their standards to the House of War. I heard many of them say you were now too old to lead them, and that I was just a clerk with no place outside a counting house. They clamored for him.'

'You showed him the letter?'

'He said he was not answerable before any but God. He also said that the next time I saw Stamboul it would be from a pike on the Gate of Felicity.'

'Those were his words?'

'They were, my Lord.'

Rüstem hurried out of the audience hall. He could not believe that the lie had worked so well. But that was the curse of being an Osmanli. Not one of them really trusted their own sons.

The garden was heavy with the scents of herbs and roses. The summer rhythm of the cicadas was hypnotic. It would be so easy to lie here and forget that the tapestry of the future, that he had woven so carefully, was unravelling in his hands.

Every law he had made, every foundation stone he had laid, every campaign he had fought had been for Mustapha. Sedition would undo everything.

'Don't listen to any of them,' Hürrem said. 'Be proud that you have a son the Janissaries love so dearly. You are his father. His sense of duty will stop him from exploiting this uncanny power he has over them.'

'How can you be so sure?'

'I cannot believe these reports are true. The Janissaries must have acted without his knowledge.'

A shadow passed over the sun. They both looked up, through the open shutters of the kiosk. The city's population of storks, who nested each year on the domes, roofs and minarets had all taken to the air over Stamboul, flying south for their first reconnaissance ahead of the winter migration. Thousands of them trailed across the sky.

'Time is running out,' he said. 'Summer is nearly over. I must ride east with the army or I will lose the throne.'

'What will you do?'

'I do not know. Who might guide me in this?'

'Abu Sa'ad?'

Suleiman considered. 'Perhaps.'

Abu Sa'ad watched the Kislar Aghasi devour the tray of halwa the pages had put in front of him. He ate slowly and with great determination, but with the utmost delicacy. When he had finished, he washed down the honeyed cakes with a little iced sherbet.

He settled back on the cushions. 'I have a message from the Lady Hürrem,' he said.

'May God preserve her,' Abu Sa'ad murmured.

'It seems she has found great comfort in our Faith. She says she wishes to glorify God in a way that will endure beyond her short time on the earth.'

'God shall smile upon her.'

'She intends shortly to bequeath a great part of her personal fortune in the form of a waqf - that is, she will place it in trust, so that more mosques may be built and maintained in the city.'

The mufti bowed his head in acknowledgment. 'Her generosity becomes such a great lady.'

'She says it is your inspiration that has persuaded her to do this. You were the one who guided her to the one true faith, and she is grateful, also, that you comforted the Sultan in his hours of trouble. She asks only that you continue to do your holy work with the same wisdom.'

It was some moments before Abu Sa'ad understood that the Kislar Aghasi was actually there to bargain. He stroked his beard thoughtfully. 'The troubles in the East weigh heavily on the Lord of Life at the moment.'

'Oh, that they might be resolved!' Abbas said. 'The Lady Hürrem has prayed night and day for God to help him through his heart ache. She would give anything to have these burdens lifted from her lord's shoulders.'

'I shall give him what guidance I can.'

'My mistress will be most relieved to hear that.'

After he had gone, Abu Sa'ad took out his prayer beads and murmured prayers of thanks and supplication, but it was always hard to contemplate the divine after a visit from the Kislar Aghasi.

God was good, God was great. But to bring his teaching to the people and to build great mosques took money. For the greater glory of God, he had sometimes to bend his soul a little to the winds of time.

CHAPTER 89

Abu Sa'ad was not the only one that Abbas visited that day.

'Sirhane,' Abbas said. 'It has been a long time.'

'Kislar Aghasi,' she said. She kept herself covered, even though he had seen her naked more times than her own mother.

He threw back the hood of his *ferijde*. 'I received your message,' he said. 'What is you want with me?'

'Gülbehar sent me.'

'I thought that she might.' He looked around the room, the gilded ceiling, the glazed floral tiles on the walls, the Aya Sofia looming through the fretted wooden grills that covered the windows. 'So this is the palace of Abdul Sahine Pasha.'

'He is equerry to Mustapha.'

'He grows in wealth and fortune.'

'Is it good fortune to live in the house of a condemned man, Kislar Aghasi?'

Abbas shrugged. 'There is nothing I can do about it.'

'Gülbehar said that there is. She says I can offer you anything - anything.'

'I have amassed wealth and power beyond any dream I had when I was a youth. But it is all useless to me. Do you understand? So what is it that Rose of Spring thinks she can offer me?'

Sirhane lowered her eyes. 'Does Suleiman know of Julia?' she said, her voice barely a whisper.

The room started to spin. Was there nothing left to believe in? 'You were her friend. How can you bring her name into this?'

'You know what is at stake.'

'I was the one who told you about her. I understand that you might betray me, but would you betray your best friend also?'

'Very soon a woman will die. Perhaps Hürrem, perhaps Julia. It is up to you.'

'Hürrem?'

'You are the only one who can save us from her now.'

'Hürrem is dust. Like every tyrant she will have her day and then she will die. You would sully your soul for these brief moments you have here on earth?'

'It is a good bargain, Abbas. The death of a witch to save the life of the woman you love.'

'She told you?'

'She told me everything; about how you courted her secretly in Venice, how you wanted her to escape with you to Spain. She still loves you too, Abbas. She said you were the bravest man in the world.'

'Yet you would still betray her to that witch?'

He wished he could see her face. Was she trembling or weeping behind her chador?

'Do it or Julia dies, Abbas. Spare me your pretty speech.'

Abbas signaled to his pages to help him rise. He spat at her feet. 'Very well,' he said and left.

Hürrem looks radiant, Abbas thought. The green cap had been pinned at an angle on her head and she wore a kaftan of pistachio velvet bordered with ermine. Pearls glistened in the insteps of her silk slippers.

'Have you done as I asked?' she said.

'I have spoken to Abu Sa'ad, as you commanded. He is aware of what is required of him.'

'My good, faithful Abbas.'

'As you say, My Lady.'

'And what shall be your reward?'

'What reward should you like to honor me with?'

'Your pick of the harem perhaps?'

Abbas smiled, acknowledging her mordant wit. 'My lady is too kind.'

Perhaps she saw the change in him for she suddenly looked wary. 'You look pleased with yourself, Abbas. Perhaps you would like to share the joke with your mistress?'

Abbas took a step towards her and his hand went to the jeweled dagger in the sash at his waist. Hürrem lowered her eyes; she knew what was coming. But the guards positioned around the room were too far away to save her.

'Ah my Abbas. At last we come to the heart of the matter.'

'I have waited for this moment for so long,' he whispered.

'Are you not afraid for Julia Gonzaga?' she said.

Abbas' fingers tightened on the ivory handle.

'There is a letter,' she said. 'I have placed it in safe keeping, to be delivered to the Sultan, should I die. What will he do, do you think, when he discovers that she is still living in Pera and is perhaps the source of gossip about his failings in the Harem?'

Abbas froze. He was trapped. He could not kill her, and he could not withdraw.

She leaned closer. 'Half Stamboul wants me dead. But you have just shown me that no matter how much you hate me you could never harm me. It makes you the most trusted and obedient servant that I have.'

Abbas slumped to his knees.

'I have a problem for which I seek spiritual guidance. A case was brought to me in the Divan that has perplexed me. I have decided to come to you for your ruling under the holy laws of the Koran,' Suleiman said. He paused to collect his thoughts. 'A merchant of good position has three sons. One of them, the eldest, he favors above all the others. He has always trusted him with good salary and good favor. When he dies, the business and all his wealth will be his.

'However one day he discovers that this son is plotting to kill him and take over his business. He cannot wait for his father to die. What should that merchant do, and what sentence should lawfully be pronounced under the *Sheri'at*?'

Abu Sa'ad did not blink. 'The Koran is clear in such matters. The son must die.'

Suleiman gave a long sigh. 'And if that servant's name was Mustapha?'

'Death,' Abu Sa'ad said.

Two days later, Suleiman mounted his horse by the fountain in the Third Court and left his palace at the head of his household regiments, bound for the east. Orders had already been sent to the Agas at Amasya to bring their troops south for the march on Erzerum. Another messenger was sent with further orders for Bayezid to come from Manisa and administer government at the Topkapi in his absence.

Suleiman knew he must hurry to reassert his authority over the army. But first he must talk to Selim and Bayezid.

CHAPTER 90

Konia stood in a vast and dusty wheat bowl on the Anatolian steppe. It was a mecca to the Osmanlis, for it was home to the monastery that contained the bones of Jalal-ud-din Rumi, the founder of the dervish order. It was also the governmental seat of Karamania, where Selim was apprenticed as second prince in succession to throne.

Suleiman had heard rumors, whispered in the corridors of the palace and the bazaars of the city, that Selim was a drunkard. The lumpish awkward youth had become a figure of fun.

Now, as he looked into his son's face, he knew the rumors were true. Selim's complexion was inflamed from too much wine. The broken capillaries on his cheeks and nose resembled a crimson spider web.

'You have heard the rumors about Mustapha?' Suleiman said.

'I do not doubt a word of them.'

Of course you don't , Suleiman thought. 'We shall settle this at Aktepe. I have a question for you: if I were to hand Mustapha to the *bostanji* , you may one day have to bear the yoke of the Osmanlis. Do you think you can bear such a burden, Selim?'

Selim beamed. 'I am your son. I was born to it.'

'All is not settled yet.' Suleiman said. 'Should Mustapha be guilty of treason, the question of the succession will be between you and Bayezid.'

Why did Allah wish to take Mehmet from me, he thought. I did not even have the chance to see him before he died. Barely a year as governor of Manisa, and the pox claimed him within a week. 'My purpose in coming here,' he said, 'is to ask you if you truly think you can bear my burdens. You have hardly earned great merit thus far in your life.'

Selim grew sulky. 'I am ready, father.'

You do not look ready, Suleiman thought. He could hardly credit that Selim was a son of his, named after the great warrior that was his own father.

Perhaps it was his fault for not paying him enough attention when he was a child. He had dedicated the future to Mustapha, and now it was too late to undo what had been done. Selim had grown without direction.

'So what are you going to do?' Selim asked him.

'I must talk to Mustapha.'

'He will only tell you whatever you want to hear. Everyone knows he is Gülbehar's creature.'

'Whoever I choose, I want no bloodshed after I am gone. You and your brothers must agree to honor my decisions.'

'Of course, father.'

'Give me your word.'

'You have it. My only ambition is to serve the Osmanlis.'

If only Mehmet had not died, Suleiman thought. Everyone had loved Mehmet. There would have been no argument, and I could have gone easy to my grave.

So next I must talk to Mustapha. Pray God I make the right decision.

CHAPTER 91

Suleiman rejoined his army on the plains at Aktepe.

He posted the seven horsetails standard outside the royal tent and sent a messenger to summon Mustapha to his presence at once.

Then he waited, prowling the carpets, long into the night.

'For pity's sake, you must not go!'

Mustapha took his mother's hand. 'The Sultan commands my presence. If I refuse, he will take it as rebellion.'

'And if you go he will accuse you of it anyway, and who will there be to protect you?'

'It is my chance to speak up against the lies spoken against me.'

'If he wanted answers, why did he not come here and ask you himself? Why did he go first to Konia?'

'I don't know.'

Gülbehar jumped to her feet, turning away to hide the tears of frustration that came all too readily these days. 'Let them accuse you of what they want. There is no proof.'

Mustapha wondered if he should tell her about the letter and his conversation with Rüstem. He decided against it. 'The Janissaries already proclaim me their leader. Where can I be safer than among them?'

'Here! You will be safer here, in your fortress, far away from Suleiman and Rüstem.'

'I must above all things obey my father. He has summoned me, I will go.'

'And what if only his *bostanji* are waiting?'

'He gave me my life. He has the right to take it back.'

'No! He has no right. I gave you that life also, I suckled you at my breast and raised you from an infant. He has no right to take you from me.' Gülbehar doubled over, sobbing. Mustapha leaped up to stop her from falling. He cradled her in his arms and led her to the divan.

He rocked her in his arms.

Finally he whispered. 'I have to go.'

Gülbehar gripped his arms, as if she could squeeze his defiance out of him. 'Take the sultanate. You have waited long enough. You have only to say the word and the Janissaries will rise with you. There is no need for bloodshed. Your grandfather removed his father from the throne and exiled him. It is within the law.'

'I cannot do it. It is impossible. I would rather die than dishonor my name before all the princes of the world and stain my soul before God.'

Nothing would move him on this, she knew. They had had this same argument now for years. The witch had won. Life was so simple if you believed in nothing but your own preservation.

'What sort of king shall I be if I give up my very soul to attain it? I shall rule without shame or I shall not rule at all.'

'Then you are a fool.'

'He will not harm me, Mother. He is a man of honor, as I am.'

She let him kiss her hand. Her eyes followed him to the door, believing she would never see him again.

When he had gone there were no more tears to cry. She sat by the window, watching the stars wheel across the face of the earth to new tomorrows, helpless in her prison, defeated by her own destiny.

The camp was in silence.

The smoke of damp fir wood clung to the air. Water carts creaked along the rutted tracks. Sheep scurried in choking clouds of dust to the butcher's tents. A group of blue-jacketed Janissaries played fortune dice by a charcoal brazier.

When they saw Mustapha they jumped to their feet and crowded around his horse, as they had done at Amasya. Word quickly spread through the camp; Mustapha had come to lead them against the Persians! The shouts became a roar and carried through the camp to Suleiman's pavilion. He was in consultation with Rüstem, and when they heard it they both fell silent and listened.

'*Padishah, Padishah!* Emperor!'

'Here comes the ghost of my father,' Suleiman said.

CHAPTER 92

Dawn.

All the previous afternoon and evening Mustapha had received the salutes of his generals in his tent, and now the camp was once again silent. The muezzin called the army to prayers; thousands of turbans were drawn up in rows, bobbing against a mauve sky.

When Mustapha finished his prayers, he made himself ready. He dressed in white, as a token of innocence, and put his letters of farewell inside his robe close to his bosom, as was customary for any Turk when facing danger.

He mounted his Arab stallion and prepared to ride the few yards separating his tent from his father's pavilion, as demanded by tradition. His Aga and his equerry, Abdul Sahine, accompanied him.

Mustapha felt the entire army was watching him. Would they reconcile or would he finally stake his claim to the throne?

He slid down from his saddle and removed the dagger at his waist. He handed it to Abdul Sahine. He saluted the guards who stood outside and went unarmed to his father.

With this, the Janissaries went back to their duties in orderly silence but not one of them had a mind for it. They all prepared to hail a new Sultan before sunset.

The pavilion was enormous, divided into rooms by curtains of billowing gold silk. The entrance had peacock blue and ruby red carpets and there were divans against each wall. A small silver topped table stood in the center.

'Father?'

Mustapha pushed aside a curtain and stepped into the Audience Chamber. Empty. The tent whipped in the wind with a sound like a whip crack.

Not quite empty. A black *bostanji* stepped from the shadows behind him. And another. Three more came from behind the curtain in front of him. One held a silken bowstring.

He saw a shadow move behind the silk. 'Father?'

The *bostanji* moved swiftly, barefoot. Mustapha was not afraid, just angry. He dodged the eunuch and stepped into the center of the room. 'Father, listen to me first! Let me face my accusers before you condemn me! This is not just!'

Outside he heard the rasp of steel, followed by shouting. His Aga and equerry were being attacked. His only chance was to slip past the *bostanji*. A prince could only be dispatched with a bowstring, his blood could not be spilled on the ground. If he could get back out of the pavilion, no one else could harm him. If he could reach the Janissaries, he would be safe.

But he would not demean himself. He had never run away from a fight before. 'Father, listen to me!'

One of the *bostanji* tried to throw the silken noose over his head, but Mustapha read his intention and squirmed away. He barreled into one of the others and wrestled him to the ground. Another came for him, but he leaped back, and the man's impetus sent him sprawling across the silver table.

'Father, I never once betrayed you! Come out and speak to me!'

'Get it done!' Suleiman roared from behind the curtain.

The deaf-mutes could not hear him.

'Call off your assassins and let us speak like men!' Mustapha shouted. 'I am innocent! Father, listen to what I'm saying!'

Suleiman put his hands over his ears and closed his eyes, willing it to be over. There was no excuse for treason. The evidence was clear. Mustapha might try to mesmerize him with his candied words, but he had seen and heard reason enough.

If I let him speak, he will sway me. Then as soon as I am compliant again, he will rally the Janissaries to him, as they had rallied to his grandfather. I will not let him take my throne. I have still so much to do.

But what if I'm wrong, he thought.

He tore the curtain aside. 'Stop!'

Too late.

Mustapha lay at his feet, eyes glassy in death, a silken bowstring around his neck. Suleiman turned away. He signaled to the mutes, 'Wrap him in the carpet and throw him outside the tent.'

He stood alone in the middle of the pavilion and waited. A soft moan, like the rushing of wind, passed through the camp. It rose to a keening of despair as the Janissaries saw what had become of their champion.

There, he thought. See what you have done. This is your doing, not mine. You wanted blood. Now you have it.

CHAPTER 93

'Give us Rüstem's head or we'll come and take it!'

He looks so unruffled, Suleiman thought. He has ice in his veins. The Janissaries swarm around my tent baying for his blood and he acts as if there are stone walls three feet thick between him and that mob, not just a few strips of gold and purple silk.

'They blame you, Rüstem,' Suleiman said.

'My lord, Mustapha was his own undoing.'

The tumult was deafening. The entire complement of Janissaries, led by their Aga, milled at the entrance, their swords drawn. All that held them back were the two sentries and the sanctity of the Osmanlis.

If just one man had the courage to ignore centuries of awe and tradition, the tide would sweep them all up and swallow them.

'They want a scapegoat,' Suleiman said. 'Since they do not dare lay a hand on their Sultan, they have decided that you will do.'

Was there a flicker of uncertainty in Rüstem's grey eyes?

'Have you dispatched a messenger for Amasya, my lord?' Rüstem said.

Suleiman was impressed. Even in the face of death, Rüstem kept a practical turn of mind. 'Yes. His wife and sons will shortly follow him to Paradise.'

'Then we have nothing further to fear from him.'

'Not from Mustapha, no.' Suleiman had to shout to raise his voice above the shouts of the soldiers outside. 'Do you not fear the Janissaries, Rüstem?'

'They will do as you command.'

'They were ready to put Mustapha on the throne at breakfast.'

'But now it is midday and Mustapha is dead. The Janissaries are like dogs. They just need a master.'

'And raw meat.'

'Indeed. Feed them and point them at an enemy and they will follow.'

Suleiman tore aside the silk curtain at the entrance and went out to face them. Immediately they fell silent.

He looked around at the thousands of faces, hands on his hips. How they hated him right now. And how he hated them. He would have had all of their heads on the gate at the Topkapi if he had his way. They were the ones responsible for killing his son.

The Aga broke the silence. 'We want Rüstem.'

'Rüstem will be replaced. The gold seal of Grand Vizier will go to Ahmed, the second vizier. But you will not harm him. He is under my protection.'

'He took our Mustapha from us!'

'I took Mustapha from you!' He would have this Aga's neck when things simmered down. The man was an ingrate. 'I took Mustapha. I, your Sultan. And you shall bear it, and you shall do as I command now! Tomorrow we march on the Safavids. There will be booty and women. If you want blood, let it be Persian blood.'

'We want Rüstem,' the Aga said, stubbornly.

'If you want him you must kill me first,' Suleiman said and drew the jeweled *killiç* from the scabbard at his waist. 'Who will be first to raise his sword against his Sultan?'

They backed down, though it took longer than he thought it would. One by one the Janissaries turned their backs and went back to the camp. Finally, only Suleiman and the Aga remained. 'Rüstem told me to arrest him,' he hissed. 'Did he tell you that?'

'You possess the written order, in Rüstem's hand?'

The Aga shook his head.

'Then I do not believe you. It was just what I expected you would say.'

The Aga turned and walked away. Suleiman went back inside. He threw everyone out and spent the next hour breaking every piece of furniture he could find.

The missive was written in white ink on black paper. Gülbehar did not need to read it to know what it said; she had known from the moment she saw the Sultan's messenger dismount in the courtyard. No, she thought, I knew before then; her son's fate had been sealed the moment he rode out of the gates.

She refused to accept the letter. She spat in the messenger's face, cursing him and his sons for eternity and tried to rake his face with her nails. Her maidservants restrained her, and the man fled, his face pale, the *kadin's* wails of grief ringing in his ears.

Sirhane knew Mustapha and her husband were dead the moment she saw the heavy-set Sudanese step from the shadows. A castrato and deaf-mute. A monster more than a man, knives and needles had excised all sentiment out of him.

There was no point in pleading for her life. Just let it be quick.

His tongueless mouth made a strange yelping sound as he came towards her. He would only leave when she was dead, with her head in the leather pouch that hung from the sash at his waist for precisely this purpose.

'Abbas sent you, didn't he?' she said. 'He thinks I am still a threat to Julia. But I would never have done it, it was a bluff, I would never have betrayed her, never. I hope she knows that. I don't mind dying but I don't want her ever to hate me.' She closed her eyes and kept her hands to her sides. Why fight? It would only prolong the agony.

The *bostanji* looped the cord around her neck. He lifted her effortlessly from the floor, the corded muscles in his arms bulging, and quickly and efficiently choked the life out of her.

CHAPTER 94

Abbas shook his head. 'There is nothing she can do about it, Ludovici. Sirhane is dead. Knowing who gave the order is futile.'

'I told her that, but I said I would try to find out anyway.'

'You have given your word before and broken it. It should be easy to do it again. I remember once you told me you would send her away from here. You promised me.'

Ludovici could not meet his eyes.

'You have placed my life and hers in danger countless times through the years because you did not get her out of Stamboul when I asked you to. Did you think I asked you on a whim?'

'I did not want her to go.'

'You fell in love with her.'

'I'm not ashamed of it. Didn't love make a fool of you once?'

'It made me a eunuch of me. It did not make me a liar.'

They fell silent.

'How does she look these days?' Abbas said, finally.

'She ages with much grace.'

'She is still beautiful?'

'She is no longer sixteen. There is a little silver in her hair. But yes, she is still beautiful.'

'I picked the fruit, but you tasted it. Do you know how much I envied you for that?'

Ludovici nodded. 'Yes, of course.'

Abbas sighed and hung his head. 'You asked me if I could find out who sent the assassin for Sirhane.'

'Was it the Sultan or his witch?'

'It was neither. It was me.'

'You?'

'She told me she would betray Julia's whereabouts to the Sultan. Suleiman is not a man who forgives or forgets. He cannot afford to. I did as you would have done to protect her.'

Ludovici's shoulders sagged.

'You may tell her this or keep it from her, as you see fit.'

'Sirhane was the only real friend she had. This will go hard with her. It is better if she does not know.'

'You should have taken her far away when I told you to.'

'I'm sorry, Abbas. I should not have lied to you.'

Abbas took a piece of halwa, then tossed it back onto the tray, all appetite gone. 'It doesn't matter, old friend. What's done is done. Neither of us is fit to judge. Are we?'

The courier galloped towards the Sultan's silk pavilion. He had ridden day and night from Stamboul. He reined in beside the seven-horsetail standard and jumped down, throwing the reins at the Sultan's equerry. He was ushered into the presence of the Lord of Life and there prostrated himself on the ground.

The message he carried was handed to Rüstem Pasha who read it to Suleiman: Çehangir had been found dead at the Topkapi. He had hung himself.

Suleiman's cry of anguish was heard around the entire camp. It echoed from the surrounding mountains, sending a shiver down the spine of the most seasoned of his soldiers. But when they heard what had happened none of them wept for him. It seemed to many of them that God's retribution had been surprisingly swift.

PART 9

Death of a Nightingale

CHAPTER 95

Topkapi Palace, 1558

By the grace of the Most High, whose power be forever exalted!

By the sacred miracles of Mohammed, may the blessing of God be upon him!

To thee who art Sultan of Sultans, the sovereign of sovereigns, the shadow of God upon the earth, Lord of the White Sea and the Black Sea, of Rumelia and Anatolia, of Karamania, of the Land of Rum, of Diabekir, of Kurdistan, of Azerbaijan, of Persia, of Damascus, of Aleppo, of Cairo, of Mecca, of Medina, of Jerusalem, of all Arabia, of Yemen, and of many other lands that my noble forefathers and my glorious ancestors (may God light upon their tombs!) conquered by the force of their arms, and which my august majesty has made subject to my flaming sword, and my victorious blade, Sultan Suleiman Kahn, son of Sultan Selim Khan.

Father.

In sundry verbal and written communications, I have appealed to my Lord for intercession against those who have sought to spread calumny against me. God knows I have never sought favor for myself, unlike others, who curry popularity with the ulema and the soldiery to raise themselves in esteem and rival our own blessed father.

I am powerless against their conspiracy, I who have never sought but to serve you. All I have is your love, and that of my gracious Mother. My fate is totally in your hands.

Yet because I do not try to sway the Janissaries and swagger on my horse I am at the mercy of those who conspire against me. I know I could never outshine the great light that you have thrown upon the world.

I worry for your safety, my Lord. Reports reach me daily that my own brother has been seen in the Porte, heavily disguised, talking with the Janissaries in their barracks and spreading sedition and revolt.

I pray that these reports are untrue for there is no rest for me knowing that my great Lord is in peril…

Suleiman tossed the letter aside. He looked grey, sunken between the two golden lions on either side of his throne. Rüstem waited patiently.

'He pleads with me like a woman.'

'He fears Bayezid.'

'As he should. Bayezid is a lion. A true ghazi.'

'As you say, My Lord.'

'And what do your spies tell you about Selim? He still drinks too much?'

'He spends all his time at the table or the chase.'

'And he wants me to protect him.'

'When the time comes, my Lord, Bayezid will take the throne from him.'

'When I am dead, let God be the judge.' Suleiman closed his eyes. 'My father murdered for his throne, and it seems my sons will do the same. I don't understand why they want it so badly. My only regret was that my father did not live longer. The mantle of the *ghazis* is like a flaming yoke. It has already cost me two of my sons.' He indicated the letter that lay on the carpet between them. 'Is there truth in anything Selim claims? Has Bayezid been to Stamboul?'

'My spies have heard nothing of this.'

'Who should it be, Rüstem? Selim is oldest. The throne should be his.'

'Bayezid is the only choice.'

'Bayezid has no great love for you, Rüstem.'

'I am growing old. I do not think I shall be here to fear him.'

Let God choose, Suleiman thought. He had done all he could. He had written the laws that would safeguard the future conduct of the Empire. Perhaps they would help the Osmanlis survive another warrior, or even a sot, should it come to that.

Yet he feared that his true legacy would be two sons squabbling over his Empire like vultures picking at the eyes of a corpse.

CHAPTER 96

Ludovici was sitting in the great hall, staring at the logs burning in the grate. Julia came to stand behind him and rested her hand on his shoulder.

'You look troubled.'

'I was thinking about what is going to happen when Suleiman is no longer Sultan.'

'You think he is going to die soon?'

'It is what my spies are telling me. He has ruled at the Grande Porte now for thirty-eight years. No man lives forever. Even Suleiman has to die sometime.'

'You will weep floods of tears.'

Ludovici smiled. 'They could make one of their camels Sultan for all that I care. But change makes me nervous. A humble merchant like myself cannot thrive in times of uncertainty. I always need to know who to bribe and how much.'

'Who will succeed him?'

'I imagine Hürrem will have a large say in that.'

'Perhaps she will proclaim herself Sultan.'

'I doubt that even she could manage that. No, it must be Bayezid. How could it ever be Selim? The man is a complete debauch. He would make an excellent Bey of Algiers - but Sultan? Even I would not wish that upon the Turks.'

A log broke and tumbled in the grate.

'And Rüstem Pasha?'

'Bayezid would rather drown in boiling pitch than have him as his Vizier. Besides, he is growing old too. Soon everything will change. A new sultan, a new vizier. For a while, the Turks might even enforce their own laws and my business will be seriously disrupted.'

The wind howled and rattled the windows.

'Which of the pashas will you court next?' she said.

'Who knows?' he said, staring back into the fire. 'The Divan is a nest of vipers, and you can never be sure which hatchling is going to survive.'

Frost glittered on the domes of the Palace as the sun rose in a cold blue sky. Hürrem shivered and drew her ermine robe closer about her shoulders. She could never seem to get warm these days, even hunched over a blazing fire.

She didn't fear death. Aba Sa'ad told her that she had guaranteed her place in Paradise with her good works. She had used her dowry to build mosques and schools in Edirne, Ankara and Stamboul, which she knew Suleiman approved of. The endowment she was most proud of was her hospital for the poor near the womens' slave market, though Suleiman had never understood the true significance of that.

But she would rather go home than go to heaven.

There was a table with a pan of lighted charcoal in front of her. She nestled her feet beneath it to keep them warm.

She stared through the lattice window, imagining the steppe somewhere beyond the violet horizon. She closed her eyes and her spirit drifted free.

In her dream she flew north over the Black Sea and the tiny specks of the *caramusalis*. Soon she broached the coast and below her was a tribe of Krim Tatar, the grass lands dotted with their tent wagons. She swooped down, jumped onto the back of one of the broad-shouldered horses and rode splashing through the reed-grown islands of the Dnieper river. Ahead she saw a city of tents and horses, and heard gypsy flutes. She waved and her mother looked up from the goat she was milking and waved back.

'My Lady!'

Hürrem woke with a start. Muomi was shaking her arm.

'What is it?'

'You were shouting, My Lady. Is everything all right?'

'Shouting?'

'Were you asleep?'

'Yes,' she said, disappointed to find herself back inside the Harem.

'Are you all right?'

'Of course I am.'

After she had gone Hürrem felt a tear course down her cheek. She was only ever happy in her dreams now. Why did she have to wake her and drag her back here to this prison?

It had brought her no happiness, this struggle for pre-eminence. There had been a brief moment of triumph when Suleiman had first chosen her, and a certain satisfaction at outwitting Gülbehar. But never joy.

And then there was Suleiman. She despised him as much now as she had the day he first chose her, thirty-five years before. No, before that; she hated him from the very first day of her enslavement, when they first brought her to the Eski Saraya,

But that wasn't what had brought on this black mood. It was the nightingale.

It had been a present from Suleiman. He had given it to her on the day of their wedding, in a cage crafted from cedar and studded with onyx and pearl. It had sung to her every day since, until this morning when she found it on the bottom of its cage, stiff and cold. She had removed it gently, cupping it in the palms of her hands, stared into its unblinking eye.

As she held it, the bird sang to her for the final time: My life is your life. You have lived out your days in your gilded cage, and the Sultan has admired you, enjoyed you and marveled at your voice and beauty. But one day your cold eye will stare at the dawn and it will be over. The cage door will never open. Your song will be gone, and you will be forgotten.

It is not over, she thought. I still have time to repay them for all the years they stole from me.

The answer was simple; the Osmanlis wanted Bayezid. More, they needed him, and if it were left to destiny Bayezid would surely overcome his indigent brother in the battle for the throne. He was the strong one, the leader, the *ghazi*.

So she would give them Selim.

The Suleimaniye mosque rose from the city like a mountain of gray marble, its domes and minarets fashioned in perfect symmetry. It had cost seven hundred thousand ducats, a king's ransom, and its purpose was to absolve a Sultan for the murder of his son.

Suleiman admired it from the window of Hürrem's apartment, his hand on her shoulder. 'It is magnificent, my Lord,' she said. 'In a thousand years, men will look at it and regret they were not born in an age such as ours.'

'I hope so,' Suleiman said. He held her tighter. She felt frail; he could feel the shape of her bones through her gown. She had been ill often lately.

She wore a green cap as she had the day he had first seen her in the courtyard, but it was a mocking echo of her youth. Beneath the kohl, henna and powder her skin was like parchment. Her hair was milky white at the roots now and all Muomi's dyes could not replicate the burnished gold of her youth.

He loved her more now than he ever had; physical passion had been replaced by a feeling of ease and intimacy that he had shared with no one else.

'It is a wonderful achievement, My Lord.'

'One day we will lie there, side by side.'

So, she thought, he is going to build my tomb on the ruins of the Old Palace, the prison where he first put me in my cage. Such exquisite irony.

He felt her tremble. 'Are you unwell?'

'It is just the cold. I shall feel better as soon as Spring comes.'

The north wind howled like a djinn outside and Suleiman shivered inside his sable-lined robe. 'You must take better care,' Suleiman said to her.

'Do not concern yourself my Lord. A few aches are to be expected when we grow older.' She turned from the window.

Suleiman waved away her *gediçli* and helped her across the room, shocked at how light she felt against his arm. He positioned her feet below the *tandir*, supporting her back gently with cushions.

'Thank you, my Lord. Please don't look so concerned. It is just a slight chill.' A *gediçli* threw a quilt over her knees. When she had settled herself, she said, 'My Lord, I would talk with you soon about the succession. I know it has been on your mind. They are my sons, and I know their hearts.'

Suleiman took her hand. '*Russelana*, Selim is a loving son, but he could never be a great Sultan. Bayezid is the ghazi.'

'He will be popular with the Janissaries at least.'

'Without the Janissaries, a Sultan cannot rule.'

'The Janissaries! For whom you have nothing but contempt.'

'There are times when a Sultan must use his sword, even if he despises war.'

'But Bayezid knows nothing else. He would spend his whole life in the saddle if he could. My Lord, I do not say this to condemn him, only to give you pause. Selim may not be a warrior like his brother, but he may prove a true knight in the Divan. As you have said, it is the law and not the sword that will ensure the future of the Osmanlis.'

'Selim is a debauch and a drunkard. He rarely attends his own Divan in Manisa. Why should we think that will change if he becomes Sultan?'

'If Bayezid takes the throne, Selim will die.'

'Let God decide it then.'

Hürrem bowed her head. 'I do not contend with your wisdom. I shall pray for both my sons.'

He put his arms around her. I have murdered my best friend and executed my firstborn son, he thought, but I have never betrayed my love for you. It is the one thing that I know in my heart has been true and good.

CHAPTER 97

Only Muomi was with her when she fell.

Hürrem had ventured onto the balcony of her apartment very early that morning. Muomi heard her singing, a Tatar song she had learned from her father, or so she said. It was cold and Muomi went to bring her back inside. Hürrem cried out just as she reached her and fell in her arms. Her handmaidens ran to assist her but by the time they laid her on the divan she was already unconscious, her breathing ragged in her chest.

Ludovici received an urgent summons to meet Abbas at the Jewish house. He hurried there in a coach, but for the first time in their acquaintance Abbas was not on time.

When he finally arrived, he gave no apology or reason for being late.

'I received your message,' Ludovici said. 'You said it was important.'

'You have lived with Muslims all these years and still you have not learned the simple art of patience.'

'And probably never shall.'

'Yes, Ludovici, the matter is urgent, but urgent in hours not in minutes. I hoped to savor our meeting today. It will probably be our last.'

'Why, what has happened?'

'The Lady Hürrem is dying.'

'You are sure? It's not just another of her stratagems?'

'She has been suffering a malady for many months now. This morning she collapsed and they have taken her to her bed. She has the smell of death about her. I know it well. There is no mistaking it.'

'But how does this affect us, Abbas?'

'You must send Julia away from Stamboul. I know you have land in Cyprus. Take her there with you.'

'But her offence was nearly thirty years ago! Suleiman must have forgotten about her by now.'

'He may have forgotten, but once he knows she is still alive he will be bound by pride and by duty to punish both her and me. He will send his assassins here into Pera if he has to. He is hardly afraid of the *bailo* of Venice.'

'But how could he find out?'

'Hürrem has held this over me for years. She put it down in a letter in her own hand and she has sworn that it will be delivered to the Grand Vizier upon her death, regardless of the cause.' He reached over and took Ludovici's arm. 'Have you not had enough? You can retire from affairs a rich man now.' He coughed, a wet, hacking sound coming from his chest. He brought the handkerchief to his lips and when he took it away Ludovici noticed a watery red stain.

'I will do as you say. But you must do one last favor for me.'

'If it is within my power.'

'My *caramusalis* may enter or leave the Dardanelles as they wish. They are never searched. My *baksheesh* to Rüstem guarantees it. Any passengers I wish to take on board are guaranteed safe passage. I want you to come with us. If Hürrem betrays Julia to Suleiman she betrays you as well. Come to Cyprus, live out your last few years in peace.'

'Peace? Does such a thing exist?'

'Tomorrow at dawn, at Galata. One of my boats will be there, you will see the Venetian lion flying from its stern - but it will fly upside down. The captain will have his orders. Just get on board and hurry below out of sight.'

'I will think it over.'

'No! I do not want you to think! I want you to promise me that you will be there. As much as you wish for Julia's safety, I wish for yours.'

'Thank you,' Abbas murmured. He clapped his hands and immediately the deaf-mutes were at his side, lifting him to his feet. He clung to them, wheezing from the effort.

'Promise me,' Ludovici repeated.

'Very well,' Abbas said.

'I will not say goodbye. We will see each other in the morning. Yes?'

Abbas forced a smile. 'The start of a new day.'

Ludovici watched him climb into his carriage.

Abbas hesitated, turned and looked up at the widow. 'Ludovici,' he called up. 'If I am not there, say goodbye to Julia for me!' And then he was gone.

'Muomi,' Hürrem whispered. The *gediçli* put her ear close to Hürrem's lips to catch the words.

'Yes, My Lady.'

'I am dying now, but afterwards Suleiman... will come to you.'

'What am I to tell him?'

'Whatever hurts him the most.'

Muomi smiled. 'Yes, My Lady.'

CHAPTER 98

Julia had never seen Ludovici like this. He seemed defeated. He stroked his beard and slumped in his chair.

She waited patiently for him to speak.

'I am sending you away,' he said suddenly.

'My Lord?'

'I should have done this years ago. It is for your own safety.'

She was overcome by a wave of indignation. Was she still just a pawn, to be pushed around the Mediterranean at whim? 'How can I be in danger?' she said.

'The Sultan may soon know you are here.'

'But surely all that was years ago.'

'It is not forgotten. Abbas is certain of it. It seems the Grand Vizier will soon know about it and Suleiman will be forced to act. These people do not forget a slight, Julia. Ever.'

'Where are you sending me?'

'I have estates in Cyprus. You will be looked after.'

Julia imagined another lonely villa, some vines, a few servants, perhaps a few books and embroidery to occupy her. A monastery for all purposes. A monastery with wine. The prospect was intolerable.

'You wish me to leave you?' she said.

'No, that is the last thing that I want.'

'Very well, then. I shall not go.'

'You don't understand.'

'I understand perfectly. I just do not wish to leave you.'

He stared at her, bewildered. 'Why?'

'Perhaps I have grown fond of you. Is that so hard to believe?'

'Yes it is. At least I never expected to hear you say it.'

'If you will come with me, then I will go. If you will not, then I will stay here. I am decided.'

Ludovici stood up and went to the window. *Corpo di Dio!* He had waited so long for her passion that this one moment of calm acceptance had taken him completely by surprise. He did not know what to say or do. He had been resigned to finally giving up something he thought he could never have. Now this.

'I do not know what to say.'

Her skirts rustled on the marble as she came to stand behind him. 'What will you do?'

'I will leave the running of my business in the hands of my undermerchant. I will let him cheat me shamelessly, while I grow grapes and turn brown and wrinkled in the sun.' He smiled. 'Perhaps the Venetian renegade has proved his point to the Republic. I should like to be happy instead of just rich.'

He remembered the first time he had seen her in the church of *Santa Maria dei Miracoli*. The angel in velvet, as Abbas had once described her. She was no longer an angel, just a woman.

He reached for her hand, and felt her fingers entwine with his.

CHAPTER 99

Abdullah Ali-Haji, Suleiman's private physician, was not a happy man. Suleiman surveyed him from the divan, ferocious in his despair.

'You must prescribe an elixir for her. If she dies, I shall hold you responsible. You will enjoy an uninterrupted view of the next sunrise from a hook on the Gate of Felicity.'

Ali-Haji touched his forehead to the rug. 'As you say, my Lord.'

A little while later a guard of eunuchs, swords drawn, escorted him through the oak and iron gate into the silent sanctuary of the Harem. They passed the hushed courtyards and climbed a flight of narrow steps to Hürrem's apartments.

The physician did not even spare a glance at the blue and white Ming vases, the gilt mirrors or the jeweled censers that hung from the vaulted dome. He was too frightened even to think. Oh that God had spared him to be alive in another time, when the Sultan did not have a queen that he loved so much!

A double guard of eunuchs lined the way so that he could see nothing beyond them, but he knew she was there. Her presence and the hush that surrounded her dominated the room. The guards who had accompanied him from the Hall of Audience stopped and allowed him to walk ahead.

Nothing was said and he wondered what he should do.

Suddenly a hand appeared from behind the human barrier, pale and limp, the wrist supported by the plump ebony fingers of the Kislar Aghasi. This was all he would be allowed to examine.

He took the hand reverently for he knew that he was the only whole man, aside from the Sultan himself, who had ever been allowed to touch her since she had entered the Harem. It was an old woman's hand now, of course, with liver blotches, and the skin was flaccid. Nothing to excite the desire.

He felt for the pulsing of the blood and gauged the temperature of the skin, as it would tell him a little about the health of her internal organs. He pinched the nails, testing for the quickness of the blood.

Her heart beats very slowly, he thought. Her body cools in readiness for death.

He must hurry, prepare an elixir to revive her organs and her vital humors. He had no wish to watch the sunrise from the main gate, no matter how splendid the view.

'Has the old fool gone?' Hürrem whispered.

'Yes, he is gone,' Abbas said. The guards filed out of the room and they were left alone. Strange how much he had hated her, yet now he admired the courage with which she faced her death. If only he had the same strength.

'I would not trust him to pare my toenails.'

'No, My Lady.'

The whites of her eyes were no longer white; they were stained with yellow and sunk deep into her head. No elixir in the world is going to save her now, Abbas decided.

Her lips cracked into a smile. 'So you are going to see me dead, after all my Abbas. That must please you.'

'Indeed it does.'

'Your candor is so refreshing. They all tell me I am going to recover.'

'I should say they are greatly mistaken.'

Hürrem turned her eyes on him, slowly and painfully. 'I have one more errand for you.'

'I hardly think you are in a position to command me anymore, My Lady.'

'You want the letter?'

Abbas controlled himself with difficulty. 'Make your peace with God. The affairs of the world will soon no longer concern you.'

'You are right, my Abbas. Muomi has the letter. She has my command upon my death to deliver it to you.'

'There really was such a letter?'

'Of course. I never make empty threats.'

'Who was your spy?'

'Ludovici had a eunuch. Hyacinth. It's a pretty name.'

'Another eunuch?'

'A delicious irony, don't you think? Take the letter as my parting gift. Go in peace, my Abbas.'

He rose to leave. Tonight, he was sure, she would die. And at dawn he would be on a *caramusali*, gliding across the Marmara Deniz and finally free.

'Do you not hate them, these Turks?' she murmured.

'My Lady?'

'What they have done to me. To you. Do you not hate them?'

'My bones ache with it.'

Hürrem closed her eyes. The effort of speaking was tiring her. 'They have made me a slave and made you a joke.'

Well, Abbas thought, even in death she does not choose delicacy over candor.

'Do you not want some measure of vengeance?'

'What does my Lady foresee?'

'I foresee Selim as the next Sultan.'

'It will never happen.'

'Who knows what will happen. Perhaps you may still be useful.' She tried to moisten her lips with her tongue. They were cracked and a little watery blood seeped from them. 'I have bequeathed you to my son's service. Perhaps you can help me in my last endeavor.'

She closed her eyes and in moments she was asleep. Abbas got up to leave but turned at the door and looked back. She looked such a fragile and pathetic figure. How could she ever have filled him with such dread?

And how, too, did he find himself in such sympathy with her at this late hour? 'I will help you,' he said. 'I will gladly do all that I can. This time you do not have to threaten me.'

He went out, closing the door softly behind him.

CHAPTER 100

'Why didn't he come?' Julia said.

Ludovici leaned on the rail, watched the domes and spires of the great city fade into the violet haze of the morning, knowing he would never see them again. 'I don't know. I never really understood his reasons for doing anything.'

'Do you think he is still alive? You don't think she has killed him?'

'My sources inside the Porte will tell me soon enough. If they killed him then we were right not to delay. And if he is well and has chosen not to come, nothing will change his mind.'

The water shimmered with pools of gold as the sun rose in the sky. The *caramusali* reached into the breeze bound for the Dardanelles. Julia remembered the last time she had been out here, the morning she first glimpsed the city that imprisoned and then liberated her. A lifetime ago.

'I shall pray for him,' Julia said.

Hürrem was dying.

It was obvious to Suleiman from the moment he entered the room. He barely recognized her. The flesh had fallen away from her bones. She looked like a skull with a tight covering of translucent skin. Her body was shrunken and tiny like a doll's.

She was propped up on pillows. Muomi had braided her hair with pearls and pinned her green cap in place. She had dressed her in a kaftan of pure white silk. It was all an absurd parody of her youth and he wanted to cry aloud when he saw her.

Muomi and Abbas crouched by her bedside, their faces dark with dread.

'*Russelana*,' Suleiman whispered. The others moved back. He sat down on the edge of the bed and picked up her hand. It was as cold as marble. 'Don't leave me,' he whispered.

'I am free, Suleiman.' Her voice had lost all gentleness; it sounded like metal on a rasp.

He brought her fingers to his lips and kissed them. 'I love you.'

Her mouth creased like a bow. There was a moment of stillness.

'Life has been cruel to you, Suleiman. But then you have deserved it.'

He stared at her, appalled. He turned to the circle of faces around the bed. 'Get out! Get out all of you!'

Abbas, Muomi and the other *gediçli* hurried out.

'I hate you,' she whispered. 'I have always hated you.'

He wondered if he had heard her correctly. He bent lower over the bed. 'What?'

'Bayezid is not your son.' She raised her head halfway from the pillow, one final effort. 'He belongs to Ibrahim.'

He looked into her eyes and watched the light die there. A flicker, like a candle in a draught, and then darkness. She slumped onto her side.

'No! It is not true.'

He ripped off her cap and veil, and the pearls that were braided into her whitened hair scattered on the marble floor. He picked up a stool and flung it at the Vicenzan mirror, splintering the glass into a thousand pieces.

Then he ran from the room.

When Abbas found him, he was curled up on the floor of his own bedchamber. His servants hung back, none of them knowing what to do. Abbas put him to bed.

He stayed there for three days shouting at the phantoms that came to haunt him. When he finally summoned Abbas, it was to order that her apartments be locked and sealed so that he would never again have to go in any room where he had once heard her laughter or felt her embrace.

PART 10

A Hermit's Rest

CHAPTER 101

Amasya, 1559

The two riders galloped towards each other at full tilt, the horses' hoofs drumming on the soft earth, the mud tossed into the air behind them in thick clumps. The first rider threw his spear and his opponent tried to slide out of the way on the lee side of his horse, but it struck him a glancing blow on his back. The mounted horsemen at the side of the arena cheered. The music of the pipes and drums became more urgent.

'Shh,' Bayezid whispered, to calm his Arab who was kicking with his forelegs, agitated by the music and the shouting of the riders around them.

His equerry, Murad, spurred up alongside him. 'Another three points,' he said, 'a good day for the Blues.'

'Soon we may be throwing real spears,' Bayezid said. He took off again, heading towards the center of the arena where two riders from the Greens were waiting for him. As he closed in on them, one of them threw his spear. It passed harmlessly over Bayezid's shoulder as he ducked beneath his horse's head. He veered his Arab suddenly to the right and the other rider had to pull up sharply to avoid crashing into him.

Bayezid reined in his horse. Before the Green realized what was happening, Bayezid was behind him. His spear struck him between the shoulder blades. The man cried out in pain and slumped over his horse.

The rest of the Blues stood in their stirrups and cheered.

Bayezid galloped back to Murad. 'What do you say, Murad?'

'I say we march today and cut ourselves a slice of barley pudding!'

Bayezid laughed. There were more whoops from the Blues as another of their team scored a direct hit with his spear and sent a Green tumbling from his horse with blood spurting from his head.

They were invincible that day. They could not lose.

Bayezid found Gülbehar in the Harem garden, in the rose kiosk. The roses that gave it its name were in full flower, a blaze of rose, gold and pink.

She sat alone, the silence broken only by the soft click of the pearl beads running through her fingers. Her lips moved silently as she recited her prayers. Her face was hidden by her veil but the deep lines around her eyes betrayed her age.

She heard him enter. 'You look so much like my son,' she said.

'I should like to be like him in every way.'

'Not in every way. He is dead. So what brings you here to this old woman's garden?'

'I want your advice.'

'What would I know of the world of princes?'

'I think you know a great deal.' He paused, choosing his words carefully. 'You know there is going to be war.'

A *gediçli* poured a perfumed sherbet into a crystal glass. Gülbehar sipped it. 'Because of Selim?' she said.

'The troubles of the Osmanlis do not begin and end with Selim', he said. 'The Turks who fought alongside my grandfather are now ruled by the grandsons of the men they conquered. The *devshirme* has burdened us with an army of bureaucrats. A Bulgarian vizier forces our fellow Osmanlis off their lands while he fills his own pockets with their taxes. Everything is *baksheesh, baksheesh.* A true Osmanli lives in the saddle of a horse not on a silk divan! He finds his power in the sword not in the size of a bribe.'

'Do you remember what the Janissaries said on the day my son was murdered? *Our hope is lost in Mustapha.*'

'I remember.'

'We need another Mustapha, and you are so much like him. You can ride. You can fight. You command respect wherever you go. I believe our hope might be reborn in you.'

'If only Suleiman thought so.'

'Suleiman was my lord for many years, but truly I do not recognize the man he has become. Look at what he has done to you. He has shamed you and exiled you here to Amasya, as he did to my son. He has all but handed the throne to your idiot brother. This time we cannot blame it all on Hürrem.'

'He knows what kind of man my brother is. It makes no sense.'

'If you are Suleiman it makes every kind of sense. He just wants to hold on to his power, and anyone who threatens him, he destroys. He pretends not to be a tyrant like his father, but he is worse. At least you knew where you were with Selim the Grim. He did not pretend to be something he wasn't.'

'What are you telling me?'

'Selim is not your enemy. Your father is. Be careful. If you ride against anyone, let it be your father. Selim cannot hurt you. Your father will bury you and spit on your grave.'

She held out her hand. Bayezid kissed it and took his leave.

Ride against Suleiman? he thought. No, that is unthinkable. Suleiman was just testing his mettle, that was all. Suleiman knew he could not let Selim remain at Manisa, just five days ride from the capital, while he lived like an exile a month's ride away. It was the Osmanli way and his father would understand that.

Suleiman was motionless but for the steady tapping of his index finger on the golden arm of his throne. He was dressed magnificently; a kaftan lined with black sable, a crimson robe with gold tiger stripes, emeralds in his turban and on his fingers. Yet he looked shrunken as if the pages had thrown an adult's clothes on a wizened child.

'It was the illness,' he murmured.

Rüstem frowned. 'My Lord?'

Suleiman jerked his head up as if suddenly aware of his presence. 'Ah, Rüstem.'

'I have come from the Divan, my Lord.'

'The Divan,' Suleiman repeated as if trying to remember what manner of thing that might be.

'I have bad news, my Lord.'

'Bayezid has sent an answer to my message?'

'He has.'

'And what does he say?'

'His reply was short, my Lord.' Rüstem produced the letter from the fold of his robes and read, 'In everything I will obey the command of the Sultan, my father, except in all that lies between Selim and me.'

'Why does he defy me?'

What else can he do? Rüstem thought. You virtually exiled him after Hürrem's death, just as you did Mustapha. 'He raises an army at Angora,' he said. 'They say the veterans are flooding to him.'

'We must stop this. While I live, they shall obey me!'

'There may yet be a way, my Lord.'

'Tell me.'

'Restore Bayezid to Kütahya. If not there, then Konia. Make some conciliation. But by assigning him to Amasya you give the succession to Selim.'

'He must obey me!'

'If you insist on this, we cannot avert a civil war.'

'They are my sons. They will do as I say!'

'I fear we cannot persuade Bayezid to stay his hand, my Lord.' He hesitated. 'It was always my understanding that you wanted Bayezid as your successor.'

'Then your understanding was at fault. You are getting old. The dropsy has addled your brain.'

Rüstem touched his forehead to the carpet. 'As you say.'

'Tell Selim he is to proceed to Konia, to guard our southern route to Syria and Egypt. Send Mohammed Sokolli to protect him with a regiment of Janissaries and thirty cannon.

'Meanwhile you shall command Pertew Pasha to go to Bayezid, to try to persuade him to return without delay to the governorship of Amasya, and to extract from him a promise of fealty. My sons will not be allowed to drag this empire into war while I still sit on this throne.'

'Yes, my Lord,' Rüstem said. He rose slowly to his feet and hobbled from the room. He would do as the Sultan commanded. Let others worry about Suleiman's successor. He would be dead before then.

'You were ill,' Suleiman said. 'You did not mean what you were saying.'

'There was a fever in my brain,' Hürrem answered. 'It was the devil who spoke.'

'Bayezid is my son.'

'Of course he is your son. I loved you with all my heart. Besides, I was close guarded in the Harem. Ibrahim could not have reached me in there. It was the Devil's lie.'

'Yet he looks like Ibrahim,' Suleiman said.

Suleiman reached out a hand to touch her, but she was not there. Tears of grief and self-pity welled up in his eyes. For thirty-five years he had loved her, loved her more than anyone. He had given up his Harem for her and made her his queen. Hürrem had always loved him. It was the illness that made her say what she had at the end.

Yet he could still hear her, as if she were in the room right now. He could see her lying on the bed, her face white, her voice jagged as metal.

He opened his eyes, almost expecting to see her. But there were only the mutes, dumb to his grief, faces blank as stone.

He remembered when he had first seen her, in the courtyard of the Old Palace, a green cap on her head and a childlike frown on her face as she worked the needle and thread. She was incapable of hate, he told himself. It was Satan speaking through her; she was already in Paradise when she damned him.

But how could he be sure? Better a drunk than break the line forever.

CHAPTER 102

In Spring, Cappadocia is ablaze with wildflowers, the rain drawing a riot of color from the sunbaked steps. Bayezid rode with Murad along a stream, between ranks of tall, spindly poplars, fields of yellow rapeseed on either side.

They reached the crest of the spur. Bayezid's army was camped below, under the towers of the Hisar fortress. He felt the warm flesh of his Arab quiver beneath him. The camp was at prayer; men were lined in rows on their knees. Heads bobbed in unison, thousands of them.

Men had arrived in these past weeks from all over; Kurds with broad scarlet sashes at their waists and woolen skull caps; Turkoman bandits in fur hats; black plumed Spahis who had deserted the Porte to come in search of the new Mustapha; and the dispossessed *timariots* in a motley selection of armor and conical helmets.

Now there were twenty thousand camped on the plain; a traditional *ghazi* army, the ancestors of the horsemen whose great grandfathers had conquered the steppes in the name of the Osmanlis.

Murad turned to Bayezid. 'You lit a flame under the Empire. See how they flock to you. You are the future now.'

'And I will not let them down,' Bayezid said.

Selim was in a black mood. Bayezid was amassing an army and still his father refused to make his move. Instead he had sent Sokolli and his cannon, with a royal command to move on to Konia to face his brother. Why did his father still sit in his palace, watching the sun move the shadows around the walls, while 'the new Mustapha' gathered strength at Angora, ready to murder him? Once again, he had been abandoned.

He emptied the crystal cup at his side and clapped his hands for his page to refill it.

Damn Bayezid. And damn Suleiman.

Perhaps they were plotting together. For all he knew Suleiman might even be at Amasya feasting with Bayezid in the seraglio, or watching him show off at the *çerit*. Worse, his brother might be intriguing with the Aga of the Janissaries to usurp the throne, as his grandfather had done.

Selim gulped down another draft of wine. Life was so unfair. His mother had never shown him any affection, and Suleiman had ignored him in favor of Mustapha and Çehangir.

Even the wine would not shake this black mood tonight. He needed a distraction. 'Abbas!'

His Kislar Aghasi stepped forward, bowing low. Why did Hürrem insist he take him into his household after her death? Perhaps he was a spy. He should have his head on a spike soon. He would think about it.

'My lord,' Abbas murmured.

'I need entertainment, Kislar Aghasi.'

'What does my Lord wish?'

'Bring on the herd. The bull is pawing the ground.'

'As you wish.'

The oil lamps had been lit in the campaign tent and his officers crowded in, side by side with Turkoman and Kurdish bandits, to stare at the charts he had unfolded on the carpet.

'Suleiman has ordered Prince Barley Pudding…' There was a grunt of derisive laughter from the others about the nickname they had given Selim. 'He has ordered him to take his army and his household to Konia, to protect the land route to Syria. From us, I suppose he means. But we have no quarrel with Suleiman.' Bayezid looked around at the hard, bearded faces. 'We will ride south to confront Selim.'

'He will run,' someone said.

'Yes, my brother would like to run. But my father has sent him a backbone, in the form of a Janissary regiment and thirty cannon. It may be a harder fight than we expected.'

'Thirty cannon will not stop us!'

'The cannons are not important, not even the Janissaries. It is Selim. Once my brother is dead, the battle is won. It is as simple as that.' Bayezid pointed to the map at his feet. 'We will draw up our army here on the plain and wait. Sokolli has orders to keep us apart, not to attack. So he will draw up artillery in a defensive posture. We will give him the charge he expects to keep him occupied.

'Meanwhile we will leave a cavalry squadron here in the hills to the west. It will be small enough to pass unnoticed, a tiny dart just big enough to cut the vein in Prince Barley Pudding's neck. When he is dead, we can break off the attack. Our work will be done.'

There were three or four dozen girls, all of them naked. They were the most beautiful girls in the Empire, none older than twenty, some as young as twelve. They had been purchased by Selim's procurators in the market at the Place of the Burned Pillar, the same place where his mother had been bought.

Selim reeled into the hall, staggering from the effects of the wine.

They were all on all fours, breasts swaying as they moved about the thick rugs, a moving herd of coffee, alabaster and olive. Abbas snapped a short ox hide whip in the air above their heads like a cattle master to keep them moving.

Selim roared like a bull and started to strip off his clothes.

Abbas stepped back as Selim plunged in among the girls. Selim caught the back of one and tried to mount her. Abbas saw her grimace in pain.

Selim roared again. Finally he was inside her and began to thrust his hips violently. Then he pushed her away and crawled after another one, his great belly sagging on the ground. He caught a fair-haired Armenian by her hips, and she wriggled in distress.

No, don't do that, Abbas thought. He'll have you killed if you resist.

But Selim was too drunk to notice. He mounted her and his fingers cupped her breasts, squeezing so hard he made her scream. He liked that. He roared again and with a final thrust of his hips released her.

He clapped his hands, and a page threaded his way through the girls with a cup of wine. Selim drained it in one draft and returned to his pleasures.

He mounted yet another girl, gripping her braids as if they were the reins of a horse. 'Damn you, Bayezid! See, I shall impregnate a whole herd of women and my sons shall swarm over the throne like ants over a corpse!'

He released the girl and scuttled after yet another; but by now the wine had slowed him and he slumped forward on his face. He tried to struggle back to his knees. The girls cowered away along the walls, but Abbas cracked the whip above their heads to force them back into the center of the room.

Selim grunted and made after the nearest one. He caught her leg, but she wriggled free and he toppled over onto his back, his belly heaving. He had already lost his erection to the wine, Abbas noted.

He made a final attempt to rise but his head fell back onto the carpets. He laughed. 'Damn you, Bayezid!' he shouted. Within seconds he was snoring.

Abbas clapped his hands and the girls fled from the room. Four pages lifted him sleeping from the floor and carried him to his bedchamber. The prince of the Osmanlis, first son of the Magnificent, pretender to the throne of the greatest empire on earth, turned over and vomited copiously onto the silk sheets.

CHAPTER 103

The dervishes had been fasting and praying for a month. Now, drunk with opium and with faces ghost-white from talcum, they filed into the courtyard. The musicians sat in a circle, cross-legged on the hard stone. The flutes began to play, the soft wailing drifting upwards as a sliver of moon rose behind the dome of the prophet's tomb. Torchlight threw long shadows on the walls of the monastery.

The drummers joined in, quickening the rhythm as the dancers began to spin, long skirts fanning out around their legs. They started their chant, saying prayers for the great ones.

The dancers inclined their heads to their right shoulders, their heavy garments giving off a low whistling moan, like the wind in the mountains.

Bayezid felt his own heartbeat speeding up in time with the music; still they whirled, until even the dancer's faces began to blur. But not one of them staggered, none of them fell.

The music ended without warning. The dancers fell prostrate to the floor, heads rolling on their shoulders, flecks of foam on their lips, in a trance.

Bayezid stepped into the circle and approached one of the dancers, a tall monk with a white beard and a brown face as wrinkled and hard as a walnut. They said he was one hundred and eleven years old.

'Holy Man, can you see?' Bayezid said.

The old man's eyes were open, but his pupils were cold and glazed, like a dead fish. 'I can see,' he answered.

'Tell me what you see for the sons of Suleiman.'

'I see only misery, corruption, and stink.'

Bayezid crouched lower, trying to make out his words more clearly. 'What of Bayezid?'

'I do not see him.'

'What do you see then?'

'A great wind that blows a curtain over everything. God's wind.'

'What else?'

'There is nothing else.'

Bayezid stood up, frowning with disgust. All these monks spoke in riddles. You could never get any sense out of any of them. He stamped away. Holy men? Holy wasters of time!

Suleiman stared at the *gediçli* kneeling at the foot of his throne. Her tight curls were grizzled with gray, but her eyes had lost none of their malevolence. For thirty-five years she had been Hürrem's slave, and hardly worthy of his attention. Now he had summoned her here by express command. Muomi alone, he realized, could possess the remedy for his grief.

'You were the Lady Hürrem's handmaiden since she was first *gözde*. Yes?'

'Yes, My Lord.'

'You knew her intimately?'

'I did.'

'I wish then, to speak of intimate matters. There is no reason to fear,' he added, 'as long as you answer me truthfully, for I am your Sultan, and your allegiance is to me, not Hürrem. She rests now and is beyond mortal retribution.'

'Yes, My Lord.'

'I want you to think back, to your first years of service. Do you remember a man called Ibrahim who was my vizier for many years?'

'I remember, my Lord.'

Suleiman leaned even closer so that now he was perched on the very edge of the throne. 'Was it possible that the lady Hürrem ever received him in the Old Palace?'

Muomi raised her head and met his eyes.

'She received him once, my Lord.'

He could not breathe.

'How?' he asked her finally.

'A bribe to the Kislar Aghasi, the captain of the Girls, before Abbas. The Lady Hürrem swore me to secrecy. She said I would die if I ever whispered a word of it.'

She is lying, Suleiman thought.

He leaped from the throne and slapped her across the face. Muomi fell back, astonished that this frail old man still had the strength to hit so hard. She put a hand to her lips, and it came away bloody.

'*Bostanji!*' Suleiman screamed and signaled to the deaf-mute who stood in attendance. The man stepped forward and drew a curved sword from his belt. With one movement he scythed Muomi's head from her shoulders.

A fine pattern of blood sprayed over Suleiman's boots.

CHAPTER 104

Wind.

It whipped at the pennons on the levelled lances and tore at the robes of the waiting horsemen. Bayezid sat immobile on his Arab stallion, his face partially hidden behind the nasal of the conical silver helmet. When he drew his damascened sword, thousands of his cavalrymen imitated his movement so that the sounds of steel rasping on sharpened blades could be heard even over the howling of the wind.

Bayezid spurred his horse forward into a walk. The line of horsemen behind him followed.

Even at this distance he could see the mouths of the cannon on the other side of the plain. They would not fire on him, he was sure of it.

'Vvt!' Bayezid whispered to his horse and it broke from its march into a canter.

Dust rose from the hoofs, a purple tail that spiraled from the plain like a trailing banner. Bayezid heard the ululation behind him as they gathered speed. He brought his sword over his head and held it in front of his body, pointing towards the cannon. He ordered the charge.

Sokolli would never persuade his troopers to fire on their favorite son.

Selim felt the drumming of the hoofs through the thick carpets on the floor of his pavilion. He clapped his hands and Abbas hurried to his side with the jug of wine.

'Where is Sokolli?' Selim said.

'He is with the Janissaries, my Lord.'

Selim took the jug, but his hands were shaking so badly he spilled most of it into his beard and down the front of his golden robe. Abbas refilled it. The last servant who had been slow to refill the *shahzade's* goblet had lost both his hands at the wrist.

'Sokolli should be here with me,' Selim said.

'With respect, it is better that he is with the gunners. Someone must direct them.'

Selim badly needed to void his bowels. He drained his glass and rushed out of the tent.

The horses had sensed the coming storm. They shook their tasseled heads and stamped their hoofs. Murad rode to the crest of the ridge and scanned the sky to the south. The horizon had disappeared. He watched the dust storm sweep across the Mevlevi monastery as if the dervishes had summoned it there.

'God's wind,' Murad muttered. 'It is headed straight for our cavalry. In a few minutes they will be blind.'

He drew his *killiç* from his belt. It was time. There were two dozen riders waiting with him in the gully. He wheeled his horse to face them. 'Now!' he barked.

Muhammad Sokolli had expected trouble.

He had brought with him from Stamboul a hand-picked squadron of Janissaries. They were veterans of the campaigns in Persia with Suleiman; a few of them had even served as young men at Mohacs. They were loyal only to the Sultan.

He had taken the precaution of deploying them in a line behind the artillery.

There were two banners of cloud drifting towards them; the cavalry from the front, the desert storm behind. He wondered which would arrive first.

'When I give the order you will fire!' he shouted over the rushing of the wind.

The men at the cannon looked at each other, then at the advancing cavalry. Finally, one of them found the courage to speak up, 'We cannot fire on Bayezid!'

The horses came on.

'You will do as I command,' Sokolli shouted at the man. 'Prepare to fire!'

Not a single trooper bent to the pyramid of musket balls beside their cannon pieces. 'Long live Bayezid!' someone shouted.

Sokolli could see Bayezid now, in his green robes - a clever choice, Sokolli thought, the color of Islam. The ground shook under their feet.

Sokolli drew his sword and turned to the Janissaries waiting in line behind him. 'Prepare to fire,' he shouted at them. They rested their harquebuses on the forked sticks in their left hands and aimed at the gunners in front of them.

Sokolli turned back to the artillery troopers. 'Fire or I will give them the order to shoot all of you.'

Still they hesitated.

'Aim,' Sokolli said. Is their nerve going to hold, he wondered? Will they force me to fire? We will all die if they do.

The cavalry was close now.

Suddenly one of the gunners picked up a cannon ball and heaved it into the mouth of his cannon. One by one the others did the same.

'Light the fuses,' Sokolli said.

They lowered the trajectories, aiming at the onrushing horde.

Bayezid saw an orange blossoming of flame along the line of artillery, heard the howl of shot in the air. The earth erupted all around him. It was if God had taken an invisible scythe and raked it over their front rank. Suddenly he was riding alone.

They were gone! Almost every man riding with him in the first wave had disappeared. He saw a horse, wide-eyed with terror, trying to rise to its feet, dripping blood from its severed foreleg. Its rider lay in several dusty heaps beside it.

He turned in the saddle. The plain was littered with more mounds, horses and men, some writhing, others lying quite still where they had fallen. The second wave came on. The ground erupted again and for a moment they were lost behind a wall of flame and dirt.

Just a handful rode on through the cloud.

A third wave, a fourth.

They had to keep coming. He turned back to urge them on.

Now he heard the hiss of arrows in flight, the clang of musket balls and crossbow bolts hitting armor. The ground erupted again, and more horses were scythed away from their riders.

Bayezid raised his sword and stood in the stirrups so they could all see him. 'Death to Selim!'

Another wave came, then another. His ragged army of bandits and horsemen did not waver. While the new Mustapha sat in the saddle, they were ready to die.

They would do it, he thought. Despite Sokolli's cannon, they would prevail.

By the time Murad reached Selim's camp, the storm had already rolled in, obscuring the horsetail standard outside his tent. Murad galloped in circles, hacking down the few guards who tried to stand in his way.

God's wind had obliterated everything.

Murad could not make out anything more than a few yards in front of him. 'Where is he?' he screamed.

He could hear the rest of his raiding party but all sight of them was lost behind the stinging barrage of sand. He raised his arm to protect his face, did not see the man who ran from one of the tents and slashed the hamstrings of his Arab. The beast bucked and screamed and crashed onto its side.

The fall trapped him underneath his horse, jarring his *killiç* from his fist and winding him. He looked around desperately for his attacker. He glimpsed the blue jacket and gray cap of a Janissary. He fumbled for the spear in its sheath on the saddle and threw it.

His practice at the *çerit* served him. The spear took the trooper through his chest. The man fell back, choking and kicking.

The crippled Arab was scrabbling in the dust, trying to regain his feet. For a moment it lifted its weight, and he was able to scramble clear. He crawled to the dying trooper and took his sword from him. His ankle was agony. He limped away.

Murad heard a woman's screams. The dust cleared for just a moment and he saw veiled figures running from a silk pavilion, darting between the horses and the silhouettes of fighting men. They had found Selim's harem; Selim could not be too far away. He limped towards them but then the dust closed around them again and everything was just shadow.

He saw a purple tent with the horsetail standard. But where were the guards? Perhaps they had been lured away by the battle in front of the women's tent. He tore open the entrance curtain and went in, dragging his injured leg behind him.

He came face to face with an enormous Moor in a kaftan of bright blue flowered silk. He gaped at Murad then fell prostrate on the floor in front of him. 'Please don't hurt me,' he said. 'I am just a harmless slave.'

Murad snorted in disgust and burst through another silk curtain into the inner sanctum. Selim lay on his belly, arms and legs spread-eagled. Murad leaned his weight on his sword and rolled him over with his uninjured foot expecting to see him split open like an over ripe peach.

He heard the rustle of silk as the eunuch followed him in.

'Is he dead?' Murad asked him.

'No, he is not dead, my Lord. He fainted as soon as he heard the first cannon.'

'Then he is fortunate. He will not feel my sword tickle his ribs.'

Murad raised his *killiç* for the death blow. Suddenly he felt as if every nerve, every muscle had been numbed. The sword slipped from his fingers and fell onto the carpet. He did not understand what was happening.

He lay on his back, staring up at the eunuch. There was a jewel-handled dagger in the slave's hand and blood smeared down the blade. 'I am sorry,' Abbas said to him. 'But I cannot let you kill him. I wish that I could.'

Everything went black.

Bayezid turned away from the whipping blast of sand and rode back across the plain, his stallion picking its way through a litter of bleeding and moaning men.

Sokolli's cannon had fallen silent. There was only the howl of the wind and the cries of the dying. A horse nuzzled a fallen rider; the Turkoman tried to crawl towards him, leaving a trail of gore in the dust.

Bayezid jumped down and administered the merciful blow, sending the man to Paradise.

They were defeated. Their charge had been halted by a barrage of sand and grapeshot. It was God's wind.

The monk was right, after all.

CHAPTER 105

Suleiman was propped on a divan in the Çinili Kiosk. The Judas trees were in blossom and the bay of Yenikapi was teeming with *caïques*, all piled high with eggplants, cucumbers and melons ferried over from the Asian shore.

'You look ill, Vizier,' he said.

'Nothing that death will not cure,' Rüstem said.

Suleiman shook his head. 'I may be wrong, but I suspect that even this late in your life you are developing a sense of humor, Rüstem Pasha.'

'I do not think so, my Lord.'

Suleiman shrugged. 'There is no answer to my letter?'

'No, my lord. Yet that means nothing, in itself. Selim may have intercepted the messenger.'

'Or he did not send a messenger. Perhaps he still defies me.'

'Why do we draw our swords against him, my Lord? Is it wise?'

'Suddenly at this stage of your life you embrace a cause? I have trusted you all these years because you never let your heart stand in the way of reason. Indeed, I often wondered if you had a heart. Now you plead Bayezid's case? Are you in his employ now?'

'My Lord, I meant no offence.'

'I am not offended. Speak openly.'

'I just do not understand our strategy,' he said.

'What is it that you do not understand?'

'The logic of it. Why destroy Bayezid? Mustapha went too far, he was a real threat. But if we crush Bayezid then the throne falls to Selim, and Selim…' He spread his hands in a gesture of despair.

'You will do my bidding in this.'

'And yet,' Rüstem persisted, 'where is the offence? He rode against Selim, not against you. Would you want this great Empire to be entrusted to a sot like Selim? Did Selim gain the victory at Konia? No, by the ninety-nine holy names, he did not! It was the wind of the dervishes and the cannon of Mohammed Sokolli. Selim is not worthy. It makes no sense to me.'

What *djinn* possesses me to speak like this? Rüstem thought. You know he will not change his mind once it is set. There is only one person who could ever manage that, and she is dead. So why provoke him? A whole lifetime you have kept your thoughts to yourself and now you are gabbling like a fishwife.

For a moment he thought Suleiman was about to raise his finger to summon the *bostanji* . But instead he said softly, 'I have made my decision. Enough.'

Rüstem bowed his head. There is more to this, he thought, but after a lifetime of dealing in secrets I shall never know this one. He struggled to his feet and left the chamber.

In his mind, Rüstem turned the pages of his personal inventory: eight hundred and fifteen farms, seventeen hundred slaves, eight thousand turbans, six hundred illuminated copies of the Koran, and two million ducats.

He was the richest man in the Empire, save the Sultan. He had proved himself a master of the game. The final book-keeping of his life was confirmation of his mastery. Yet with death beckoning with one skeletal finger, he struggled with the lingering suspicion that there was something that he had missed.

The great drum in the courtyard of the Janissaries had not sounded for many years. It beat now, its echoes reverberating from the walls of the palace, hastening the last-minute preparations. Suleiman mounted his horse by the fountain in the Third Court, wincing at the pain in his knees. He led the army out.

They crossed the Bosporus at Üsküdar, and by that afternoon the column was winding its way through the Cyprus groves at Çamlica, forcing the heavy-laden wheat carts off the dusty road. Runners jogged at Suleiman's stirrup; the plumes of his guardsmen bobbed behind him.

He tried to shut his mind to the rigors of the journey that lay ahead of him. At least twenty-five days of hard riding to reach the fortress at Amasya; then a long campaign in the heat and dust, hunting down his own son like a wild boar.

I am too old for endless days in this saddle, he thought. Each step of the horse jars my bones. I have made so many laws, but in the end the Janissaries, the cavalry and the cannon were the only laws the Osmanlis really understood.

But he would not allow the line to be broken; if Bayezid would not bend to his will, then he would be made to submit.

CHAPTER 106

From Erzerum, the Anatolian plateau rose into soaring snow-capped peaks and plunging valleys. Ranged along the mountain road were the shuffling remnants of the great army that had assembled on the plains of Konia. Only a few thousand were left, many of them wounded. The Kurds and Turkomans had melted away, back to their villages.

Bayezid and his ragged band climbed higher until they were swallowed by gray clouds. The road snaked along a gorge, scree crumbling beneath the horse's hooves. The rock walls here had been polished by centuries of horses and donkeys who had hugged the cliffs to keep from falling into the chasm on the other side of the path.

The wind tore at his robes, threatened at times to dislodge him from the saddle. The high passes were deserted save for the occasional lumbering brown bear. They passed a tarn, black and crusted with ice.

They were deep inside Armenia now. Lake Van was a steel-grey mirror. A falcon wheeled over their heads, its cry piercing the rush of the wind.

The past few months were a jumble of skirmishes, all fought on the run. Bayezid had said goodbye to his wives at Konia, and had just his four young sons with him. They were guarded day and night by his personal guards. They were his treasure now, the prize around which he would gather a new army.

They had to find a way to survive, to regroup. He would not throw himself on his father's mercy because he expected none. Look at what happened to Mustapha.

The shepherd's hut had been built in the lee of the ridge. A trick of the eye made it appear as if it were floating among the mountains.

Bayezid turned to his lieutenant. 'We will camp here tonight. I shall make my headquarters in the hut there.'

'Yes, My Lord,' the man said and hurried away to relay the order.

The hut had been abandoned for the imminent winter. There were four stone walls with no shutters on the windows and no door. The floor was bare earth, and the smell of animals was strong. A long way from the palace at Topkapi, he thought.

A rainbow arced across the valley, chasing a shower of rain through a rent in the clouds. The light had turned a sulfurous green, and a chill wind stirred the grass. Thunder echoed around the passes.

What was he going to do? There was nowhere to run, and his followers no longer had the numbers or the will to fight. He had to find a way to survive.

As morning broke, a chill mist drifted down from the mountains. The wind had wrecked their tents during the night. Men stumbled through the camp wrapped in blankets silent as wraiths.

Bayezid ate his breakfast without appetite; yoghurt laced with raw onions and salt, diluted with cold water and eaten with a little dry pita bread. He heard shouts from the camp and jumped to his feet, spilling his bowl, thinking that Suleiman's scouts had found them. A rider, dressed in Persian light armor, had appeared on the ridge above them. Bayezid's battered army rose to their feet and glared up at him.

As he entered the camp, he was disarmed by Bayezid's personal guard and led through the scowling ranks of Turks to the shepherd's hut. Bayezid received him sitting cross-legged on the rich silk carpet that had been spread on the floor.

The rider executed a formal *salaam*. 'I bring a message from the Shah Tahmasp,' he said.

Bayezid nodded and the lieutenant took the letter from the courier and handed it to him. He read it through quickly, then read it a second time, giving himself time to think.

'The Shah offers us sanctuary?' he said finally.

'Suleiman has made an enemy of Persia,' the courier said. 'When Sultan Bayezid ascends the throne, our Shah hopes to find a friend at the Sublime Porte at last.'

The wind gave an eerie moan as it gusted through the open windows. Ascend the throne, Bayezid thought. For now, ascending the next ridge is as much as I can hope for. This offer is anathema, of course; yet it would give us a chance to draw breath without my father's cavalry sniping at our heels. We are cold, dispirited and defeated. There are more wounded with us than able men. What choice do I have?

'You will wait while I consult with my officers,' he said, but as the man was led away, he already knew what his answer would be.

Suleiman looked up at the mountains. A heavy band of cloud clung to the peaks and high passes.

'He has gone,' Sokolli said. 'He has crossed the border into Persia.'

'To the Shah?'

'He offered him sanctuary. My spies say Bayezid has taken a hundred of his men with him. The rest have gone back to their villages.'

Bayezid, you fool, Suleiman thought. While you remained in the Empire you had a chance. Did you not know my army was on the verge of revolt? Whole regiments of Janissaries were refusing to march against you. The patrols I sent out to hunt you down have returned already, their horses still fresh.

If you had defied me just a few more weeks, winter would have closed in and I would have been forced back to Stamboul. I could never have persuaded these men to come back and fight you again in the Spring. They loved you. They loved how you charged at their guns at Konia, loved how you fought on, even when I brought my whole army against you. They love you every bit as much as they hate Selim.

The one thing they cannot forgive is for an Osmanli to accept the mercy of a Persian. When you crossed the border, you left behind everything they thought you were.

Even the Janissaries will curse you now.

CHAPTER 107

She did not perform her *salaam* as she entered the room. But she is an old woman now, Suleiman thought, not at all concerned about the consequences of offending me. Strange that I loved her so much once; now it is like meeting a stranger.

'My Lord.'

'It has been a long time,' he said.

'As you say.'

He sat down beside her on the divan. 'Are you well?'

'As well as one can expect at this great age. And you, my Lord?'

'My legs swell, and I ache all over.'

Gülbehar fingered the prayer beads in her lap. 'So what has brought you here then, so far from the comforts of the Porte?'

'I wish to be reconciled,' he said.

'I cannot believe that after all you have done, what you did to my son, what you did to me, that you can still hope for my friendship and good favor.'

'I am your lord. You still have a duty to me.'

'Am I then obliged, by Osmanli law, to forgive you? Because, if that is what you are saying, then you should sentence me now. I despise you, Suleiman.'

He rose to his feet. There was a blue and white porcelain vase in the corner of the room, the height of a man. Suleiman drew his *killiç* and smashed it with one blow. He stood among the shards and shouted at her, 'I am your Lord!'

'You are my son's murderer.'

'I gave him life and he turned against me. What did he expect?'

'He was innocent. You are a butcher, just like your father.'

411

He swayed on his feet. 'We shall not see each other again,' he said. He sent the sword clattering across the floor and stormed out.

Gülbehar returned to her prayers, the pearls clicking between her fingers while a *gediçli* brushed away the shards of broken porcelain.

There was a nimbus around the moon. Below it, the Zagros mountains glinted in the moonlight, alien and ice white. As if I had been exiled to the moon itself, Bayezid thought. He shivered in his fur pelisse.

He heard the ring of hooves in the courtyard below. A rider jumped from his horse, leaving a page to hold the reins. He shouted the password to the guard and ran inside. Perhaps this was the news he had been waiting for.

How many times had he gone over this in his head? What else could he have done? Mustapha did nothing and Suleiman executed him. He himself had acted like a true *ghazi* and Suleiman had thrown his entire army against him. How was it possible to understand such a man?

A log broke in the grate in a shower of sparks. There were footsteps on the stone flags outside. The Shah entered. 'I have good news,' he said.

'Your messenger has returned from Stamboul?' There had been many messengers riding back and forth in the last few months.

'Yes, a time and a place has been agreed. He wants to meet with you.'

'Where?'

'Tabriz. He is coming there in secret. Everything is arranged.'

'And Selim?'

'Selim knows nothing about it. It seems that your father has reconsidered. The Shadow of God Upon the Earth has remembered he is mortal like the rest of us.'

'May I see the letter?'

'There was no letter. The message was entrusted to my man's memory.'

'That is unlike my father.'

'He is being cautious. He didn't want Selim to intercept his courier and be forewarned.'

'Did he tell your messenger his purpose?'

'He wants to be reconciled, Bayezid. He said there has been enough bloodshed.'

'When do we meet?' Bayezid asked him.

'We leave tonight,' the Shah said.

Selim is just thirty-four years old, Abbas reminded himself. But already he looks like an old man. His face is so bloated from drink that his eyes look like two small currants sunk into a custard. His body is gross beneath these fine gowns that he wears.

Selim was slumped on the divan picking at a large tray of halwa on the silver table beside him. He took three of the pastries and popped them in his mouth.

'You have news, Kislar Aghasi?'

'I do, my Lord.'

'From my father?'

'He has left Amasya and rides east.'

The negotiations had dragged on for more than a year. It seemed Bayezid was worth much less to Suleiman than the Shah Tahmasp had hoped. It had been whispered that the Shah's starting price had been Mesopotamia.

'He looks sick, I hope?' Selim laughed and sprayed half-chewed pastry over Abbas' robe.

'The Lord of Life cannot spend as long in the saddle as he once did.'

'Does he have his army with him?'

'No, my Lord. My spies say he has a squadron of Spahis and a regiment of Janissaries.'

Selim clapped his hands. A page appeared, holding a pitcher of wine and a jeweled cup. Selim held the cup out to be filled. He swallowed it in one draft.

The page refilled the cup and withdrew.

'That's all. What is his purpose, do you think?'

'They say he will meet Bayezid at Tabriz. There are whispers of reconciliation.'

Selim jumped to his feet and the wine spilled across the carpets. He put his knuckles in his mouth to stifle a scream and began to shake. Not again, Abbas thought. This is like minding a child.

No one moved. Finally, Selim fell back onto the divan. He bunched the corner of his robe in his fist. 'I have been betrayed,' he said. 'Wine! Where is my wine?'

Abbas silently withdrew, drawing no attention to himself. He had no interest in Selim's hysterics. He had lived too long under the tyranny of princes.

CHAPTER 108

Moonlight rippled on the tiled domes of the Blue Mosque and burned like phosphorus on the chill ribbon of the Aji Chai River. The sound of flutes and drums carried on the cold air. Yellow light flickered from the shuttered windows of the citadel.

In the great hall, slave girls dressed in silk and gossamer danced while the guests gorged from the silver plates on the carpets in front of them. The Shah sat in the center of the room with his guest of honor, Bayezid.

The Shah leaned towards him. 'Suleiman regrets what he has done to you,' he said. 'Perhaps you will allow me to mediate. It is not too late. I will help you now and when you are Sultan, Persia and the Osmanlis will be allies.'

'What does he want from me?'

'Just that you stay your hand until his death. Selim will take the throne on his death but that will not matter. When you return to Stamboul the Janissaries will never support him over you. You will take what is yours.'

Bayezid had no appetite for the food, or the promise of women later. The delegation was due the next morning and he wanted to have a clear head. The Shah was right. He must learn patience and cunning from now on. He had been too impulsive in the past. There would be time enough to see Selim's fat head on a pole.

He was aware of a cold draught on his back and realized that someone had entered the hall behind him. Latecomers. He glanced up for a moment, then returned to eating.

'Who are our guests?'

'They are expected,' the Shah said.

Then Bayezid heard it; a familiar sound if one had lived in the palace, something between a bark and a cough, like a dog trying to swallow a piece of gristle. It was the noise men made when they had no tongue to speak. The sound of a mute.

The Shah smiled, with genuine regret. 'I am sorry,' he said. 'Your father insisted.'

'My father?'

'It is a poor bargain. Four hundred thousand gold pieces. My mullahs thought I should hold out for Baghdad. All very well for them; they would have gone to hide in the mountains if your father had marched here with his army. I decided to take the money instead.'

'You pledged me protection!'

The Shah shrugged. 'You say what it is best to say at the time. I am truly sorry. It is a very poor example of our hospitality. I wish it could have been another way.'

Bayezid span around. There were five of them. One of them was the man they said had murdered Mustapha, a huge Sudanese. Each of them held in his hands a loop of thin red silk.

Bayezid's hand went to his *killiç* but one of the Shah's bodyguards had anticipated this and caught his wrist. Two more guards pinned his arms behind him. Bayezid looked at his sons. God help me in my sorrow; they were too young to understand, too young to die. His eldest started to run and one of the Persians caught him, laughing.

'Could you not have spared my boys?'

'Boys grow up to become men. Suleiman was quite specific in his demands.'

'Then let Selim be his epitaph,' Bayezid said. The silken bowstring was around his neck and he was jerked backwards over the *bostanji's* knee, choking. His hands clawed instinctively at his throat but once the noose was in place there was no reprieve.

The children were next. The Shah watched with a frown of disgust. He did not hold with the assassination of children. He took a sliver of spiced lamb from the plate in front of him and chewed reflectively. Statesmanship was an indelicate business at times, but it had to be borne.

A woman was screaming in the courtyard below the window. The *bostanji* wished his men would do something to shut her up.

Bayezid's youngest son was still only nine months old. He had been conceived before the battle of Konia and his father had never seen him.

As the *bostanji* bent over the cot the child looked up and smiled. His hands began to shake and he dropped the bowstring.

He went outside and gave the guard two gold pieces and the bowstring. He waited. A few minutes later the man reappeared and fled down the steps. The coins tinkled as they rolled along the stones.

The *bostanji* sighed and went back inside.

If you had been a girl, he thought, I would not have to do this. He felt for the leather pouch at his waist. If he did not return with it filled, Suleiman would have his own head.

He readied the bowstring and closed the door behind him. As he approached, the child held out his arms.

CHAPTER 109

It was a long journey from Venice to Konia, from the *Campanile di San Marco* to this lonely place, surrounded by stone *caravanserais* and the black yurts of nomads.

It was a lonely place to die.

They found Abbas in his cell slumped face down on the rug. A white kitten was licking at the bloodstained handkerchief clutched in his left hand.

'Consumption,' the physician muttered. Or perhaps poison. Still, death was infinitely preferable to being the Kislar Aghasi to Selim. Or there might be other reasons. Who could know? The less you knew, the better. Knowledge could be dangerous.

It took six pages to lift him and carry him out of the iron-studded door of the Harem into the waiting cart. The physician remained behind to examine the room. Abbas had been writing a letter. Quill and parchment lay on the table beside the body. The letter was unfinished. In fact, he had only written the salutation.

'Dear Julia,'

The Chief Eunuch writing to a girl? Well, it did not matter now.

He screwed it up and threw it in the fire.

After the wardrobe page had left, after the final offering up of prayers, Suleiman was left alone. He lay on his quilt listening to the sound of his own labored breathing. Sleep would not come. He got up, went to the latticed window and looked at the stars.

She must have lied, he thought.

You cannot believe the ramblings of the dying. It was her illness talking. Of course she loved you.

'But how can I be sure?' he said aloud.

He thought about how she looked the day he first saw her, so lovely, with her burnished copper hair braided with glittering pearls, the green taplock cap on her head.

She could not have deceived him for thirty-five years. He had given up his harem for her and made her his queen; the first Osmanli sultan to give a woman such an honor.

He went back to his bed and tried for sleep once again, but it was no good. The room was full of ghosts; Ibrahim, Mustapha, Bayezid.

He wondered if he would ever sleep again.

'What men call empire is worldwide strife and ceaseless war.
In all the world the only joy lies in a hermit's rest.'

*from a poem written by Sultan Suleiman the Magnificent,
discovered after his death in 1566.*

GLOSSARY

bailo: Venetian title for the resident ambassador.

baksheesh: Bribe.

bareta: Hat worn by Venetian gentlemen, usually black.

bastinado: Form of punishment that involved caning the soles of someone's feet.
caique: Light skiff used on the Bosporus.

caramusali: Turkish merchant ships.

cerit: Traditional Turkish sport played on horseback.

Consigliatore: Member of the ten man ruling council of Venice.

devshirme: Forcible recruiting of soldiers and bureaucrats from Christian subjects.

Doge: Venetian head of state.

duenna: Chaperone, usually an older woman.

Enderun: Interior Service of the Ottoman Imperial Court.

gözde: A favorite.

gömlek: Chemise falling to mid-calf.

kadin: Slave girl who has given the Sultan a child.

Kapi Aga: Chief White Eunuch.

killiç: One-handed, single-edged, curved scimitar.

Kislar Aghasi: Chief Black Eunuch.

Padishah: Emperor.

Seraskier: Commander-in-chief and minister of war.

shahzade: Male descendant of the Sultan.

timariot: Cavalryman who received land in return for service.

EPIC ADVENTURE SERIES

Colin Falconer's EPIC ADVENTURE SERIES of stand-alone tales draws inspiration from many periods of history. Visit the fabled city of Xanadu, the Aztec temples of Mexico, or the mountain strongholds of the legendary Cathars. Glimpse Julius Caesar in the sweat and press of the Roman forum, ride a war elephant in the army of Alexander the Great, or follow Suleiman the Magnificent into the forbidden palace of his harem.

2000+ five-star reviews.
Translated into 25 languages.
3000+ pages.

A fantastic read' - Wilbur Smith

All books are available on Amazon in Kindle eBook or 6x9 inch paperback.

Find them at www.colinfalconer.org.

ABOUT THE AUTHOR

Born in London, Colin Falconer started out in advertising, then became a freelance journalist. He wrote for radio and television before writing his first novel. He is best known for historical adventure fiction inspired by his passion for history and travel. His books have been translated into 25 languages.

If you enjoyed this novel, please consider leaving a review online.

If you would like to be kept up to date with new releases from Colin Falconer, please follow him on Facebook or visit his website, www.colinfalconer.org.

Printed in Great Britain
by Amazon

26450386R00243